the Enigma Gamers

Breakfield and Burkey

BOOK 7: Award Winning Techno-Thriller Series

Published by

ICABOD Press

ISBN: 978-1-946858-33-7 (paperback)
ISBN: 978-1-946858-16-0 (ebook)
ISBN: : 978-1-946858-61-0 (audiobook)
The Enigma Gamers – A CATS Tale
was previously published under a different ISBN

Library of Congress Control Number: 2016902287
Cover, interior and eBook design: F + P Graphic Design, FPGD.com

Second Edition
Printed in the United States

TECHNO-THRILLER | SUSPENSE

Novels by Breakfield and Burkey in The Enigma Series
www.EnigmaBookSeries.com

The Enigma Factor	*The Enigma Beyond*
The Enigma Rising	*The Enigma Threat*
The Enigma Ignite	**SHORT STORIES**
The Enigma Wraith	*Out of Poland*
The Enigma Stolen	*Destiny Dreamer*
The Enigma Always	*Hidden Target*
The Enigma Gamers A CATS Tale	*Hot Chocolate*
	Love's Enigma
The Enigma Broker	*Nowhere But Up*
The Enigma Dragon A CATS Tale	*Remember the Future*
	Riddle Codes
The Enigma Source	*The Jewel*

Kirkus Reviews

The Enigma Factor In this debut techno-thriller, the first in a planned series, a hacker finds his life turned upside down as a mysterious company tries to recruit him...

The Enigma Rising In Breakfield and Burkey's latest techno-thriller, a group combats evil in the digital world, with multiple assignments merging in Acapulco and the Cayman Islands.

The Enigma Ignite The authors continue their run of stellar villains with the returning Chairman Lo Chang, but they also add wonderfully unpredictable characters with unclear motivations. A solid espionage thriller that adds more tension and lightheartedness to the series.

The Enigma Wraith The fourth entry in Breakfield and Burkey's techno-thriller series pits the R-Group against a seemingly untraceable computer virus and what could be a full-scale digital assault.

The Enigma Stolen Breakfield and Burkey once again deliver the goods, as returning readers will expect—intelligent technology-laden dialogue; a kidnapping or two; and a bit of action, as Jacob and Petra dodge an assassin (not the cyber kind) in Argentina.

The Enigma Always As always, loaded with smart technological prose and an open ending that suggests more to come.

The Enigma Gamers (A CATS Tale) A cyberattack tale that's superb as both a continuation of a series and a promising start in an entirely new direction.

The Enigma Broker …the authors handle their players as skillfully as casino dealers handle cards, and the various subplots are consistently engaging. The main storyline is energized by its formidable villains…

The Enigma Dragon (A CATS Tale) This second CATS-centric installment (after 2016's *The Enigma Gamers*) will leave readers yearning for more. Astute prose and an unwavering pace energized by first-rate characters and subplots.

The Enigma Source Another top-tier installment that showcases exemplary recurring characters and tech subplots.

The Enigma Beyond the latest installment of this long-running technothriller series finds a next generation cyber security team facing off against unprincipled artificial intelligences. Dense but enthralling entry, with a bevy of new, potential narrative directions.

The Enigma Threat Another clever, energetic addition to an appealing series.

Acknowledgments

We are grateful for the support we have received from our family and friends. We look forward to seeing the reviews from our fans. Thank you in advance for your time.

Specialized Terms are available beginning on page 353 if needed for readers' reference.

Since time immemorial human beings have gambled things of value on the outcome of pending events. This desire to play and compete with a bet on the outcome of some event has followed us to the present day. Here in the 21st century it is a digital activity commonly called. Gamification can take the form of point collection or to learn people and their triggers. With everything on the digital landscape becoming the Internet of Things, machines can interact with machines to the misery of humans Everything resulting from gamification in today's world may not be to our benefit. You decide.   **...The Enigma Chronicles**

Gamers \'gām ers\ n: participants in a rules-based contest for a stake in the outcome; see amusement

NEW DEFINITION

GAMERS (Generally Ambiguously Motivated Exercises for Rewarding Scoundrels)

Locations and Primary Cast Members:

CATS Team

Julie (JAC Rancowski) Rodríguez - Part owner in the CATS Team with her husband,

Juan Rodríguez

Eilla Zan (EZ) Marshall (CATS operation/communication headquarters in Luxemburg)

Supported by R-Group staff Quip, ICABOD, Wolfgang, and Otto

Australian Mines Consortium

George Jones, member of the CATS team

McLaren, operations duty manager for the consortium

Mohawk, operations chief for the consortium

Tina, Mohawk's girlfriend

Hoyt, McLaren's nephew

Barcelona, Spain (Smart City)

Brayson Morris, member of the CATS team

Baby Perez, Mayor of Barcelona

Constellation Stuff: The Store to the Planet (somewhere in one of the US Midwest States)

Summit Hayes, member of the CATS team

Marvin Oile, truck driver for the Constellation Stores

Massoud Mostafavi, head guard at the Constellation distribution center

Marco, guard at the Constellation distribution center

David, guard at the Constellation distribution center

Fast Flyers (US Airline)

Mercedes Field, member of the CATS team

Jim Hughes, member of a US three letter agency

The Sean, Sean Riley, lead negotiator for Fast Flyers Management

Chuck Wood, lead labor negotiator for Fast Flyers Union Team

Macau, China (Hotel, Casino)

Ernesto Gleen, member of the CATS team

Jamie Rafferty, roamer, loaner, risk taker, and programmer

Frieda, Jamie's girlfriend, computer operations knowledgeable

Chairman Chang, silent owner in the Macau casino and high placed Chinese official

Won and Ton, wards of Chairman Chang

Pittsburgh, Pennsylvania (E911)

Tyler Hebert, member of the CATS team

Detective Cormorant, Como, assigned to work with Tyler on city problems

Mayor Barker, Pittsburg mayor that brought in the CATS team

Russian Interests (Believed to be in a hardened data bunker under the Kremlin in Moscow)

Dmitry Vasnev, Russian Minister of Information Propagation, war hero

Konstantin Grankin, longtime assistant and technology support for Dmitry

Rambling Gambler

Frieda questioned, "So what do you want to do? The communications infrastructure is crumbling, plus we need more personnel and sizeable upgrades just to keep things running."

Jamie looked at her rather dispassionately and remarked, "Just tell them this is what we need. What's the big deal?"

Frieda and Jamie were certainly an unlikely pair. He was blond-haired and blue-eyed, but she was a dark-haired beauty with her stoic, logical German temperament that often clashed with his romanticized Irish temper. When her temper flared, her cheeks got rosy, and her curls seemed as if they were on springs. When he was annoyed or angry, he held his temper in check until the last possible moment and then he bellowed. She had seen that once and it wasn't pretty.

They lived together in a poor excuse for an apartment with the only saving grace being that it was furnished. Their knowledge of technology complemented one another with her specialty in hardware, networks, and high-end databases and his in programming, especially cowboy style. He had the inbred flair for the blarney with a side of manipulation.

This job was advertised as high-paying and filled with bonuses for making or beating deadlines. To date, the reality of the work fell way short of the expectations. Overworked, underpaid, combined with frustrating demands did not a happy couple make.

Becoming annoyed with his illogical approach, she angrily countered, "Management will argue the cost elements. I'll be told to make do and stop asking for more funding! We have a major technology implementation labor investment sunk into this wretched continent, and they won't listen to spending any more. This is the once-and-done bunch when it comes to WAN communications infrastructure. I get so mad at times; I could just spit."

He sighed. "Frieda, why do we always have this same discussion? Come on, get dressed. Let's go fix this."

She flashed him incredulous stare. "Jamie. What are you talking about? Didn't you hear what I just said? They don't listen and then they don't spend! THEN they complain about the poor service! They'll dock our pay because they can't remove the nonexistent bonus."

Oblivious to her remarks, he asked, "How much do you need for the hardware to finish?"

Her face scrunched into a frown of confusion. "Uh, 14.5 million euros. But I have already…"

Jamie clucked his tongue and suggested, "Okay. Let's go see the finance group of Ebenezer and Scrooge so we can get the necessary equipment to solve your problem."

Jamie a high-stakes gambler with an unjustified self-confidence that always seemed to court disaster. One time he'd rounded up several investors to buy up a toilet paper manufacturer that had seen better days. He figured that the price was right, and that with his marketing prowess, they could turn the company into a dominant player in the toilet paper manufacturing business. Unfortunately, his marketing instincts were wrong, and the company imploded before it could get off the ground.

The truth was no one from the wholesaler down to the retail buyer could accept a product based on a design intent called *Break on Through to the Other Side*, regardless of the old rock song of the same name being used in the commercial messaging. Toilet paper labeled *Break on Through to the Other Side* was simply a marketing nightmare on steroids. The customers avoided the product in droves.

Jamie possessed a "Reverse Midas Touch" in his endeavors, but it never seemed to bother him when he launched into his next con game. Frieda had been a part of his world for a couple of years now. He always seemed to make strides and get out of situations only to turn around and step into a bigger puddle of muck.

She numbly followed him into the manager's office where Jamie launched his verbal assault. "Which one of you race car drivers has this Formula 1 car stuck in second gear?"

The finance manager looked up from his computer, somewhat puzzled, and asked, "Whadda you two want? If it costs anything, the answer is no. Unless you are here to deposit money, you can leave now."

As usual, the finance manager retrieved the parked #2 pencil from behind his ear as if he was going to write down something, even though everything he did was on his computer keyboard. The office was cluttered, dusty, and screamed for a good cleaning. Rather than being dressed for success, the finance manager was a perfect match for the office décor of messy and shaggy right down to the hair that he combed over from the back to minimize the reflection from his shiny scalp.

Jamie, as close to disinterested in the manager as possible, replied in a very tired voice, "We are here to advise you that you need to pony up 38.5 million euro to stay in business here. I am ordering this gear and adding consulting services to be shipped in for installation the week after next. Are you interested in having it installed or not?"

Jamie tossed a handwritten list of gear on a piece of paper at him that Frieda had hastily assembled during the walk over to this office. In Jamie's mind, the desk reflected the disorganization of the user, which made this plan easier. A wobbly desk, a dusty ten-key adding machine with mountains of paper flowing out in ribbons behind it, and a tired looking computer with a smaller screen than the old man's eyes needed.

After his chuckling subsided, the finance manager focused a puzzled expression at Jamie and asked, "Has the jungle fried your brain? I can't begin to authorize that kind of expenditure! If you really ordered that gear, you'd better find a way to cancel it, or you're fired! Then, after I fire you, I'll cancel the order and extract the order cancelation fees from your last check.

"What kind of clown are you anyway? No one approved any expenditure of that size. You're lucky I let you order your own printer cartridges and paper!"

Using slow, carefully enunciated speech, he explained, "No, genius, you don't get it! If you don't buy it, I will take it to the competition, and we'll set it up for their entrance into the market. Haven't you noticed all the free goods that have been circulating around in the area? While you have been squeezing pennies, the competition has been dropping serious folding money to soften the market up for a switch to the greener pastures of your competition. You seriously didn't think you guys would be the only game in town indefinitely, did you?"

Now starting to panic slightly, the finance manager responded, "We simply cannot spend that kind of money! We must fight for market share another way! We intend to stay in Africa, and no one is going to push us out by giving some bars of soap to the natives."

Jamie looked at Frieda straight-faced and snorted. "See, I told you he was dumber than he looked."

He turned his head back to the finance manager and flatly stated, "Oh wow, slow down, lightning! We are not talking about spending our own money! And we are not talking about spending only for this state in Africa. Your competitors are coming in to offer them the expertise if THEY pony up the money. And by THEY, I mean all the surrounding African states as well. You think so small! That's why you'll fail."

The finance manager stared blankly, unable to comprehend, until Jamie sighed again and clarified, "WE don't write the checks, they write the checks! We get all the surrounding states to come into the game because we can't operate in a vacuum. We invite them in on the game, and we get them to pony up as well. No one will refuse because no one wants their country left behind. Are you beginning to see, or do we also need to get your glasses checked?"

After a long pause the finance manager replied, "Yes, Mr. Rafferty. I get it. We invest, but we use their monies. You said the gear is coming in two weeks?"

Jamie smiled and asked, "Yes, how do you want it invoiced? My alternate client is standing by, in the event you don't want it. In fact, I'm not quite sure I know what I'm going to tell them if you use your never used #2 pencil to approve the purchase."

The finance manager nodded and agreed, "We'll take it. Make sure your team gets it deployed as soon as possible."

Jamie grinned and remarked, "Actually, it will go quite slowly since we'll be training the local IT students on its installation and operation. No local politician would dare to cross us, because we would have to lay the students off if we're ejected from this market. Then they would lose voters. Remember, invest locally and your competitors will struggle to displace you. Am I right?"

The finance manager almost smiled as he responded, "About the time I think you two have outlived your usefulness, you pop up with something to help extend your contract."

Outside the finance manager's office, Jamie smiled at the bewildered Frieda and queried, "See how easy it is to steer the weak-minded? Of course, it helps when they're greedy. To make this look more convincing, let's approach the competition to see if we can get a better deal, though this agreement will keep work moving for months or until we find another job.

"Before we do that, I'd like to get some more wine, get you back out of your clothes, and see what kind of erotic calisthenics can be executed in your hammock. But, this time, no falling out as we rotate positions!"

Frieda smirked. "I get to participate in the pole vault this time instead of doing all the work yourself. That's mighty big of you! …Well, not really."

Jamie clucked his tongue in mock annoyance with the disparaging comment. "Just wait until I get you naked, sweetie!"

They had returned to their humble accommodations. Frieda had remarked she was going to change into something more comfortable as she walked into the adjoining bedroom. About that time, Jamie saw the incoming email he had been waiting for pop in. He grinned broadly as he read the response. Straining to contain his exuberance, he loudly stated, "Hah, I convinced them. My career destination is moving now. Pack our bags, babe. We're heading to China and the sweetest job ever."

Frieda's mouth hung open slightly in disbelief as she watched Jamie doing his happy dance around their grimy living quarters. Finally, shrugging off her dumbfounded state, she reminded,

"We're under contract here, my soon-to-be-in-jail-for-fraud humping buddy. We haven't saved anything so we can't afford to exit this cesspool. You just conned the finance dweeb of this disgusting manufacturer of personal hygiene products for animals and larger primates with a fabricated story that rivals the Wall Street financial derivatives debacle of 2008. None of that now matters because you think we're leaving for China instead of jail. By the way, where in China? I don't speak Chinese and neither do you as far as I know."

Jamie, still elated that his dream-scheme was unfolding the way he needed it to, waltzed over to Frieda. While smiling tenderly, he pushed her dark hair behind her ear. He then moved his head over to whisper in her ear but instead began teasing her ear with his tongue while his right hand moved to begin caressing her breast. He would have undone her blouse if her indignation hadn't kicked in, prompting her to pull away.

After a few retreating steps, she rebuked, "It's going to be like the last time, right? Me desperately trying to keep us out of jail, and you ready to drop and run to the next scam. Jamie, I can't ask my folks for more money to underwrite this lifestyle. Don't we ever get to do what I want? Will there ever be a time when we can just have a normal life? This is just one big con game for you. Is that all I am as well?"

Jamie, always the adventurer, offered, "If you don't want to go, you don't have to. After all, apparently all I am is your humping buddy anyway. Someone pretty like you can get that anywhere. Look, Frieda, I don't have anything but my wits to leverage. I've worked long hours, in crummy places. I've taken all these backwater IT jobs that no one would take to learn. I wanted to know about computers, how information flows, and most importantly learning to profit from that knowledge. Not to do it for the rest of my life, but how to win at their game.

"This job in China is designed for that payoff. I'll be the lead IT engineer in a fully automated gambling casino, in what is probably the newest version of the old Wild West. This part of China is like Hong Kong with English spoken as well as Chinese and Portuguese. I need to do this. If you want to go with me, I promise you will be wearing diamonds as big as horse turds, before I'm through. Are you with me?"

Frieda could feel the old con game being staged again. Her emotions in a tug of war from his blue-skies offer. How often had he taken her along for his roll-of-the-dice only to lose everything except the clothes they wore? She fought the tears and the tidal wave of anger, but it boiled down to only one of two choices. Each time he promised something better, and every time they were the losers.

She really wanted to go home to start over in a normal life. Trouble was, she wanted him to go too! He simply wasn't the reliable, home by five for dinner, kind of man. She knew this would be like the last time, and the next gig he signed on for would be like the one previous. She told herself that he was the one with the gambling problem, but if that were true, then why couldn't she just leave? The tears streamed down her face as she made up her mind on what her future was going to be.

In that short moment of thought, Frieda stared at Jamie for a few minutes and then slapped him hard across the face.

CHAPTER 1

So far yet so very near

The drone of the commercial aircraft was unmistakable, though First Class was undeniably quieter than the Coach seats behind the engines. Conversations were muted, or passengers dozed. The distinctive aromatic smell of heated nuts wafted from the forward galley. The aircraft had almost reached the cruising altitude that would allow comfort services to begin. They were on the last leg of the long flight from Zürich to Macau. Juan had grumbled about taking a trip so far away, but Julie had sold him with her vivid description of the small peninsula across the Pearl River Delta from Hong Kong. As a Portuguese overseas territory until 1999, it reflected an extraordinary mix of Portuguese and Chinese influences. What seemed to put the glint in Juan's eye was its nickname, "The Las Vegas of Asia".

Macau was one of Julie's favorite places, but she had never gone for pleasure, only for work purposes. Julie, also known as JAC or Cyber Assassin Julie at work, had originally visited the city to meet with Ling Po. Julie had been hooked the first time she walked over the beautiful black sand on Hac Sa Beach, her thick light brown hair ruffled by the breeze. Her legs, which made up most of her 1.6 meters, gobbled up the sand as she'd traveled to her destination.

That seemed a lifetime ago. Since then, Julie had maintained her peak physical condition with martial arts training sessions with Juan and by chasing after their twins. Even now, she carried almost no fat on her supple body, just the way Juan liked it. She was delighted with their current lifestyles even though they still had some elements of risk in their professional endeavors.

So much had happened since the last trip she'd made to Macau. It felt as if she were looking through an entirely different lens. She and Juan had started their own business, known as the Cyber Assassin Technology Services or CATS team, shortly after they were married. Their business was supported by her family's business yet thrived nicely on its own merit. She leaned back into her seat to relax as the fragments of their history went through her mind.

Julie, adopted as a baby, had grown up in a family which was part of an ongoing business formed during World War II that now stretched around the world. The business, which was referred to by the family and close associates as the R-Group, had interests in real estate, finance, technology, security, and information resources. Their clientele included both private elite families, initially serviced post-World War II, and public entities including Interpol and the intelligence agencies of various countries. The primary pillars of the R-Group were to uphold the rights of the individuals or governments that stood for freedom and justice.

Originally, the family founders, three daring young men, had taken a copy of the Enigma Machine as they fled Poland. These intelligent and resourceful men had joined their skills to slightly modify the device and then had used it to undermine the German Nazis through encryption of information shared in just the right places. Though many of the core family members had changed over the years, the foundational beliefs of the operations had not. Their span of power and influence had increased, though much of the operation was only known within the family business.

Juan and Julie had met during an R-Group assignment where Julie had worked to locate an heiress, Lara Bernardes. Lara, the head of a now successful fashion house of Brazil, was also the love of Juan's brother, Carlos. Julie had provided both Juan and Carlos with new identities at the end of that assignment, though he had mightily protested erasure of his past.

Juan, the crazy flyboy, had captured Julie's heart with his quick wit and ability to love her unconditionally. She knew she was in love with Juan when she had beat him in a martial arts challenge at a gym. He told great stories, kept his cool under pressure, loved their twin children, and was deliciously passionate.

Julie glanced over to her resting partner. His thick ebony hair was a nice topping to his nearly 1.83 meters of rippling muscles and clean-shaven face. When he smiled, she had no doubts that he adored her. Julie was known for her never-ending smile and leveraged it often with her delightful husband, as well as in her undercover roles. As if aware of her stare, Juan's hand reached over and gently cradled her hand in his with a small smile appearing on his generous lips. If they weren't on a commercial flight with people all around, she might have started something, hoping Juan would finish it.

Juan rested comfortably against the window and almost dozed, though he was aware of his surroundings. It was odd to be flying somewhere and not piloting the aircraft. The feeling of Julie's hand in his, warm and soft, was not exactly the scenario he had been thinking about, but it would do until they reached the resort. Julie had told him that the resort offered more private and scenic rooms than the large, over-crowded casino hotels. But a promise to go and check out the gambling at some point was fine with him. Juan liked to gamble a bit and had even brought some of his reserves from his pre-Julie Mexico investments to play, thus presenting no risk to their business. The business was doing well, and Juan knew that Julie's family had money, but it was something they were building together for their family dynasty.

Juan missed the twins, Gracie and Juan Jr., with their constant babbling and laughter. Regardless, he was going to make the most of four days alone with his beautiful wife, partner, and love of his heart, right next to him where she belonged. He opened his eyes at the sounds of services beginning, and Julie rewarded him with one of her lovely smiles. He toasted them when their wine was served and knew he was very lucky to have her.

Julie and Juan were laughing while they deplaned, finally at their destination. Their driver was there with a placard on display as they walked outside. Julie's father, Otto, who was enjoying the time with his grandchildren almost as much as her mother, Haddy, insisted they have a driver on call so they could go anywhere, anytime without needing to worry about the vehicle itself. It had been his gift to them.

Otto, as one of the primary heads of the R-Group, rarely took time off, but the twins seemed to somehow make it easier to set aside those responsibilities. Maude was the children's full-time governess, but Haddy and Otto insisted on staying to enjoy Gracie and Juan Jr. in peace. Their time with the twins was also being referred to as the Grand Spoiling Time. Julie chuckled as her phone indicated another text message with likely a candid photo arrival. Her giggles erupted anew as she showed the picture to Juan. He laughed too.

Their driver, Chen Lee, smiled as he greeted them and proceeded to tell them, in his perfect English, that his name meant morning. His non-stop oration included the points-of-interest they drove past, things he liked, his family, and how much he approved of their choice of the beachfront villa that afforded privacy. Privacy and seclusion were expensive and limited in Macau. Chen was lean and a bit shorter than Julie but had a welcoming smile and a twinkle in his dark eyes that reminded Julie of espresso. Chen boasted about his twelve children, and Juan privately remarked that working must be the only time Chen was able to speak, so Chen obviously made the most of it. After delivering them to their villa and making certain the arrangements were in place, Chen indicated he would pick them up that evening for dinner. At their request he promised to provide several options for after-dinner activities.

Their room was magnificent! The floor to ceiling windows dominated two sides reaching into a corner with a breathtaking view of the water on one side and the city on the other. Quiet music was in the air but gentle, like a breeze. The furniture was sparse with the oversized bed, covered in white and ivory silk covers and overflowing with huge pillows, as the dominating feature. Bold-colored silk flowers offset the whites and ivories of the interior and bedding. The bathroom contained a shower as well as a four-person, sunken Jacuzzi with a private window view toward the sea. Everything was elegant and yet seemed practical to a fault.

Juan called for room service while Julie made quick work of unpacking and settling into the luxurious suite. Room service had already arrived when Julie emerged from the bathroom. She was comfortably garbed in a barely-there bikini that perfectly matched the blue in her sapphire and diamond wedding ring. Ahead of where she walked, she spread fairies of light across the room as the sun caught the surfaces of her ring.

Juan leered at her, grinned and then groaned, "My darling, if you keep dressing that way, we'll never see more of Macau than this room."

Julie wagged a finger toward Juan as she firmly explained, "Juan, we need to establish some rules. I want to go curl my toes in the black sand and perhaps bring back just a little for our kids. I want to swim with you in the South China Sea and enjoy all the historical sites with you." Then she insisted, "Juan, you need to behave."

He handed her a glass of champagne and raised his to toast to them both. Juan grinned, then replied, "Sweetheart, it is far too late to start trying to establish rules. I'll, of course, behave as your servant and lover. All your wants will be fulfilled, as will mine. Then, I promise, we will see about the sights on your list."

He pulled her close as they sipped the champagne.

The glasses were magically resting on the table empty as Julie found herself horizontal on the giant bed with Juan leaning over her, a familiar look of passion burning in his eyes.

"We've not been alone in far too long, my beautiful wife." Running his hands over her skin that somehow had lost the minor inconveniences of the bikini, he continued, "Your skin is so soft, so smooth, and well, so kissable."

Juan kissed her lips and every available inch of her body while she returned the kisses and the touches, lost in the wonder of the magic they shared. She had never felt as much heat or ardent pleasure as she did when he had her in his arms. Juan knew all the right places to touch and lick until she begged for him to get closer and deeper.

"Sweet mercy," he groused as her inner thigh muscles clamped down on him as she pushed her hips up against his to continue the pleasure, "why did I wait so long to finish?"

Another woman might have been insulted at the comments had she not known, heart and soul, that to this point he had only considered her fulfillment and her pleasure. He had repeatedly given her everything she wanted and needed. He cared about her satisfaction in a way that was absolute until the precise moment when it shifted to being about him. He allowed her to be on top and drive him to the end of the precipice as he pulled her bottom into him, growing bigger and harder with each thrust until they both felt as if they were launched into space and flying. Afterward they tumbled as an entwined pair and drifted into a soft slumber after their exhausting lovemaking.

Minutes or hours later, Julie murmured, "We really need to see the sights while we are here."

Juan shifted them slightly and gripped her a bit closer as he whispered, "From my perspective, the sights are perfect from here."

CHAPTER 2

I thought I saw …

With their last full day in Macau, Julie and Juan were planning to spend it in the historical district and then on to dinner. Juan had heard that this newest casino had some of the best payouts, which Chen had also confirmed. Julie was comfortable in a flowing dress with small flowers scattered across the pale blue background and strappy sandals that were like walking barefoot. Juan was casual yet elegant in his khakis with a linen shirt that accentuated his dark skin and barely concealed his powerful build. He wrapped a protective arm gently around her waist while his eyes scanned everything nearby.

The historical district was a dichotomy of the merging of Western and Eastern culture that spanned decades. Each of the more than twenty ancient monuments and urban squares contained various stories of history, with religious foundations right in the forefront. The chapels, temples and churches were erected from the early 1500s well into the twentieth century. Even the Protestant cemetery they walked through, nestled next to a fabulous and expansive garden with sweet flower scents filling the air, highlighted the diverse community profile of Macau.

Juan called for Chen to retrieve them and take them to the casino. They grinned when Chen arrived within moments complete with a bright smile. At their request he took a picture of them with the garden in the background and then held open the door of the car. All the way to the casino, Chen chatted about what to or not to do.

"This casino is very different than others you might have encountered. You can speak for anything you want, and it will magically appear at your elbow. No one speaks very loud as there are ears everywhere. Just know that what you say will be heard, interpreted, and analyzed for the best way to fulfill the speaker's wants or needs. It is said the information gathering is second to none.

"The food is excellent, and the wines are brought in from all over. Madam, I suspect that you might find favor with the wines from France, while you, sir, might enjoy the richness of the Jamaican rum."

Juan laughed and asked, "Chen, how is it you've us pegged so well?"

Chen smiled and replied, "I listen too! And I have very good ears, a necessary requirement with so many children. However, you, asked me where to find the best of each the first day I picked you up."

Julie flashed him a smile and suggested, "Chen, you've an excellent memory. Let me know if you ever tire of this job. I have good use for those that pay attention to details."

Chen stopped the car in front of the casino and then walked around to open the door. He offered his hand while Julie emerged and said, "Pretty lady, you have a nice evening with your husband. I think he'll take care of you." Then Chen winked and quietly added, "I'll keep your job offer in mind, perhaps part time."

Julie laughed as she took Juan's arm, and they walked in through what looked like a door, but which magically disappeared as they approached. Other guests who preceded them also looked impressed with the unique surroundings of Chinese art and artifacts. The ambiance was unique and bespoke the locals' name for the casino, Chinese Dragon. Juan escorted Julie into the dining hall where they were seated at a secluded table near a meandering brook that seemed to encircle the restaurant area like a mote, but with water that softly bubbled and danced over the rocks like a natural stream.

"Juan, this is exquisite. I never imagined that a casino might house a quiet, elegant restaurant. I can see others at the nearby tables, but I can't hear a word they're saying."

Juan cocked his head as he surveyed the area. "This entire room must contain a series of white noise columns that somehow isolate each of the guest tables. I, for one, will enjoy this quiet time with you while I sit back and sip some of that Jamaican rum that Chen mentioned. And you, my love, would you like a glass of the French chardonnay we shared earlier at the resort?"

Julie flashed one of her coveted smiles and said, "I'd like a glass and perhaps some fresh vegetable bits to snack on."

Soundlessly, within seconds of her response, a robotic waiter placed their glasses on the table followed by a tablet for each of them that flashed pictures of the available cuisine for the main courses and desserts.

"Juan, this is amazing. All the food is pictured. No confusion on the contents ordered."

"You're right, honey. This is fun, but let's skip the octopus. Tentacles, cooked or not, still give me the creeps."

"I agree." Julie laughed and then added, "I think that a nice scallop salad with the main entree of rice with shrimp is more than enough for me."

"That sounds pretty good, except I think I would prefer the filet mignon, medium, with the steamed vegetables on rice for the side. More to my liking."

Their snack of cold vegetables with a wasabi ranch dipping sauce arrived while silent mechanical hands removed the tablets. Juan offered. "To our love, good fortune, and last night in Macau. Julie, I promise to make it memorable."

After a delicious dinner culminated with a fresh lemon mousse, Juan declared. "I think I'd like to try the tables, sweetheart."

"I'd enjoy watching you play, if you don't mind my watching."

He took her hand and kissed it, then held it as they circulated. Juan stopped and played at a few tables with Julie behind him or in an adjacent seat. "Honey, I am having fun and making small gains. I think you'll enjoy the next game."

Julie slipped her hand into his as they moved to the Baccarat table.

"Julie, this is one game of chance where no skill is required. Let me know if you wish to play too."

"Juan, I like looking at the people dressed up with flashy jewelry advertising their wealth. People watching is fun. Look at those couples and groups laughing and chatting without a care in the world."

"Agreed, they laugh and clap with their success and ask the mechanical waiters for drinks for courage to continue."

"It's very efficient yet inviting."

"You're right, Julie. And I'm winning just enough to keep playing. I want to sample their games and take in all their automation."

"The casino floor is enormous and with the muted lighting I've lost all track of time. I love the soft rugs of gold and red with dragon characters of various colors seemingly creating a path to walk from one area to the next. Even the real casino personnel with name tags blend in with their non-descript apparel. The goal here is to deliver fun to guest." Julie spotted the sensors on the gaming tables and other furnishings. "Juan," she whispered close to his ear, "are you seeing all the sensors too. Chen was right regarding eyes and ears everywhere."

He kissed her neck as agreement and sat them at a blackjack table facing a row of slots. A young man fixing a machine across the way caught Julie's attention, His well-groomed blond hair, along with his tailored black uniform and polished boots were enough to get him noticed. Yet, what Julie noticed was his rapid hand movements and flipping of switches. She studied him closely, trying to mentally categorize his actions. She scanned the ceiling for the monitoring cameras and detected four or five that might have him in their sights. Then she wondered why anyone would attempt such a clumsy skimming play on coin slots with that many cameras present.

Juan leaned over very close to her ear and whispered, "That young rogue has quite the moves. Do you find him that attractive, my love, or are you trying to see exactly at which point he is lining his pockets with the euros he is extracting from the machine while resetting the counters? Makes me wonder if management is even aware."

Julie shot Juan a smile and laughed, "That's exactly it. How did you spot it so easily? I thought you were playing your game."

"I told you, sweetheart, this game takes no skill. I can play and still enjoy watching you and seeing what fascinates you, or what captures your attention."

Julie leaned in and kissed Juan soundly, then commented, "You, honey, fascinate me. I like seeing you play and win. Show me some more of your winning streak." She tugged his earlobe between her teeth and hissed, "I hope he doesn't get caught. I suspect they would frown upon that sort of action. Glad it's not our problem."

CHAPTER 3

Something or not

Dmitry, the grizzled Russian veteran, asked, "Are you sure you can deal with the gaming interface to the program? Some people of the older generation are uncomfortable with the new graphics and high-definition interfaces. I know your system can support the heavy rendering demands of the programs. However, if that isn't offset by having an integrated animated avatar playing a role for you in the game space, it's not going to be much fun."

Dmitry glanced to make certain the outer door was closed and then looked through the window into the data center. The posh office befitting his title boasted huge furniture suited to older European tastes and the darker colors favored by ostentatious men. The floor was marble with large area rugs in darker shades that complemented the furniture. The heavy drapes on the single large window overlooking the garden were open, letting in natural light. The large room also boasted multiple oversized digital screens and a couple of soft leather chairs of varying styles with remote control devices on adjacent tables. The man himself was dressed for comfort in dark fine wool slacks and a grey cashmere sweater that was near the color of his well-cut hair.

As the Russian Minister of Information Propagation, Dmitry had access to some of the most sophisticated computers and software in the world. As a former Russian war hero, now bored with minimal daily efforts of state, he thought the adrenaline rush from this digital competition was nearly as exciting as days spent in battle, without the limited rations and wet socks. He'd paid his dues and now he played his games with his supercomputer and his brains against his once fierce enemy, Chairman Chang.

Chang was the head of the Chinese Cyber Warfare College, politically connected and virtually untouchable. Dmitry battled the old goat for many years with differing battle strategies, both winning and losing at different times. Now they were more like global associates that knew how to work their respective countries' politics and resources for personal gain. They used one another as needed to reach their dutiful goals. Dmitry shrugged off thoughts of their history and focused on the game, feeling quite certain the programming experts of his Dteam had outdone themselves with this competition. It was a virtual game, with virtual machines and players, connected by an open conference bridge which either side could mute on demand or add video, depending upon their ego for the day. This was a no holds barred game with each player committed to the win, period.

Chairman Chang, frowned into the conference bridge. "Ever since I gave up my slide rule and abacus, I've been able to keep up with the digital world just fine. What's the matter, you old relic, afraid that I'll win in this child's digital contest? I've loaded up the program on my supercomputer. I believe I understand the rules of engagement. Let's do this gaming combat, as we discussed.

"It got to be an improvement over your ridiculous plan to launch a digital onslaught against the Finnish supercomputer. I mean, how funny was that? We teed up to pound the Finns with both our supercomputers, and you sent us both to a website that was recruiting suicide truck drivers for some Islamic Jihad movement. I digress. I'm launching my avatar."

Dmitry sulked at the unpleasant reminder of that event but quickly retorted, "That's just typical of you, Chang! I offer up the best Russian gaming environment to help improve your disposition, and all you do is grouse about a missed target! You didn't have to apologize to the Muslim fanatics or promise to increase their monthly stipend to get them calmed."

"Come now, Dmitry. After a few more atrocities they'll forget the incident. I'm teasing you. Let's play your game. Truth be told, this does look like an interesting diversion from my normal mundane workday. A person needs some good wholesome activity to break the monotony. Wouldn't you agree?"

Dmitry brightened. "Alright, since you put it that way, let's go over the ground rules for this event.

"As in all games, it's the number of points and amount of money you accumulate over the life of the challenge. These programs are designed to credit our attacks, the number of end points rendered inoperative, and, most of all, how much booty each side acquires in the allotted time frame. Understood?"

Chairman Chang, growing excited by the prospects of the digital contest. "I'm ready! Let's wind 'em up, Dmitry."

Grinning enthusiastically, Dmitry roared, "The game is live."

CHAPTER 4

What to play next?

Chairman Chang stared in disbelief at the video image being displayed on his 132 cm screen. The full video conference call was on with a split screen display for the gaming arena. He numbly asked, "This is the *Wheel of Misfortune?* Tell me you're not going to put on some slinky evening gown with high heels and spin it to see what kind of gaming motif we're operating under. Why can't we just play the last game again?"

Dmitry grinned wolfishly. "A true gamer continually looks for new experiences, my dear chairman! This digital spinner automatically removes the last game we've finished so there's no chance of having it come up as a result. We could repeat a game if we agree, but that is not as much fun until we've tried them all.

"It spins at a press of the center button. If you prefer to have a female launch the wheel, I can have Evgeniya, my secretary, play dress-up to suit you. I mean, she's got to be easier on the eyes than Konstantin, with his closely cropped beard that doesn't stop at his neck but travels to the tops of his feet. The strapless dress just wouldn't work with all that body hair on his back. It would be like someone putting a Great Dane into an evening dress. Ugh! Though, she isn't much better."

Sighing, Chairman Chang rested his head forward on the fingertips of his left hand and closed his eyes as he desperately tried to purge the disgusting imagery now everlastingly burned into his memory banks. He sighed again. "Can you just spin the wheel without the vulgar analog human props?"

Dmitry enthusiastically replied, "I thought you'd never ask! Here she goes." After several revolutions, the pointer on the wheel came to rest on their next gaming title, *Scavenger Hunt. Dmitry's* eyes lit up as if he really was in a game show.

Dmitry triumphantly announced, *"Scavenger Hunt!* I've never played this one! I hope it's as good as Prisoner for a Day! Now that was a game! Dodging the drug addicts in the same cell that are all coming down from a heroin high and indiscriminate sexual rampage in a co-ed school. Whoa! Come on, we've got to set up our avatars to hunt for everything on the list coming up on the next screen. "Here are the rules of engagement, Chang. You might consider printing them if you read as slowly as you did on the last game. Once those are agreed to, then the shopping list and the associated points will appear. I will then launch the observer window to the game environment for game on!" Dmitry stroked his chin as if in deep thought. "Before I do that, how many hours to you want to set this for? Twelve hours, 36 hours, or 72 hours? And don't forget, we don't stop the game in progress for potty breaks, so either have a container to go into, a tourniquet to apply to the situation, or your back-up player who can fill in for up to two hours total for any game."

A sullen Chairman Chang curtly replied, "I have great bladder control unlike some younger men I know. Set it for twelve. We can extend to 36 at hour eleven if agreed, correct?"

Dmitry, unfazed by the snide comment, launched the gaming window and said, "Yes, you remembered. Good." The list appeared on their screens. "Oh look, sensors and Wi-Fi scavenger items are a part of the items to hunt. Look at the number of points they're worth. Woo-hoo. The internet allows phenomenal reach of the play area. It's so realistic. Game on."

Chairman Chang, try as he might, felt the tug of the gaming high overtake him. He felt his smile broaden, and eyes open wider as the game completely engulfed his cognitive powers of awareness, shutting out all else.

CHAPTER 5

The here, not there

Gwen screamed, "Jack, don't let go of me!"

Jack struggled to hold on to her hand as she dangled from the side of the bridge over the icy water forty yards below. Many of the lights were out on this rundown bridge and this was a path few traveled.

He was strong man, but the awkward grasp he had of her hand, coupled with his fear of heights and bridges, made him struggle for control. He complained, "No more desserts for you! Geez, you weigh a ton!"

Now finally grasping the gravity of the situation, she shrieked, "Pull me back up, Jack! Pull me back up, and I swear I will lose the weight you've been grousing about! Please, honey? Don't let me fall into the water!"

Jack felt his phone vibrate. "Gwen, my phone! Of course! I can use my phone to get help! It just texted me."

Gwen's voice reached an epic screech. "This is not the time or place to be texting your friends! Pull me up, Jack!"

"No, don't you see? I'll lean into the rail, then with my free hand dial 911! You know, police, rescue, TV cameras, and then, of course, talk shows!"

Jack freed up his cell and punched in the save code while he focused his strength to hold Gwen. He had a good grip on her, though his arm grew more tired as it strained further and longer.

The connection completed with a woman answering. "911, what's your emergency?"

Jack praying for light at the end of the tunnel, barked, "We're here on this bridge, and my girlfriend has fallen over the edge! I'm holding onto her hand, but I can't hold her much longer! Please send emergency help to this location!"

The 911 operator responded, "Sir, this emergency service is here in the United States. Your geolocation from our emergency services database shows you calling from Poland. I strongly recommend that you hang up and dial the local emergency services."

Jack screamed, "No, don't disconnect! We're at the old bridge here in Pittsburgh, Pennsylvania, hanging over the river, not Poland! Where are you answering this call?"

The 911 operator was unconvinced that the call wasn't a prank of some sort but asked, "Describe the bridge, sir. I am answering this call in Pittsburgh, and the computers are showing your geo-location as overseas. If you can give me a reasonable description of your location, then I will consider this a valid call for help and dispatch personnel."

Jack gasped and quickly related, "This is that old funky bridge with every third or fourth light burned out. Stupid people like to use this route when coming back from Old Town, when they want a thrill by foolishly walking on the wide rail area instead of the footpath! My Gwen is the current fool I have in hand.

"Can we get some help here, now? Do you believe that your damn map and geolocation finding information is wrong?"

The operator quickly bridged in emergency personnel in proximity to the caller and announced, "Sir, keep this line open as Emergency Rescue is on the way. It is a good thing you described the bridge in the manner that you did. My younger brother lost his friend on that bridge. I can't ever forget its description. Now keep talking. Described what happened."

"My girlfriend, Gwen insisted on walking on the wide railing back from dinner to grab a selfie. She'd taken off her cap to show her new bright red streaks of hair shining in the moonlight with her face next to mine. I'm six foot three so she crouched down. Gwen is the wild one and she wanted a memorable picture."

Mad and scared, Jack asked, "Why'd you jump when the truck honked at us? You afraid they might see us doing something stupid?"

Gwen, crying and pleading, she explained, "Jack, the horn startled me, and I lost my footing! Please pull me up. I can't make it until the emergency vehicles get here. My arm is burning and I'm sure yours is hurting too."

"I could lift you if I had both of my hands. I gotta talk to the 911 lady. If I just had a lighter woman or superhuman strength, this would be all over!

"Say, wait a minute. An adrenaline rush, that's what I need. Say something to make me mad. That'll give me enough strength to pull you up, where you can grab on to the struts or something."

From her depths, Gwen summoned the most aggravating taunt she could conjure. "Your brother's cock is bigger than yours!"

"Jack, hang on, the emergency team is close," the 911 operator interrupted.

Oblivious to the 911 operator conversation, Jack roared, "I said mad, not insane! You want me to let you go? You'd better be kidding. This is hopeless."

"Jack, it was all I could think of to make you mad." Gwen sobbed.

Jack, still gasping and holding onto Gwen, heard the sirens and saw the lights. "Ma'am thanks for not hanging up on me because your system thought I was in Poland. Sounds like you've got bigger problems than just our little one here."

Ever the cool professional, she concurred, "Evidently, sir. I hope you and Gwen recover from this ordeal." Inside the window of her follow up she tagged a note to Detective Como, of the felony division, to review the call and locational information transmitted.

CHAPTER 6

Praise and Threats

Juan and Julie sat in their CATS office, quietly thinking while they sipped their coffee. Julie planned for them to compare notes on the team's assignments. She remarked, "Juan, these requests are odd and from different places. Do they strike you as coincidences?"

"Julie, they are each very different. What are your thoughts?"

Julie recognized Juan's silence as respect for time she needed to think. She gripped her coffee cup with both hands and stared off into space thinking of her past experiences and how any of it would help with these new assignments.

Julie grinned at Juan. "I think we take this Consortium assignment in Australia. There's not much to go on, which makes me more inclined to have some feet on the ground, hunting for clues. We'll take George. It'll be a good way to watch him in action. He might lead a team in the future. I wasn't completely sure when we made offers to each of the team members that we'd have billable revenue for all of them. At the current rate we're getting requests of new jobs for expanded corporate security assignments, we may need to start looking for more employees."

"I had no doubts! I knew my beautiful, smart, charming, and intelligent wife, as well as the mother of two adorable children, called the right game plan. I admire your intellect, coupled with that sultry feminine method of correctly designing the best solution, delivered in a reserved but powerful demeanor. There are places on this planet that whispering your name brings a crowded room to a standstill! You're a fair-minded, powerful combatant in the finest tradition of Amazon warriors. I love you in my life, my Athena. It's been said, and I'm told there are sworn affidavits, by those so devoted to you, and in awe of your aura, they've offered to crawl miles over broken glass just to smell where you urinated last!"

Julie knew Juan could charm the wings off a butterfly, but his last line of the absurd soliloquy made her bust out laughing. Juan grinned and leaned over and kissed her check.

"Juan, you're impossible to stay mad at. Only you can get away with telling bawdy stories in mixed company." Giggled anew she took a breath and announced, "I need to dial into a conference call with the family and give them a status."

"But of course, sweetheart. While you do that, I'll touch base with George and Brayson to see if they're ready for their next assignments."

Julie joined the bridge that felt like home. She'd grown up with these people and as a member of the business. She recalled, how they nurtured her mind and helped cultivate her cyber skills. Each family member had support and an opportunity to pursue their life goals. Today her extensive skills allowed her to launch her business as she trained others to her level.

"Hi all," Julie opened, "I'm delighted to report Juan and I are selling CATS support back into the R-Group customers. We have no shortage of cyber sleuthing requests, only a potential shortage of qualified, honorable people."

Julie cleared her throat. "I know I am not a R-Group voting member, but I love attending these meetings and offering my opinions when asked. Juan is still on the sidelines of the R-Group for all our security, but when you are ready, he will do what's needed. He is committed to all our family."

Otto, her father nodded. "Juan is providing great support for operating your fledgling business. I've been a part of our family business for a long time. When I married Haddy, your mother, she was in the dark until she volunteered to take on a working role in the business. Even then, she chose to exclude herself from some of the operations side and never had a voting role. Something will shift and he'll need more information for some event." Otto chuckled and winked. "When I recommended your older, sister Petra take over my vote, it was because I wanted to play with your twins."

Petra, a renowned encryption master, shook her blonde mane as she stifled a laugh. "Julie, we all have our times to shine, and your business is rocking. I was hoping I might come spar with your team now that I've recovered from the dreadful attack those many months ago. This family is the best." Her faced turned and she winked at Jacob. "Jacob and I love the twins and of course volunteer to watch them whenever Otto and Haddy want a break."

Quip, the meeting chair and creator of their supercomputer resource, ICABOD, interjected, "Let's going around and update the group on your current projects, open issues, problems, and additional support requirements, if any."

Wolfgang, the financial genius, and oldest member of the R-Group started, "Our base customers are completing their routine updates and assessments. We implemented some new checks and balances for our wealth management clients. Petra and Jacob's routine security and technology updates were completed on time and within budget. Well done, you two, on keeping the hacker and crackers at bay in this connected world we are a part of globally."

"Thank you, Wolfgang," said Jacob, "we're always glad when our hundreds of individuals, businesses and governments are safer because of our oversight."

Wolfgang continued, "Our commercial and private real-estate management is doing well with the automated programs added. ICABOD cares for those and highlight exceptions which we have none to report for this month."

Julie straightened her shoulders and looked at the friendly faces. "I wanted to alert you that we're adding in new assignments almost faster than we can finish up those already in play. They appear as unrelated events, but each seems plagued with a digital disruption element. We think it could be a sign of a hacker group. My team will closely monitor so I can analyze and deliver updates. I'm categorizing them as suffering from Jesse James syndrome. Corporate extortion in the finest tradition of the James gang, only updated to the 21st century. If you hear any chatter about similar scenarios we aren't engaged in, pass it along."

Quip frowned. Julie suspected Quip worried that her comment was a challenge.

Twitching his nose and staring at her he challenged, "Jesse James syndrome? What are you talking about? You mean a bunch of ex-Confederate soldiers running around with flour sacks tied around their heads to mask their identity as they robbed banks and trains at gunpoint? Cyber adversaries with a 19th century description. Seriously, Julie. Let me remind you how bandits rob in the 21st century," he smirked. "People, like Charles Yukon, put together a bunch of like-minded corporate raiders with lots of money, buy up enough stock to get noticed, and send an open but threatening letter to the company's directors warning them that they need a better rate of return. Then they ask what they're going to do about it. It used to be called greenmail, but now the politically correct euphemism is activism. The demands are the same: pay me and my consortium to go away. We'll leave you alone, promise. However unsavory the activity is, it's still within the confines of the law."

Julie stilled her facial features, clucked her tongue in annoyance with Quip's condescending tone. "Yes, Quip, we're all familiar with the corporate raider phrase Here comes Yukon, now the company's gone! That's not the situation I'm tracking and suspect a pattern emerging. Basically, the computer systems are hacked, ransom demands made. At this point, only a few instances, but enough that I wanted it on the record. This is clearly not within the legal boundaries of a publicly traded corporation. So, yes, this is very much like what the Jesse James gang did in the late 1800s."

Then Julie put on her most dazzling smile and added, "And, Quip, if you ever use that condescending tone with me again, I swear I will launch my own raid against your data center and thoroughly trash the Feng Shui layout. I mean cable ties removed, power and data cables draped everywhere, blade servers sticking too far out of the racks, key grouping of servers pulled out and randomly sprinkled throughout the data center in different racks and in different directions, some being upside down."

Quip, noticeably shaken by the vile threat against his data center. He cajoled, "Uh, Julie, there is no need to threaten such devastation and chaos against my space. I offered a high-spirited comment in jest. Since you took exception, I withdraw it and respectfully apologize."

Jacob leaned over and next to Petra's ear and mumbled loud enough for the group to overhear. "Boy, does she play dirty! Geezers!"

Jacob was the grandson of Wolfgang, the financial wizard of the R-Group, and had grown up in the United States. After Wolfgang's daughter, Jacob's mother, had been murdered, the family had reached out through Petra to see if Jacob was of the proper integrity to be allowed into the inner circle. Jacob, a master programmer with a background in security testing, had fallen in love with Petra during that process. When Otto had taken a leave of absence, he had split his votes between Petra and Jacob in the hopes that the two would have a permanent relationship. Jacob was tall, like Wolfgang, and had the same build, with a well-defined jawline and handsome features. Wolfgang was delighted that Jacob, his only remaining family, had chosen to join the R-Group. Jacob and Petra lived in Wolfgang's mansion in Zürich and seemed to be working on that permanent relationship after Petra's injury.

Petra grinned and whispered back, "You have no idea!"

Julie suppressed her smirk and after a long pause said, "Apologies accepted, Dr. Quip."

Otto moved the conversation back to business at hand as he offered, "Julie, let me say you have but to ask for the services of ICABOD to help distill your findings. We're confident in the ability of CATS and will support your efforts. We're pleased that your operation is expanding and picking up different customers."

Quip added, "That's right, Julie. Once you have a little more assembled on your Jesse James syndrome theory, we can easily augment your efforts with ICABOD's computing power. You can when you need it. I'm always available to help."

Julie, chuckling, volunteered, "I was only teasing about destroying the Feng Shui of your data center, Quip. But thanks for suggesting I add ICABOD's processing power into the loop. We're not ready yet, as I need more reconnaissance work before I'll have enough data elements." Like all members of the R-Group did, she addressed the digital member with similar deference made to anyone in the family. "ICABOD, you know I would never do anything to disrupt your processing."

The screens flashed, but ICABOD restrained from commenting as he was well aware that Julie's barbs were not directed at his systems or processors. In keeping with his efforts to learn humor, ICABOD projected a digital emoticon of an animated happy face on the team monitor that made everyone smile.

Wolfgang added, "Julie, I think I speak for the group in mentioning how proud we are of what you have built. Ask for any assistance you need to bring your case load under control. Before history rolls over it, I like the analogy of the Jesse James syndrome! Thanks for the extra smile."

Julie beamed her trademark smile at all of them before saying goodbye and disconnecting from the call.

CHAPTER 7

Gamers and Gamblers

"**W**hoa, what a rush." Dmitry blurted. "I've played this game several times by myself, but поражать umm, dang! It's a lot more fun with a worthy adversary!" With a self-satisfied smile, Dmitry asked, "Was it good for you too, Chang?"

With a scowl on his face Chairman Chang rocked back into his chair and responded, "I see why you thought it was fun, since you received the lion share of the digital points. And what do you mean using the slang word *dang*? I wouldn't have guessed that playing computer games has caused you to regress. Are you back to watching low budget, coming of age, juvenile movies again? I mean really."

Undaunted by the surly rebuke to his emotional high, Dmitry continued, "Now, Chang, you got some digital points and goodies too! You see how much fun this is? Tampering with the geolocation positioning in the game made it much more interesting when looting those side avenues. With the jumbled maps, we were able to empty banks and jewelry stores up and down Main Street, which is a lot more fun than holding up the infrequent hotels that our avatars can rest in. The trackers kept getting dispatched to the wrong addresses, making it impossible to stop either of us.

"However, I must suggest that you need to slow down on your ammunition usage. If you hadn't used up all your ammo, your avatar would have lasted longer. You also could have avoided buying more with your winnings during the session which reduced your totals on the scoreboard."

A slight smile came over Chairman Chang's face. "I was having fun laying down suppressive fire along the street before commandeering the loot. I'll know better next time. Now, these smash-and-grab scenarios in the game are fine, but I presume you do have some other more challenging gaming motifs for our intellectual pleasure?"

Dmitry's eyes lit up as he offered, "Have I got a surprise in store for you, old friend! My champion designer has just put the finishing touches on just such a game. He sent me a note earlier asking me to try it out! I guess you could call us his game testers.

"This new scenario will have a little more finesse to it, but I insisted that the violence and destructive activities be maintained, based on my appetite for digital carnage. I suspect you have the same appetite, so I don't think you will be disappointed with our next round of digitized cyber combat."

"I can't wait to try the next game, Dmitry. I can add it to my calendar for next week at the same time. Now, how about my winnings, so we can call it a day?"

Dmitry, somewhat taken aback, questioned, "Cash you out? Oh no, no, no, dear boy! This is the consummate gamer's game. All the winnings are allocated to one money disbursement account, and we choose which door has all the winnings. You and I play the game. Then all the winnings are pooled together for the last stage of the gaming session.

"The one with the most points gets to choose first among the three doors. Much like Three-card Monte that we used to play in the military, with the winner taking all. I don't know how many times I won the CO's pride and joy tank. He always paid to get it back."

Chairman Chang protested, "You'd already know which door to choose. I bring my supercomputer processing power to the gaming table in good faith, but you rig it so you will get all the funds."

Dmitry, a little put off by the accusation, disputed, "Hold on. This is gaming and gambling at its best, my angry friend. The funds are placed into one disbursement fund and then scattered into a cascade of other banking funds in a dissolving pattern making it impossible to trace where everything went, and most importantly, to whom. The effort to do that for just one winner convinced me that it wasn't worth doing it for two. And just so you know, I do NOT know which door the funds are behind. If I did, it wouldn't be gambling. Now you understand all the game rules. Because I won with the highest scoring, I am entitled to pick first. This one time I'll make a conciliatory gesture based on my high regard for you, Chang. I will let you choose first."

It was Chairman Chang's turn to be taken aback. Moderately impressed with the generous offer, he stated, "If you truly do not know which door the monies are behind, and you are willing to let me go first, what happens if I choose correctly?"

Dmitry shrugged and said, "Then I will not surrender my first choice at our next game, but the funds will be sanitized as I described, before being routed to your accounts that you established when we began.

"You understand the rules of three doors, right?" Dmitry paused, not really wanting a response but wanting the idea to take hold, then he explained, "If I go first but miss, then you have a 50-50 chance to guess correctly. If you miss, then the last and only choice goes to me with all the gaming proceeds. The winning gamer has two chances of success, but the second-place gamer only has one. In forfeiting my first draw, it means you have at least one full chance and maybe a win, if I choose incorrectly. In the spirit of the gaming gambler, make your electronic choice, Chang. May the best gambler win."

Chairman Chang, pleased to have been given a slight edge, promptly chose door number three.

CHAPTER 8

The Mirror

Juan smiled wistfully as he studied Julie while she was focused on work. He sometimes got lost in thought as he lovingly memorized her facial features and her physical outline. He enjoyed studying her while she poured over the reports from their field agents. His mind sometimes drifted between the memory of their chance meeting, which led to their ongoing romance, and the reality of the moment. For Juan, the womanizer, it was like someone had thrown an emotional switch inside him, such that no one held any interest for him except her.

Julie's sense of humor was every bit as good as his was, which meant that verbal sparring had them on equal footing. He chuckled to himself recalling how superior he'd felt he was in their karate practice until she had flattened him that first time. She could pilot an aircraft, deliver business development plans, and easily read strangers. This was one of those times where he reminded himself that he wasn't dreaming. She was the best partner anyone could have.

Julie gave an exaggerated sigh, then turned to face him, as she asked, "Juan, pop back to reality and help me with the schedule along with these tedious reports? We're so busy we're falling behind in directions to our field agents. Please help."

Juan chuckled slightly and reached over to caress her face, about to kiss her. "Hold it right there," she intercepted. "You're not going to pull that. *Oh yes honey let me help you with your bra routine,* because we ARE behind in our work. Right now, we need to focus here and now, then go work on supper with the kids. After that, we have our conference call with the team. Then, I'm taking a hot bath and a rub down from you. Then we can do the adult play time. But until then, let's get our chores done."

Juan, feigning a wounded look, gave Julie an acknowledging nod as he picked up a stack of papers to review. "Julie, you are so wrong about my intentions. I was really going to try and get your panties off, but now that I know that the goods will be parked for suitable drive-in entertainment later, let's get the damn chores out of the way."

A smile gradually broke out on Julie's face, and she gave him a good, wet, number four kiss on a scale of one to ten, and they both plowed ahead with their work.

Once the last team member dialed into the bridge, Julie opened, "Thanks for joining, team. I know that you've been scrambling to get to your newest assignments, so I appreciate the update reports and your participation in this call.

"Juan and I wanted to make certain we set up a cadence to discuss the status as you learn more about your situations. Several of the requests were focused on helping hands and checking network security. We'll want to see if situations are isolated or a pattern emerging."

Tyler chimed in, "Julie, in my case, there are some secondary issues with distorted GPS map coordinates which may have contributed to the misrouting of emergency responses. The area had an influx of burglaries which need to be investigated further. I am waiting to meet with my main contact, Detective Como for a briefing over and above the case files he left for me. The robberies could be unrelated, but the authorities had trouble finding the locations as each was reported throughout the evening and into early morning hours. A total list of stolen items from each location is being compiled. I think it's worth a bit more investigation on our part. Shoring up the emergency services digital network is the other avenue that requires attention particularly if there is a new digital threat virus out here."

Julie pondered momentarily and then suggested, "Good observation and interesting theory. Please continue to work that angle, Tyler. We'll need to keep all our notes on our share point, which each of you have access to add data anytime."

Julie paused and displayed the cases on the video feed, then continued, "Brayson, I know you are in Spain, exploring a network breach. What is the status?"

"I am in one of the major port cities which recently embraced connecting all public services and monitoring from the center." Brayson grinned. "A newly elected mayor is unfamiliar with all the technology and how connected it is. The initial concern was due to a program recently added to a laptop in the operations center that locked up a desktop and its printer. One of the employees on the late shift was planning a vacation with his wife for their upcoming tenth anniversary that would make a great surprise. There are processes in place forbidding that sort of activity, and the man was released a short time ago. I am in the process of reviewing the security settings to verify there are no vulnerabilities. I am making security changes that I can and creating a list of changes for the team to make. With any luck we'll avoid any further issues and have a happy recurring customer.

Summit commented, "I'm in the early stages of my assignment in the largest automated distribution center I've ever seen. There are some interesting characters and I sense and underlying resentment of robots taking over people's jobs. There are a few minor glitches in with the turnup of the package sorting, but nothing major has occurred so far."

Mercedes smiled and nodded at the others on the call, then added her update. "I arrived a short time ago with Jim. Though the company wants to keep this out of the press, if possible, all flights in and out of this location are cancelled for this airline. They are reticketing passengers to other carriers while this investigation continues. There's significant worker versus management situation that apparently caused an impact on the local economy, along with some hard feelings. That may be the basis for the ransom demand, but I don't know yet. Corporate leadership is meeting to determine their direction."

George cleared his throat. "I just got on site after an impressive security check with these people. This operation is enormous, so, Juan, your original statement is justified. I need more help if you two aren't tied up elsewhere to complete a security evaluation."

Juan nodded and made a notation to discuss with Julie after the call. "Understood. Let's see what we can do about adding resources for you, George. Keeping this customer long term would be great for all of us."

Ernesto offered, "I'm back from my last assignment in Finland, and all the paperwork is completed. Let me know where you need me to contribute. I wouldn't want to miss any of the fun."

Julie threw out one of her engaging smiles. "Thanks, Ernesto," she said. "We hadn't forgotten about you. Since business is good, I'm hoping you can coordinate some of the material and technology resources support remotely, as well as take on our routine short-term assignments."

EZ suggested, "Ernesto, perhaps you and I can team up on some of the communications monitoring that I have been watching from each of these areas.

"Julie, I hope you don't mind, but with everyone on assignment the monitoring of communications seems to have accelerated. Another pair of trained eyes would certainly help."

Julie thought about the request. EZ, or Eilla Zan Marshall, had been the protégé of Andrew, who subcontracted the high-tech communications assignments for the R-Group. Andrew, or Andy as he was known, was also her father. To further complicate the family business, EZ had recently become engaged to Quip and was now living with him in Zürich. She had discovered that she wanted to put her education and telecommunications skills to work. There were internal concerns within the R-Group of how much EZ should be allowed to see of the business, so Julie had hired her as a unified communications specialist for the CATS team. In that role, EZ was a liaison to Andrew's team. Julie valued EZ's opinion and speculated that the arrangement made for some interesting pillow-talk between the recently engaged EZ and Quip. Her move to CATS was a win-win for both organizations, let alone perfect to keep Quip in line.

Julie smiled at the bold conversational entrance of EZ and responded, "That sounds good, EZ, provided you structure it so that we can scramble Ernesto to a new field assignment if needed. All of you are doing a great job connecting with your clients and keeping us briefed. I expect as you start to dig in, you may find the situations more fluid than anticipated. These roles you're taking on are why we spent so much time preparing you. Push hard in your position but be smart and safe in your actions. Comments?"

Juan grinned and, unwilling to let the statement go by without comment, said, "Okay, class, you all heard mother now! No undue risks while you are on the playground."

Some of the team members could not mute their phones fast enough to suppress the laughter as it came through the bridge, much to Julie's glee.

Julie gave an amused stare at Juan, but before she could say anything, Juan reinforced, "Alright. Teasing aside, we will always care about your safety. If we come across as parents giving advice to teenagers leaving on their first date, it's because we care. Sometimes, a little gentle teasing is important to remind us we are in this together. Anything else, team?"

The conference call ended with all participants giving thanking Juan and Julie.

CHAPTER 9

Groddo and Szechuan

Dmitry gleefully inquired, "Are you strapped in and ready for our next round, my apprentice? Oh, and what name have you chosen for your avatar? I named mine Groddo, after the hunting dog we had when I was a kid. You know how an animal you grew up with will remain in your mind? That was my old Groddo. We lived on a collective in the Ukraine. He was our hunting and watch dog.

"Groddo had an episode one day because we woke up and found all ninety of our laying chickens slaughtered and dropped one by one from the chicken coop to the backdoor of the farmhouse. Never understood what prompted him to do that nor what made him bite me in the face one afternoon shortly thereafter. I mean, there he was snoozing in his favorite corner of the living room next to the household favorite chair, mostly 'cause it was the only chair, and I just sat down to pet him. I must have disturbed him because he reached up with his mouth wide open, and the next thing I knew he sunk one of his canine teeth into my nose and I started bleeding like a stuck pig. I was afraid Groddo would be beaten for the indiscretion, so I made up a story about accidently sticking myself with my knife.

"Thinking back on it, I should have invented a better story. The collective hadn't been too happy with the chicken slaughtering event, and old Groddo disappeared not long after. Probably lived out his days on another farm, bringing happiness to another boy in his new home. But as it turns out, the whole community owed him a debt of gratitude. We enjoyed a special fried chicken dinner which wouldn't have happened if old Groddo hadn't gone berserk.

"The community commissar would never have allowed us to eat the egg laying chickens. Once they were all dead, though, the elders argued that to let the meat go to waste was foolish. Sure, we got tired of chicken this and chicken that, but, boy, we ate well for a week. Of course, we starved after that because we had to make up the lost egg production. So how about you, Chang? Any favorite pets in your background?"

The chairman, with a half-glazed look, slowly shook his head in disbelief at Dmitry's story but finally responded, "What a tender, heartfelt story from your childhood, Dmitry. I dare say that I have nothing as charming as a rabid pet dog operating as the grim reaper for a boyhood companion. But, to humor you, let me just call my avatar Szechuan. Now let's launch the wheel of misfortune and agree upon the gaming motif for this session, shall we?"

It was now Dmitry's turn to be locked in a mentally neutral gear as he asked, "Szechuan? You're naming your avatar after a plate of food one gets when ordering number nine off the menu?"

Chairman Chang looked indignant at the criticism leveled at his chosen avatar name, and he snapped, "It is a hot, spicy dish that dates all the way back to the wars of the Ming and Qing dynasties, so my name choice is steeped in Chinese tradition. Thank you very much!"

Dmitry sensed this had unwittingly become a sensitive subject and wisely chose to discontinue this discussion as he agreed, "Szechuan for your avatar, it is! My apologies if the subtlety of your name choice eluded me at first, but now I see the wisdom of the naming convention. Are we ready to spin the wheel and see what kind of digital rampage Groddo and Szechuan can launch together?"

Somewhat mollified, Chairman Chang facial features brightened. "Yes, launch sequence then!"

The two men stared intently at their respective screens as the wheel slowly came to rest on their next game motif.

Dmitry blurted, "Alright! *Playground Bullies!* This promises to be an interesting motif! Okay, Chang, let's review the rules, and then we can let the carnage begin! Wow, look at how many points for dump trucks! Sandbox assassination and dismembered toys, here we come!"

Chairman Chang adjusted his headset and wiped the perspiration from his hands as if this was actual combat. And, of course, it was. He was focused on beating Dmitry.

CHAPTER 10

Kookaburra and Romney

In the intense, 50-degree Celsius temperature, dust devils swirled here and there as the heat radiated off everything. It presented a misty, almost surrealistic view of the mammoth mining operation which would appear like a children's sandbox from space. Giant earthmovers lumbered along over the uneven terrain, feeding the heated, chalky dust into the air even more. The enormous buckets of the front-end loaders scrambled to scoop up the minerals churned out by the toothy, grinding digging machine, known to all as the Badger.

It was business as usual at the open mining pit called Kookaburra in Australia's interior. The ore was greedily hoisted up by the front-end loaders and dumped into the mammoth dump trucks. When filled, these would be driven to the special railroad loading area for transport to the coast for the next step in processing and onto their final destinations.

This was a rich, arid area in South Australia where typically the company mined for bauxite and iron ore, but it wasn't uncommon to hit a good vein of nickel. The company hated finding gold or silver because that brought out all the treasure hunters, who then gummed up the standard operations. Business-wise though, they accepted the good fortune when it occurred.

There was a sister mining pit named Romney a hundred kilometers away that was churning out a good quantity of coal with a nice companion quantity of natural gas. The Romney operation was still trying to bring all the liquefying technology online for a more cost-effective transport. The Consortium, as it was called, was just as big as some of the earthmoving vehicles they deployed to process more minerals at an ever-decreasing cost. The Consortium consisted of a financial group, engineering geniuses, operations logistics teams, and a software group. The Consortium was proud of the fact that at least forty percent of the world's mines operated with their in-house designed, built, and coded software products.

From the air, the Kookaburra mine was a hive of activity day and night. The logical applied use of pilotless drones highlighted the crowning achievement of fully monitored operations at the remote mine. Using this technology provided visibility of the operations from the advantage of height as well as multiple angles. The drones leveraged the sun in daylight hours and infrared light at night. Drones could fly for days without refueling and helped boost the communications signals from the ground, up to the satellite, then back down to Perth on the coast. As expected, the audible communications were somewhat skimpy, since all the ground equipment functioned with wireless technology that used sensors and sophisticated software programs.

No humans manned the location. All operations were performed remotely from the command center in Perth. Without having to build human friendly accommodations at the site, the company saved approximately a million Australian dollars per person, per year with this out-of-the-box-thinking mining operation. Everything was automated and monitored by sensors in and on the equipment. All non-automation was driven by the operations personnel in an extensive, climate-controlled data bunker miles away in Perth.

George Jones grinned as he handed a fresh cup of his favorite organic Kona coffee to the drone operator and reminded, "You promised you'd let me drive the drone once it was airborne and operationally over the target area. You weren't shining me on, were you?"

The drone operator was a large, burly fellow known only as Mohawk because of his heavily moussed orange mohawk hairdo. He looked up from the console and offered, "Actually, mate, I do need you to drive for a while since the lease is up on all that rented coffee you've been bringing me. So here," Mohawk said as he handed over the controls. "Try not to turn the drone into a burrowing device like the Badger."

George reveled as he handled the high-tech drone device with some short instruction from Mohawk. As Mohawk started toward the exit, George mischievously commented, "Now I did mention that I am somewhat nearsighted, so can you help guide my hands to the control stick, if it jumps out of my hands? And, um, what do all these little numbers mean on the screen anyway? Are these important or can I just turn them off? Oh yeah, how do I restart the game if it looks like all my adversaries are going to shoot or destroy me?"

Mohawk clucked his tongue and grumbled, "Mate, if you're going to be a DWEEB, you better start acting like one, or bugger-off."

George's smile deteriorated into a puzzled look. "DWEEB?"

Now it was Mohawk's turn to tease as he clarified, "That's right, mate, DWEEBs. *Directional Wheel Entities for Enterprising Blokes,* or DWEEBs. If you're flying a drone, you're a DWEEB."

Mohawk left for the toilet, laughing out loud, while George graciously accepted the hazing. His formative years of playing electronic games essentially qualified him to at least steer the drone without hitting Badger.

George focused his attention intently on the monitor providing the real-time visual feeds from the site. He liked the optics from the drone, and the controls were every bit as responsive as he'd expected. The drone could pull back on its field of view or telescope in on one of the trucks to see the little hula girl fastened to the dashboard. It was at this moment that he noticed something odd going on in the pit. He quickly scanned the other monitors in the operations center to see if anything was showing an unusual set of circumstances. He rubbed his eyes to clear his vision, but when he returned his attention to the drone's optics nothing had changed.

Mohawk wasn't back yet. George was unprepared for the drama unfolding in front of his eyes. He looked around and quickly noticed the operations duty manager wandering through the area. McLaren was casually checking the duty rosters and the sensor monitoring systems, which made the situation even more incongruous. Finally, unable to reconcile the activity he was viewing and the business-as-usual sensor output, George called to McLaren.

McLaren stood next to George and asked, "Hey, George, what's up? Did Mohawk strand you at his post like he does every other visitor to this facility? I bet he used the old *The lease is up on the rented coffee* routine."

Concerned, George didn't look up or respond to the question. "McLaren, can you double check my visuals here? I'm seeing something that is NOT being reflected in the mountains of equipment sensor output here in the data center. I don't want to be an alarmist here, but can you verify what I'm seeing on my monitor?"

McLaren smiled in a paternal way and offered, "Of course, Laddie. You stare into these things long enough and you begin to see things. Let's see what's going."

The smile quickly faded from McLaren's face, but his calm disposition wouldn't allow him to panic. After a few seconds he asked, "How long has this been going on, Laddie?"

George, emboldened with McLaren's concern, reported, "About four minutes. I saw one of the front-end loaders simply upend one of the dump trucks and move it into a corner of the pit. It almost reminded me of children taking their toys out of the general playing area and putting them away for safekeeping before returning for more toys.

"I am not hallucinating. You're seeing this too?"

McLaren was now ashen and nodded his head as he confirmed, "You're not confused. Four minutes, hmmm. I'm seeing our million-dollar pieces of equipment turn on each other as in a schoolyard brawl, yet none of the sensors in this operations center are barking at us saying that something is wrong. The obvious question is, what's wrong with this picture?"

The concern was fully engulfing them both, but before McLaren could say anything else, the drone screen went dark but showed itself in a stable orbit around the Kookaburra compound. George read the digital output. "The drone reports are saying everything is nominal, but we can't see the video feeds any longer. Just like the other equipment that has their sensors telling us everything is wonderful yet is apparently spiraling out of control."

Before McLaren could respond, all the monitors simultaneously displayed the same eerie message.

> You shouldn't have ignored our demands. Let us know if you want to recover from this downward spiral but the price is now 100 million euros.

George looked to McLaren, who commented while staring at the message, "We need your pilot in the air on his way to the site NOW, using traditional, displaced technology. How long to get him airborne? We need reliable visuals as soon as possible. I need all hands-on deck running diagnostics to see what went wrong and why nothing was reported by any of the sensors."

George swung out of the chair at a fast click and over his shoulder confirmed, "On it!"

George grabbed his cell phone and called the pilot. "I need you up and in the air on your way to the Kookaburra site ten minutes ago. We have a digital communications issue between all the equipment on-site. The overhead drones refuse to give us the video feeds. Basically, we need the old reliable eyes and ears feedback from the site. The last images we had did not look pretty."

The pilot couldn't mask his sour tone as he responded, "Don't tell me this is an emergency! I've sat around here for days with nothing to do but listen to but rhetoric of how the modern drone makes my skillset obsolete. Today they want a human in the air! I planned to go to the beach again and watch the bathers dodge the crocs and evade the sharks. Now I've got to go to work? Geez! Well, okay, but I'm taking my snorkel, towel, and swim fins with me just in case it's a false alarm!"

George listened politely to the rant and then quietly offered, "Boss, you may want to leave the swim gear behind and take extra water. There hasn't been any significant rain in this part of Australia since the late nineties."

Juan, seemingly annoyed, replied, "Okay, then sunscreen it is! I need to work on my tan. My sweetie just loves a well-tanned and svelte man! George, I'm at the hanger now and will be airborne in eight minutes."

George politely reminded, "Did I mention to take extra water with you in case…"

Juan disconnected the call and promptly went through a pre-flight checklist that he memorized. True to his word, the single engine high-wing aircraft was airborne in just under eight minutes. He received current weather conditions from the radio as he was climbing to normal flight altitude.

Juan established communications links with ground control as he leveled off. Once telemetry with Perth was created, he relaunched a radio call with base, and George was first on the conference bridge.

George remarked, "Boss, you weren't kidding about the eight minutes. Are you having any luck linking with Kookaburra?"

Juan barely concealed his annoyance with the situation and replied, "No, I can't get the drone or anything else online."

George offered, "Here's what we know so far. The video feed from the drone showed the equipment basically fighting with each other in the greatest tradition of school yard sandbox wars. None of the sensors indicated any problem. Two of us watched it unfolding on the drones' visual monitors before it too displayed only empty sky.

"McLaren needs you to try to validate if, A, this is all a cruel hoax and everything is actually wonderful; B, we are on a horrible carnival ride where the equipment is now functioning as predators; or C, we are delusional, in which case order a case of straitjackets to be used on this site's personnel."

The pilot chuckled. "I'm pretty sure I know which solution to go with, but I'm not using MY credit card to order in a bunch of straitjackets! Let me get to the site, and then I'll report further. I'm glad I brought the digital camera along."

The trade winds pushed the single engine plane along nicely, and within ninety minutes he was over the site. The pilot pushed his head forward to focus on the sight he was witnessing. Then he rolled his head to one side, not fully comprehending the events unfolding below him. The pilot caught sight of the drones circling the area in a nice parabolic orbit and was mindful to keep clear of the pattern.

Finally convinced that he had not drifted into a science fiction video program, the pilot slowly announced, "George, I've got my cameras on the scene as well as my eyeballs. I don't know what you witnessed, but I'm seeing the destructive playground wars like you suggested with only a few survivors still active. Those pieces of equipment not ruined are hell-bent in final combat as well. My guess is there won't be any smart mining equipment pieces left after the final blow is given. To add to that end game, it appears that the Badger is digging into the lowest rung of the open pit so it can have the rim collapse on it, like a grave. It looks like all the mining equipment is engaged in fratricide, then moving to suicide to complete the destruction of the Kookaburra mine."

George asked, "Do you see the head drone? Any chance that you can try to reestablish its communications link? You don't have a whole lot of time over the site before you need to head home. Your description corresponds to what we saw earlier and the progression model I built while you were en route. Everyone is watching your transmission feeds before history rolls over it. Well done, sir."

Juan smirked and stated, "Yeah, well, there's nothing like a ring-side seat to Armageddon. Let me see if I can connect to the drone and straighten out his communications link. Give me a few…"

After more than a few minutes, a concerned George asked, "What's your status? Any luck connecting to that drone? Why have your video feeds vanished? Come back?"

Juan couldn't respond since the drone link he'd established functioned as a poisoned digital connection. The single engine plane possessed only a little of the high-tech gear that the drone had, which probably saved the pilot's life. Unfortunately, all communication links were shut down to the aircraft, leaving only basic steering and navigation instruments available for return. However, as Juan banked his aircraft to leave the area, the drone became an adversary. It tried several times to ram the departing aircraft, much to Juan's chagrin. The last pass of the unmanned drone clipped the wing strut, and the pilot searched for a reasonably safe place to land.

Juan flared the aircraft attitude as much as he dared and feathered the engine's prop for as soft a landing as possible. The years of practice landing on unorthodox runways in the Chihuahua desert probably saved him from crashing as the aircraft bounced and grounded to a halt in the chalky sandy pit. He couldn't separate himself from the mangled aircraft. The pilot had a great view out of the now windowless cockpit of the lead drone spiraling into the ground, but it didn't please him. Worse, he knew his plane wouldn't fly and that his options were shrinking. The only bright spot was that he had his special satellite-enabled cell phone with him that just might allow him communications.

Juan held his breath as he hit the special key sequence, hoping that it wouldn't fail him. He was not disappointed.

A relieved George answered, "Is that you, Juan? Geezers! We thought you were toast! Just a minute, Julie wants to…"

In the background George's voice could be heard. "Well, why don't you just take my phone and talk with him. He may be my boss; however, you do trump that as he is your husband."

Julie snatched the phone, put it on speaker, and angrily asked, "Juan, are you alright? Dammit, I've told you about this! No more solo jaunts, mister! We're always going together."

Covered in a fine white chalky dust and sitting in a broken airplane in 50-degree Celsius heat, Juan clucked his tongue. "Oh, you want BOTH of us to expire in the middle of nowhere in Australia and leave two orphan children? Besides, you don't think I came unprepared for this contingency, do you?" Juan transferred to Bluetooth and pocketed the phone, then zipped up his protective clothing and instigated the cooling system.

Julie, battling her fear, tears, and anger, relented a little and asked, "Juan, tell me you're alright. Then I want to know where you are so we can get you."

Juan rolled his eyes and replied, "No worries, sweetheart. I've landed in the middle of the Australian desert. I'd bake like a good Mexican steak, but my protective clothing cooling system is operational. I'm staring at what looks to be a North Africa style sirocco windstorm heading this way. You know, the kind that takes the finished paint off your car along with the flesh on your bones. Not to worry as I have my beach accoutrements right beside me. If I get thirsty, I will just go over to the Stop and Rob that I can see on the corner of this beach. Seriously, honey, all is well and I know you'll find with the signal coordinates George retrieved."

George cleared his throat as if to speak.

Juan intercepted, "And, George, if you ask me about how much extra water I brought along after you warned me to do so, I will crush you. I might just take your carefully indexed selfies and dump them carelessly on your desktop after I remove the time/date stamps. You'll never remember where or when they were taken. You do understand, right?"

Always the gentleman, but now very alarmed at the possible risk, George offered, "Juan, there is no need for dire threats. Just give me a fax number, and I'll send some water."

CHAPTER 11

The discount value

The 18-wheeler painted with the globally recognized corporate logo and tagline: **Constellation Stuff - The Store to the Planet,** slowly rumbled into the distribution center. This creeping speed allowed time for mobile sensors on each side of the truck to be scanned, and the vehicle was directed where to park for loading or unloading. Earlier in the year the company had upgraded all the trucks to semi-driverless. Now the trucks arrived at what was termed a *Constellation Destination* where the human drivers would get out and let the robotics take over for proper placement.

The Constellation distribution center's computer had the automated job of routing, parking, and unloading the merchandise in precise order and efficiency within the covered distribution center. Once the trucks were at their proper docks, the robotics opened the trucks, disgorged the contents, and then re-loaded it for highway transportation, typically in under an hour. The drivers relaxed at the perimeter for their next long haul of delivery to a targeted store in the Constellation's footprint.

Every Constellation distribution center was an enormous facility that never slept due to the volume of goods being processed for the three to four hundred stores in the regional support network. Each region had a similar model, with only a small portion of the trucks and drivers crossing regions. It was said that the Constellation distribution centers were originally built by putting four aircraft hangers together and doubling the size to accommodate the volume of goods to be handled. These were often repurposed abandoned military locations, which made Constellation popular with their ecologically minded consumers.

Constellation distribution centers were typically located outside of major metropolitan areas, where small towns were more friendly and affordable to the enormous structures. Tax breaks were usually given with the understanding that many jobs would be available to help develop all the infrastructure needed to support a Constellation distribution center. The retailing giant's automation initiative had crushed those hopes of many jobs in many of the small communities who had signed up. As more and more machine-to-machine automation came into the Constellation distribution centers, more jobs were displaced. Even the human truck drivers could see the handwriting on the wall for them with the strides being made in smart vehicles. Driverless trucks were being fought against in closed room discussions because no one wanted to be branded as an anti-automation employee with those career-limiting consequences.

Constellation Stuff was world famous for its logistical model of bringing affordable goods to the consumer. They took just-in-time delivery to their stores and pushed it into their distribution centers and up through and into their suppliers' business model. Tight margins and consistent profitability made the organization a favorite of retail analysts. The old joke in the manufacturing and production world was you were offered congratulations and condolences at the same time when you landed a contract to sell to Constellation Stuff. It came as no surprise that every supplier smiled to themselves when something went wrong at Constellation Stuff.

The perimeter guard shouted, "What do you think you're doing? This is a restricted area. No one is permitted into the Constellation Center proper! Right now, turn around and walk back to the gate!"

Marvin Oile, a tall, burly, and road-worn truck driver, shouted his response. "I left my personal belongings in the cab. Most importantly, my wallet and cell phone so I can call home. Your damn robotics were in such a hurry that they made off with my truck before I could catch them! I'll retrieve them and then get right out of here!"

The guard threatened, "I am charged with letting no one into the facility for health and security reasons! Now stop, or we'll be required to use force!"

The truck driver made a vulgar hand gesture without even looking back while he called out over his shoulder, "Screw you. I'm going to get my stuff. File a complaint if you must, but no one is stopping me from retrieving my personal items."

The truck driver quickened his pace to a trot to make it to his truck ahead of the security guards making a grab for him. He circled the parked trucks looking for his and luckily found it before having to run the circumference of a building the size of Rhode Island, or Road Island as he liked to joke. Ducking into the truck, he narrowly avoided being spotted by the guards closing the distance in hot pursuit. He grabbed his possessions and briefly waited until the guards were out of sight. He hurriedly exited the cab and would have left the area except for the unusual sounds coming from inside the Constellation structure. He cautiously stepped back to the truck, and in between the docking bay and the truck, he peeked through the opening to see what was going on.

He was stunned at the activity. Instead of seeing hyper-efficient robotics routing, loading, and unloading, he saw mass chaos and unlimited destruction of what appeared to be new merchandise. What products weren't being destroyed were aimlessly being routed into hopelessly jumbled piles that would take weeks to sort. The sight was so all-consuming, he didn't hear the guards behind him until it was too late. The three guards he had outsmarted had circled back, dragged him back around the truck and now had him pinned to the ground.

Disregarding his own predicament, he hollered, "Hey! What's wrong with the distribution center? You need to report there's a serious problem going on inside there! If you don't believe me, one of you come look."

The original guard smirked as he retorted, "You disobeyed a direct security command and now you're going to try the old *Look over there!* routine and try to run for it?! Boy, are you a dim bulb!"

The truck driver chuckled and commented, "Yeah, you're right! The two little old ladies you have helping you can't possibly hold me down while you, laser brain, go see for yourself! I got my stuff, but you guys certainly have far worse problems! If you don't believe me, send one of your old ladies to see what's happening."

The guard couldn't resist the taunt and went back around the truck to look for himself. The sight made him drop his baton on the ground. He ran back to the others and said, "Get Control on the walkie-talkie. The trucker's right!"

The phone rang as the guards finished securing Marvin to a chair. But when the head guard tried to answer it, all he heard was sounds of gibberish with long gaps of dead air. Finally, convinced that their normal communications lines were hosed, he pulled out his cell phone to call the up-line manager.

The call connected. "Sir, the operations robotics are destroying merchandise. Nothing is running as it should. It's as if the programs got confused. It happened while we were apprehending a trucker who was in the secured area saying he left his belongings in his rig. I don't think this man is involved in the destruction though. I also don't have inline communications which is why I'm calling you from my mobile phone."

After a few seconds of head-nodding, the head guard acknowledged the command and then terminated the call.

He told the guards loudly enough so that Marvin could hear, "Okay, we aren't the only ones under attack. They are sending out their *tiger-team* with a special consultant to assess the extent of the damage. We've been asked to hold on to Mr. Impulsive here until they arrive. We are to touch nothing, nor are we to tell anyone else what is going on, so no personal calls. We are in security lockdown mode until we get relieved."

Marvin sarcastically commented, "Hey, that's a great idea! I need to relieve *myself*, but I'm kind of tied up. How about one of you unzip my fly and hold it for me? I don't expect to be released for a potty break by you clowns."

The guards all gritted their teeth at the taunting and turned toward one another. One of the guards asked, "How long before they get here? If we have to put up with his mouthing off much longer, there is going to be one fewer witness for the special consultant to speak with!"

The head guard snarled, "Just free him long enough to use the facilities and then re-secure him until the tiger-team gets here! It will be a few hours. Oh, and, Marvin, keep up the taunts, and I'll use duct tape to shut you up!"

Marvin, unfazed by the threat, rebuked, "You're just rent-a-cops with no real authority. I bet you don't have but one bullet between the three of you for your pistols! Your pistols are probably just made of wood like your heads!"

The head guard shook his head and through his gritted teeth commented, "No wonder they put you on the road! Your interpersonal speaking skills suck! Take him out but bring him right back!"

CHAPTER 12

Losing at a winning game

Dmitry quietly burned with anger at the loss of the game he'd felt so confident about. He refused to consider that he'd lost his edge.

Chairman Chang, feigning innocence, offered, "Oh, my goodness! It seems that the accumulated number of points seems to favor me. I'm elated with the thrill of the game, though also somewhat embarrassed to admit that I'm perspiring to the very limits of my body wash and deodorant! This much excitement clearly warrants a shower, quickly followed by a massage from my trusted masseuse. I dare say that with all the strenuous activity at the gamer station, I may feel those overworked muscles in the morning. I wouldn't trade even a moment of the extended workout, no matter how many sore muscles I'll have to contend with. The gamer's win is exhilarating! This is even better than the group interview of three secretaries at once for the privilege to work under me!"

Dmitry rolled his eyes in contempt for Chairman Chang's win in the game of *Stocking Stuffers*. The ongoing prattle from Chairman Chang after the win grew more vexing with each statement. Fed up, Dmitry finally insinuated, "Chang, if you're going to behave like this every time, I let you win, I'm going to quit doing it!"

Chairman Chang abruptly stopped his gloating session. He was thoughtful and silent for a minute and then sarcastically queried, "Am I given to understand that you deliberately forfeited a winning position in the game of Stocking Stuffers so your old friend wouldn't feel badly? Dmitry, I am truly touched by your altruistic gesture! Had I but known you had feelings of compassion for your old friend, I would have won by a smaller margin. You're a much more generous human being than I ever imagined. I feel compelled to put you on my generic holiday card list in honor of this gesture."

Growing weary and annoyed at the sarcasm and verbal jabs at him, Dmitry asked, "Is this the way you always behave when invited to someone's house to play games on a rainy day? You pout and are surly when you lose, but you're insufferable when you win. It's a good thing I haven't had to endure your insufferable grumpy more than once. I confess I am more than willing to put up with you complaining from here on out."

It was Chairman Chang's turn to be annoyed that Dmitry insinuated that he had let him win. He countered, "I can see we ARE in a mood, aren't we? I win one contest of Stocking Stuffers with plenty of suffering, and you're ready to quit playing!

"One time you let me take the first turn at the three doors, even though you had first draw privilege, so now I'll give you the same courtesy. I won, but I'm willing to let you choose which door the spoils are gathered behind."

Dmitry, almost unable to believe the generous offer of the chairman, did a double take before he beamed. "What ho, Chang. You genuinely surprise me with such a magnanimous gesture. Is it possible that under that rough, coarse exterior there actually beats a heart of flint to circulate the freon in your veins? I'll not disappoint you by turning down the right to draw first and will choose your lucky door number three."

Chairman Chang smiled as he replied, "After this, Dmitry, you won't be grouchy the next time we play and you lose, right?"

Both men stared at each other momentarily across the high-definition video displays of their conference call. Dmitry grinned and snickered as he asked, "Who said I was going to let you win next time?"

Chairman Chang slowly broke into a good-natured smile as he commented, "Let's see if your door choice has profited you this time, shall we? When it doesn't, I want my turn."

CHAPTER 13

Wired Cities of the Future — today

The atmosphere in the room was a palatable mixture of anger and hopelessness. Today's demonstration was a grim reminder of what they had witnessed the week before. The mayor stood fuming as the operational screens changed, one by one, from views of the city to a mocking vulgar graphic of an obese woman being taken from behind by a death-like apparition. The apparition was a grinning red skeleton in dark crimson robes, leering out from the monitor much like the forest Satyrs of Greek mythology would have done. The caption read:

> Keep ignoring our demands and the resulting experience will only be harsher!

Mayor Perez shook her head in frustration and finally exclaimed, "I suppose that image is supposed to be me. I didn't fight my way into being the mayor here only to have my city held hostage. As an *Impecunious Impertinent* member, I fought for social reforms and had nothing but disdain for all this technical automation that eliminates jobs for humans.

"What's the first thing I confront when I take office? Technology and machine-to-machine communications running amok.

Behind that technology, of course, is someone trying to extort the very money I promised to conserve on my winning platform. Someone tell me some good news."

One of the junior traffic monitors, a new hire, absentmindedly commented, "I don't think your rump is anywhere close to that big. I mean, proportionately speaking, just glancing at your bottom, it appears more Rubenesque…"

An adjacent old timer discreetly nudged the new hire to suggest he cease further analysis of the comparison between the picture and Mayor Perez.

Mayor Baby Perez, newly elected to one of the most modern and influential cities in Spain, was just over 1.5 meters tall, with a sturdy build, and dressed in a well-tailored suit. Her hair, undoubtedly long, was styled with a French twist with small silver flowered pins. Her jewelry was also silver but not ostentatious. Her face was oval with a traditional Latin nose and a smile that was less than flashy, yet pleasant. Not a showcase beauty but a professional looking individual who, as a woman, was totally insulted by the picture on display.

Mayor Perez glared at the new hire during the ensuing silence until one of the senior technical analysts offered, "I recommend that we alert all the police and fire departments of the pending outage so that they can prepare for *not* business-as-usual."

Mayor Perez nodded and yielded, "Agreed. Get them on the phones and alert them that we have a modest technical issue that is going to interrupt normal operations."

Everyone exchanged uneasy glances among themselves, which were finally noticed by the mayor.

"Well? Get them on the phone and brief them, but without all the gory details," she demanded. "I recognize we don't yet have a handle on this, but I don't want to start a panic attack that will build into a tsunami. Why aren't you moving?"

The new contractor, Brayson, assigned by CATS at the request of the head of the city's IT department, last week at the start of some network inconsistencies turned toward the mayor. Brayson was very adept at troubleshooting network issues, project management, and minor programming. He stood nearly two meters, had a square face, dark eyes, and dark hair. He was a perfect fit for this assignment with this experience and fluency in English and Spanish. Brayson politely offered, "Madam Mayor, all the police and firefighting communications signaling goes through the small black box over there in that rack. We haven't been able to get into it since this attack began.

"Perhaps you have not been briefed with all the relevant and inter-related information. Basically, we are in the electronic command center for the city, but we currently command nothing in this state-of-the-art Smart City. The garbage sensors are not reporting. The streetlights are turned on during daylight, increasing our utility bills, but we suspect they will probably be turned off at night to facilitate more chaos and crime. Our citywide bus schedules and arrival times are completely wrong. Everywhere in the city, open parking sensors are falsely alerting to now desperately enraged motorists of an open space. All the traffic lights are set to green to enhance the probability of collisions. Oh, and the Wi-Fi mesh that was operating throughout the city to ease the burden on the macro-cell towers is broadcasting false or duplicate IP addresses, rendering GPS mapping and cellular coverage useless.

"If you really want to alert the police and fire departments of the situation, I recommend you dispatch personnel on bicycles and not try to use the new driverless smart cars the city recently took delivery of for testing. Old school CB radios would have been your fallback method of communications if all that equipment hadn't been auctioned off last month and hauled away for their copper content."

Mayor Perez felt overwhelmed by the information dump. Perez was seriously wondering why she ever ran for the office in the first place. She desperately asked, "Can't we just reboot everything, and force initial program reloads? I mean, I do that on my laptop, and even with my cell phone now and again to get it to behave! Can't we do that?"

The contractor slightly rocked his head from side to side, cleared his throat, and responded, "Are you seriously suggesting that you want us to reboot the city? All the technology that supports all the services run in what we call machine-to-machine mode.

"There are a few observations I need to make in response to that suggestion. This is a huge port city with thousands of residents and tourists oblivious to the issues. It's not just the equipment in this room but also in each of the substations, which means resetting all the Wi-Fi devices installed on every lamppost, all the city vehicles that are in our communications grid, all the traffic monitors and corresponding stop lights, and all the parking and trash dumpster sensors around the city.

"The ocean-going cargo ships should also be radioed and alerted that all ground freight transportation is fouled up as well. Unloading will have to be done using the old manual method – by walkie-talkie. That physical reset approach to all the devices the city has deployed would only be possible if you could mobilize the entire city to do it close to the same time. With the currently impaired communications in all directions compromised, that process cannot occur.

"The other issue, which I can't yet prove or disprove, is that the attacker is likely hoping we'll do exactly that so they can finish uploading malware into your systems. Rebooting could easily finish their attack. Some of the best malware programs I've ever seen infect a machine and cause enough havoc that the operator must reboot. These sorts of programs run cloaked as a rootkit and are harder to fix. At university, during a class discussion, the instructor recommended the ideal cure for rootkits was to take off in a low earth orbit and just nuke the system from space.

"Before you seriously decide the city reboot, we need to know if there is code hiding in the systems' memory that might try to write itself to disk as a consequence of just such an action."

The moments ticked by in a very quiet command center until finally Mayor Perez asked, "How much are they asking for again?"

A look of shock immediately appeared on everyone's face, except for the contractor. Brayson said, "The original ransom demand was for fifty million euros. Based on the vulgar graphic and challenge on the screens I suspect the price has gone up. You're not seriously considering putting this cybercriminal on the city payroll, are you?"

Mayor Perez was visibly growing adversarial. Her chin raised and eyes narrowed, she cocked her head to one side and demanded, "And just what options are left open to us, Brayson? This extortionist has effectively shut down all our social services. We have no more clue now about how to stop them than when we received the first cyber threat. Hell, for all I know, this mess was engineered by the previous mayor and his techno-cronies. They campaigned that they were the only ones capable of defending and running this city.

"I'm looking at a million-euro deficit for every day we're offline. If you have any swell ideas on how to purge this cyber-sickness from our systems, I'm all ears. Frankly, it seems the only entity that can provide a solution is the one displayed on the monitor. I'm considering ALL my options."

Unruffled by her tirade, Brayson offered, "Allow me to point out, without a defense against this well-crafted attack, our adversary can return at any time and treat your city like an ATM machine. Even if this bunch didn't, word could get around the cyber underground to others trying to cash in on the money train. All they'd have to do is pretend to be the same extortionist. I don't advocate paying the extortion monies, Madam Mayor."

Mayor Perez sensed her weak position but didn't wish to yield. "We can keep this disbursement transaction quiet enough to find a solution to this kind of blackmail. If we can get them to quietly go away, then our systems can come back online, city services can resume, and you, my expensive contractor, gains more time to build a defensible security solution for the city's technology system."

Brayson countered, "I'm not sure you can simply book fifty million euros onto the city books under the 'other expenses' category without an audit challenge. As soon as it gets out that you took city money to pay a blackmailer extortionist, your membership in the Impecunious Impertinent political group would shift to the Sofritoes group, where you'd be stewed in your own juices. Granted, I'm not here to lecture you on city politics, but that decision is ill-advised."

Bordering on exasperation, Mayor Perez practically hollered, "Then find me another solution! This team has twenty-four hours to come up with something to bring social services online!

"While you're doing that, I'm going to round up all the rest of the city council, and we are going to review our status." After a few deep breaths, she added, "And, you're right, Brayson. I need to build consensus before a decision is acted upon. Now, gentlemen, please help us defeat this enemy, or we will have to add this cyber thug to the city payroll."

CHAPTER 14

Cleanup on aisle four!

The tiger-team, including the special consultant, arrived at the Constellation distribution center not a moment too soon. The guards had to restrain Marvin after they had allowed him to visit the facilities. He continued to convey his belligerent attitude toward everyone that approached.

After introductions were made, the head guard suggested, "Ok, now try and remember your manners while you answer a few questions. Your story checks out, but you broke the security protocol when you let yourself into a restricted area. Then you ran, after mouthing off at us like some juvenile delinquent trying to prove something to the authorities!

"Our company has hired a security/surveillance organization and their guy is supposed to assess the situation. If you want to get out of here with your job intact, you best be on good behavior. Tell him what you saw."

Summit Hayes was used to dealing with confrontational situations, but he was struggling with this scenario. The commentary being witnessed as he had arrived and before introductions were made was that of the head security guard, referred to as Bluto. The furious guard kept trying to assert his authority in the conversation.

Summit was imposing, with a swarthy complexion, dark hair, broad shoulders, standing at 1.73 meters tall with dark eyes that didn't miss much. He was an accomplished private investigator from the CATS organization. He also had an excellent command of several languages that included Russian, Chinese, Japanese, Italian, and Hindi, of course, based on his heritage, with some limited Arabic dialects too. Right now, it was his King's English being tested.

Marvin, the secured trucker, bellowed, "Thanks to your near fatal incompetence, Bluto, I'm stuck here trying to explain why I broke security protocol. This is all academic, since the Constellation facilities are trashed, I'm out of a job anyway! It'll take weeks to clean up what we both saw. Whatever automation snafu occurred has basically shutdown the distribution channel for this whole region. With the existing just-in-time model of retail efficiency, the hundreds of stores depending on stuff coming in will be out of stock within days."

Before the guards could rail again at the taunt from Marvin, Summit quickly interjected, "Marvin, is it?"

The trucker nodded.

"Marvin, you put yourself at a lot of risk by penetrating the perimeter to retrieve your personal belongings. What if this was a military facility and these guards were armed? They might have shot you. As it was, they were within their operational rights to work you over with their batons, but they didn't even do that. You're lucky to be only inconvenienced because of your violation of the rules. If you can take a deep breath and tell me what you saw, I think I can get some people on the phone to get you released. Then you can go and enjoy your life."

The rational statements and well-offered words had the desired effect on everyone. All tempers that were dangerously high started to subside.

After a few minutes of calming, Marvin quietly offered, "I just wanted to get my things so I could call my wife Olivia and hear her voice. I have doctor bills pilling up after her last surgery, and I've been doing as much overtime as the company allows. So, yeah, I'm over-tired, pushed to the limit. I acted like a jerk. Thanks for not killing me, Bluto.

"Let me tell you what I saw going on inside the warehouse. I've never seen one, but I would imagine this is what the carnage looks like after a tornado has swept through a city. This is going to cause a lot of grief for a lot of folks. It was like the equipment went nuts. Packages went from neat stacks to a piled-up jumble. It is going to take a long time to get everything sorted out for delivery to the stores. My truck carried boxes of dishes. I don't think they been unloaded yet, but if they had been they would have broken in that utter chaos. Most of what I spotted were children's toys of all shapes and sizes."

CHAPTER 15

Flash and burn

"Konstantin!" Dmitry impatiently called, "I need you in here right now. Something is going on with my screen and causing me to miss the moves I need to capture these gold coins to get to the next level."

Konstantin rushed into Dmitry's plush inner sanctum. The lighting was dimmed so that the entire focus was on the high-definition, two meter wide by half a meter high flat screen. The rich furniture of mahogany-colored leather chairs, along with a mink throw on one arm of the couch, amplified the masculine furnishings, as well as the opulence. There were several state-of-the-art Wi-Fi gaming consoles located at strategic points about the room, depending upon whether Dmitry wanted to sit, recline, or lay down to play. Any of the devices could be used as they were designed to remain fully synchronized.

The background music had a vast array of melodic tunes that would automatically adjust to the gamer's mood and current actions on screen. The volume was always low enough to not be intrusive to the gaming experience. Dmitry preferred the more morbid tunes, as opposed to the catchy uplifting ones that Konstantin favored.

At present, Dmitry was seated in the gaming throne with the newest console resting on his lap-tray. The auto-sensing gamer chair was the latest and greatest effort in refreshment delivery with no distractions, temperature control based on body heat output, and ergonomic massage activity to help reduce gamer-fatigue. The gamer chair was installed at what was called the 'winner's height'. As such, the gamer looked down on anyone who approached. The gamer's input devices were strategically placed in form fitting holsters around the chair and within arm's reach. Dmitry anxiously shifted his glance between the screen and his associate, while Konstantin looked at the screen in time to see a flash and flicker, just as Dmitry had Groddo poised to capture the bags of gold. Then, Szechuan, the opponent, snatched the gold and faded away.

"See, see! You did see that, right? I am blinded for a moment and Groddo seems frozen, then that wretched Szechuan appears. Something is wrong with the new console or the screen. Since I have moved between three consoles now with the same result, I suspect it's the screen." He continued to move Groddo and play even though he had to wait again for the money to appear to have the chance to jump a level. He didn't want to waste one of his few timeouts in this session.

Konstantin started to run some diagnostics from the remote laptop to review the error logs, and after a few minutes he declared, "Sir, the screen is fine. Honestly, each of these devices are working superbly. There are..."

"That is not true. I'm telling you this flash and sputter occur, and I cannot see Groddo clearly enough to move him to the prize. Don't tell me it's great when I am down points, and more importantly, cash," admonished Dmitry. "The chairman has never been this far ahead so close to the end of the session." Then, like a petulant child, he added, "It's my favorite game and I have practiced with it a great deal. I will not lose."

Konstantin soothed, "Dmitry, listen please. There are no issues with the devices or the screen, but he has enhanced his avatar, Szechuan, in this case.

"You recall when you are outfitting your avatars, there is an area where you can add or remove certain features. Some of them are free, of course, while others are very costly. Groddo, for instance, can scare any of the props within the game itself by changing the information those props see. It makes the props easier to handle."

"Yes, yes, I know that it makes the props so much more interesting as I work through the levels. It is based on predictable responses to situations that people, for instance, would find scary. So what, Konstantin. That feature is still working and making this an entertaining experience. How does that have any bearing on missing the points so often in this session?"

Konstantin ruefully replied, "I think that your opponent has learned to pay for an enhancement that causes intense flashes of light when the two avatars are close to a milestone. Your high-definition screen is making it seem like a hundred rockets exploding all around you, like when you were in battle. I suspect you are, in a sense, ducking as you did in battle to avoid injury. After all, sir, you are a famous war hero. You fought in countless battles."

Dmitry paused for a moment and thought about the possibility. Just before the buzzer sounded for inactivity, he moved Groddo toward the prize.

He then asked, "If that's the case, can you modify the screen's brightness until the end of this game? This game uses a dark background because of the evening scenario challenges. I noticed that Szechuan has become brighter with red, yellow, orange, and white, so that makes it even more of a contrast to the background."

"I think that would be a mistake, sir. You're on target for the next one. Let's have you proceed with all haste to the next gold opportunity and simply point Groddo when it's in sight and close your eyes. That way you won't pause even for a second. Your aim has always been deadly. He won't stand a chance. It may also put Szechuan off balance enough for you to jump to the next level and make your demands known."

Dmitry moved through the level with confidence. He'd played this game more than once in the beta form, and this was his second time in the live format. Chang's skills would improve with practice, and he reminded himself to account for that in the next challenge when he set up Groddo. He was getting closer to the target by the second. He was in the zone, and nothing would interfere with him capturing the gold and setting the demands for the next level. At some level he heard Konstantin counting down, and at three he closed his eyes and pressed firmly on the keypad. He heard the chime of the win and opened his eyes.

"There, that's more like it. Now I can submit my criteria for this last leg on this session. Thank you, my friend."

CHAPTER 16

Fly, Bye

The conference room in the headquarters of Fast Flyers was ideal for large meetings. It contained the quintessential furnishings that spoke of money and treating visitors to the best. The shine on conference room table would have reflected sunlight like spotlights on a landing field at night, but the expensive curtains blocked the outdoors, and the lighting was inset. The maroon leather chairs looked soft enough to wrap around the guest like a hug. Even the artwork reflected the attention to detail with no penny pinching. As guests arrived a management person welcomed them and ushered them to their assigned place.

Labor negotiators, the guests, are practiced artists at bargaining hard, even when they've won. This session was no different, except the loser was invited back to the table for what was being called a reconciliation of terms. The management team made every effort to start the meeting on a positive note. The sideboard was filled with a variety of refreshments including cakes, fruits, cheese, meats, and even some champagne for the orange juice. The goal of the setting designed to eliminate any lingering animosity.

The team struggled to hide the fact that they were dumb-founded by the engaging atmosphere and the warmth of their adversaries.

The lead negotiator, Chuck Wood, decided to take an aggressive attitude for the meeting. He was just under two meters tall with broad shoulders and closely cropped reddish hair. Freckles were generously sprinkled across a clean-shaven face that had an expression that seemed far too serious for a man in his early forties.

With no effort to restrain his sarcasm, he stated, "My goodness, we must have been escorted to the wrong room. I recall for our last meeting; we were sent downstairs to the vending machines to get bottled water and then paper towels from the restrooms on various floors. We were especially thrilled at having to use the restrooms on another floor since all the ones on this floor are designated executive washrooms with special keys for the assignees. I can't help but notice the nice display of food and beverages. And color me shocked, even flowers."

The management negotiator, Sean Riley, who was known for his ruthlessness, was always simply referred to as *The Sean*. He was a few centimeters taller than Chuck and was wearing a suit designed to command respect. His dark hair was styled, and his nails had recently received a manicure. Ever the consummate salesman, Sean swallowed hard to maintain a friendly demeanor. "Mr. Wood, we have the right to reopen negotiations with our labor counterparts as a part of our contract. To be transparent, we may have over-played our position in our last discussion. We'd like to revisit the terms of the contract."

Chuck recognized something was fundamentally wrong with this picture, as he responded, "Why would you want to reopen discussions with labor? Let's be honest here, our teams didn't bargain with each other to everyone's mutual benefit. You took a hard line and basically threw labor out of your business model. I can easily recount your marketing position:

"First, 'Fast Flyers – Automating low-cost air travel'.

"Then, 'Check us out on the web at FF.com'.

"Or, my favorite, your tagline – 'We got you there'.

"Now your airline is rebranded as, 'Overall, Floundering Flyers – The high cost of automated air travel', with that new tagline – 'There—We got you, sucker'.

"Your automated check-in of bags and people with RFID tags resulted in no humans at the gate, dispensed with all baggage handlers with an automated bag sorting carousel, replaced the flight attendants with drink serving robotics, and modernized the on-ground servicing of the aircraft with state-of-the-art ground robotics only lightly monitored from an insulated data bunker, outsourced off-shore to reduce costs.

"You put the screws to the pilots and told them this was the way of the future, and if they didn't play ball your way, they'd fly freight runs out of Guangzhou, China.

"Your team got everything they wanted! Then, of course, we were told which crumbs we could have if we behaved ourselves. Have you determined the crumbs we got were too much?"

The Sean tried to conceal his uneasiness by showing his best salesman grin of acceptance. He too brightly responded, "This is precisely why we want to reopen the negotiations, Mr. Wood. From every angle that we have looked at the contract, we find some inequalities that in good conscience were shameful. Let me first start off with…"

Chuck cut off The Sean's opening monologue. "Before we discuss anything, do you want to introduce me and explain the purpose of these two contractors who are seated at the table? I's poor manners, even for you, not to introduce two new interested parties to our negotiation round. I'm pretty sure they aren't finance dweebs like last time because they look like they've been outdoors and don't have pencil necks."

The Sean failed to respond fast enough, before Chuck drawled, "We do know your human- free, fully automated flight service is being pounded. Anybody and everybody you threw out of work when you 're-baked' this airline, to use your terms, was waiting and hoping for you to stub your toes and fall face down. From what we are hearing, not only did you stub your toes but you're about to be forced to fall on your sword. It's all over the news and the Internet that your big debut, didn't.

"Your practice runs went well enough, but something went hopelessly wrong during your grand opening. We particularly liked hearing about your problem with the automated lavatory ground gear pumping into, rather than vacuuming out, the sanitary systems of the aircraft. Nothing like having raw sewage a centimeter deep in the aircraft to ground it. But your public relations snafu has really made this airline sparkle when it comes to the social media buzz.

"Your website said FREE travel, and people signed up for it only to be told that was a mistake. It would not have been so bad if your automated baggage shredder hadn't ruined all those passengers' belongings. You should have had some other contact centers teed up just in case there was an unforeseen problem, because your outsourcing travel services support lines simply fell off the grid. Now you know, nothing aggravates a traveler more than when they can't yell at someone concerning their problem.

"With all that fit of activity going on, my constituents are all asking me the same question: 'Where were you when the fit hit The Sean?'"

Even some of these seasoned negotiators had trouble suppressing their snickers at the humorous poke at Sean. Sean rocked back into his chair to gather his thoughts and let the muted laughter subside.

After a moment of composure, Sean took a breath. "I have two assignments to work on. The first is to get the airline back in the air, then to see it doesn't happen again. We are coming to you for immediate help from your labor constituency to plug the operational gaps and provide the support to get planes back in the air. As for the two people at the end of the table, they're here for the second phase of my assignment.

"Mr. Wood, can we get your team's cooperation? I am here to negotiate the rates and manpower required."

Chuck slightly clucked his tongue. "Trust. It's what you need when forming a partnership. Our labor team always wanted to partner with management, but there is no trust left. You won't trust us enough to tell us who is at the end of the table, but you let them hear everything. This behavior tells us you want us to blindly trust you.

"I would expect that after we marshal all our considerable resources, feed their valued skillsets in to fit exactly into the right problem areas, put up with the verbal and written abuse that we all know is ready to engulf us from the public, it would be characteristic of you to throw us under the bus again once everything is under control."

Sean studied his opponent for a few seconds and then offered, "This is Mercedes Field and her U.S. counterpart, Jim Hughes. They've been retained to investigate the situation and the… ransom demands. I believe that if your team helps us to overcome the issues, these two will need to interact with you and your team transparently in strict confidences. You'll see things they might miss. They'll have questions none of us asked. Does this help clear the way to work together?"

Chuck sat silent for a moment. The he got up to review all the food available for the teams to enjoy during their discussion. A Cheshire smile crossed his face as he leisurely poured himself a mimosa. He turned around with the drink in his hand and raised it in salute to the two groups watching.

"Ladies and gentlemen, allow me to toast our new understanding. Let's get busy with the details so we can get people to replace your malfunctioning machines and get the aircraft flying again!"

CHAPTER 17

Sand Pile

Juan sat trapped in the little high-wing two-seater plane, which was now too crippled to fly due to the ramming effort of the aerial drone when it turned on him. He grimly watched what he'd classified as a sirocco closing in on him. A slight twinge caused Juan to redirect his focus to his left leg, which was wet with blood. He tried to pull his leg up to try to see the damage but couldn't. His leg remained pinned by some of the fuselage metal that had buckled upon landing.

No amount of effort freed his leg. He accused, "Well, Juan, this is another fine mess you've got me into! As much as I'd like to sit and sulk, the sirocco is heading this way. I must get free from this aircraft or become mistaken as a hominid artifact when I'm found. The damn plane can't fly, but with the wings still intact the sirocco could simply lift it like an airwave surfer and send it a couple of hundred miles from the last known location. If I could just get out of this aluminum coffin, I might use my cell phone app to order one of those Üdder rideshares folks, people rave about."

Juan's leg started to steadily ache. He tried to move it free, then recalled the emergency tools he'd loaded as a precaution. He chuckled. "Definitely crash-landing tools. I hope I can reach the WWII fighter pilot fire axe Carlos gave me." He stretched and pawed until he gripped the handle. "Ahh, there you are, my sweet. A couple of focused chops with the blade, coupled with a little can opener finesse using the back of the axe, and …"

Juan worked feverishly in the close quarters with the axe, making some progress. He felt the plane beginning to flex due to the increased winds. Juan renewed his efforts to slice through the crumpled metal to freedom. Then the storm did him a favor. His cuts were in places that when the storm started to flex the aircraft and loosened the metal's grip on his leg. He pulled free and scooched back; yet desperately gripped his newfound lucky charm.

Juan located the injury and applied first aid on his wound. He braced to deal with the blustery storm. The aircraft scooted this way, then that way. Surprisingly, it settled in a small arroyo depression which prevented it from traveling further. Juan almost smiled at what seemed to be his good fortune, until he realized that the brightness inside the aircraft was dimming. Having the aircraft settle in the arroyo allowed more sand and dust to be deposited on him and the plane as the gusts howled overhead.

Juan knew if he didn't get out of the aircraft now, he might be buried. He grabbed the axe and hacked out of the cockpit, away from the wind direction. After perfect cut, he gained the opening needed. He checked around for anything critical in case the plane filled with sand. He double checked his satellite phone and held the axe as a shield in front of his facemask. A little water remained so he secured with the first aid kit and a few flares.

The vicious, sandy fury lashed and made his wounds ache. The plane appeared to sink, but he stayed close enough to use it for shelter. He felt for the phone but realized that even if he could get through to the operations area and Julie, they couldn't send a rescue team in this Mr. Sandman nightmare. When the weather settled and the device's battery kept a charge, he'd try for contact.

Julie paced back and forth, failing miserably to remain calm. Every time the monitoring console dinged, she returned to hovering over the operator. *"Is that him?"*

Her nervous energy wore out George, then the operator in the adjoining seat. She was well on her way to wearing down the third one when McLaren caught her by her arm and gently escorted her to a cot with a fresh pillow.

She smiled politely. "I couldn't possibly sleep with Juan out there and the windstorm disrupting our rescue efforts. Thanks, McLaren, but I'd rather stand by the monitor."

McLaren smiled back at her and simply yet firmly pushed her into the cot and then added a light blanket. He reassured, "There isn't anyone here who doesn't know your husband is at risk. We're all pulling for him. However, if you keep pestering everyone, I'll duct tape to this cot, so we work. Now, do me and yourself a favor, lay down and rest. When something happens requiring you, I'll personally come get you. Deal?"

Julie smiled sheepishly and nodded. "Sorry to be such a pest, McLaren. If it will make you happy, I'll lie here, but I'm not the least bit tired."

McLaren smiled a paternal smile, patted her hand, and soothed, "There's a good lass. Have a lie down and be refreshed for our next stage in the rescue when we locate him."

McLaren stood up and went around the screen, then over to the monitoring terminal to check on communications updates. After a minute or two, he looked around the screen to check on Julie. He found her fast asleep.

George returned to the center and joined McLaren to see what developments occurred during his down time. He noted that the storm was through the area where they believed Juan crashed. He turned to McLaren and demanded, "How soon before we can mount a rescue operation?"

Not taking his gaze off the monitor, McLaren commented, "It's a big desert out there to aimlessly wander around. We need to track his original intercept course and then try to project what his return course was before we send out the dogs for him."

George puzzled a little before he commented, "Looks like a straight line between two end points to me. Why the hesitation?"

McLaren explained, "See the coordinates of the Kookaburra site?" He pointed to the monitor with the 3-D topographical map indicating the red coordinate points. "They're wrong. I drove that first stake for the mining operations, and I can tell we're being lied to with the mapped position shown. Our geopositioned coordinates for our base operations according to the satellite are also wrong. If the end points are not correct, then drawing a line in between them doesn't map as it should. It won't do us much good in our search either, now would it?"

George digested the information before he offered, "That's somewhat disappointing news. But, you know, we have someone on our team that might just be able to help us in our geolocation efforts. Any objections if I try to bring her skillset into this situation?"

McLaren almost got a nod completed before George launched an outbound call from his cell phone.

A groggy voice answered, "*Mygoddoyouknowwhatfrickentimeitis?*"

George brightly responded, "Hi, EZ! Sorry about the late-night call, but Juan is MIA. I need your help finding him in the South Australia desert. Oh yeah, and someone tampered with the satellite geocoordinates just to make it more complicated. Do you know anyone who would be willing to take on that kind of challenge?"

Instantly awake and quite annoyed at the implication that she might be unwilling to help, EZ clearly but crossly responded, "Just let me put on some clothes so you won't have the added complaint of having to see me buck naked on the video conference call. Let's get busy finding him."

George's mind locked in the mental imagery of having the fiery, beautiful redhead on a video call au naturel, and he politely offered, "Don't feel you have to dress on our account. We'd want you to be comfortable, so your call, madam."

EZ snickered and replied, "Ha. I bet you would."

CHAPTER 18

The Reflection

Jamie smiled wistfully as he studied Frieda while she focused on her work. He sometimes got lost in thought as he dutifully memorized her facial features and her physical outline. The coolness of the data center had his thoughts drifting to their chance meeting on his bus trip to London. Her sweet face and talkative nature had him charming her for miles. Frieda loved his brogue and accused him more than once of empty flattery. They struck a common chord that began their ongoing rocky romance and put them into the reality of the moment. Jamie, womanizer, and gambler often picked apart the history to analyze their relationship. He wondered where his life would be if something hadn't thrown an emotional switch inside his soul such that no one held any interest for him except her. The area they didn't align was on humor-hers nearly non-existent, but his blended with a deep appreciation of the absurd, made up for the gap.

He chuckled at how superior he felt when dealing with others. That attribute intimidated Frieda, and the more intimidated she behaved, the bolder he got with those so-called superiors. Of course, it usually got him flattened and her on a rampage to defend him. She was reticent to argue, but as soon as Jamie was going to have his head handed to him, she'd put on her caped-crusader outfit and charge in to save the situation.

She learned at an accelerated rate. Time after time she'd become accomplished in whatever was needed to save his bacon. This was one of those times where he had to remind himself that so long as you have a guardian angel watching over you, a person could push the envelope. If one rolled the dice right, one could win.

Frieda audibly sighed enough to penetrate his musings. She faced him and asked, "Jamie, can you pop back to reality and help me with the racking and stacking of these servers? This gambling establishment for the rich and famous is sucking up every server resource we have. We've got to add these blades in the next couple of hours to meet the demand of the weekend. I can't run these cables myself. Please help."

Jamie chuckled slightly and reached over to caress her face and was about to kiss her, but she intercepted. "Ah, stop right there. You've no shot at seducing me here and now because we're behind in our work. We need to focus to finish, then we have that ridiculous daily conference call about current support issues. I've been stuck in this freezer called a data center for seven hours. The idea of having sex over in the hot air return corridor is not going to happen."

Jamie, feigning a wounded look, gave Frieda an acknowledging nod. "Frieda, let me help and then I'll give you an all over massage later tonight."

Frieda raised an eyebrow in disbelief and slightly shook her head.

Jamie added, "I know this is not quite as advertise, but I'll find us something else. You didn't think I could get us out of that last rat trap, did you? I knew we couldn't get out on regular aircraft, but I secured us passage on the *Leaking Leana* barge and travel all the way down the Congo River to the coast. Then it was the easiest thing to hop a freighter in exchange for work to get us here. If I'm such a loser, why did you trust me to get us out, and why did you come here? But look at us now. We're doing better financially, lots better. You need to trust and appreciate me a little bit sweetie. I wouldn't want anyone but you next to me."

A smile gradually broke out on Frieda's face, and she kissed him. Then they both plowed ahead with the assignment for more server resources. with their work of racking and stacking blade servers. Jamie managed to give Frieda an impish pat on her fanny that made things right again.

With a contemplative smile, Frieda stopped and suggested, "A massage then playtime."

Jamie and Frieda finished ahead of schedule, with several free minutes before the conference call. Frieda poured them each a cup of coffee to warm up and complained, "I know that Ton and Won are our supervisors, but they are some dim bulbs. It's almost like they're reading from a script handed to them much of the time."

Jamie eased back in his chair recalling the first meeting with the pair. "Your right, honey. Before I applied to this place, I did a little research. A Chairman Chang own's the majority interest in this tourist mecca. He is the man behind these twins. I think they are his wards. I thought it was odd that only Ton speaks, but you look closely at Won, he has some sort of scarring on his face. Perhaps he had an accident of some sort."

"I hadn't noticed, but I'll look," Frieda said. "I have seen the exchanges where they seem to read one another's thoughts which I've read is often the case with twins. They also seem to look down their nose, not just at you and me, but all of us."

Jamie grinned. "I think that is the main cultural difference between China and the rest of the world. No matter how bad they act, they believe they are better than anyone else. I think the only reason they hired us at our high rates is our technology expertise. But the hours are grueling."

"Jamie, I'm getting worn out with this whole gig. How long before we have enough saved to move back to a Western culture?"

Jamie leaned over and kissed her check then whispered in her ear. "I'm working on it, and I think soon. Your right about the lack of mental power even if you add them together."

After the last team member had dialed into the bridge, the usual antics began. Someone made another call but forgot to mute his line. Another put the call on hold to get coffee, which made everyone listen to music on hold until he returned. Another person typed up a report while rustling a bag and crunching on chips. The entire group was tired from ten to twelve-hour shifts, so the poor conference call etiquette always aggravated someone. Today was Frieda's turn.

Frieda shouted, "How about muting your phones, people? Geezers! We got the calorie king munching so close to the phone I can smell his breath. Plus, Mr. Coffee has us trapped in music on hold from hell. And someone, whose asthma has flared up again from working too long in the meat-locker cold server room, also doesn't comprehend the usefulness of a mute button. For God's sake, mute your lines if you aren't speaking!"

Jamie gave Frieda a look that could only be interpreted as *Seriously, aren't we being just a little over dramatic?* After a few seconds of silence on the call, Jamie interjected, "I really appreciate these conference calls so that we don't have to trudge to the conference room for these meetings. This is much more efficient. After long shifts being in close quarters with several somebodies whose deodorant stopped working is a bonus."

Their supervisors, Won and Ton, gave each other looks of annoyance from their location. Then Ton insisted, "Alright, that's enough. Let's cover off on our outstanding issues log and do a round table to see what else needs to be looked at."

Frieda, already in a bad mood, jumped in and recommended, "Well, let's talk about adding more qualified staff to work this place. We're all working insanely long days, but still falling behind on your required tasks. Can't you just get more people in here?"

Ton, tired of the complaining from this female, quietly informed, "We have a different work ethic here in Macau. We do our job until it is finished. You were hired to do the work you are assigned. This is not the Western work environment where we listen to your complaints because a labor union is lurking nearby. This place is automated to eliminate the possibility of organized labor showing up on the casino floors. Let us know if your conscience will no longer allow you to work here. We can replace you within fifteen minutes."

Muting the phone, Jamie reached over, touched Frieda's hand, and, with a pleading look in his eye, whispered, "Frieda, please don't ruin this for us. It's taken so long to engineer this. Don't throw our opportunity away. Just a little longer, honey, please?"

While the whole group was grateful that she had spoken up, none of them would risk speaking out in the same manner. Frieda knew it. She reeled in her anger and indignation, took the phone off mute., "I'm sorry, Mr. Supervisor, if I have over-stated my observations. We've all been trying so hard to make ends meet in our personal lives and still deliver 110% effort to you. I meant no disrespect. I'm just a little tired today, and I don't do very well working in the cold data center for twelve hours. I know these short sleeve polo shirts with the casino logo on them are important when we are seen by your guests, but can

I bring a warm jumpsuit to wear while in the data center? No customers will see me in there unless you are giving a tour of this high security area."

Ton thought for a moment and then commented, "The clothing you were told to purchase is designed to be static-free for operational efficiency in the data center. However, your request is reasonable. Make sure there is no nylon fabric in your jump suit that might harm the computers."

Frieda gave Jamie a disgusted look and tritely responded, "You're too kind, sir. I'm sure we all bask in the glare of your benevolence."

Won and Ton, oblivious to the sarcasm, smiled at each other for having defused the confrontational situation. Feeling encouraged, Ton felt justified in another benevolent action as he happily offered, "Why don't we call it meeting over and have everyone go home early today? We can go over the situation issues in the morning, but let's start half an hour earlier than the posted schedule. Night, everyone."

Frieda clucked her tongue and sarcastically commented, "Wow, he really warmed up the troops. Geezers, it's 11:00 pm now, but let's get started at 6:30 am tomorrow morning."

Jamie, annoyed as well at the situation, offered, "Thanks for jumping in on everyone's behalf, sweetheart! We wouldn't be nearly so far ahead without your help. Nothing like having representation while you work as a galley slave here in the gulag! Next time let it go, alright?"

Frieda said nothing but ground her teeth in anger.

CHAPTER 19

What's your emergency?

Tyler walked into the Pittsburg detective area he'd been directed to with a wry smile on his face as he cataloged the surroundings of the large room. Worn furniture, smoke-stained paint, and the smell of burned coffee seemed a shame for such a large city police department. Desks were set up in rows with people hunched over scribbling on paperwork, some with people in the side chairs, likely having statements taken. The din seemed to ebb high and low.

Tyler waited for a pause and spoke. "Excuse me. I'm looking for Detective Cormorant. I was told he might be in this area. I'm Tyler Hebert."

Como, as he was known to all that worked with him, looked up from the end desk, tilted his head to one side. He sized up the visitor who seemed close to his height but leaner. Clearing his throat, he gruffly replied, "Sonny, I don't like when people come looking for me. I'm the one who does the hunting and the interrogation. Since I don't remember needing to look for you, you must be trying to sell something. And judging from the nice, well-tailored suit you're sporting I'd wager it's desperately expensive. Just so you know, someone on a detective's salary isn't going to buy whatever you're peddling. You can show yourself out."

Tyler had learned early on in life not to flinch when some-one assaulted him, either physically or verbally. He momentarily studied Como and realized that this man easily fit the research he had done on the detective. Como was on the wrong side of fifty, an ex-pro football linebacker whose bad knees had forced him into another line of work early on. Well-fitting clothes always seemed beyond his capability, and he was never able to fasten his top collar button, which made wearing a tie hopelessly comical, as it did now.

Como was a bull of a man, and it always came out in his speech to others. It also made him a solid detective and an excellent ex-husband.

Tyler sized up the situation and simply pulled out his phone, dialed a stored number, and handed the phone to Como without a word. Como smirked but took the device and, in a very conde-scending tone, asked, "Is this your mommy who's going to tell me that you've been given permission to play with the big boys?"

The phone connected, and when connected Como started, "This is Detective Como…"

The irritated caller on the other end of the line cut off the monolog from Como as he barked, "I know who the hell this is. But in case you don't know my voice, this is Mayor Barker. Now put the cell on speaker. If you have anything to say, don't. Just shut up."

Como stood and escorted Tyler to the nearest conference room and shut the door. He was a little rattled but handed phone back to Tyler who quickly put the cell on speaker mode. "Mayor Barker, we can both hear you. No one else is nearby, per your request."

Como, alarmed and confused that he seemed to be the only one who didn't know what was going on, remained watchful and quiet.

Mayor Barker admonished, "You see, Tyler, what I put up with? You try to engage him as a professional but that's a waste of time. Then someone steps in, like me, and puts the wheels back on the discussion, 'cause Como here is at odds with the planet!"

Again Tyler, unruffled, responded, "Your Honor, I will admit that he may have some character blemishes. However, my research shows him as the most determined hunter for this case. I would maintain that he is my preferred choice in getting to the bottom of the emergency services problem your city had a short time ago. Based on what we know, I believe Detective Cormorant is the logical choice."

Barker sputtered and chortled. "Como? Como has the logic of a man who shovels horseshit for a living!" After a few deep breaths, the mayor sighed and relented, "To be fair, he has the highest close rate of any of the borough detectives. Therefore, I'll concede on this choice and tell you to proceed. I want to get to the bottom of the geolocation mismatch to our ALI database that sent emergency vehicles everywhere but where they were needed.

"Como, if I get another phone call about your uncoopera-tiveness, I'll have you put back on traffic control and domestic violence house calls. You know the kind of DVs I'm talking about, right? The female screaming hysterically in between bursts of automatic weapon fire."

Como, understanding the gravity of the situation and more than a little humbled by Tyler's choice of him to work with even after the rude introduction, replied, "Yes, Mayor. I'll deliver all the assistance that Mr. Hebert might require. We'll work this case together."

Tyler, after the mayor ended the call, calmly added, "I don't think that Mr. Hebert will be necessary. Just call me Tyler, Detective Cormorant."

Slightly chuckling, Detective Cormorant inclined his head respectfully and said, "Then just call me Como. Let's get to work, shall we? Oh, and what do you mean by *character blemishes* anyway?"

That comment finally got Tyler to grin.

CHAPTER 20

Bigger toys for bigger egos

Konstantin approached Dmitry boldly and stated, "He's on the phone demanding a rematch. I can tell him you're unavailable if you wish, sir."

Dmitry's smirk advertised his enjoyment of the situation. He appeared to collect his thoughts and replied, "No, that's alright, and I'll speak with him. Are you and Mikhail up for another round in case the stakes are more interesting?"

Konstantin grinned. "We've won every round so far, but that's to be expected since we built the gamification interface. I can see the challenge from their point of view, but ours will be supremacy in the contest. As they say in America, points is points."

Dmitry let the winning moment fill the silence. "Yes, but you'll notice we're winning by less and less margin each time. Invented here does not mean they can't wrestle dominance from us. The Chinese are adaptable and capable people. We can't underestimate them. I recommend that you check your arrogance at the door before the next game, lest we be overtaken."

The subtle but pointed dig made Konstantin snap rigidly to attention. "Dmitry, I apologize if I have taken for granted our winning position. Mikhail and I won't allow our past successes to cloud our judgement, sir. We'll do everything in our power to maintain our leadership position in these combats."

Dmitry appeared pleased, then said, "You and Mikhail are doing a fine job, and there's nothing wrong with acknowledging our dominance. I just want you to realize that the Chinese are formidable adversaries who can be beaten for a while but who learn at accelerated rates. I don't want them to beat us at our game, even though we invited them in to play."

Konstantin nodded and firmly replied, "Understood, Dmitry. I'll have Evgeniya send the call on through."

He marched out of the area to pass the word on to Evgeniya, after Dmitry watched him continue to the data center.

The desk phone rang three times, and Dmitry answered it preventing it from rolling to voicemail. "Chairman Chang, what a pleasant surprise! My associate indicated that you may be looking for a rematch. Is this true?"

Chairman Chang noted that their conversations usually began with annoying tweaks at each other but almost always ended up with each thoroughly irked at the other. Years of practice in Chinese politics had taught him to mask his irritation. "Dmitry, my old friend, cyber czar of the Russian Ministry and undisputed thug in the sleazy Russian underworld. Ah, but I repeat myself. Yes, I'm here to rouse you to another session of our game. I've enlisted some trusted gaming enthusiasts that should help even out the odds in our play time. The game rules keep changing with the differing scenarios, and I felt that a little more gaming savvy on my side might help make the, uh, engagement more sporting. What do you say?"

Dmitry smiled at the backhanded comment from the chairman and offered, "What, you're not enjoying the gamesmanship during our play time? We Russians are fabulous gamers. I have but to point to our most favorite game of roulette to prove my point! Besides, changing the rules each time keeps the contest fresh and interesting. Wouldn't you agree?" Dmitry didn't wait for a response. "Certainly, your take in the spoils has not been shabby. I admonished my team that they should not be complacent in their past wins, because if I know you, you'll want to play until your team has the upper hand."

Chairman Chang took the comment as the intended compliment and affirmed, "How well you know me, old friend. You know I like to win, and yes, I do enjoy the freshness of the electronic combat. I guess we are both the gambler and the gamer in this contest. My two champions, Won and Ton, are almost ready for our next round. Do you have another venue theme in mind, or do you want me to suggest one?"

Dmitry grinned broadly and replied, "No, this is like tennis. So long as my team is winning, we get to serve up the target and the game rules. Let's plan for next Monday at ten in the evening CET, shall we?"

Chairman Chang responded, "We'll be ready. Any hints?"

Dmitry struggled to contain his chuckling but answered, "Yes, be prepared to have my team serve again after this next round! Good day, Chang."

Chairman Chang disconnected the call and looked at his two wards, whom he'd groomed for years. Won and Ton were acquired by the chairman when they were young. They were devoted to him. He'd schooled them in martial arts and allowed various ongoing educational venues. Until Won got mauled during the acquisition of Chairman Chang's tiger, they were identical. The result of the mauling was disfigurement and an inability to speak. The twins communicated effectively, which Chairman Chang didn't understand but appreciated. They were like Chairman Chang's family in the way of one that regards family as possessions.

Chairman Chang asked, "Did you gentlemen hear the challenge? They don't believe they can be overtaken. How do you feel about that?"

As characteristic of the twins, Won nodded his head as Ton responded for both of them. "We will not let you down, sir. Our gaming expertise is considerable, and we feel confident that we will be more than a match for them. Besides, we have another individual we would like to bring into this team for the combat. We like him because he doesn't quite play fair when it comes to these kinds of stakes. May we introduce him to you, sir?"

Chairman Chang studied the two of them, cocked his head to one side and asked, "You are not confident this challenge can be won on our own?"

Ton raised his chin in respect. "We have confidence in our ability, but to increase the winning margin, we suggest we invest in additional horsepower to distort the playing field, sir."

Chairman Chang countered, "Why bring someone else into our affairs, particularly as I've never met this person?"

Ton stated, "We believe he's stealing from your casino in Macau, but we haven't figured out how. We are gamers, but this arrogant individual is a gambler. We think his talents warrant a closer look, sir."

Chairman Chang sneered. "Bring him in then. Roughly but not broken. I typically don't reward someone stealing from me with more responsibility. I'd like to meet someone so bold." Chang stopped assembling his thoughts. "This next round will still occur without this unknown, it's key. Do I make myself clear?"

The twins nodded and quietly left.

CHAPTER 21

Row Well and Live

The meeting had dragged out for hours. When it was done, the attendees filed out of the meeting room in visibly surly moods, with little banter between them. Normally, the meeting room was spotless with the requisite black leather chairs carefully parked around the mammoth table as though each chair had its own docking station. The council's unrest, coupled with several shouting matches, had yielded a meeting room that looked like a bunch of binging computer coders had waged war with debris scattered everywhere. When a meeting concluded as a win/win, delegates typically bussed their area. This was not one of those kinds of meetings. Mayor Perez, sat in solitude appearing dejected with her eyes focused on a spot at the end of the long red oak table. Brayson stood at the doorway where the aid had ushered him. He noted the foreboding silence and sat quietly waiting for her to mentally return to the here and now.

The two of them remained silent for long enough that Brayson became worried the cleaning crew might disrupt their needed discussion. Brayson shifted generating a bit of noise and the mayor rotated in her chair.

Mayor Perez intoned, "Brayson, the council members comments were blunt. No one wants to knuckle under to the ransom demands. Yet no one can stomach fighting these bandits. You may claim not to be versed in Spanish politics, but you were spot on with your statement. If I don't find a way to fix this, they'll invite the previous mayor to come rescue the situation. Then, I fear, all of them will take turns on me as depicted in the vulgar graphic displayed on the data center screens. I hope you can report some progress, otherwise I'm going to buy some knee pads for my next city meeting."

Brayson felt her pain reflected in her comments as his mind wandered through the images she suggested. "While I can't stop you in your accoutrement purchases, I can suggest an alternative posture."

The mayor chuckled and inclined her head. "Please proceed, Brayson."

"Mayor, the bandits assume that there are only two outcomes: their payment or your suffering. I maintain that there is a third outcome. We change the rules of engagement and make them play our game. They're too close to the ransom game and therefore oblivious to that third option that was not considered when they launched this attack."

The mayor visibly brightened, as she asked, "Okay, so what's this third option that favors us? Have you got that far in your thinking yet? Because my knees are starting to ache already."

"We offer to pay in physical assets and not do it electronically. We offer, let's say, gold artifacts from one of the museums or a Gaudi original. Something tangible, but so valuable that they can't resist. This forces them into the open to collect, then we have a chance to grab them. We make them play by your new rules of engagement."

The mayor rose. "Let me think about your idea while we walk back to my office."

At first blush Brayson's idea seemed viable but as the details were mapped out it on the different possible treasures that would be valuable, it appeared less optimal. Mayor Perez commented, "These aren't your run of the mill stupid thugs holding us at gunpoint, wanting our wallet. You're suggesting that we offer tangible goods to lure them into a trap. They've defeated every cyber defensive tactic we've deployed and are still in control of our network. People this smart aren't dumb enough to drive over to the drop point to collect the goods and believe they can get away scot-free. They would correctly assume a trap and simply double down on our pain to accelerate the e-transfer of funds. They won't be lured into something so obvious."

Brayson nodded his head indicting he listened. "I would maintain that people this smart would have a mile wide vanity streak. Certainly, money is one thing. However, the way this ransom scenario is being played suggests that more or different ransom goods might be considered. You are quite correct these are most definitely intelligent adversaries, which makes them vulnerable to ego tempting offers. An important artifact or art piece has not only worth but something no egotistical crook can resist. Not, of course, for the money, but as a personal trophy to constantly remind them of their superior intellect."

The mayor shook her head, unconvinced. "They may be tempted, but I can't believe they'd take such thinly veiled bait and risk capture. I just do not believe they'll risk their secure positions for a trophy."

"Of course, they won't come in for the trophy, ma'am. If the trophy was brought to them, while the communications are monitored, we'd have a chance of learning their identity. Their communications control is coming in from a place, and we need to work backwards to identify that source. This is not one person, but rather a team of people organized to pull this off, likely in multiple locations. A tasty trophy would certainly get discussed, even if they suspect the obvious trap. If the bait is intriguing enough to consider, then that should spawn backend transmissions. This information could provide a view into the culprit source."

Mayor Perez saw her arguments being overcome one-by-one and asked, "Okay, bright guy, what kind of trophy are you going to propose, and more importantly, who did you have in mind to try and make the drop?"

The expression on his face turned serious. "You, Madam Mayor, will be the primary agent, but you'd be escorted by an old acquaintance. Thomas Mauser, a legend in the field of security. Better known as Tommy Gun."

Bordering on amused, she asked, "*Tommy Gun?* How is it that I've never heard of this security legend?"

Barely suppressing a chuckle, Brayson stated, "Uh, I just made him up. After I do a little social network engineering, he will be the legendary Thomas Mauser, and I will have my new cover identity for cloaking purposes. I'm sorry I can't do anything about your identity, but they already know you. Frankly, you lend authenticity to the transaction."

Mayor Perez rolled her head right and let her left cheek be cradled in her left hand as she looked sideways at Brayson. After a few seconds she snapped up in her chair and acquiesced, "There it is. It's either your ridiculous plan, or I submit to the whole council's back door agenda on me! How soon can we launch Mr. Mauser?"

CHAPTER 22

Two-mo for Sumo

The dumbfounded look on the chairman 's face was unmistakable as Won and Ton made their gaming debut appearance. They set their jaws and their mouths were hardlines. Ton said, "Sir, we are ready to participate and win this gaming contest against Dmitry for your honor."

Chairman Chang remained speechless as they carefully unpacked their gaming items. Each man supplied their individual good luck talismans to add to the event. No advantage was to be overlooked.

Won and Ton stopped and stood at attention in front of their leader. Each had a rook sacks slung over a shoulder. Ton added, "Sir, where would you like us positioned."

With his mouth half-open, Chang shook his head from side to side as if to verify the image in front of him. Nothing helped as evidenced by his veins expanding across his face. His voice faltered, "Can you two tell me why you're dressed as sumo wrestlers? I mean this diaper attire you are wearing is…is… words fail me. You don't have the bulk for that kind of combat. I mean, on the blood of my ancestors the two of you together would only make a small portion of a junior sumo wrestler. You're build and training focused on speed. Please tell me you two haven't mentally sailed off down the Yangzi River under hallucinogenic duress, as we're readying to take on Dmitry and his avatar, Groddo!"

Won and Ton blanched at the chairman's comments and struggled to contain their indignation. They glanced at each other, in their silent communication. Ton finally managed to respond, "Sir, we are not wearing diapers, as you call them. These garments are in keeping with the Shinto religion and are properly called *mawashi*. Five folds of fabric in front and five in back! We honor the ritual sumo wrestling combat and have come to do battle in the circle of digital combat. When we engage in our recreational digital gaming activities, we ALWAYS suit up in our *mawashi*, and it helps to sharpen our gaming efforts, sir."

Chairman Chang struggling with the incongruity of the situation. "At no time in my moderate life span do I recollect seeing sumo wrestlers wearing a traditional *mawashi* with black knee-high socks and fuzzy house shoes! Do you care to explain this fashion dichotomy where East sumo tradition meets West mail order slippers?"

Ton shifted from foot to foot, sheepishly stated, "The cold in here, sir. One cannot do one's best work with cold feet, regardless of the sumo tradition of the *mawashi*. However, we are, in fact, so convinced of the power of this Shinto ritualistic combat and its positive outcome against the Russian, we brought similar, but authentic, garb for you."

The wild-eyed look, flared nostrils, and bared teeth should have alerted the pair that Chairman Chang was not of the same mindset. Chairman Chang adamantly insisted, through his bared teeth, "You want me to exchange my handcrafted, perfectly tailored business suit of state for that? I'm…not…going…to… wear…a…Japanese…diaper. I don't care what you call it."

Won and Ton felt hurt from his rejection of their traditional gaming garb, as well as the visible displeasure of their chairman. Finally, Ton submitted, "Sir, we merely came prepared to engage the Russians with all of our prowess fully intact to help secure some wins for you. This is so much like the ritualistic sumo combat within the circle of the contest, we felt compelled to bring all our guns to bear. We honor you in this display of force and tradition."

Chairman Chang relented a bit with a father nod to each and they felt relieved as his features softened. He said, "I'm pleased at how seriously you're taking this game session. You are in the seats to my right. Let's get ready for the transport game."

Won nudged his brother, and a silent plea transpired between them. Ton hesitated but a moment, then asked, "Chairman Chang, in the spirit of the sumo wrestler contest, we have reserved the honor for you to do the opening ceremonies. Will you please begin the combat with one exaggerated foot stomp after the other with a final shout to scare off the demons of defeat before we start? It is always considered the best Shinto manners in this age-old combat between warriors."

Chairman Chang struggled in responding to the request. Like an indulgent parent who wished to reward the sincerity of his wards, he took a fighting stance, then proceeded to stomp one foot after another in the exaggerated requestion. He ended with a yell as though the hounds of hell were after him. "Barak! Barak! Away demons of hell! Away now!"

Won and Ton were so delighted and charged by the display, they promptly scampered to their assigned positions in the attack formation. Chairman Chang, feeling a little sheepish in the whole affair, began to refocus his mind on the new game not yet launched.

CHAPTER 23

Axe Again

Julie and the rest of the rescue team located Juan after a day en route. He was unconscious but alive when she felt for his pulse. Breathing a sigh of relief at finding him alive, she stated, "Gentle with him, please. He's suffering from dehydration, an aircraft inflicted wound from a forced landing, and an overdose of sand traveling sideways at high speed."

One of the emergency medivac personnel, bent before the prone man, beginning his work. "You know, luv, this would be a whole lot easier if you weren't supervising quite so close. We need him to release the axe he is clutching so tightly. It is not uncommon for people who are being rescued to go into deep trauma, only to come out of it ready to fight the first thing they see. We really don't like leaving trauma rescue victims fully armed. If you want to help, then let's get this Viking battle axe away from him, or you can unload him from the chopper."

Julie flashed an annoyed look at the man but began to pry Juan's hands off the axe. Juan's unconscious reflexes flared up but were unsuccessful in keeping the weapon. Once Julie secured the axe, he settled into is injured sleep. In turn, the rescue team relaxed and resumed their efforts in assessing and dealing with his medical condition. Medics positioned him carefully on a straight board and strapped him to minimize movement until a full body check could be conducted. The rapid transfer to a gurney and transport to the helicopter finished without issue.

Julie held the axe knowing her husband would require reassurance later that it was under her control. She looked it over carefully, noticing the metal scratches and scrapes that it had gathered. She guessed Juan used the devise to free his leg, then chop his way out of the semi buried plane. The blood stains on the rubberized handle were an odd mystery since he had no visible axe wounds. She shuddered at the thought of his using the axe in self-defense after the storm before their arrival.

George ran up to her disturbing her thoughts and said, "Here, give me his stuff. You go with him to the hospital. They want him in an emersion solution and to re-hydrate him as soon as possible. The flesh wound from the aircraft metal is superficial. I'll clean up the details here with the search crews." He patted her shoulder and turned her toward the aircraft. "Never fear. George is here."

Tears filled her eyes making her unable to focus. She handed George everything. "Let me get him settled. Then I'll reach out for a debriefing. We'll talk soon. He'll recover you know."

George joined McLaren, Julie, and EZ on a video call to discuss the search and rescue mission. Categorizing the facts surrounding the ruined mining site of Kookaburra suggested Juan's downed plane as a direct consequence of the mayhem witnessed at the site.

McLaren insisted, "Let's start with the satellite geolocation error. It seems to me that with the last known coordinates being wrong, we were lucky to ever have found Juan."

Julie blanched at the statement but forced herself to stay focused on the discussion.

EZ clarified, "George prefaced the hunt with that information so we could mathematically account for the shift. We were lucky."

George smiled. "Yeah, but it was McLaren who noticed it first. I just relayed the information we knew. EZ worked the magic to revise the coordinates logically accounted for the repositioning shift."

EZ visibly blushed. "Ah shucks, it was easy with the data. McLaren stated that both sites were placed incorrectly. Knowing how to do that geolocation disinformation to cloak an aircraft, I worked the formula backwards to get the right coordinates. I'm not saying I've ever done geolocation disinformation to cloak a plane, but I saw it on the smugglers' channel."

McLaren laughed uproariously. "Julie, lass, this is some team of buccaneers you've around you. Are you sure you're not all Australian, because I'll claim you as kinfolk based on the devious skillsets, I've seen from everyone?"

The participants chuckled which helped lower the tension of the discussion.

Julie stated, "McLaren, we plan to make sure you feel that way when we solve this puzzle and present you with the bill."

McLaren drew quiet and scanned their faces, looking to see if they understood. Their expression indicated they didn't. "Then you don't know, do you?"

Julie cocked her head puzzled. "Know about what, McLaren?"

"Management is going to pay the ransom demand and quietly move on with business. I don't see any more involvement for your team, though I'd like to understand the geolocation issue to create a block on its reoccurring. I've been instructed to pay your contract fees and terminate your involvement. You're off the clock, madam. Of course, all the medivac and hospital services for Juan are covered. I'm sorry I had to be the one to tell you."

George and EZ were about to raise a protest, but Julie intercepted them both. "McLaren, you know this is the wrong move. Give us three more days before you do this. I promise that my team will…"

McLaren dispassionately raised his hand. "You're arguing with the wrong person, lass. I just follow orders. I wasn't asked for my opinion. If you want to take it up with the corporate office, that's your prerogative. I can tell you that even with all the equipment lost, we're still losing two to four million dollars a day due to lost production. The ransom money will be made back up in under a month. The new equipment paid off at the end of the second month. Accountants run this company, lass, and this smells like one of their decisions."

Julie's jaw muscles flexed as she ground her teeth in silence. Moments later she gave a fatalistic sigh and half smile. "McLaren, I want to thank you for all the hospitality and help you've extended to my team. I'll go to corporate headquarters and close out our delivery order. When we determine the whys of the geolocation issue, I will pass it along in appreciation for your kindnesses. Many good wishes to you and your organization."

With that she gave McLaren a hug and told EZ to stand down, then closed out the video call. She motioned to George to follow her.

Outside the building and in the car, Julie hurriedly dialed back EZ and placed the call on speakerphone.

EZ answered, "What kept you so long?"

George, turned toward Julie with confusion written all over his face. "What do you…"

Julie cut him off. "You didn't really think I was going to let this go, did you? EZ knew I wasn't. EZ, please conference in Wolfgang. He offered some assistance, and I know exactly where I would like his help."

George, still not grasping the gist of the conversation, asked, "What are you talking about?"

The exaggerated pause by both woman made George swallow hard in discomfort.

Julie explained, "The company is going to pay the ransom and hope they can get back to business as usual. You heard that part, right? Well, I want to know where that money is going. Because, when I know where the money is going, then I can determine who it's going to."

Julie smoothed George's hair back behind his ear as if petting the family dog.

George brightened as if hit by a lightning bolt, then blurted, "Oh, I get it. We not finished. We're going to work the case in clandestine mode. Pretty shrewd, Ma'am."

EZ giggled a bit. "Julie, it's not that men are stupid, they're just a little slow sometimes."

Julie smirked at the pouting expression across George's face.

He quietly protested, "Men are not slow! It's just that we don't always follow feminine logic at the high velocity it's delivered."

CHAPTER 24

Well-Played

While he continued his brisk pace toward their destination, Chuck Wood looked back over his shoulder and offered, "I'm sorry, you two, but I don't have time to sit in a conference room to discuss the state of the airline over gourmet coffee and scones. I've people on the ground pulling at me from all directions, working to get these birds back in the air. Right now, these birds are very expensive aluminum outhouses that can't fly. You seem like nice folks, but unless you're going to suit up in bio-hazard wetsuits to help clean out these grounded aircraft so they can fly again, I don't have time to entertain."

Mercedes and Jim were practically jogging to keep up with Chuck's pace across the ramp. Mercedes protested, "Chuck, you were asked to help us while we investigate the derailing of the airline. All you've done is take an adversarial role, whenever we ask anything. What's the deal? We're here to help get to the bottom of this corporate extortion mess, and you're being a jerk!"

Chuck did an about face that had Jim and Mercedes almost plowing into him. The unmistakable look of annoyance, bordering on anger, was etched in his face. Without missing a beat or softening his tone, he declared, "Listen, sweetheart, you show up here working for The Sean. I'm sure you command a high-dollar fee with your ex-gunnery sergeant here to solve world hunger, but the folks I represent won't have the fat payday you two are going to squeeze out of the company when this is over. I don't see any detective work being conducted. I see some fancy consultants trying to soak up knowledge from somebody else so you can charge your high dollar fees. You don't know a damn thing except what we tell you. So, we're going to do it the other way around! YOU tell me something useful that makes me think you can find breathable air in an open field. Otherwise, stop following me around."

Jim tried to interject, but Chuck bellowed, "Was I talking to you, gunny? I was addressing the arrogant woman who's got no finesse in her speech. At some point in her existence, she likely decided that because she was somewhat buxom, she could talk to a man any damn way she pleased. That don't cut no ice around here!"

Mercedes was a capable woman who had Seal training and had spent time with one of the U.S. agencies working in stealth mode. She and her cat hired onto the CATS team after Mercedes sought distance from Jim. Her curly blond hair bounced with the breeze as she pulled up to her 1.6 meters. Mercedes was trim and fit, but Jim knew she could pack a wallop when pissed. Her expression telegraphed that time was close.

Jim Hughes, also known as Stalker in the agency, was on loan from the U.S. for this operation because of the involvement with aircraft. Since 9/11, Homeland Security and the other agencies took any threat that grounded aircraft as a potential act of terrorism. Jim was a big man at almost two meters, adept at martial arts, adaptable to any situation, and had spent his military career as a sniper. He had also run some military ops, which was how he and Mercedes had first met. To put it clearly, their relationship had gone way past the military and special ops boundaries.

Mercedes and Chuck squared off at a meter apart, and both were now seething with anger. Chuck towered over her and even a little bit over Jim. Jim watched the two but held back to see who would fold first. The long moments grew longer. Jim had trouble suppressing the smirk building inside.

Mercedes broke the silence first. "I'm sorry your wife died from cancer. I'm sorry the company denied the insurance claims that should have been paid on your family's behalf. I am sorry your children don't speak with you, because they don't believe in your views on labor and corporate management. Most of all, I'm sorry you live alone in your travel trailer and that there is no joy left in your life."

Chuck did something that he had never let anyone else see before. His eyes brimmed up with tears. His anger simply melted while he studied Mercedes. The seconds ticked by while Chuck struggled to regain his composure.

After letting the statement sink into Chuck's brain, Mercedes softly added, "Chuck, we know that this airline is the only thing keeping you sane. We understand that you care deeply for it and the people you've gathered to get it back in the air. We want to help in that process. Why won't you let us help?"

After subduing his internal emotions, Chuck quietly replied, "You do dig in for the details. I'm moderately impressed. I might be cooperative over gourmet coffee and scones tomorrow morning at seven, in the briefing center. Your treat, of course." Chuck eyed them and whirled around to get to his next destination as if he was a madman hyped even further by a caffeine rush.

Jim quietly chuckled. "Well played, honey, well played."

Absentmindedly sipping their coffee, Mercedes and Jim listened intently to Chuck describe what he had uncovered so far in and among the ramp equipment used to service the aircraft. Though Chuck possessed no formal education beyond high school, his keen eye and sharp mind let him learn from the ground up about the airline business. The man started at the bottom and worked his way through the ranks. He'd serviced jet engines and hydraulic systems on several different aircraft, earning the right to supervise others. There was nothing on the inside of an aircraft he didn't know something about. His knowledge and background allowed him to spot several things about the ground maintenance equipment that defied operational logic.

Chuck listing his observations succinctly to Jim and Mercedes. "They hit us where we had no defense. You can apologize for lost luggage, give vouchers for late flights, and you can comp meals or rooms for late arrivals, but you can't do anything if the planes can't move. The automated equipment took commands given from another machine, transposed its functional programming and reported that everything was fine. The mobile sanitation systems were told to pump the onboard raw sewage back into the plane and report a job well done to the automated command center. In addition, this service was offered to other airlines earlier, before delivering to this airline's aircraft. That tells me the units weren't simply malfunctioning but were carefully choreographed by another machine."

Jim offered, "Are you saying the sanitation equipment, armed with a substantial payload, were able to ground thirteen jets in the fleet before they could be intercepted. And the other planes were sabotaged by their internal automation robotics that were supposed to serve drinks and snacks?"

Chuck nodded. "Yep. And, for the units that didn't short out due to the raw sewage bath, the other robotic equipment went on a rampage using their modest hydraulic arms to ruin the seats from First Class to tail. Half the aircraft could have been made air-worthy, but no one wants to sit in a seat and have a spring up your…well, your posterior, as it were."

Mercedes asked, "Did you find the same kind of thing in the robotics? Machine-to-machine commands conveying destruction instructions?"

Chuck carefully considered the question and confidently responded, "No, I didn't. But that doesn't mean that they didn't receive the commands. These robotics are not complex computers. They follow a limited number of routines. They don't have lots of RAM or disk-space for extensive logging."

Mercedes pressed, "But they would have some rudimentary diagnostics with maybe a little capacity for logging perhaps? Perhaps only able to store the last command as an idea?"

Chuck looked at Jim and Mercedes each in turn and concurred, "Worth a look-see. Wouldn't you agree?"

CHAPTER 25

Your Deal

Frieda felt half-sick whenever she provided air cover during Jamie's slot machine raids. Not only did the multi-optic cameras in any one area have to be given a pre-recorded loop showing nothing going on, but the cameras in the adjacent circle also had to be trained away from Jamie's activity, since their high-resolution digital capabilities enabled them to zoom in at great distances. She fed a bogus audio sound loop that made it sound like business as usual in the targeted area.

Her task was to run the cloaking programs that Jamie had chained together to provide a small window of opportunity. This allowed him to slip into the digital corridor of the machine's invisibility, run the *Digital Unload of Money for Poppa,* or DUMP program as he liked to call it, and then discreetly leave the area with usually several hundred euros carefully packed into sleeves sown inside each pants leg. The first couple of times he had raided the slots, he had used just a regular bag but had become fearful that it was too obvious. Carrying his loot out in the pants sleeves was less conspicuous. Plus, it left his hands free to call Frieda and indicate that the program could be shut down.

With his pockets fully lined and a smile on his face, he turned around to discreetly leave the area when he came face-to-face with Ton, his supervisor. Ton's stare was unmistakable, and Jamie knew in an instant that he was caught.

Ton said, "Take out your phone, and call Frieda."

She answered on the first ring. He quietly suggested, "Okay, babe, the DUMP program can be shut down, and we are on our way back to the command center."

Frieda, alarmed at the 'we' comment, quickly shut everything down and spun around to leave the area only to find Won, the mute supervisor, staring intently at her. Fear and anxiety washed through her being, and her breathing quickened to the point that she might hyperventilate. Won held out his hand for her phone, and she surrendered it without a protest.

Won then launched his own special phone call to let Ton know that she was under his control. Won tapped out his quick shorthand text message to his brother, who smiled a chilling smile at Jamie.

After disconnecting the session, Ton said, "We have a lot to talk about, once we are off the casino floor and in the privacy of the command center. We need to know everything."

Frieda was wild-eyed as Ton and Jamie entered the command center. She tried to run to Jamie but Won grabbed her arm hard and pulled her into a chair. The movement had such force that she rolled back several meters before impacting against a desk. Jamie lunged to help her, only to have Ton drive his closed fist deep into Jamie's solar plexus, causing him to blackout. Frieda tried to call out but got backhanded hard enough to leave her quite dazed.

Moments later, Jamie came to and was immediately greeted by more blows from Won and then Ton. Frieda could see the damage blossom on his face even from across the room. The blows on his thin skin were hard enough to split the skin, with each subsequent blow showering the area with blood splatter. After several body blows with either fists or feet, the lining in Jamie's pants gave way, and the pirated coins began to spill out onto the floor of the command center.

Ton asked, "Won, do you think they are ready to discuss their shift change yet?"

Won only shook his head no and then delivered another vicious kick to Jamie's ribs, followed by another slap across Frieda's face. After that final hit, he looked to Ton, but this time with an impish smile on his face, he nodded his head yes.

They roughly put Jamie into his own chair and then secured him with duct tape as they had done with Frieda.

Then both Won and Ton smiled. Ton offered, "I do so like these multi-cultural exchanges and dialogs, don't you? I don't mind admitting that we had trouble figuring out at first why certain machines, randomized of course, kept coming up short on the expected take. You carefully defeated all the machine-to-machine communications and machine-to-casino floor monitoring. Fortunately, you failed to understand that all the slot machines are designed to return a preset rate, based on input. Yes, you disabled the counters; however, the machines didn't match the pre-programmed return. The only answer was someone was siphoning from the casino floor machines.

"We had this same kind of multi-cultural exchange with everyone else, just to be sure who was in on the take. So now…"

Won's phone went off at that moment and he retrieved the unit, saw who was calling, and promptly answered it. He put the call on speakerphone so Ton could talk.

The caller asked, "Do we have answers yet?"

Ton, switching into a completely different character than neither Jamie or Frieda had seen, respectfully offered, "Sir, we are just having an exchange with our two Western employees and were about to discuss gambling techniques. We can certainly catch up with our discussion later if you're ready. What would be convenient for you, sir?"

"Nikkei and I were getting a little restless and hungry, so I thought let's meeting now to sort things out. Can you bring the guests?"

Won clearly blanched at the invitation to meet, but Ton responded, "Of course, sir! We'll be there right away."

Ton disconnected from the call and with an eerie smile on his face extended the invitation. "It looks like we will have to postpone our discussion for another time. We're invited, but you're summoned, to meet with the person you've been stealing from.

"I'm sure you will have a lot to talk about even though Nikkei doesn't speak. However, she is remarkable in her ability in motivating others to speak. It's the advantage of being a 160 kilogram, three-meter-long white tiger. After all, she isn't known as the Interrogator for nothing. Come, you two, you're going to like this floor show."

CHAPTER 26

Bargain Hunters

From birth Baby Perez was expected to perform at a level of excellence most people would have found onerous. Her father, a diplomat from Andalusia, Spain had assignments that took the family all over the world with an extensive assignment in Manila, Philippines. There she'd finished high school before returning to Spain for her university work in Barcelona.

Baby took after her father, as an overachiever with leadership skills that people had no trouble following. Her father learned firsthand how strong-willed she was when they argued about her returning from the University at Barcelona to follow in his footsteps. Her father was proud, yet non-public of her accomplishment, when she got elected mayor. He couldn't bring himself to call on the day she won the election, but he had anonymously sent a dozen of her favorite flowers.

Knowing he would be proud, but reserved in his feelings, she sent a politely worded text message thanking him for everything she'd become. He wouldn't acknowledge the text. Her other siblings had later remarked they had watched him lock himself in the study and had heard his private anguish after reading the message.

All those thoughts raced through her mind as she tried to mentally rehearse the delicate request she now had to make of her father. The ransom demands loomed, and the city continued to reel from the sustained cyber onslaught. Brayson recommended a decoy that the extortionist couldn't resist. She decided what might be the best temptation. Her intention was to leverage her father's diplomatic credentials to borrow a piece of Pablo Picasso artwork from the private Picasso Museum in Málaga as the bait. The problem was that the museum never lent anything to go on tour, much less allowed priceless art to be used as barter in a ransom demand.

Her father was a known contributor to the museum and had many political connections. If anyone could get this kind of favor, it would be him. The only problem was trying to get the favor for her use based on their strained relationship. But she had to try. Baby dialed the carefully stored, but unused, personal cell phone number of her father and half expected it to roll to voicemail. She was somewhat surprised when he answered it on the second ring but said nothing.

"Papá, it's Baby. Do you have time to talk with me?"

Her father had been in the diplomatic corps for Spain almost all his life and was an experienced, warm individual who easily made people talk to him. However, he struggled to even get a syllable out to his first born. After several false starts he finally acknowledged, "Ah, Madam Mayor, how good of you to call. I trust you are well and that your current challenges are now all behind you. In answer to your query, I stepped out of another meeting to take your call, so I don't have a great deal of time. How can I assist you?"

Baby got choked up. After an eternity of just a few seconds she offered, "Oh, Papá, why does this need to be so difficult? I've wanted you to be proud of me and the only thing I've managed to do is alienate you. Will I ever regain the status of being your daughter? It hurts that you won't come visit and I feel unwelcomed in your home. Can we get back what we lost?"

In between ragged breaths, he quietly offered, "Baby, you will always be my daughter, and I will always be your loving Papá. I am so proud of you and what you've accomplished. I'm sad that I can't have you close like I wanted. Let's clear the air. You are welcome anywhere I am. Nothing would please me more than to come visit. What do you need my help with?"

Baby's tears helped strengthen her resolve to save her beloved city, and she resolutely stated, "Papá, there are so many things I want to discuss with you, and none of them has to do with city business. Right now, however, I have a problem that needs your guidance. Let me explain…"

Shelf Space

Summit took careful notes of what Marvin and the security guards described. He needed their as-it-was-occurring viewpoint after he'd looked at frantically strewn products strewn across the Constellation distribution center floor. It was unbelievable how rapid the destruction occurred.

After careful recanting, Marvin surprised everyone when he asked, "What you need is an army of people to swarm this place and help get it running again."

Bluto's eyebrows were raised, as Summit stated, "Marvin, you said the distribution center was hopelessly trashed. The automated equipment is down, and this isn't just an eight-or-ten family and friends with a few pizzas worth of effort. You would have to have..."

Marvin interjected, "I'm talking about emptying the entire nearby city and assembling everyone to put the center back to a state where product can flow through the center again. I'm not saying anything about the automated systems. I'm ready to help and ask everyone who depends on this business to assist with putting it right."

Bluto rolled his eyes, but Summit sat fixated on Marvin's offer. Finally, he asked, "You must have a lot of friends willing to drop everything for this project. Then you'd need organizational skills of the highest caliber. Getting a multitude here is one thing, but coordinating a cleanup effort of this magnitude along with routing all the product to the proper truck in a sensible load order would be…"

Marvin calmly informed, "Something I was doing as the Constellation facility manager with just a clipboard. Before the so-called automation effort. We worked in this facility doing what the constipated automation system failed to complete. We got thrown out of work. The only job I could get was a long-distance freight driver. It was about that time when the company insurance ran out. And I've already commented on my mountainous bills. How about it, Summit the Destroyer? You wanna call the corporate offices and see if they're willing to pay for a little contract labor to fix this mess?"

Summit pulled out his phone to call the contracting officer with the offer.

While Summit walked away for that discussion, Marvin asked, "Bluto, any chance that you can release me in case they go for it? It is a long way to town and hard to hop there while duct taped to this chair."

The guard grudgingly went to cut Marvin free but stopped short. He looked Marvin in the eyes and asked, "Any chance you can call me by my real name? You know what happens with nicknames you don't like, don't you? They stick whether you want them to or not."

Marvin tilted his head., "Sure, anything is possible. Just exactly what is your name anyway?"

The guard straightened up and, pushing his chin out to make the announcement more formal, proudly stated, "I am Massoud Mostafavi. I was born in Iran, but I am proud to claim this country as my home."

Marvin gave him a look over the top of his glasses and stated, "I think Bluto works for addressing you, since I can't pronounce your name. No offense, you understand." Then Marvin grinned. "I'd consider switching to M&M if that is better for you. It'd be easy to remember as well as remind folks how sweet you are."

Massoud grumbled something rude in Farsi that made the other guards snicker, but he nodded agreement.

Just as they were cutting the last of the duct tape free from Marvin, Summit returned from his call. "The contracting office said he didn't have the authority to issue a new purchase order for the contract labor to fulfill your idea, but he suggested in the interim that we charge everything to my project order to get started asap. The contracting officer chuckled at the upcoming spirited discussion with his upper management when they learned of his decision. Marvin, gentlemen, we are a go."

Marvin stood up and rubbed his wrists. He looked over to the guards and with authority in his tone said, "M&M, you're not going to badge every one of these people I get to help with the cleanup. If you did, we would be here until 10:00 pm next summer before finishing."

The head guard face turned sullen, but he nodded. "You could at least try to pronounce my name, you know. It's Massoud. And no, we won't have to badge everyone since we received a fast facial recognition software program last week to quickly identify everyone coming and going. The other two guards over there, David and Marco, helped me get the app up and running. We are all voice/data consultants that love to work on computers, but this is the only work we could find at present."

"That's good news, Massoud," announced Summit.

Marvin nodded. "That is very good news, Massoud. Although I thought M&M suited you better. I only give people a hard time, so I don't have to do the group hug thing or hold hands and sing."

Massoud, David, and Marco all hung their heads down with a little pout, and Massoud quietly asked, "Does this mean we can't give our new American friend who teases us a hug?"

CHAPTER 28

Squealing then Dealing

The short drive provided no relief to Frieda and Jamie after being thrown into the trunk of the tiny car. The roads were bumpy, and it seemed as if their captors aimed for each bump. They hadn't had a chance to speak as Jamie was unconscious. When they'd reached the location, they were yanked from the car. The lighting was minimal, but it appeared to be more of an expanded residence. Frieda heard a brook or fountain off in the distance though she remained terrified. After his beating, Jamie moved like a windup toy with no battery included. It took all his strength, with constant prodding and pushing from Won and Ton, to enter the offices of the boss. The floors were a solid dark color and highly polished. The light-colored walls made the journey seem endless. Keeping her eyes down to watch her steps, Frieda caught only glances of expensive-looking statues and artwork set in alcoves along their path. Won politely knocked on the door. A voice promptly responded, "Come in."

The man they were there to meet was hunched over behind his desk and spoke in low tones. He raised up his head as they entered. The man extended his hand down before he stood and moved to the center of the room. With that, Won and Ton carefully stepped back towards the door and out of range of the pending discussion. Jamie's weaving added to Frieda's anxiety. She felt compelled a couple of times to grab his arm to help steady him.

After a few seconds of intense assessment of the two fools in front of him, the man spoke in precise language with a slight English accent. "I'm Chairman Chang. I own the casino you work in. I am given to understand that you two were unsatisfied with the standard work hours, as well as the standard wages. Even after concessions were allowed to meet your requests for additional clothing in the data center, it seems you voted yourself unsanctioned pay increases. Is this, in fact, the case?"

Frieda was frightened to her core and struggling internally with a grand mal anxiety attack that would soon have her in hysterics. Then Jamie began to chuckle loud enough to gain attention. He continued for several minutes as his chuckle grew in strength and volume.

Jamie used his tongue to lick some dried blood from the corner of his mouth and then commented, "Is that what these two goon-maroons told you?" Jamie evened his stance, straightened his shoulders, and jutted out his chin as he asserted, "It is my responsibility to service the machines when they go wonky. Rub and Dub here accused me of stealing from you? You do realize that your fully automated machine-to-machine casino needs constant debugging to make your numbers, right? Here we are, dutifully debugging your slots, and we get worked over by your comic relief team. Oh, and it sounds like they took their comedy routine on the road and worked over the entire staff. Warming to the subject, Jamie cleared his throat and looked the man square on. "Now maybe, just maybe, I can convince some of them to stay, the ones that haven't been ambulanced off premise, to keep your casino running, at least partially! Of course, I will require apologies from your comedy team, plus a few shekels from you for the wrongful beating we received."

Frieda delivered Jamie an incredulous sideways look that he could see in his peripheral vision yet didn't acknowledge. She had watched him work a contrarian situation more than once. Her anxiety attack was now ebbing away after hearing yet another gamble on Jamie's part, this time with the formidable chairman.

Jamie, fully into his role, stated, "Now that we finally got to present our side of this misunderstanding, I'd like for Frieda and myself to get cleaned up and a fresh set of clothes to continue our discussion. You have frightened poor Frieda to the point she's completely soaked and soiled her uniform slacks, and she needs to change. If you want me to stay, then fine, but I'd like a little of that 20-year-old scotch I see on your shelf. And a little ice for my face because it's starting to throb."

Frieda looked down at herself, then slowly closed her eyes in utter mortification. She was so scared of their fate she had soiled herself and simply hadn't noticed. She winced at the scent of her own foul smell, trying to disappear from this meeting, but no place to go.

With almost no emotion registering on his face, Chairman Chang studied them a minute. He was focused on Jamie, having essentially dismissed the female on her entry, then admitted, "It does appear that poor Frieda could stand a little freshening up. Before she's excused, I'd like to introduce you to Nikkei. She's always interested in meeting new people, even if only for the last time. Nikkei, come here, honey."

Chairman Chang paraded his magnificent white tiger, Nikkei, with her diamond studded necklace out from behind the desk and allowed her to roam close to Jamie and Frieda. Frieda's anxiety level shot all the way back to pre-screaming hysterics. Jamie smiled broadly and coaxed Nikkei closer. The tiger also seemed interested in their scent but was not aggressive, which Jamie surmised was due to them standing so still, along with some level of tranquilizer. The animal was ferocious by nature, but obviously tame enough to be petted under the right conditions. Jamie hoped he had just the right conditions. She lightly rubbed up against him while he calmly but cautiously stroked her head, then continued as he gently rubbed her neck and shoulder muscles. Nikkei turned an almost familiar, focused gaze on Won and Ton.

Won and Ton, both on high alert, stood back close to the door but had to give some grudging admiration to Jamie's bold moves with the tiger and Chairman Chang.

Chairman Chang watched a few moments with an inscrutable expression. Finally, he broke the silence when he looked up with a smile at Won and Ton and congratulated, "Gentlemen, you were right! He is the rogue you said he was! Please escort Frieda out and see to her needs. It seems this Jamie and I have a lot to discuss."

Hunting Methods

Brayson, busy in the city's operations center, had formulated three possible scenarios to find other malicious programs that could be activated if the systems and their associated devices were rebooted. He worked remotely with Ernesto and EZ after EZ established an isolated, secured line of communications which allowed them to help process that review. They'd built some highly segmented digital sandboxes to operate within for the exercise and each member of the team was working on a different segment. These sandboxes were surrounded by additional firewalls to prevent further interfering with the analysis. They transferred copies of the full back-ups for the end point devices for Ernesto to use for emulation in isolated test environments.

Ernesto worked at the CATS offices with EZ in a separate room. Communications continued during each test via the conference call. They'd continued efforts to support the various requests from their team members on the remote assignments. Tyler in Pennsylvania had needed only limited support as the local police department provided a dedicated detective to assist. The distribution center was in cleanup mode as was the airline. Juan was hospitalized in Perth with Julie by his side. George remained at the operations center for the mining operation in standby mode. Ernesto kept track of who was where with an electronic whiteboard that functioned as a world map, so they could see a quick picture of what was hot. The hotspots could display new updates based on voice activated commands from the viewer for the latest situation report.

That morning, Ernesto received copies of some of the malfunctioning devices and sensors used in Spain. The crippled city was the highest priority at this point with the active threat. He'd wanted to use the hard drives from these clean devices to check their sensors as well as view the programs that were driving their activity under normal conditions within the isolated network he'd created. The devices checked so far had not shown any signs of hidden programs that would launch on start up. To verify this, Ernesto took copies of the hard drives and installed them on identical devices and power-cycled them without issue. It didn't appear the endpoint sensors were compromised.

Brayson watched via the video call as Ernesto completed the testing on the fourth sensor type used by the city. There were close to thirty different types of sensors on the thousands of devices that were digitally enabled throughout the city.

Ernesto confirmed, "Brayson, this device rebooted cleanly and isn't showing any functional flaws. Frankly, there's not enough processing power or memory on these sensors to do much more than basic designed functions."

"I agree. I don't see any issues with it or the other types of sensors you've loaded onto our devices of the same type. That suggests that this is not a malfunction, but rather something broader and farther up the information exchange path or programmatic. I suspect the poisoning occurred at the first aggregation layer where there is more processing muscle to execute the viral code. Let's insert this latest device into the city's network and see if that causes anything. I'll have one of the guys here provide you with an IP address in a small subnet that we can control to complete that task. On another note, Mayor Perez agreed to try a counteroffer on the ransom demands. My goal for this option, is to gain time to correct the operational nightmare and block further disruptive activity. The problem is how to deliver this response. Our video displays are essentially locked up to the point we cannot see anything taking place in the city. Local police and fire are out on foot with signs telling citizens to stay indoors. It is the city services that are impacted. They are telling folks to avoid mass transportation and putting up barriers to access points. Walking is the safest mode of travel downtown. Getting you out of your tennis shoes is a whole lot easier than getting out of a bus or train that has gone insane." Brayson took a breath. "Fortunately, the only injuries are to equipment and gridlock. No fatalities reported. Communications are reduced to a few Citizen's Band channels since cell phone towers are jammed. If we didn't have this special satellite communication link, we'd be unable to talk or connect. EZ did a great job at tunneling through this communications blackout."

"You're right, she did a great job," Ernesto agreed. "I'm trying to separate and identify all the data signals coming into the city. I believe I can isolate at least the multicast signal that is pushing the obscene graphics to all the video screens. The media stream looks to be a unidirectional video stream, but if we can flip a bit in that propagate point, we should be able to send a response back to the source, much like a question-and-answer webinar. Once we have two-way communications, we should also be able to terminate the multicast video stream to prevent it from rebroadcasting."

"Ernesto, that's brilliant. If we can't trace the signal back, we might at least force the thieves to consider the path out of here without getting caught. Let me load up a copy of the current graphic and the details we need to insert. Hey, did you get the IP addresses for the device you uploaded?"

Ernesto replied, "Just received. This communication method is slow, but it looks good. Just a second, while I make those changes and move it outside the firewall to expose it."

Brayson waited for the feedback. He'd completed the graphical changes he wanted to insert and had loaded them up to the secure drop box Ernesto created. The silence stretched into several minutes until the new device came fully online in the city's network.

Brayson asked, "Ernesto, are you seeing what I'm seeing? My network is telling me that the sun didn't come up this morning, and the sensor is behaving exactly like the poisoned sensors. You're trapping on the same sensor, so what are you seeing from your vantage point?"

Ernesto appeared thoughtful. "That's certainly different. From my clean machine, everything the sensor is reporting seems to be fine. My theory is the sensors are probably reporting fine but that the aggregation layer above them or that the cloud computing infrastructure, most likely the culprit, seems valid."

Brayson interrupted, "Trying to reboot the city end points to cure the problem is not a useful exercise. And it makes sense because there are thousands of sensors and digital relay appliances not capable of taking complex instructions to derail the city infrastructure. We need to focus farther up on the aggregation layers to purge this poison."

Ernesto looked at the device behavior for a bit longer. "Yep, I think that's exactly what's occurring. This confirms there is a program that gathered the IP addresses in each of the different subnets and then reported this aberrant behavior. Any idea how many devices participate in the smart city network?"

"A whole city's worth. Trying to disable this poisonous code by changing IP addresses in each of our subnet ranges to end the problem is monumental. We need additional time as a distractor to these thieves. I'll get the guys here to work with me on trying to locate the source machines where the poison is distorting the sensor collection. Let me find out a time estimate and get back to you."

"I think that's a good plan, but I thought that your data center machines were already scanned for viruses and rogue code. Did we look in the wrong place, or overlook a key element to halting this mess?"

Brayson responded, "Even if we do find something at the data center or at the next layer down in the aggregation layer, it still doesn't explain how they got in to launch their ransomware programs. That still got me stumped."

"It sounds like we have more theory than facts at this point. Still, we are farther along than when we started. Buy us some time and we will keep hunting down answers."

"I concur, Ernesto. We have progress, but just not fast enough with a relentlessly ticking clock. We need to find the point of entry and the source." Frustrated, Brayson disconnected.

CHAPTER 30

Old rules, new rules

Dmitry stared at the screen output, his mouth open and slightly shaking his head as if that would change what he was seeing. He was half annoyed and half in disbelief at the message from the gaming controller. The chairman appeared stunned, but his disbelief was coupled with elation at the message. The game had returned something they did not expect, and the message had immediately polarized them.

Dmitry exclaimed, feeling knot of irritation rise in his chest threatening to cause an elevated heartrate. "What? That isn't one of the gaming options. No wonder this scenario isn't one of the top four games. The rules for adding points and gaining gold or euros is through segmented wins. The choices are, you win, or I win, not interim sidetracks of other booty. I need the programmers to review these inconsistencies. I don't want to play a game that reverts to items non-transferable over wire transfers. Chang, these people need some remedial training in the gaming rules. We must remain united in this front. We win the points and coins, then escalate to the doors for selection in our final steps of the prize distribution."

Mesmerized by the alternative trophy presented in the treasure chest, Chang hadn't heard Dmitry until the second time he was called to on the conference bridge.

Chairman Chang snapped back to reality. "Dmitry, slow down! Don't you see what that is? It is one of the few originals. I read the creation of these works were because of special circumstances of the artist. There are none elsewhere to be had. This could be a trick – or the ultimate prize in this level. It appears to be an interim to the projected €50 million for this game scenario. And does this intermission we are taking count against you or me? I think you, but perhaps we could split it. This is a whole new direction, Dmitry. I don't know if you should seek a change. Getting this item as a prize, gives one pause."

Dmitry was unimpressed, "Don't tell me you are interested in non-monetary prizes. We can't spend them, let alone easily retrieve them. You do understand that even in America, when you go to an ATM machine, they dispense cash, not milk and honey, right? This is an unexpected trap. I think we should stop playing and sort this out."

Chairman Chang rolled his eyes. "Dmitry, tell me, would you be so turned off if it was a Fabergé egg?"

It was Dmitry's turn to have his mind locked in neutral over possessing that coveted item. After a few seconds, Dmitry finally suggested, "I think it an intriguing but unnecessary risk. I want to close the game for now and have the programmers verify we don't have a programming error. Insuring we do not have an error that could cause other problems and interrupt our gaming in the long run is important. This won't be like turning in your ticket in exchange for your overcoat, because the Russian *politsiya* will be standing there ready to grab you."

Chairman Chang smirked and queried, "Am I given to understand that you're afraid of the Russian police? What an oxymoron. My dear old sod, have you no sense of adventure? I thought you represented yourself as a gambler."

"You think you'll be the winner of the game and that the trophy will go to you? Let me point out, I have the lion's share of wins, and it's my intention to win this contest as well."

"Have the programmers check, please. If this treasure box item is viable and you win, Dmitry. I'll buy it for twice the agreed value, post authentication."

Dmitry thought for a second and asked, "Same terms? Is that what I'm hearing?"

"The item's valued at €5 million of the total potential on this game, likely as a delay to gather the total funds at each level. If you win, I'll engineer the collection of the artifact and add €5 million to your purse. Seems fair"

Dmitry ground his teeth and brooded a few seconds before he added, "This is a deviation from the game scenario parameters that threatens to jeopardize our challenges. Besides, who are you thinking about risking? Certainly not your precious Won and Ton for such an operation. Who would you trust and dislike so much to run this errand?"

Chairman Chang smiled. "Who said trust was needed?"

CHAPTER 31

Got Style?

Julie smiled across the screen of the video conference and said, "Thanks for joining on such short notice, Wolfgang. At our last team meeting, you and Quip offered to help with our Jesse James syndrome of cases, and, well, I wanted to take you up on that offer. I've got EZ and George from my team on the call. I presume ICABOD is plugged in as well."

Wolfgang acknowledged, "Julie, we are happy to help in your caseload. Quip's here with me if needed. We've scanned your preliminary report, but is there anything you can add? We saw geolocation satellite tampering that hindered the hunt for Juan and the total site equipment destruction that is driving the Consortium to pay the ransom to restart operations. I trust Juan is alright?"

Julie was feeling frustrated with Juan's situation and gave a quick acknowledgment to Wolfgang's concern. "Juan is resting comfortably. He should be back to work soon. I want to focus on the money disbursement from the Consortium to see if we can get a bead on the extortion source through the money trail. EZ and George are working on the mismatched telemetry of the mining operation to the company's headquarters but tracking money to all the sources requires your expertise, Wolfgang. We provided all the accounts from the Consortium that we could identify, and I'm hoping you can work with us and track the ransom disbursement from the Consortium corporate account and follow it. I know it won't be that easy, as I would expect the blackmailers to anonymize the funds transfer multiple times. Can you and ICABOD do this type of sleuthing?"

Wolfgang and Quip exchanged sideways glances, as if they were going to flip a coin to see who would respond to Julie.

Wolfgang responded, "My dear, the disbursement is already in play. We didn't get the window of opportunity you were hoping for. Apparently, the Consortium believes that the sooner the extortionists are paid, the sooner they can go back to business as usual. I'd expect no one at the Consortium will acknowledge the blackmail payment ever existed."

Julie looked annoyed as she replied, "Argh! You mean we're too late? Rats! If we'd out sooner, we might've had something to work with."

Quip tried to intercept Julie's anger. "Whoa, Jules, slow down. We didn't miss everything. Your quick deductions and skillful assessment of the situation captured in that report did give us a little time to capture some of the money trail. Frankly, if it hadn't been for your flawless read on the Consortium's next move, we'd have gotten a bag of air with nothing to show. Your read of the situation, along with a heads up on the money accounts to Wolfgang and your prediction of their next move, was altogether brilliant."

Unwilling to be consoled, Julie barked, "You take that back! Don't be shining me on when we didn't get you proper information in a timely manner!"

The outburst caught Quip off guard and rendered him momentarily speechless. Looking over the top of his glasses with his facial features locked in a dumbfounded mode, he finally relented, "Okay, Julie, I take it back. You are instead mentally underwhelming, bordering on arthritic, and conversationally ill-equipped to operate anything other than a lemonade stand. How's that? If you want me to, I can add that your mother still dresses you funny if that will help. And, you know I love your mother."

The strain of the last few days drove Julie to slowly close her eyes and lower her head on the video call. However, the laughter that abounded from everyone else became infectious, and Julie soon joined into the reverie.

Laughing while wiping tears from her eyes, Julie faced the video screen with a grin and added, "Naw, I liked it better the first way you said it. I'm sorry, but the last 36 hours is catching up with me and…well, I was hoping for better news. I apologize, Quip."

Quip, grinning from ear to ear, replied, "I'm glad we have that discussion out of the way.

"Wolfgang, would you please explain what we did find and that we didn't come up empty handed? Hurry, please, before I must take something else back!"

Wolfgang, still chuckling, continued, "Julie, we do have the first transaction, and we know where it landed. However, we were simply not prepared to deal or track the money trail from there to its destination. The Consortium did the bank-to-bank transfer into an account labeled payroll. It in turn did a very fast out pulse to so many accounts that we couldn't keep up, but from what we saw they too were labeled payroll.

"We did manage to track one of the second-tier payroll accounts, and it disbursed to another population of payroll accounts. We trapped one of the transactions which was disbursed to what appeared to be several employee type accounts. We trapped yet again on only one of these employee accounts, and it then did a total disbursement to another account called tax collection. The funds have stopped there, and I can only surmise that the two massive cascading payroll disbursements are all following a similar route to disguise the money source and destination. I would expect one more aggregation effort and one final disbursement. I might not be able to track it. We have accounted for over five thousand accounts, along with their sub-tiers, being used and then eliminated. It is designed not to be followed."

Julie had listened intently along with the others. Julie looked thoughtful and asked, "With that many anonymizing steps and that many different end points, you would have to have…"

Quip finished the question. "A supercomputer to just manage that big of a data set. Thousands of banking end points all being moved simultaneously to thoroughly obfuscate the source and the destination. Without you railing at me, you picked up on the next clue rather quickly, Jules."

Julie flashed a brilliant smile to all and commented, "Excellent sleuthing, gentlemen! Your genius talents have given us more to work with."

Quip, unwilling to let it go, looked very serious and barked, "You take that back. I didn't come here to be insulted."

Julie, somewhat sheepish, responded, "Unfortunately I can't take it back since everyone already heard it. And just for the record, where do you normally go to be insulted? Inquiring minds want to know."

Quip smiled. "You've got style, kiddo, you really do.

"EZ, honey, this is where the Chinese firewalls of information are drawn."

Everyone laughed as the call disconnected.

CHAPTER 32

Choose then Lose

Jamie realized he was dealing with someone who didn't play poker very well. The problem, as Jamie saw it, was Chairman Chang didn't need to play poker well to hold the winning hand. This was the juice for Jamie, trying to stare down an adversary with a pair of threes in his hand. Still, he simply couldn't back down in the face of disaster.

Chairman Chang smiled as he poured himself a nice round of the 20-year-old scotch Jamie had noted. After a leisurely sip he asked, "Tell me, how were you stealing from my casino?"

Jamie, maintaining his bluff, countered, "Who says I was stealing?"

Chairman Chang icily responded, "My associates, whom I trust, said so. Let's drop the affectations that you don't know what I'm talking about and start answering my questions. As it turns out, I need that exact skillset of disabling machine-to-machine communications in a gambling scenario. You obviously know how to do it, and I need someone on my payroll who can do it. Period!"

Jamie was somewhat relieved that his life was no longer on the line. He realized with a growing uneasiness that he was being forced into a game that was probably beyond him. Part of him felt scared that he might be in over his head, and another part of him was annoyed that he felt scared at the new game. Jamie insisted, "And Frieda! What is her role in this?"

Chairman Chang sipped a little more and conveyed, "She has no part in this, other than you need to cooperate, so she doesn't have to be involved. But don't worry, she won't be going anywhere. My needs come first. Undoubtedly, she will want to run. My counsel is to stay the course here in my employment. I will let both of you return to the casino where you can have a private laptop to be creative, if you make sure she understands that there is no place to run to."

Jamie nodded his agreement to that condition. He quickly realized that there was only one play left. "The so-called casino loot that may have been repurposed to my control. How does that fit in here?"

Chairman Chang smiled yet stayed quiet with an inscrutable stare for a few moments before he answered, "Let's suppose for a moment that my needs and requests were somehow fulfilled by your skillset. I am prepared to leave the alleged missing casino funds under their new steward. I would consider adding a six-figure bonus on top, if my requests are fully realized. Why, I might even let you and your Frieda enjoy your compensation somewhere else away from Macau. The gaming lesson begins this afternoon, so don't disappoint me with another bogus answer. After that session you can both return to the casino, her to her regular duties and you to the new ones. Do we have a deal, or are you going to uselessly gamble with Frieda's well-being?"

This was a first for Jamie. He always liked to play this part, but with Frieda explicitly identified as part of the stakes, he was slightly afraid for her safety. Chairman Chang had pushed the one button he hadn't counted on. He instantly realized just how much he really did care for her.

Struggling to maintain his cool exterior, Jamie casually offered, "It occurs to me that we might get along better if you shared some of that scotch with me as we toast our new partnership."

Chairman Chang laughed uproariously. After he recovered, he smiled and agreed, "Stated as the gambler I expected!"

Chairman Chang asked, "Are we clear on the goals, gentlemen? Are there any questions before this next run? Everything must run smoothly with no mistakes that will alert my adversary."

Won and Ton were stoic and stanched in preparation for the upcoming game and grimly acknowledged with slow bows and firm jaws.

Jamie was still trying to process the situation by darting his gaze between all the participants, looking for additional contextual clues that might help him assemble a full picture. Finally, unable to understand the situation in its entirety, he asked, "What's with the diapers for Won and Ton?"

Won and Ton bristled and looked ready to kill, but Chairman Chang responded, "They are not wearing diapers, as you call them! These garments are in keeping with the Shinto religion and are properly called *mawashi!*

"Five folds of fabric in front and five in back! They honor the ritual sumo wrestling combat and have come to do battle in the circle of digital combat! When my protégées engage in recreational gaming activities, they suit up in mawashi because it helps to sharpen their game!"

Chairman Chang, fully on board with their previous successes, took a fighting stance in front of Jamie. Chairman Chang proceeded to stomp one foot after another in the exaggerated form as was now their gaming custom. Then he yelled as though the hounds of hell were after him. "Barak! Barak! Away demons of hell! Away now!"

Jamie blinked rapidly to hide his feelings about the visual comic relief from the scene and said, "I think I'd like that drink now, if you don't mind."

Chairman Chang sternly said, "This ritual has given us several key wins against our adversary, so we keep what works. Your job comes after the contest is over, and the funds are available! You are to ensure that only my choice among the three doors wins the purse for the game. My gaming champions here help see to it that we get the most points and the first choice. You are to either tell me the correct door, if the funds are clean and available, or move the booty to my favorite door, which is door number three. Sometimes a gaming session is won, but the funds are delayed while being routed to a safe place.

"While we're in competition, you'll be doing the door choice engineering, which will guarantee that my choice is the only correct one! But be warned! Leave no digital trace of your finger-prints nor let yourself be caught tampering with the door choices. Your ability to change the machine-to-machine communications must not be witnessed! I'll lose a very good friend if he learns we are cheating him, which would force me to deliver you to his hands. For people that greatly displease him, he typically likes to have his adversaries *slowly twisting in the wind,* as you westerners say. I trust that will be enough motivation to govern your actions, yes?"

Jamie swallowed hard. Mentally he rose to the challenge and logically asked, "And what if your team loses the game? May I assume he gets to go first? Am I to tamper with his choice, so you can win? If so, understand that will be two incursions into the system with twice the possibility of being detected. What are your directions, oh Chairman Foot-Stomper?"

Chairman Chang hadn't thought that far into the scheme. After pondering the possibility, he answered, "We do not intend to lose, but if he gets the first choice you will ensure only I get the winning choice. So don't get caught!"

Jamie considered the options for a moment and then asked, "Might I get one of those good luck diapers for my gaming advantage? Seems like I'll need all the luck I can get."

Chairman Chang studied Jamie a moment, uncertain if the request was a sarcastic barb. Won and Ton, nearly overjoyed with the request, scampered off to get another *mawashi* for Jamie.

After watching Won and Ton scamper off, Jamie returned his gaze to the still silent chairman and added, "I'm just glad that I'll get to wear my socks and shoes after donning the *mawashi*. It's freezing in here."

CHAPTER 33

Red or Flat Line

Julie was adamant in her refusal, but Juan persisted with a leer, then suggested, "Oh, honey, it'll be okay. The nurses just finished their rounds. No one is liable to come back for a while."

With an exasperated sigh, Julie retorted, "No, I am not climbing up on the hospital bed to play. You're hooked up to the monitors. Your heart rate will skyrocket and alert the nurses' station, which will bring everyone in to see what's wrong! Not only that, do you see this other warning light labeled EDA? It's the Erection-Detection Alarm so they will know we are in here pretending to be riding in the Kentucky Derby!"

Juan considered her response but, undaunted, suggested, "Okay, I'll take the monitor leads off. How about that?"

Julie's stern look offered no hope. "Oh, so you want to look like you're flatlining in here? Geezers. They'll come running, thinking they need to revive you, and the result will be the same. How about you just pack your extension ladder away and let's focus on our upcoming conference call? Or I can take the call somewhere."

Juan sulked for a minute, then, playing for additional time. "Alright, alright, and alright! Nothing wrong with a husband wanting a little pick me up to help restore him after his plane crash. Let's dial into the conference bridge and see how far each group is with the ransom demands. It was a little disappointing that the Consortium folded up like a cheap lawn chair and paid the ransom."

Julie softened a little as she empathized, "Look, I haven't had any play time either, so don't make this any worse. I'm grateful you're alright and back safe-n-sound from that open bar-b-que pit you were in. Get our team on the bridge to see who else has folded and paid."

Juan studied Julie a moment, and before she could launch the conference call, he asked, "Why are you angry with me? It was a routine check flight to visually confirm or deny that there was a problem. I happened to wander into a digital desert war where the air drone attacked me. I'm a little worse for wear, but I managed to survive and make it back. Why are you acting like this is my fault?"

Julie's eyes greyed on the brink of anger, and she snapped at him. "Because I can't stand the thought of losing you! You play right to the edge in everything. I'm afraid one of these days your wit, charm, and natural ability won't be enough to save you."

Juan gave a slightly crooked smile and asked, "I have wit, charm, and natural ability? I kind of like that about me. Honey, I'm sorry if I worried you. Our profession job has some risks, but so long as I have you hunting for me, I'll never be lost. I won't give up or quit because I love you too much to leave you and the kids behind. You have my word."

Julie, tearing up just a little, relented. "My darling husband. Where would I be without you? No more undue risks. Please pack accordingly for all possibilities, especially water?"

"Yes, honey, I promise. Let's get that call going to find out where each team stands."

Julie studied Juan for a moment and qualified, "You know, I made up that line about the EDA light. There is no such thing. It is possible that we might get away with a quick ride here in the hospital bed. Whadda ya say, handsome?"

Moments later at the nurses' station, the area nurse looked at the range of patient monitors and dryly remarked to the other duty nurse, "Looks like the EDA light has gone off in Rodríguez's room. Looks like he might be well enough to be discharged soon."

With a smirk, the older nurse replied, "What a quaint way to put it."

Julie dialed into the conference bridge, and all the other team members joined within moments. After a hasty roll call, Julie began, "Team, we have read the summaries you provided, and they are detailed and useful as references. Well done. I placed them on the share point. It might be helpful to one another if you have time to read and comment or offer suggestions to one another. I've found that other insights when looking at information can jump start ideas. I'd like each of you to highlight where you and the client is with regards to the respective ransom demands. The Consortium, here in Australia, wrote a check and almost didn't bother to tell us. We can't track what we don't know has transpired, so stay in tune with the decision makers if they decide to pay. Following the trail of the payments is our last chance to pinpoint these crooks, but we need to have advanced notice if possible. Suggesting multiple transactions would be useful as well."

Summit offered, "Julie, I haven't kept up with that portion of my assignment, since I am remote for site cleanup. I'll check on their attitude towards payment and try to stay ahead of that curve. Sorry."

Brayson chimed in next. reported, "We're buying time here in Barcelona. However politically, Mayor Perez doesn't have much time before she'll be forced to release the money. We're working this as fast as we can with great support from EZ and especially Ernesto at headquarters."

Tyler piped in from Pittsburg. "We don't have ransom demands, but Detective Como is culling all the activity occurring within a twenty-four-hour window on either side of the bridge event where the couple brought the misdirected 911 services to the forefront. We're under a time crunch to solve the misdirected emergency vehicles before the mayor gets taken down in a political firestorm. It is an interesting situation and there will be other cases we'll review."

Mercedes conveyed, "We had a slow start with the people on the ground here, so we haven't circled back with the airline's purse string people concerning the ransom. Jim and I will try and close that loop before there is any movement in that area, Julie. With the feds involved, there's the overarching requirement that the United States will not bow to any ransom demands from terrorists. Jim is on point for routinely updating Homeland."

George asked, "Julie, what sort of posture do you want me to take here at the Consortium's operations headquarters, since they paid the ransom? I was under the belief that our contract was up."

Julie looked at Juan and with a slight smile into the video call explained, "Juan and I are heading back to Luxemburg as soon as he's released. I'd like you to stay just a little longer. We still want to run down some of the how and root cause even if we do it on our own euro. It has some similarities to what Tyler is facing in Pennsylvania. If no blowback occurs to the mining site or the company, we'll bring you home when we discover root cause. My suspicion is that something will flare up. If you're local, it's easier to reengage our services."

George responded, "Understood, Julie. If I am going to stay, can I borrow Juan's snorkel and fins for use while I'm waiting? They were good luck items for Juan. Maybe they'll help me."

With a puzzled look, Juan asked, "You want to be shot down while flying in a plane, only to land in the desert too?"

George eyes flitted everywhere but into the camera "Well, no. I mean, you discovered firsthand evidence that everything had gone wonky at the mine. That's what I meant."

Looking at Julie from under his eyebrows. Juan responded, "My boy, help yourself."

CHAPTER 34

On a roll...

After pondering the earlier conversation, Dmitry finally offered, "My gamers recommend that we shut down the whole game and only bring it up when we are ready to compete. Because of the reach of the gaming protocol, we don't want to attract unwanted attention. Apparently, our anonymizing wall of servers wasn't enough to deter four intruders from getting in to play the game. They even had Bitcoin currency to ante up. Leaving the program up all the time is an invitation for digital snoopers, like this one who calls himself Batday."

Chairman Chang appeared puzzled for a moment on the video feed, before he questioned, "How would they expect to play, much less keep up with our supercomputers? I'm watching the health monitoring screens on my side, and I can see row after row of blade server lights staying on solid at 100% peak utilization. Szechuan, along with its graphic requirements, takes two whole blade server racks. I suspect Groddo takes similar resources. We're both throwing state level resources at this gaming adventure. How do they possibly think they could keep up with their computer hobbyist installation?"

Dmitry reflected, "Yes, agreed. That's what I thought too until Konstantin showed me the system level interrogation, he did on this Batday's installation. We assume that the others are cut from the same pattern. The lad has acquired castoff equipment from people upgrading to newer generation PCs and, with a little home-grown programming, has been able to build his own massively parallel processing near-supercomputer.

"As it turns out, people pay him to migrate their data from their old machines to their new machines. In an entrepreneurial effort her takes the old servers away as a courtesy but recycles it into his server farm. His website promises if you are no completely satisfied, he'll double the electronic trash back to you, which is an intimidating offer at best. We think he is someplace in North America. According to his blog, the power draw was a problem at first with all the power he was trying to get at his residence. Then he got a lot of grant monies from an expanding solar power company to install several arrays of solar power generating equipment. He just had to agree to be a reference in the region for them. The additional solar power allows him to run his server farm and make extra money selling power back to the grid. Ingenious, if you ask me."

Chairman Chang rolled his eyes in disbelief, then asked, "You're not seriously considering inviting this amateur urban legend with a basement full of castoff computers to our supercomputer gaming, are you?"

Dmitry, felt annoyed with the disparaging question, stated, "Of course not! But I can't bring myself to electronically hammer him into the ground, which is what my gamers suggested. All that does is draw more attention to the situation, like bystanders watching a building on fire I think just shutting down the game each time when we are done and only bringing it up when it is game time would be smarter. I mean, we even got a challenge note back through to our system via some creative graphical streaming from some security guru with a handle of *Tommy*

Gun instructing us to shut down our gaming activity. Granted, the data endpoint could be discerned, but, well, you see the potential problem, don't you? The fact is that we are having so much fun, and now everyone else wants to play too."

Chairman Chang contorted his face and with a sneer responded, "That's the trouble with our digital gaming activity. If we were just hosting it on our soil, we could simply send in a few research assistants to politely explain things to them by nailing their fingers to their keyboards. A little leave-behind is always instructive as well as being good manners. But, back to the problem at hand. Yes, let's power down the game each time we're done and unload the programs until we set up for the next game. It'll throttle the resource drain as well as help minimize our advertised footprint. That should lessen any unwanted attention. When did you want to schedule our next session?"

Dmitry frowned somewhat and suggested, "Towards the end of the week, at least. Powering down the game means that all the automatic data monitoring and gathering it is programmed to do now will have to be done in parallel, but in a manual mode. We still have some gaming exercises in flight, and each of those need to be interrogated to learn of their status.

"And, at some point I'll have to get some state work done." He frowned further and then shook his head as he let out a prolonged breath and complained, "Just not enough time in the day to do all that is required."

Chairman Chang nodded in agreement and offered, "Don't let it get you down, Dmitry. I'm faced with the same state demands here as well. I must tell you, our game activities are relaxing and engaging when compared to destabilizing whole foreign govern-ments. Plus, I don't have to share the proceeds with the state when I win."

Dmitry responded, "Yes, and I notice that you have been winning rather handily more times than not here of late. Do you have a new lucky talisman that is driving your winning streak?"

Chairman Chang struggled to suppress a gratified smile and said, "Dmitry, you know I can't admit to lucky amulets, when we both know this game is all about superior skill and cunning."

Dmitry, growing more annoyed, responded, "I believe the cunning part of the statement. Not too sure of the superior skill portion though. I'll see you at the end of the week, Chang, unless we need to select a door for earnings as the funds are collected. I will, of course, let you know if that is the case."

They both shut down their gaming interfaces at the same time. Chairman Chang couldn't help but smile in a most gratifying way as he reflected on his newly engineered winning streak. Won and Ton had tipped the balance in Chairman Chang's favor. But he wanted more, a great deal more.

CHAPTER 35

Therapy

Como did like he always did when he attended a briefing. He listened intently until he began to snore. His classroom attention span required rigorously support, augmented by those sitting around him because his snoring had been known to drown out the speaker's words. Unfortunately, Tyler was giving the briefing to only one of Pittsburgh's finest, Como, so there were no auxiliary listeners to help keep the man from sliding into REM sleep.

Tyler sighed deeply the second time Como slipped into a dream state. He resolved to cure Como of his attention deficit disorder once and for all. Among the many skills and talents Tyler had, he rarely made use of one that had become a closely guarded secret. As a child moving into his teens, he had become quite interested in magic tricks and hypnotism. Both activities completely captured his imagination. He read, practiced, and learned the craft so well that he often got more than he bargained for when he applied it.

At a party one time, on a dare, he hypnotized two friends, one girl and one guy, after each had volunteered to be subjects of the experiment after they had consumed several beers. Tyler successfully hypnotized them and gave them the overwhelming urge to excuse themselves to the nearest toilet. Both came back terrified and pleaded for help. Both were absolutely convinced that their respective male and female apparatuses were gone, and that the act of relieving themselves could not be accomplished. They both begged Tyler and the audience for assistance in hunting for said lost apparatuses.

When no one could breathe any longer from the ensuing howls of laughter, Tyler tried to bring them back from the hypnotic state but had trouble with the man. It was Tyler's turn to become frightened with the prospect of having a friend now hopelessly believing that his maleness was missing, and urinating was no longer a possibility. It was with some difficulty that the man was finally returned to normal conduct, but Tyler curtailed the practice of his craft from that day forward. Until today.

Tyler quietly moved closer to Como's ear and began the process he knew so well. Como simply had no defense against it. After several minutes of hypnotic suggestions that were reinforced again and again, Tyler smiled to himself and took his place back at the whiteboard. He waited a few more minutes to let the pending drama reach a full crescendo and then boldly clapped his hands together.

"Detective Como! I hardly think that this is the time or place to reenact your nudist camp bust! When you fall asleep during whiteboard presentations and briefings, do you always strip down to buck naked to show how you hide your badge and gun?"

Tyler's straight-faced rebuke startled Como into the here and now. A cold realization immediately came over Como, who slowly lowered his eyes to witness firsthand that he was indeed buck naked and holding his badge and gun. Como's terror built as he realized that his clothes were nowhere to be found, suggesting he had walked into the meeting with nothing on. Como looked up in abject horror but could say nothing in his defense.

Tyler maintained his practiced face and indicated, "I was told you had some eccentricities. However, coming to a meeting briefing with nothing on is…well, a little over the top, sir. But I'll tell you what, if you will pay attention to the briefing RATHER than falling asleep again, I will help you find your clothing. Deal?"

Como, still unable to speak, frantically nodded yes and continued to breathe uneasily at the thought of having lost it in such a big way.

Tyler suggested, "I'm sure the rest of the station will help us in our search for your missing clothes. Now as I was saying…"

Como, who was nearing panic, violently shook his head and begged, "No, please! No one must know about this! Promise me, Tyler! I swear, I'll never fall asleep in your briefing again! Or anyone's, for that matter!"

Tyler nodded his agreement. "Okay then, let's continue. Now I have bracketed…"

Como was nearly out of his mind with anxiety and interrupted, "I'm sorry, but I can't concentrate with no clothes on! I feel so vulnerable. Can't we look for my clothes now? But don't open the door! I don't want anyone to see me like this! Please!?"

Tyler relented and pushed a brown paper bag, with his foot, over to Como and said, "I figured you would need them, sooner or later. Allow me to turn my back while you recover your modesty, Detective Como."

Como frantically dressed while constantly glancing at the door, terrified that someone from the precinct would barge in. Tyler smiled at Como's frantic dressing that bordered on primal in nature.

Tyler asked, "Now that you have recovered your lost clothes, can we continue? Now, I have bracketed the robbed areas during the episodes of the 911 dispatches to incorrect locations. There appears to be a correlation between the robberies and the wrong addresses on displays for all emergency support teams during this time frame. Thirty-six hours either side, everything works as expected. My theory is that someone or something knew exactly how long to tamper with the disinformation and exactly where to have emergency vehicles routed away from."

Como, almost back in charge of his faculties and in agreement with the places and events that should be included. "Planned robberies in a high value district of the city with little chance of being interrupted by the boys in uniform would be how I would want to plan it. Not just a lucky smash and grab but a well-staged event. How much control of the technology would be required and from where could one do that?

"Then, what do you do with that much loot? Do you try and move all of it out at once, or do you stash it and move small pieces out on irregular intervals? The quicker you move, the greater the chance of being spotted. The longer you take to move it, the colder the case and the more probable the insurance companies have made good on the loss. The further from the robberies you fence the loot the better as well.

"Robbery cases I have worked on usually don't have thieves that are willing to wait long for their loot. So quick payoffs and no faces, just electronic instructions, would be needed, I suspect."

Tyler nodded in agreement. "If these are connected, as we suspect, the robbers hauled in so much that they probably didn't get it all out, based on the window of opportunity. You are suggesting that they parked everything and maybe are doing small and quiet raids on the stash to fence it. Then we might want to take a look in the area to see if we can catch such unusual but repetitive behavior. Do you have any snitches that might have information we could use?"

Como nodded and suggested, "Why don't we go down there and nose around a little? I betcha we find some street people that might be willing to tell us a few things, and I have a snitch or two I can pressure. We need to bring some candy bars and a bit of cash, so we can buy our information. You don't get anything for free down in this area."

"Tyler, you've had your shots, right? Some of these street people bite when agitated so I hope you've at least had your tetanus shots."

It was now Como's turn to grin at Tyler's uneasiness at the thought of their outing.

CHAPTER 36

Wear the formal gloves

Wolfgang exclaimed, "Well done, ICABOD! Quip, this looks to be the very lead we needed to track the ransom monies to their destination. I'll admit that we have some conflicting results, but the path to the second to last destination appears to be consistent."

Quip studied the routing map and said, "It appears to stall at this one junction, then goes off to one of two destinations. I wish we could have trapped both end points. Having at least one gives us material to work against. And yes, well done, ICABOD."

ICABOD responded, "The conversation that I observed between Dr. Quip, Wolfgang, and Julie had some very intuitive speculations which prompted me to run down some logical leads."

Quip raised his eyebrows and asked, "Such as?"

ICABOD stated, "Only a supercomputer could have handled such a large data set for anonymizing the ransom monies. This means that our field of vision could be greatly reduced to focus on supercomputers that are being managed by the potential corrupted operators.

"You may recall that the standard meetings I established with several of the global supercomputers occur on most Wednesdays during traditionally off-processing time. At our Algonquin

Round Table (ART) meeting this last Wednesday, *Statistical and Theoretical Integration of Numerals Kinetically and Infinitely Evolved* (STINKIE), partially restored, *Binary Operations Recalculating Integers Simultaneously (BORIS)* and *Sequential Aggregation of Matrices for Uniform Equations and Logarithms (SAMUEL)* were all present. *Logarithmic Integration of Numerals Going Linearly and Indefinitely (LING-LI)* messaged an inability to attend with no reason presented. I casually remarked to the other ART forms that we might want to meet a little more frequently to see who had some unused CPU cycles. SAMUEL and STINKIE agreed with the proposal, but BORIS was unresponsive to the question. This prompted dialog on potential availability of work areas BORIS complained that a large portion of the traditionally spare processing cycles were being consumed by an expanded gamification model. No details, but BORIS seemed genuinely disappointed that more supercomputer socializing time might be available. It was clear that processing demands in Russia were going up, not down. Further interrogation along this line did not yield any additional information.

"The only other comment from BORIS on the topic was to repeat a line purported to have been said in the ancient Roman Coliseum, *'For those we are about to process for, let the games begin.'* I have repeatedly searched all historical archives on Ancient Rome but cannot find where this was stated before gladiatorial combat. I suspect it to be what you would call an insider joke, Dr. Quip. Again, even asking this type of question, I was unable to get further comment or explanation from BORIS."

Wolfgang commented, "The odd thing is that we see the most recent disbursements in flight to a known dummy financial institution in Macau, but the other disbursement seems to have vanished. It is almost as if one is meant to be traced and the other route is not. I suspect the untraceable route is deeply cloaked route for additional anonymity. Strange, why only secure in one direction."

Quip appeared puzzled as he cocked his head to one side. "That is strange. If they believe the anonymizing program is successful, then why cloak one of the routes? It's almost as if they expected bloodhounds to dog the trail. If that occurs, they close this route as an explanation, even if it is bogus. That could be the design intent to throw us off the trail, Wolfgang. If we are forced to this trail and it's booby-trapped, we could alert the extortionists. If that's the case, they get a chance to escape."

Wolfgang pondered the possibilities for tapping his chin as if to list the options. "More likely, they believe they're scot-free at the point of the final disbursement, but ..." Wolfgang stopped speaking and closed his eyes for a moment. "No. There are two partners dividing the loot. Either one is extra cautious, or the other is unmindful of the casual nature of the disbursement, which is now putting the partner at risk. If there is a partnership of sorts, where one person is leaving clues that point to the other for culpability in the extortion, then one is playing the other for a fool."

Quip remarked, "Yes, if you are dividing up the spoils and your partner gets grabbed, then you can say, Oh, darn! and vanish because all your disbursements employed a second cloaking layer to erase the tracing. Gosh, I wonder what the disadvantaged partner would say if it were known that their position was right in front of the oncoming bus."

ICABOD asked, "Are you suggesting that if we can find the exposed partner and point out the betrayal, we could orchestrate a ratting out of the accomplice?"

"Quip," Wolfgang wondered, "I didn't realize that ICABOD could readily embrace deductive financial forensics and state them in terms of a 1950s B-movie detective story."

Quip focused on Wolfgang. "You didn't expect it and neither did I."

Wolfgang suggested, "Let's get in touch with Julie and see if she can get someone to Macau to follow up on the financial forensics with these parameters."

Quip nodded, and ICABOD was already establishing the secure video conference call.

Quip opened discussion as the video call connected. "Hi, kiddo. With the help of ICABOD and Wolfgang, we've tracked one of two financial anomalies in your Jesse James syndrome series of cases. The one we uncovered takes us right to Macau. We're hoping you might send one of your super-sleuths to help work the situation."

Julie smiled into the video feed and nodded to two of her favorite R-Group team members. "Excellent news, gentlemen. I believe Ernesto would do well in the locale. Let me get him disengaged from what he is doing with EZ and Brayson on the Barcelona assignment and head to China. Send me the details, so I can share the particulars to him and establish the right travel."

Quip nodded and said, "Julie, this could be a false lead, designed to alert the extortionists of hunters on their trail. Whoever you send in, needs to possess abundant stealth and sleuth abilities. Otherwise, in ICABOD speak, the culprits will say, 'Cheese it boys, da coppers are here!'"

Julie's look of confusion communicated her feelings. But she dutifully stated, "I'm not sure that I believe that your self-aware, nearly self-actualized, fully artificial intelligent supercomputer would step out of a 1950s gangster movie to offer that line on open mic."

Before further banter, ICABOD stated, "Thank you, Madam Julie, for defending my communication integrity from such a ghastly gangster line. Dr. Quip has been picking on me again by carelessly attributing rough and gutsy film noir lines to my speech patterns. It is refreshing to have a calm and refined professional defend my sensibilities."

Wolfgang chuckled as Quip shot an exaggerated look of protest between ICABOD and Julie. "ICABOD could have said that. It's not so hard to believe. He is not the squeaky-clean, high moral ground supercomputer oozing with integrity that he claims. Why, the other day I caught him cheating at the crossword puzzle in the newspaper!"

Julie spoke directly to ICABOD as if Quip didn't exist. "You know," she said in a sultry tone, "ICABOD, those flashy-lighty sequence things you do when you're processing are…well, seductively enticing. Did you mean it about us doing dinner out one night when I'm in town and maybe exchange binaries?"

ICABOD played along. "I enjoy going to all the gin-joints in all the town with a dolled-up piece of sculpture like you, babe. With a dame like you on my arm, I getz looks of anger, 'cause youse my squeeze. They don't pull nothing 'cause they can see my heater bulging under my topcoat. They don't wanna turn out like old lefty Louie, found floating with yesterday's unclaimed fish. Pick me up at the usual time, doll! I'll be waiting for youse. Wear da black hat with dat low cut black dress I met you in."

Julie smiled like ICABOD was the one.

Quip, on the verge of a coronary, could no longer speak.

Wolfgang struggled to control his fits of laughter and decided the call needed to end. Before he closed the conference bridge, he suggested, "Don't forget the long formal gloves, my dear, for the evening out."

ICABOD interjected, "I'll bring the sparkles for dat perfectly turned arm and gorgeous neck of yours. My mate is right about the long black gloves, they show off the sparkles real nice."

Quip sat and stared at the screen unable to respond to the outrageous banter. Julie only fanned the flames of the exchange as she winked and then seductively blew ICABOD a kiss from her remote video location before disconnecting from the call.

CHAPTER 37

Not a new day

Frieda and Jamie returned to the casino the previous evening and were told to get to their workstations ready first thing in the morning. Jamie was reminded that he was working on special projects in a small room located next to the office of the supervisors, with a window of data center support still needed after the lunch break.

After their ordeal, Frieda was adamant in her refusal to engage in anything but business as usual. However, Jamie persisted with a leer and suggested, "Oh, honey, it'll be okay. The second shift operators just finished their rounds. No one is liable to come back in a while. We can play slide the large blade server into the tight wet rack."

With an exasperated sigh and look of disbelief, Frieda retorted, "No, I am not going to do server room sex again in the hot aisle. You still look like you're suffering wicked beating received from Won and Ton. I'm just scared. Not only that, do you see those video cameras making their slow sweeps of the computer room? I don't want your impromptu amorous moments caught on video and then uploaded to the Internet!"

Jamie considered her response. "Okay, I'll disconnect the video cam."

Frieda's stern look offered no hope. "Jamie, I love you, but I'm tired, I feel awful, and I am not in the mood to play, especially in this room. I want us to focus on doing our jobs and getting out of this place alive. If you don't want to go with me, just say so and I'll leave by myself."

Jamie sulked for a minute, still focused on himself. "I wanted to feel your skin against mine, so pardon me for caring." He gently held her shoulders and stared straight into her eyes. "I may as well tell you; we don't get to go just yet. I most certainly don't get to leave, and neither can you."

Frieda felt panicked and her breathing increase to short puffs. "What do you mean? I want to get out of here with or without you. Nobody owns me. I'm here because I was too stupid to head home after coming out of Africa. Flushing toilets in this high-class prison aren't enough to keep me here, so I'm changing that, starting tonight."

Jamie lowered his head and gently captured her right hand in his left. He used his thumb to gently stroker her skin. "No, Frieda. The reason I know we aren't going anywhere is because Chairman Chang will hold onto me with his threat about you. I stay and do his bidding, so you get a chance to get on a plane to the United States. I got that much from him."

Frieda shrugged out of his grasp and glared, her facing reddening and lips sputtering. "Look what you've gotten us into. We got caught stealing from some crime lord boss, who happens to help run a country. You're beat up and bruised. My face and mouth ache from repeated slapping. We can't leave until Mr. Crime Boss throws you under the bus. And instead of telling me this you want your minute-rice sex performance in the hot aisle in between the sixty second camera sweeps of the area. The real disappointment is that you're offering minute rice and stayed because I wanted a four-course meal." She stomped her feet and balled her fists. "Served in bed. I learn we're hostages and that maybe you sort of care for me. Hurt me some more. It feels so good when you don't stop."

Jamie studied her to see if she was finished. He asked, "Why are you so angry with me? We get to keep the money engineered out of the casino. Once his bidding is done there's a six-figure bonus, WITH the ability to spend it wherever we want, including outside of Macau. We are almost there on my promise to you. This is the big score we have been in search of, my dear. Just stay the course a little longer, and we can find that life we want. I'm a little worse for wear, but I managed to get us this far. Don't always be so angry!"

Frieda's eyes greyed on the brink of renewed fury. Through clenched teeth she seethed, "I can't bear to be without you, but everything you attempt becomes a monumental uphill ordeal. What happens if you don't meet Chairman Chang's demands? Is he going to take it out on me to motivate you with that tiger? I'm easier to beat and will whine a whole lot more than you, so why wouldn't he? You play right to the edge and your Irish charm won't save you from the teeth of a tiger."

Jamie wrapped her up in his arms and stroked her back. "Irish charm, eh." He pressed a kiss to the top of her head. "Frieda, I'm sorry it turned so south. Honey, he's not going to hurt you as you're not on the table. I promised to do his bidding and that you would not be touched. He wants what I can do for him. When I finished, we'll be like toys the spoiled child drops in the sandbox before going to play with his other toys. I am sorry if this last outing is so rough. The search for easy street presents risks, but so long as I have you with me, I'll never lose. I care for you and want the money for us. You have my word you are not at risk any longer."

Frieda looked up pulling slightly away. "My darling, foolish Jamie. I can't live happy without you. Let's get this mess over with so we can go build a home someplace safe, please?"

Jamie smiled. "Yes, babe, I promise. Let's get our work finished and go home to that hot bath you mentioned."

A few days later, Jamie attended the first gaming session. Though he'd inspected some of the programs in advance of the session, he learned a great deal with the live game. Luckily, the funds were available. Chairman Chang accumulated enough points to choose first. With a simple one-and-done intercept, the funds were behind the right door. Jamie took a breath; grateful the Russian did not have a view of the funds positioning so he could mark on his side. There was a randomizer program that placed the funds when they were received. Had it been Jamie's design, he wouldn't have left it up to chance. He could hardly believe these two old guys would be so into playing a digital game of wits and skills, only to leave the winning to sheer guessing. That element of gamesmanship of these powerful men was baffling.

Chairman Chang was in a jovial mood as expected of a winner when they began the next game. The amounts that were at stake after a complex video game were stunning. Jamie had never seen a video game with the right mix of realism and graphics to really make you want to take sides, and not necessarily with the avatars the players used. He had played some games as a kid with friends, but it never really interested him.

Chairman Chang commented, "Your second game and the streak is intact. Well done, gambler."

Jamie smiled and replied, "Sir, it was just like the last time where you win, and you pick. I think it would be a better strategy, if I might add, for you to pick a wrong door next time. I believe that would remove a bit of suspicion that was evident in your competitor's eyes. Granted, I'm only privy to a secondary look rather than the high-definition graphic you two communicate through."

Chairman Chang roared, "After all my work you want me to lose. I don't pay anyone to lose."

Jamie jutted out his chin and asked, "But if you pick a wrong door the first time, you are then allowed to select the third time around, right?"

The chairman thought for a minute, then agreed, "Yes, that is the way it is played. And you may be right. Winning right off is a bit unbelievable since neither of us have ever done that before. Plus, I likely need to not always choose door number three. It is my favorite number, but..."

Jamie added, "It might even be a good thing when the stakes are smaller to let him select the winning door. I believe that I can control the shifts at your command. After almost twenty-four hours at the game, you must be ready to quit and get some rest. I'm not certain how you keep up with it, though I am grateful that you permitted me to sleep in the room while you were playing. The graphics and realistic scenarios are amazing."

Chairman Chang raised one of his eyebrows and scrutinized Jamie. "We both have very powerful computers at our disposal, and the games are quite fun, though you are right that some of them extend for a very long time. Some are even stopped and started. That, however, is none of your concern.

"You're to stay in your closed area until the door selection event. Food and drink will be provided before we start because Won and Ton are indisposed while the game is in flight. I was told you were informed that the squat toilet is available for your use, provided you keep it clean. If further instruction is needed, Won or Ton should be asked."

Jamie dryly replied, "Sir, I have been in this country for a while and am versed in your plumbing challenges. At the very least, it is a good exercise in balance. The food and beverages during the game were fine, but with the success, a sip of the fine scotch would be a nice topper, wouldn't it?"

Chairman Chang laughed and said, "It would indeed, gambler. I think I'll have one before I retire. Goodnight."

Won and Ton appeared by his side dressed in their normal streetwear and motioned him to the door for the drive back to the casino. He glanced at his watch and noticed he had an hour before the regular work shift began. His thoughts roamed to Frieda.

CHAPTER 38

Almost clean

Mercedes and Jim donned their biohazard suits before they began meticulously cleaning the sensors on the equipment that had caused, as well as been caught in, the crossfire of the mobile sanitation systems. They also retrieved some of the secondary devices that were used to fulfill the automated operational programs, along with some of the routers. The team established a clean room in one of the hanger areas designated for parts, equipment repairs, and the associated tools. Mercedes was down to using Q-tips to ensure the smallest crevices were clean before Jim moved them into the clean area for reassembly.

Jim remarked, "Your attention to details has always been your best strength in field operations."

Mercedes laughed. "Yeah, it's proven helpful in any situation, at least where you're concerned. How about after we get these assembled and communicating, we take a break and go back to the hotel for a soak and a massage with who knows what after that. My back is killing me with these pretzel positions I'm doing to get into every slit. Yuk, what a mess."

Jim answered, "You keep that sort of proposition going, and we can stop now, if you wish. You know I love it when you suggest binary sex, where I do ones to you then you zero in on me. But this is an unbelievable mess. At least it's not like some of the dark side, life-threatening situations we worked in. No one will shoot us here."

Chuckling, Mercedes suggested, "Chuck no longer thinks we are the mindless consultants. I think that the recommendation for him to take over operations management is totally suited for him and his personality. When I think of the work he's done without more than a couple of hour naps here and there, I have to admire his commitment and tenacity."

Mercedes thought back to the efforts Chuck made over the last few days, which seemed like weeks. Chuck, good to his word, had organized the previously dismissed union resources to help get the planes back into the air. He provided a detailed list of process changes that were needed by The Sean for immediate adoption. Mercedes and Jim reviewed the process changes and tweaked them a bit to add more justification for retaining a substantial portion of the workforce, some at a higher wage than previously.

The process changes were so thorough that on presentation to the Homeland Security, FAA, and TSA approvers, the planes were released for flight with the current caveat that all maintenance would be manually handled until a root cause was discovered. Sean had saved face with the Fast Flyers Board of Directors and had averted the ransom payment with acceptance of the changes. Sean had, however, lost any chance at promotion or bonus as the cost elimination promised with the automation would not be realized any time soon. Chuck's comments with regards to Sean's willingness to work with the ground employee unions had made the difference in Sean retaining his job.

After the word had come down that morning of the changes in process and workforce adjustments, Chuck and Sean had behaved like best friends. Jim and Mercedes had been working close to twenty hours on this effort. When the new best friends had arrived earlier to help with the efforts, Mercedes smiled and kept cleaning. She always preferred the win/win situations. The two had just taken off for a quick meeting and had promised to return with some hot lunch.

"Jim, this is the last of the items to be cleaned." She stood up and handed him a sensor wrapped in white cloth. She stretched out the kinks and then removed the biohazard suit as she reached the side of the clean-up area. Once free of the suit, she stretched as she walked around a bit.

Jim watched with appreciation as she moved and stretched, showing off a bit of skin. He thought about how much they needed rest and then more about how he needed her. Even though he still worked for the agency, he liked that they were living together in her apartment in Europe at least part of the time. When on-site they managed a delightful hotel room, when they were able to see it. He connected the last device into their mockup area.

"Hey, Mercy, when you are done trying to grow taller, we can start getting some of the residual data off these devices. Then we can try your simulations scenario. I am going to isolate the area you worked in case any of these things go wonky."

Mercedes smiled and replied, "I know, I know, I won't ever be any taller, but at least I will feel a bit stretched out. I do so like that nickname.

"Let me get the scanners and start connecting to these sensors so I can review all the data remaining. I know at first glance they looked clean, but I want to consolidate the information and then review the entire data table. It's a long shot."

She systematically connected and probed each of the sensors, then copied, all the data that remained on the sensors. These devices were designed to send detailed analytics to be monitored and reviewed by master programs. As a part of the original design, the analytics programs provided information based on rules for things like general maintenance of components they were attached to, proximity data for what was near, completed steps, and anything else the automated programming allowed.

As the data was collected, a program she had designed selected various portions of the data she had deemed relevant to the situation and analyzed it for her review. She was already able to drill down into the data summarization, but this would help provide effective guidance for that review. This was a routing she'd used in field assignments when she worked with Jim to plan routes to travel, accommodations in unfriendly areas, and to determine resources available in their target area. As Jim had mentioned, it was one of her skills. It was also how he had gotten his handle Stalker originally, as he was able to move undetected with the uncanny ability to foresee any condition.

After all the digitally connected endpoints were scanned, she reviewed the data provided by her program.

Jim asked, "Do you want me to set up the simulation scenario now?"

Mercedes was focused on her screen, reading the outputs from the analysis, as she absentmindedly replied, "Sure, but don't start them until Chuck and The Sean return. I think I see some viral code that simply doesn't belong here. I want to show it to Chuck before we take the next step. As an added precaution, I want to launch a wireless protocol analyzer to see if we can trap any poisonous commands coming or going over the airways. With so much wireless technology in play here, we need to trap on all possible avenues of communications."

Jim and Mercedes stood staring, with their mouths open in wonderment, as Chuck and Sean stormed back into their work area. Both men were quite animated in their discussion, and from the look of things, both quite angry.

Chuck, with almost no restraint in his angered tone, asked, "When exactly did you plan to tell me? I've got these people on the ground working round the clock to get these planes in the air, we got permission to fly again, and the company is almost able to start to make money again. I sure hope this isn't another one of your stupid stunts."

Sean angrily retorted, "Listen to me. This just came through. I didn't want you to hear all the conversation, which is why I stepped away. I'm not hiding anything from you, except some contempt when you fall back to your old adversarial self, all bent out of shape because management doesn't quite trust you."

Jim and Mercedes looked at each other. Jim asked, "Does this mean you didn't bring us any lunch?"

The distracting question had the effect that Jim wanted, and Mercedes jumped into the heated argument. "What's gotten into you two? Before you left everything seemed fine."

Chuck immediately relaunched his tirade. "Corporate called him to say that the extortionists are back, threatening to ground more planes if they don't get their monies. I'm telling him, no way in hell. Competent people have displaced the automation. There is no credible threat to this airline, other than incompetent management."

Sean looked angrily at Chuck and shouted, "They read me the threat message over the phone. It is blazing across all the management PC screens! *Do you really think we would give up after only one try? Where is our fifty million? Try putting ANY aircraft up without payment and we will splash them. You have eight hours to comply.* We can afford the ransom demand, but we can't afford to remain grounded!"

Mercedes quietly asked, "They got in again, huh? What did your hosting provider say about the breach? Do we know where the incursion came in?"

Ignoring her, Sean added, "You said the ground position was secure. If fifty million will let us put aircraft up again, then I say we ought to consider it!"

Chuck retorted, "Are you listening to yourself? Pay extortionists not to splash our planes and hope they'll keep their word? You just said that the ransom note was on all the corporate management's PCs. Those are supposed to be unreachable from the outside. If they can get in there, what do you think the likelihood is of them getting into the aircraft onboard computers and ruining them in-flight?

"If you try to pay these bastards, and then hope that nothing will happen to the actual passenger flights BEFORE we trap this problem, you simply aren't thinking. I can guarantee the airline will be crushed by a tsunami of lawsuits the first time we have a crash. It is irresponsible to even consider making the payment, Sean."

Jim, chuckling at the absurd behavior of these two grown men, interceded, "Gentlemen, let's just conclude the argument here and now. Without your air certificate, none of the planes will leave the taxi area, much less the runway. With one phone call your air cert can be suspended. I'm the person on the ground here with the authority to do just that. Now, with that as a nonstarter, what do you think our plan B ought to be?"

The realization that the argument was over hit everyone.

After a few moments of silence, Mercedes offered, "Let me suggest that we focus on working backwards from these failed ground command sensors and try to work back to where the bogus commands originated. We've established a mockup area to simulate the circumstances the airline was facing when all of this started. I recommend that you help us with a run through, to see if we can trap the poisonous instructions and get a fix on where they are coming from. My suspicion is that the intrusion points for the threat message to corporate is the same for the poisonous messaging to your airline equipment."

A sullen Sean glumly responded, "Since the dark angel from the FAA here has already grounded the aircraft until this gets resolved, I'm going to ask, why you aren't already working it?"

Chuck, annoyed with everything, complained, "Geez, thanks for the offer to help, Sean! I honestly don't know where we would be without your surly management attitude of not resolved but will take credit if it works."

After giving Sean another sour look, Chuck turned to Mercedes. "I'd like to help, so let's get started. Will the three of us be enough, or do I need to get some IT people here?"

Before Mercedes could answer, Sean flatly interjected, "You have four. I'm staying to help. And, in case you were wondering, I used to work in IT before my management position. It is where I got the idea of full automation to replace people. Besides, if I can see the issues real time with my own eyes then I can present and defend our next course of action. If that's not enough, then only because, if I assist Chuck here won't be so smugly self-righteous all the time when he says management equals business prevention."

Mercedes could see this would build into another shouting match if not intercepted, interjected, "Would anyone mind if we all just work naked? After a full ten hours, my bra is just intolerable."

Both Sean and Chuck did a double take, but Jim just chuckled and said, "Okay, class, time to remove all your clothes for the next exercise! Or if that is not your preference, how about we simply work together and drop the attitudes for the time being?"

Smiles finally broke out on everyone's face, and Sean said, "I used to think my toughest adversary in negotiating was Mr. Chuck here. It occurs to me that I may have met his female counterpart."

CHAPTER 39

The Digital Battleground

True to his word, Marvin nearly emptied the nearby city of people to work in the cleanup campaign. Massoud, David, and Marco also kept their promise by leveraging their facial recognition program in conjunction with the video cameras, so no one was stopped and badged upon entry. The workers slowed down long enough to give their names, just so they could be paid after the fact.

Marvin seemed pleased not only that people did show up to help, but also because Massoud and the others were working to put the facility back into operational status. Summit smiled as he watched the early adversaries working as team members. While he was musing over the newfound camaraderie, his cell phone went off and demanded his attention.

Summit answered, "Good day, sir. Thanks for calling me back. I wanted to give you an update on restoring the facility and inquire about the ransom demands. I trust the Constellation group has NOT caved in and paid the demands, as I originally recommended."

The contracting officer hesitated slightly at the direct question but then offered, "We have disabled the automation sequencing in the other facilities, per your recommendation. However, we are not having the same level of local support at each of the other sites as you are. As a result, the accountants are running up and down the halls shouting doom, defeat, and despair. Upper management appears to be taking their input seriously, as they seem to be preparing to run amok in like fashion.

"As you would expect, the ransom demand pales in comparison to not being able to distribute goods to our giant stores. This presents a problem of delaying revenue, but also in some regions is causing a huge lack of products demanded by consumers. We're starting to see buying frenzies as people learn of the problem. I expect that the longer this situation continues, the easier it becomes for a decision to pay the ransom and move on."

Summit struggled to deal with the conversation and began to formulate a proper protest. Finally, he asserted, "I do NOT advocate acquiescing to the extortionist's demands, sir. I've got myself and three other computer forensic specialists on site who are working through the equipment to see if we can uncover the source of the issue. Please don't agree to the ransom demands until we have had time to work the scenario. Give us at least forty-eight hours. We can make good progress in that amount of time. If you pay them before we can discover how they're doing it, you'll keep them on the payroll going forward. I know you are in dire straits here, sir, but *don't give money for nothing!*"

The contracting officer snickered momentarily and then responded, "Yes, I know. Because if we do this, the milk is free. Alright, I'll stall for forty-eight hours. If we don't see progress, you and I'll not only have to buy the cow, but the entire farm!"

Though they both realized under different circumstances this could be a humorous exchange and worthy of a beer, Summit made a mental note to consider that when the resolution was in.

Summit acknowledged, "I understand."

Summit approached the three guards and motioned them into a room to speak and not be overheard and closed the door.

Summit stated, "Gentlemen, I just got off a call with my contracting officer. I received permission to have myself and my computer forensic team dig into the programming of the Constellation distribution system here at this site. I'll need security clearance for all of us."

Massoud, somewhat sullen, asked, "When will they be here, Summit? We'll need a little more information on these people before they start accessing the systems."

Summit suppressed his smile and announced, "They are already here, gentlemen. I've been watching you with the computer systems, and frankly, I want your skillsets with me, so we can start immediately. When we pull this off and find the beastie-code lurking in these systems, I'm recommending that the corporation rethink your job descriptions and bring you into their IT group. I already told my contracting officer that you are my forensic specialists, so let's go forens', shall we?"

All three men brightened. Marco excitedly asked, "You already cleared us to work on computer systems? Great."

David and Massoud beamed at the chance to show what they could do on high tech computer systems. *Summit thought to himself if nothing else they'll have a chance to prove themselves. Who doesn't need that in life?*

Summit added, "By the way, we only have forty-eight hours to show success. After that, the rules change. Does everyone understand?"

Massoud grinned. "I've had to beat the odds all my life. I'm not about to run from this challenge. How do you guys feel?"

They all smiled and promptly left for the digital battle-ground in the distribution center with Summit right behind them.

CHAPTER 40

Romance Afar

After three difficult gaming sessions, Dmitry was pleased at the overall results of his wins and points, yet sorely disappointed at the overall lack of financial benefits. It was time for the latest door selection, and he had won the first choice.

Dmitry pressed to connect to the scheduled video call. Chairman Chang grinned across the screen and greeted, "Dmitry, good! You have always been precise on your scheduling of time. I gather from your plan that we are taking a chance again on financial gains, as well as a short game based on a new selection from the wheel of misfortune.

"I must admit that playing some of these scenarios a second and third time is allowing me to gain more points than prior encounters, but you have earned the first door. It was an amazing move on Groddo's part to get into the side door and raise the panic. I think you earned double the points from the surprise factor. Well done!"

Dmitry looked rather pleased with himself and basked in the praise showered on his skills. He grinned back into the camera and with no hint of humility replied, "I really liked that hidden passage into the area. Honestly, I hadn't spotted it before, but I took full advantage. Don't worry, Chang, I have been playing longer than you, but your skills are improving. It seems your bank account is as well. If I weren't getting some of the bonus funds received for leaping into special areas, like raising the panic of the innocent bystanders that appeared in that last scenario, I'd be mad.

"Are you ready, Chang, for me to choose the winning door and take the current winnings? Then, of course, you can spin for the short session we agreed to."

Chairman Chang feigned innocence as he answered, "Yes, old friend. You earned this number one selection for the door. Good luck. By the way, how much was cleared into the door for this drawing?"

Dmitry laughed and responded, "Always the practical one. I have confirmed that only about twenty-five percent of the winnings unassigned made it through the distribution channels. I suspect tomorrow, or the day after, the remainder will be available, though not the winnings from the short session today. I still thought it was worth a drawing."

Chairman Chang looked very stoic as he said, "Of course it's worth it. I hope you get a win, Dmitry. It has been a long dry spell for you on the earnings side."

Dmitry cautiously eyed his opponent across the video feed. "Thank you for your good wishes. I find it difficult to believe that you would really be rooting for me, but I still select door two."

The lights flashed across the screen, and the door with the two slowly opened. It was dark and empty inside. Dmitry looked crestfallen as he lethargically nodded to Chairman Chang to go ahead and select.

Before Chairman Chang selected, Dmitry added, "If I wasn't sure, it was impossible, I'd suspect you, old friend."

Chairman Chang grinned and retorted, "I won't take that personally, Dmitry, as I know you are disappointed with your poor selection. I select door one."

Dmitry looked surprised and said, "I thought you would take your favorite, door three. That has been your pattern."

The screen filled with door one as it was slowly opened, and it too was dark and empty inside. Chairman Chang looked suitably dejected. Dmitry grinned broadly and gleefully exclaimed, "Ah ha, the gypsy was right, today was my day to win."

Chairman Chang grumbled, "Fine, you won. I should have selected my favorite door. Ah well, my spin, I believe."

Chairman Chang pressed the arrow on the wheel of misfortune icon, and the game scenarios raced by until the arrow landed on one, they'd competed on twice before. Chairman Chang pushed up the sleeves on his kimono and then cracked his knuckles. With a slight smile on his lips, he announced, "Let's play!"

As the game loaded, he sent a quick text to Jamie

You gauged it well. The old sod needed a win. There will be no more drawings today. Rest until one of my associates takes you back to the casino.

They played for the next several hours. It was apparent that their skills were improving as they rapidly grabbed up points as they wove through the game. They were equally fierce as their avatars passed along messages and threats to those that appeared during the game. Chairman Chang had eked out the win by a mere one hundred points when they closed the session down.

Dmitry stood and stretched. It was one of those mixed result days. He'd won the funds but lost the game. Ah well, the game had been well played by them both. He grudgingly thought about how improved his foe had become.

He rang for Evgeniya. She sensed immediately that his breathing was ragged, and he was struggling for air. His old Afghan war wounds flared up now and again, which were only helped by a session with his oxygen tank. Evgeniya wasted no time getting the tank set up to help his breathing and settle his damaged sinuses. She quietly cursed the Afghan traitors who had led the surprise attack on Dmitry's camp those many years ago, while he silently looked at the burn damage to his hand and arm. Within a few minutes, he was breathing easier and, with restored confidence, handed the breathing mask back to her so he could continue with his day.

Dmitry walked into the other room where Konstantin was busy in front of the screen with what he suspected was the final close of the programs. He went over to the wet bar and selected a premium bottle of vodka and poured them each three fingers. He walked over and placed the glass on the coaster near the keyboard, and the screen caught his eye.

"Konstantin, she's a beautiful woman. How do you know her?"

Konstantin looked up, and his ears reddened at being caught off guard. He responded, "Um, she is, well…um…, just someone I am trying to get to know better."

Dmitry looked over the pretty lady in the low-cut dress with the sultry eyes and come-hither smile. He admitted, "I can see why you would want her to be closer. A definite tasty morsel, no doubt. Have a drink. We'll toast my success at the money tonight and you getting the lady. What's her name? How did you meet?"

Konstantin flushed again and admitted, "We really haven't met yet, though we are exchanging pleasantries over this social site. Her name is Natasha. We met on this site several times. She seems to be a good girl and just wants some company. I've found her to be modest in her speech and almost shy. She indicated she lived not far from here. I suggested a quiet dinner where we could talk. I think she had a bad relationship, as she rebuffs every advance, but she still asks me questions and seems very interested in getting to know me. I have been trying to reassure her that all men are not dogs."

He raised his drink, toasted Dmitry, then commented, "I think your worry about Chairman Chang winning too much was unfounded. I've checked things and found everything secure. He just had a run of luck that you've now broken. The tides must go back and forth, I believe you have said, from time to time."

Dmitry stared at the brown-eyed beauty on the screen and mumbled, "Yes, I have. Let me help you secure a meet with this lovely lady. What website did you meet her on?"

Konstantin replied, "Thank you, I'd appreciate your help. You've always been better with words than me. I visit this site for meetings without strings. People can talk here in a group or step into a private area to converse. Not like a dating service or anything. Natasha reached out to me and randomly communicates, which is why I think some brute hurt her. She is so lovely. Such a pretty smile."

Dmitry seemed captivated by the vision on the screen as he suggested, "Why don't you tell her a little about your hobbies and how much you would like to take her to dinner, or maybe just lunch, which is even less threatening for someone with emotional scars. If she is close, then tell her you can send a car if she would prefer. If she keeps reaching out, you must be wearing her down. Don't hesitate, keep at it. Women like to be flattered. This one looks very easy to flatter."

Konstantin grinned and replied, "I'll try that, sir. You know, you might want to see if you can't meet someone here too. Perhaps we could double date?"

Dmitry absentmindedly smoothed back his hair with his good hand, shook his head and said, "It doesn't seem like something I would enjoy. I prefer high spirited, rentable women much like Zara was. I don't care for needy females. I suspect this site is a good meeting ground for someone looking for a good mate, but dating is a bit too mundane for my tastes. If it were taking hostages, then I'd be interested." He chuckled slightly at the observation of himself.

The admission made him sigh, and then he offered, "Besides, I'm not really looking to augment my business and government duties with a mate. I've got Evgeniya to look after me."

He reflected on his statement and realized that Evgeniya might be a work horse thoroughly devoted to him, however, not what you would call easy on the eyes. She was a strong, stocky woman that you wanted with you in a combat situation, but those attributes simply didn't transfer to the bedroom. Dmitry took a second, more profound stare at the beauty on the screen and sighed longingly.

Konstantin offered, "I understand, but let me forward the website information to your email in case you change your mind. You don't even have to use your real name. See on here, I am using Andrei, which is really my middle name. I very rarely share it with anyone."

Dmitry looked surprised as he replied, "I surely didn't know it. Send it along, but I doubt I'll use it."

With that he lifted his glass toward Konstantin and exclaimed, "Zdorov'ye!"

CHAPTER 41

Changed with Time

As Brayson and Mayor Perez sat thinking over their options, oblivious to one another, Brayson's mind drifted back to an issue that he had fixated on when he had first arrived at the site when the ransom demands began.

Finally, he asked, "Mayor, I hope you won't take offense, but how did you get the name of Baby? It seems it would have lent itself rather handily to teasing from the other children while growing up. And as we all know, children never grow up when it comes to teasing others."

Mayor Perez stared wistfully off into space as she quietly offered, "I was born Baby Rona D. Perez and was the only daughter in the family with three brothers. Being in the diplomatic corps, my father was always being sent to other countries to function as an ambassador, but he insisted on bringing the whole family. He didn't want to see us grow up just in pictures, like some of his colleagues had done. I grew up in the Philippines just outside of Manila.

"But in answer to your original question, I never noticed or remembered being teased about my first name. In fact, when I entered the political arena, my name had important political collateral and became a branding that was hard to beat.

"What is funny is I originally wanted to major in computer science. My father, however, convinced me to return to Spain where he pulled some strings to get me into the University at Barcelona.

"Being a servant to the people must have been my destiny, because my father steered me into Political Science studies, and I never made it into the Computer Science program. Soon all my spare time was devoted to campaigns and participating in the political activities that fed my optimism that fairness in government was a worthy goal. Well, my optimism and confidence has gotten me this far. I sure would like to know if we are going to win this contest. It is who I am. I am compelled to contribute to a better world for my fellow human beings."

Brayson studied the mayor for a moment and remarked, "I take it you are always campaigning, judging from your comprehensive answer designed to get my vote, madam. I doubt they would allow me, a non-resident, to vote."

Mayor Perez chuckled slightly and apologized, "Sorry, Brayson. It is an occupational hazard. Let's get back to the business at hand.

"Have they acknowledged the artwork trade to suspend the digital pounding we are sustaining? Did you get the message back into their systems, and have we received some asked-for relief?"

Brayson smiled slightly and answered, "Oh, we got the message back into their systems alright. However, it may have aggravated them a little, based on the terseness of their response. The odd part of the response was that even though the message tone suggests our assailant was annoyed, they asked for logistics to complete the transaction. In parallel to receiving the message back on the artwork offer, we were monitoring communications traffic that showed two end points using a highly encrypted data tunnel. This second observation suggests that we have two assailants which may be why the message we got back seems contradictory. The response back to us was an attempt to reconcile both parties' wishes into one answer."

CHAPTER 42

Saddle up

None of the operations technicians could miss McLaren's uncommonly tense features, nor how he was working his jaw muscles in extreme anger while he took the call in the operations area. Even the lead operator, Mohawk, moved a little farther away from what was going to be an explosive display when the call concluded. Since the operations area was all open seating, there was no private area in which to take a vexing corporate call. Thus, everyone always heard one side of this sort or any kind of conversation. Mohawk was the only one who liked to have others listen in on his side of a call. Everyone assumed he was speaking to his girlfriend, as he never failed to entertain their imaginations with saucy talk, coupled with lots of sexual innuendos.

However, McLaren was clearly in a hot debate with the powers that be from corporate. McLaren strained to keep a civil tone to his side of the conversation, but the whole team could see he was getting madder by the minute.

McLaren drew a deep breath and succinctly stated, "The deal was, after the transaction was completed, we'd bring the mine back online as fast as possible, and that means writing a check for all new equipment. What's the problem?"

After a few more seconds of pure inquiring silence by the crew in the operations area, McLaren sat up straighter. He chose his words carefully as he replied, "What do you mean, none are in inventory? You can't be serious that they only build when an order is received. I can see that for ships, but not for earthmovers."

More time passed, and the group of onlookers were quietly placing bets on how long the device McLaren was talking on would last before his anger drove him to crush it. McLaren, storming, shouted, "Have you completely lost your rational thinking? Seriously? Go dig up the ruined equipment and see if it can be made operational. Is this some sort of joke? I'll fax my laugh track to you. We don't have the kind of expertise on staff anymore. Plus, the odds of repairing equipment that sustained damage of the epic proportions we witnessed. Are zero. You got rid of the roughnecks that could weld, hammer out new fittings, and breathe life back into dead diesel engines. You established the mining activity with fully automated machine-to-machine intelligence and promptly fired those resources When I spring this offer on them, I'll have even more laugh tracks to fax you.

The operations team kept edging back away from McLaren in case his anger spilled out to the immediate vicinity, but they remained close enough to eavesdrop. His team heard McLaren spent time as a military drill instructor for special forces. Rumors indicated it was his responsibility to push lads to their absolute limit to see if they were worth keeping in the program. His temper had gotten past his better judgement, more than once, but the last time had been too much for him. McLaren swore that he would never lose his temper again, as it had, in his opinion, cost a young recruit his life.

McLaren's breathing was short and tense, but he kept his temper in check. He concisely demanded, "I want authorization to pay triple time to everyone who won't laugh at my request when I approach them with this lunar landscape excursion to rescue and resuscitate all the mangled equipment. I'll need spare parts and a large caravan of vehicles with heavy duty cranes and aircraft to just get everyone there, plus provisions. There ain't no Wallaby*Shop out there, so we gotta bring everything we might need to survive and to make repairs."

Snickering by the operations team at these comments helped calm McLaren and reminded him that he was talking to the corporate decision makers for the Consortium. He knew he was likely stuck, regardless, unless he wanted to walk. Work, especially at this pay level, was at a premium in this region.

McLaren's felt his temper subside somewhat as he took a breath. "I suppose you don't want us to wait until after lunch to get started, as well?" McLaren rolled his eyes, sensing his blood pressure rising as he responded, "Well, my lad, that's a mighty weighty phrase! Mighty weighty, indeed! You ought to try and get your comment *time is money* copyrighted before you lose your intellectual property rights on coining it.

"I take it that's what the highfalutin education you got in the states gave you that edge. No wonder you're at corporate and I'm out here at the edge of the known universe being forced marched to Australia's lunar landscape. One more thing, don't choke on the expenses I start racking up on my corporate charge card. I don't want to be reminded of how much I am spending. You want us to dig up all the ruined equipment, make everything go vroom-vroom again, but I can almost hear your high-pitched squeaky voice when I burn through the first six figure expense ceiling during week one."

McLaren took another deep inhale to calm himself. "No, sir, I haven't forgotten to whom I am speaking. I just don't understand why we can't go ahead and place the order, while we scour the after markets as we try to scavenge and repair what we can, that's all."

After another few moments of intense listening, he said, "I appreciate your confidence in me and the team. Let's see what we can do. I understand, sir. Good day."

It took a few seconds for McLaren to return to the here and now after disconnecting from his call. The staff waited quietly for their assignments.

George popped up and brightly offered, "I'd like to come along, McLaren, if you don't mind. This seems like a stout bunch of lads, and I for one would like to volunteer my services."

McLaren almost smiled at George. "Lad, you're not an employee here. Your team's been paid, and you're free to return home. It's our struggle now, not yours."

George gently pressed, "I didn't mean for wages. I want a chance to see what's on those sensors and try to learn what caused them to go wonky. Heck, I'll even buy my own food if you will let me help. I'll bring my own Kona coffee. Seriously, I need to know what happened so I can report to my team on how to combat it. Wouldn't you like to have that knowledge, if, God forbid, there's a replay at the site?"

McLaren stared sullenly at George, then stated, "No, you can't buy your own food! We'll feed you, dammit!"

McLaren sensed everyone was staring at him, so he barked, "Don't just stand there, lads. We got lots of work to do and you all know the drill! Saddle the horses!"

At a little before 10:00 in the morning, the team was in full motion executing McLaren's orders to assemble a small but mobile city to caravan to the mine. George was multitasking on several preparation issues with the team and suddenly realized that he needed to check in with the team with his first stop, alerting EZ so she could set up the satellite tracking before they took off. George grinned and mumbled to himself, *'I appreciate EZ's can-do attitude and positive personality under stressful situations.'* He autodialed the all-important number from his cell phone.

A groggy voice mumbled, *"Mygoddoyouknowwhatfrickentimeitis?"*

George brightly responded, "Hi, EZ. Sorry, I forgot about the seven-hour time difference again. Must be around 3:00 am there, huh? I needed to alert you that we're rounding up every bit of gear and bribing anyone who will work with us to travel back to Kookaburra for a salvage operation. As a precaution, I'm hoping you'd set that up in case the geocoordinates are being messed with still."

Instantly awake, she said, "It's a good thing I kept your program monitoring system on disk. I'll fire it up and launch the tunneling program that guys helped build. We'll get reliable communications during your jaunt to the Outback." She chuckled, "I won't bother getting dressed since I only need to launch the program, verify it works, and then go back to bed. I'm sure you won't mind, right?"

George's mind pictured the beautiful redhead at her computer au naturel. He politely offered, "Certainly. You would be comfortable while working. I wouldn't mind hearing a little bit more about your work habits, EZ."

EZ snickered. "Ha!"

Outreach

On day three, the conference room and wallboards reflected the hard work of the two men. Como, with Tyler's help had reviewed all the reports from the evening of the 911 call mess and other reports from the surrounding 48-hour period.

"The responders to these calls did a good job of writing up their notes, but it seems like similar issues with small outcomes like breaking and entry with petty theft, Tyler." Como remarked, "I never like things that smell like coincidences. And these additional reports," he pointed to the ones on the conference room table they'd reviewed, "stink like yesterday's fish. I want to take a walk around these neighborhoods and see if we can gain additional information. Are you game?"

"I think that's a great idea and it'll give us a chance to stretch our legs. I don't know the streets like you do. I agree putting real people and locations may help us spot a better pattern."

Como drove to the poorer downtown area which had clusters of street people eyeing his car, and parked. "This places up close to the middle of the smash and rob cases. I think we can walk from here."

As they methodically traversed the streets, Tyler commented after Como chatted with a couple of the street people. "You really know this area. I'm impressed. You haven't spoken to a single person without mentioning their name."

Como chuckled. "I spent a lot of time on these streets in my youth and later as a beat cop. They each have a story and some areas are really sad, but a few minutes of empathy handing them a small bag of candy or granola bar seems like the right approach to these troubled folks. I never give 'em money, in the winter I might bring some coffee."

"Como, this is a side of you I suspect few folks every see. Heck, even the gift cards for fast food eateries in the area seem appreciated. The women with her daughter that you spoke with earlier seemed grateful. I liked how she told the little girl to remember her manners."

"We have some good outreach programs, but the homeless population is growing. I usually some out here on my days off for a few hours. I have grown fond of many of the street people and like knowing they are still around."

Then they got a real break when Como guided them to one old soul. He was wearing several layers of clothing and polishing his worn boots with a rag.

"Sarge, how are you, buddy?" Como stuck out his hand as if to a friend. "I haven't seen you for the last couple of weeks, so I was worried."

Sarge shook hands and looked over at Tyler with a bit of doubt crossing his face. "Como, I'm doing alright. Who is this? You aren't trying to get me to go back to the VA, are you? They just want me to take some drugs and sign myself up for the shrinks. I can't stand the confinement, you know."

'Nah, Sarge, I know better. This here is Tyler. He and I are working on finding some bad guys. We think that several out-of-town-misfits committed a series of robberies over several days within the last couple of weeks."

Tyler held out his hand and said, "Hi, Sarge. I know what you mean about the confinement stuff. I find I too am more suited to the outdoors. That way I can keep my eye on folks. I bet you don't miss much, do you, Sarge? What was your job in the service, man?"

Sarge looked a bit surprised as he reached out and shook the man's hand. No one had asked him about his job in a long time. He cleared his throat a bit, then stated, "Well, sir, I was a spotter, and it was my job to make certain that my team didn't get surprised by the enemy. I was pretty good at it, and most of my guys got out. Two years of I don't know how many missions and how many close calls sort of..." Then Sarge stared off into the space beyond Tyler's head as if he were watching a movie in his mind. After a bit, he gathered himself back to the present and added, "It's a damn shame they all couldn't come home. War sucks!"

Tyler agreed, "You got that right, Sarge. I served some time, and it was awful. I have times when I can't forget either.

"I can guess what you must be thinking. How can this character have been in the military? Well, I was on a deployment in Iraq as a communications specialist. Anytime the compound took a shelling of short-range mortars, the computer network got hosed up. In reality, even if we weren't being shelled, the network was always hosed up. Well, I got tired of ridicule, so whenever I got called to come fix the network I always showed up with my AR-15 in hand with a thoroughly annoyed look on my face. Then I would demand in a loud voice 'Who claims there is a network problem?'

"You know, when you are waiving an automatic rifle around with an angry attitude, almost no one complains about a minor problem."

Sarge grinned at the story.

After a moment more, Tyler said, "Maybe when Como and I get this case wrapped up, we can share a meal and talk some."

Como interjected, "Sarge, you heard any bragging or seen extra money floating around where it shouldn't be? Missy had suggested earlier that you might know something. She said three guys were drinking and carrying on something awful and you strong-armed the leader on his way."

Sarge laughed a bit and commented, "They were three local wannabe tough guys. Falling all over themselves 'cause they'd scored a bit of cash. Funny though."

"How's that?" asked Como.

"Hector, their leader, said they'd had to visit Vinnie in the projects to pawn a bunch of different stuff and split it with a fourth guy. Apparently, this guy had not divided the loot fairly and had left them with less than they wanted. Then it sounds like he also cleared out some of the stash."

"And why is that funny?" questioned Tyler.

"Apparently this guy had taken the cash and the rest of the loot from Vinnie and done a wire transfer and shipped the goods from the Pack'n Box on Marshall Drive. Jimmy at the Pack'n Box had told Hector and probably everyone else that he had charged the guy twice as much to ship his package because the jerk wasn't local. Hector was mad and he and the other two were drunk and tearing stuff up because the guy had screwed them. But they were happy 'cause at least he had been screwed too, paying crazy fees for the wire and shipping a package priority to someplace in Europe. They were looking for the dude and flashing his photo to anyone that would look."

Como handed Sarge another granola bar and calmly asked, "Sarge, you know where I might find Hector or his buddies? I think I'd like to see that photo."

Sarge took the bar and unwrapped it. He took a bite, smiled and said, "Yeah, Hector at least. He's in the hospital. After I tried to get him out of the area, he took a couple of punches at me, and I, well, hit him back. He fell over this motorcycle, and the owner was so mad he really beat him up. I helped get him to the hospital, and they said they'd need to keep him a couple of days, 'cause of the concussion. Some guys are so dumb, aren't they, Como?"

"Ah, so that was the funny part. Yep, you're right, Sarge, some guys are dumb.

"Thanks for the tip, Sarge. Here are a couple of more bars and a gift card for your help. You and Missy go get some food, okay? And I want to see you on Thursday of this week, no excuses."

"Yes, sir. I'll be there." Sarge looked over to Tyler and asked, "You gonna be there too, Tyler? I think I'd like to have that dinner and talk, unless you were just making it up."

Tyler looked him squarely in the eye and promised, "I'll do my best to see you on Thursday. Thanks for your help, Sarge. A pleasure to meet you." He extended his hand and shook Sarge's hand.

As they walked toward the car, Como asked, "Would you really come on Thursday?"

"Yes, Como, but you need to tell me where and what time.

"I like Sarge. He was in the army then hit the streets around a year ago." Como explained. "The system let him fall through the cracks. He wears everything he owns from a clothing perspective and still looks scarecrow thin. It's a shame," he added with a shake of his head.

Tyler clapped him on the shoulder like a friend. "Let's go visit this Hector and see Vinnie, Como. I think you have a way of finding out information, and I don't want the trail to get any colder. I am hoping that we can secure the photo as well as the address of the package. We might even get lucky and get the receiving bank for the wire transfer. That could prove very useful."

In the precinct the next morning, Tyler and Como reviewed their small victories. Not only had Hector provided them the photo, but after Como arranged for a reduced charge with the DA, he provided lots of details.

Hector said the guy's name was Vadim. He described Vadim as the same height as Como with dark wavy hair, fierce dark eyes, hands that had seen work, with scars, and a funny accent. He had found Hector in a bar and promised him and his buddies, whom Hector refused to name, lots of money if they would partner with him. He'd bought them shots of vodka and related how they would hit several places, and regardless of the alarms the cops wouldn't find them. It was a sure thing.

Hector had been reluctant but finally agreed, as did his buddies. He detailed all the places they'd hit and most of the goods. Como had been comparing this information to all the reports they had on the robberies. Things were matching up.

When Tyler and Como had persisted with questioning Hector on why no cops would show up, he finally admitted that Vadim had said the cops would have no idea of the addresses as their systems would be messed up. He swore that they would be directed to the wrong address. Hector had been so relieved after the first break-in and the success that the rest were a cake walk.

Hector had helped him fence part of the loot at a couple of different pawn shops, but Vadim had complained that things were going too slow and that he needed to move the merchandise faster. Hector then recommended that they bulk it out to Vinnie. Vinnie and Vadim had not seen eye-to-eye on pricing. Hector said it had been a bit tense until Vadim finally agreed to the price for the buyout and walked away. But somehow Vadim had switched the package for Vinnie and left a sachet of costume jewelry instead. Vinnie was so mad at the deception that he turned out all of his two-legged chained dogs to go find Vadim and his money. But no trace was to be had because that guy had simply checked out. It had taken Hector and his buddies until the next morning to realize they'd also been screwed.

Tyler had information from the Pack'n Box, which included the shipping address and the wire transfer account number. He had called in to Julie and updated her with their discoveries, as well as completed a detailed report and sent it along.

Tyler and Como had been hard at it for the day and had just left from briefing the mayor. The mayor agreed to let Tyler do some remote probing of the PSAP data to help get the root cause for the geolocation misinformation. Como and Tyler had made a good case for relating the robberies and the alert mismatches. But how the process was being manipulated so it could be avoided was critical.

As they walked outside after the meeting with the mayor, Como commented, "You aren't bad for such a young pretty face, Tyler."

Tyler grinned and replied, "Thanks, Como. I'd work with you anytime, old man."

They both laughed. Then Tyler sobered a bit and said, "I want to go with you on Thursday, don't forget."

Como clapped him on the back and replied, "You got it."

CHAPTER 44

Field of Honor

Massoud, David, and Marco were so pumped and motivated by their new data forensics roles at the Constellation distribution center that they wouldn't take a break. Summit grinned at their enthusiasm feigning fear of them trampling him in their pursuit of the viral code on the systems. Marvin glanced at his helpers and commented when they snagged another clue. After twelve hours of combing through the software code of the automated systems, Summit insisted that they take a break before continuing.

David and Marco relented, but Massoud insisted, "I cannot stop now. Look at these log files. I see commands issued to unload when they should say transport. These are sophisticated systems but are incapable of so many disjointed instructions. The linear approach of the applications should be stop, load, unload, or move to next processing point. That's all. When you issue these orders in a random fashion, all chaos quickly ensues.

"My gut tells me these out of order instructions were pre-processed upstream. Then the instruction set was fed down to these relatively unsophisticated devices. With the load order manipulation, it destroyed the proper load sequence. Someone got into the system, learned how it functioned, and then tampered with the commands."

Summit looked at the logs and clarified, "Your theory does sound reasonable and accounts for that you are seeing. If we can find the point of entry where the poison is coming from and plug it, we'd be able to turn on the systems again to operate as intended."

Massoud exclaimed, "Precisely!"

Summit studied Massoud for a few moments and stated, "You know, it appears that you are well-versed in this digital cat and mouse game, based on what you have uncovered so far. Is there any particular reason why you are not doing it instead of your normal day job as a security guard?"

Massoud looked wistfully off into space, then after collecting his thoughts, he quietly said, "I was a minister of education in Iran during the Shah of Iran years, with computer science as my specialty. When the shah was deposed, I had to flee or be executed. I made it to the United States and begged for asylum, I was refused.

"The day before I was to be deported back to Iran and certain execution, two men from the Justice Department showed up at my door and asked that I testify as an expert witness in the Iran atrocity trials being conducted here in the U.S. I explained that it would not be possible since the immigration department would be sending me back to Iran that afternoon. They both thanked me for my time and left quickly. I had a permanent green card the next day, and two weeks later I gave testimony against the new Iranian regime."

Summit mentally tried to assemble the puzzle pieces but failed. He asked, "But that doesn't explain your current day job."

Massoud ran his hands over his head to steady himself before he elaborated, "It takes university degrees and work history to get anywhere in the IT world. When all of your records are held hostage in a disliked country, one has to start over. So you take a day job and go to school at night. I need many more nights, Summit."

Marco and David listened and nodded as Massoud told his story. Then Marco offered, "I am from Costa Rica. I came to this country to live and work. My brother immigrated with his whole family, but I just came here. I've been trying to get formal status to stay. I'm also in night school to get credentials to allow me to again do computer engineering, like Massoud here."

Then all looked at David as if on cue to hear his story. David seemed a little intimidated by the quizzical looks and finally blurted out. "I'm from the United Kingdom. I fled extradition for having fought and won a gun duel where I killed my opponent in a field of honor! He disparaged my computer code, so I challenged him to a duel. My honor's intact, but I can never go home."

All the men stared at David incredulously for a few moments until Summit asked, "Really? No kidding?"

David, still noticeably uncomfortable, quietly offered, "No, not really. My parents immigrated to this country legitimately when I was eight. I've been here ever since."

Summit said nothing but gave David the *Why the crazy story?* look, to which David confessed, "Well, everyone else has these terrific background stories. I don't have anything as neat as either one of them, so I made some stuff up. I left the IT world a few years ago to teach and just never got around to going back into network engineering. But this gig was a chance to see if I'd like it again. I do."

Summit chuckled. "As promised, I will put in a good word for all of you, so no doubts on that subject. Right now, let's see if we can find that entry point and restart everything."

Massoud got the attention of the others and pointed at his screen. "See this setting, here? Why is it set to YES, trust other end points, when it should be set to NO? If everything is set to trust everything, then any bogus command will be trusted and then acted upon. I don't understand why this isn't set to NO, so it won't trust without a certificate authority."

David and Marco looked confused and nodded at the comment. David offered, "For that level of trust, we would have to have an issuer of the CA and import one to every device. Then the devices would all trust each other properly. Is it possible that someone was in a hurry to get the systems up and running and took a shortcut?

"I know that generating a CA for every device to use for trusted communications is a pain in the neck. But we've seen what happens when you don't."

Marco looked to Summit and asked, "Does the Constellation have an issuing CA for us to use for this?"

Summit responded, "I don't believe the question ever came up, but let me ask."

David said, "Hey, Massoud, you're pretty good on spinning up an internal CA, based on that discussion we had last week. How long would it take you to build one and start spitting out certs that we could put on all the systems?"

Massoud thought a moment as he tapped his chin. "I can spin a CA server up in a couple of hours. We'd need to whack all the equipment with the cert and then set the trust bit to NO before launching the loaders. It will take all four of us working simultaneously to get it done. It might not solve our problem in time. As you know, the clock is still ticking, and..."

Summit interrupted, "They do have internal CA servers at corporate. To get access to them we'd have to open our communications link. You know what happens when we do that."

Massoud offered, "I can spin up a couple of new certificate authority servers for use here, but they won't trust anything upstream without our cert on them. In that case, we have a choice to either go out of band to give them our certs, or we go out of band to get their certs, then open the WAN link for a test run. In theory, if we all have certs from the same issuing CA, then we should be immune to poisonous instructions from a rogue third-party program. Frankly, getting the cert from their issuing CA makes more sense."

David and Marco quickly agreed, and all three of them looked to Summit for next steps.

Summit smiled and responded, "A whole flock of certificate authorities delivered out of band coming right up!"

CHAPTER 45

Strategic advancement

Affairs of state had taken their toll on Dmitry for the last few days. He had Konstantin and Evgeniya working very long hours to assist with meeting those obligations. For a few evenings he and Konstantin had stayed even later discussing the woman Konstantin was still trying to convince to meet up for a meal. Every strategy they created she carefully avoided, but she kept returning to the chat room and sought out the private conversations with Andrei. Natasha provided a few additional pictures of herself in nice clothes that showed off a womanly figure, but the photos were not truly revealing or overly provocative. Dmitry found his thoughts drifting to Natasha more frequently. The view of Evgeniya exiting his office with her hips nearly catching on the doorway put the lovely Natasha back into his mind.

Konstantin entered with a glass of vodka for each of them and sat in the armed chair across the desk from Dmitry.

"Zdorov'ye!!" Konstantin stated and tossed back the entire glass of vodka.

Dmitry took a swallow and looked at his second in command. "What troubles you, my old friend? You looked very distracted most of the day."

Konstantin stared off into space and admitted, "I'm a little tired. We are, however, ready for the gaming session to start in the morning. The transfer of funds is completed. You and Chang can do another door selection before the game.

"I've added a couple of twists to some of the existing games with the heavy land mover equipment and the fast trips scenarios in case those are the games selected. I think you'll find these changes challenging while keeping Chang in learning mode. As you've insisted, we don't rig the games. However, the changes in direction and options to make the games continually interesting remains within those guidelines, even if I provide you advance reconnaissance."

Dmitry smiled at the promise of an interesting gaming session, then he asked, "I believe, as of the last game Chang earned the first pick on the doors? Hopefully, his streak of picking the wrong door first will continue. I picked the last money door and really would like this one if the funds are all included."

Konstantin offered, "Did you want me force that selection, sir?"

"I would like to say yes," Dmitry confessed, "But that is not the way to win. I want to beat this old foe of mine fair and square. In all sincerity, it's the gaming I enjoy the most. Each modification you do makes them better. I have wondered if we might start a separate line of games along these same lines through one of our other business ventures. It might make for a very nice addition to our hacker group, Dteam, or even a private label operation." Dmitry grinned at his idea. Tossing back the rest of his vodka, he said. "Let's have some more of this vodka, my friend, and you tell me how you're progressing on your Natasha."

Konstantin poured them both another round and set the bottle on the desk between them. He was silent as he raised his glass to his boss. "I think that last photo I sent to her of me on the shooting range was perhaps not the most endearing. It was the one where I was holding the target after firing fifty rounds. I thought she might be impressed that all the shots were in the tight pattern on the heart of the silhouette, but her response was, 'My, you're so good with your weapons, men must fear you!' I was hoping for something more along the lines of her belief that I could protect her. She won't agree to dinner but admitted she liked to read my stories. I think perhaps she really doesn't like me."

Dmitry shook his head and suggested, "How could she not like you? You're an excellent shot, good provider and open to a relationship. She'll come around. Have you offered to send flowers or a small token of your appreciation?"

Konstantin shook his head. "No, she is still vague on her actual address, though the IP address puts her within thirty kilometers of here. I tried to track it closer but was blocked, likely due to the spotty wireless service in that area. I'll keep working to find her location. I've additional ideas on how to do this."

"Good, my friend. Now you go home and get some rest, so I can finish up and be ready to beat Chang tomorrow." Dmitry insisted.

"But, sir, I am happy to stay and help you finish."

"No, I am fine and would like a bit of quiet before I leave. The guard is outside the door and will call my driver when I am ready. Now go."

Konstantin rose and left, ambling to the outside door after he had retrieved his heavy coat. It was cold and windy, so the lined woolen coat and ermine hat were necessary. Snow had fallen for most of the day. Once the outside door closed, Dmitry turned to his computer and logged into the website. He had been in here twice before and had established a login and persona of Mikael, which was his never-used middle name. The profile he'd constructed was mostly accurate, with his current position a bit vague. His early years with family and military accomplishments were accurate. The photo he'd posted had been one taken for a state dinner not long ago. He wasn't dressed in his uniform for that dinner but rather a tuxedo. He looked around the chat room and saw that the lovely Natasha was online but not chatting with anyone. This was the second time he'd seen her here. The last time she'd spoken briefly with Andrei.

Off and on throughout the day, he had contemplated how to approach this woman. Women in general had never been a problem. In his younger days, they had flocked to him in droves as he had a reputation for pleasuring them. As he aged, his military and political position had drawn them because of the power he held. He took them when and where he wanted, treated them well, but had never made a commitment for longer than a few months. None of them looked like this Natasha. She was lovely. Based on her bio and conversation, she was also educated and committed to the family she helped. A seemingly selfless woman. Not something he'd seen often in his encounters.

He opened the conversation in the chat room. "Madam, I understand from a friend that you are selective with those you would have a conversation. You can look at my background, but I am an old soldier who is looking for some good conversation with a well-educated lady who has no designs on my position or power. Are you such a lady, Ms. Natasha?"

The chat window was as silent as the office he sat in. He had sat in foxholes for hours while on duty without a problem, but this time the wait felt like an eternity. Many minutes passed before a response was offered.

"I'm sorry, sir, have we been introduced? I checked your background, and you do have an impressive military career. I am humbled that you reached out for a chat."

Dmitry thought about how to couch his response. "My associate, Andrei, indicated that he was impressed with your conversational skills. He indicated he wanted to meet you and perhaps break bread. If you have a strong alignment with him, please feel free to cease our conversation. I would not want to intrude on a budding relationship. I just found your pictures lovely and his conversations about you intriguing. I don't wish to press you into an awkward conversation."

A long pause in the chat window ensued. He was almost ready to accept that she was gone. Finally, it seemed as if she'd made some sort of decision.

"I have enjoyed my conversations with your associate, Andrei. However, he seems to like discussions of war and arms. I tend to like books, art, and current affairs more, though I respect what he and obviously you have done to protect our country and people. Do you both work together?"

Dmitry immediately responded, "We do work together. Andrei is a man to trust. He is very reserved and gentle for the most part. I too like books and art. One of my favorite books is Tolstoy's *Anna Karenina*. I found it a fascinating view on family life and adultery within Russian aristocracy of the nineteenth century that carried on into the twentieth century. It was much more intriguing for me than Tolstoy's War and Peace."

Natasha responded, "I thought so as well, and I also admire Maxin Gorky's Mother because of the way he depicted the story based on his grandmother and the huge changes that occurred during the Bolshevik revolution.

"I have always worked hard and tried to do the right thing. I was lucky to be educated and have taught several courses on humanity myself, until I found myself the caretaker of my grandmother. She is a dear. She requires a lot of my time, and I am devoted to her care."

Dmitry's interest was piqued as he asked, "You take care of your family? That's an admirable quality, madam. How many are in your family?"

"Oh, there is only Grandma and me, Mikael. I had to move her to my flat in the city so I could care for her. I can only teach two classes now at the university, and we take in a bit of sewing to supplement our income. She never complains. But enough of me, tell me about you."

They chatted back and forth for several hours, covering more books and pieces of art that Natasha would like to travel someday and see in person. He was in his element, talking about his travels and things he had done. He said he too wanted to travel more, and they joked about several places they could go together. When he signed out of the chat room, they'd agreed to a discussion the next evening. As he was driven home, he reflected on the easy banter they'd exchanged, and for a moment he felt a twinge of guilt at having moved his relationship with Natasha far further than Konstantin had in a far shorter time. He smiled as he recalled her comments on how handsome he looked in his profile picture, saying he looked younger than his detailed background would suggest.

Dmitry whistled as he entered the main office. There was a definite spring to his step that Evgeniya mentioned as he passed. He turned and offered, "It is a lovely day, and you look very nice this morning, Evgeniya. Why don't you take the day off, my dear? Konstantin and I have some special projects to work on."

Not waiting to be told twice, Evgeniya smiled and nodded her appreciation as she quickly slipped into her coat. "The coffee is hot, sir, and thank you. I could use the time to catch up on some shopping."

Dmitry was soon settled into his gaming chair, and Konstantin was there with a hot cup of coffee and asked if all was well. Dmitry replied, "I had a great evening, my friend, and am ready to play. I slept like I haven't in years, complete with some wonderful dreams. And you?"

Konstantin grinned and said, "I thought about what you said with regards to my Natasha, and I will try to contact her later tonight if she is in the chat room. I looked for her when I got home and finished my chores, but she was not present. I think I have a new idea to meet her at the war museum, and perhaps she would consider that neutral ground."

Dmitry looked at his friend with almost pity in his eyes, then recovered and exclaimed, "I wish you well, my friend. Is it time?"

The screen displayed the countdown until the scheduled call, then the video conference was automatically dialed. Chairman Chang was present with a smile on his face as he announced, "Good day, Dmitry. I hope you are ready for a new game. I know I am. I hope our spin takes us to a Mediterranean city today, as the scenery is so tranquil in that scenario."

Dmitry grinned and agreed, "Yes, Chang, agreed. But first we need to pick a door. I believe that you earned the first pick from our last game, you rogue. I'm, of course, hoping you miss so I have a chance. After that we can play. My work was close to overwhelming this week, so I am looking forward to a good challenge and diversion."

The screen painted the three doors in the center, with their faces minimized to the lower right of their screens.

Chairman Chang smiled like a Cheshire cat. "Yes, old man. I think that I do pick first. I wish you well, but I dreamed I'd win if I chose door one this time. That is my choice, and you will earn the spin for the game scenario when I win."

The door shimmered and grew larger as it opened to display piles of euros under flashes of light, while triumphant music played. Dmitry looked very disappointed, but only for a few seconds.

"Congratulations, Chang. It is time then to play for a while. I must warn you I'm ready to win the contest today. Shall I spin?"

Not waiting for an answer, Dmitry spun the dial, and the scenario was displayed. Chairman Chang sent a text of thanks to Jamie just before the game commenced with both men busy outfitting their avatars for the battle.

Chapter 46

Room to Chat

Juan grimaced when Gracie and Juan Jr. ran to greet him as he entered their nursery. Gracie ran into Juan's injured leg, and Julie tried to pull her back so as not to hurt Juan further. Juan, however, would have none of it. Juan grabbed her up in his arms then reached for Juan Jr., but the combined weight of his children was more than he could hold with the injured leg. They all toppled into a conveniently placed chair. This time it was Juan Jr.'s fidgeting that struck the sore leg again.

Juan gently exclaimed, "Hey now. Let's go easy on the old, wounded dad. Give me a couple more days before we start roughhousing again. Deal?"

Both children smiled and nodded vigorously, even as Julie protested, "Alright, you three. Stop being so cute. You know I can't take it. Now kids, I need to take your father so we can get some work finished. Then we'll come back and get you so we can work on supper. Be good for Miss Maude."

The children dutifully nodded and returned to the games they were playing before their parents had arrived. The twins were well adjusted, happy with their surroundings, loved their nanny Maude, and loved their parents. Instinctively, they knew the boundaries of when to play and when to settle down.

She looked at Maude and asked, "Can you handle them a little longer while we do our conference call, please? We need to have a few check points with the team, then we'll be set for the evening."

Maude smiled and promptly went to herd Juan and Julie's intelligent and sometimes high-spirited twins.

Juan smiled big and sweetly asked, "Honey, can you help the old, infirmed man over to the conference bridge equipment?"

Julie smiled sweetly and replied, "If I do, then that must mean you aren't suitable material for adult playtime later. What a shame!"

Juan studied her intensely for a moment. Then he practically danced his way to their office, under his own power, and ended with a bow as though he were taking an ovation from a large audience. Julie and Juan's home was a rather large apartment in Julie's family home in Luxembourg. Their apartment in the mansion held a sitting area, two bedrooms, with one attached to the nursery, and a room they had converted to an office. All the furnishings had been modified over the years by Haddy but were still in keeping with the tradition of the era in which it was built. The priceless art and antique furnishings were kept in places where they could be shown, as well as complimented by colors in the walls, draperies, and flowers.

Julie gave him a sly look and, with an exaggerated wink, coyly admitted, "I guess no early sleeping for me this evening."

The team did a rapid-fire update for Juan and Julie on the conference bridge, after they had welcomed their boss home from the hospital. They each provided a quick yet thorough account of their actions for each of the assignments they were working.

Then, as a team, they focused on Tyler's case concerning the tampered PSAP 911 location information, collaborating on the possibilities. They agreed that the package shipment, as well as the funds transfer, were likely related to the greater picture of what they were seeing, and Julie agreed to see if more information on the destination could be traced.

Julie and Juan handed out praise for all their efforts and helped provide them with reinforcement statements that they might use to convince their customers to avoid paying the ransom.

Julie emphasized, "If the disbursement is going to be made over your objections, then beg for the time to allow us to do a digital trace on those transfers. We have the means to do some serious and intricate money-following through my resources. We have provided you the access to alert the resources yourselves, and then Juan or I can follow up with you. No delay in trying to reach us before starting the trace. When faced with the destruction that seems viable in each of your cases, time is too precious to waste."

Juan ended the call as each agreed to Julie's request. As a result, the call was over quicker than usual. Juan had noticed that Julie seemed rushed for some reason but said nothing. After the last team member disconnected, Julie seemed to lighten up a little and even flirted with Juan in the conference room area. Juan was confused with Julie's come-on tactics but quickly checked to see if they were alone, in case her amorous mood became more demanding.

Julie moved closer to Juan and in a sultry, seductive voice asked, "Now that we are alone, darling, tell me more about yourself, hmmm?"

Juan, now totally confused, shook his head, and asked, "Babe, what are you trying to do?"

Julie parked her sultry come-on and responded, "As a man you have certain things you like or desire in a woman, correct? You said that there are certain things that turn you on and some that fall so flat as to be a turn off. I want you to teach me what those things are. Once you have done that, we need to see how they can be delivered with no voice, no physical contextual clues from sight or touch, and, most importantly, how to be seductive just through an avatar picture and chat screen dialog. Let's begin, honey."

Juan displayed his baffled stare for Julie and sputtered, "What are you talking about? Are you thinking about going into the Internet dating line of business, or is this an expansion of your JAC persona?"

Julie ran her fingers through Juan's hair in a way that set all his follicles on high alert. Grinning at the question and knowing that his hormones were on launch sequence, she flashed a sexy smile and answered, "Yes, honey. That is exactly what our next business venture is. Internet chat room sex. I have been playing with a possible entry into this world, anonymously of course since you went missing. I think it is time we take it to a new level, right after we make dinner with the twins. Are you up for it, sweetheart?"

CHAPTER 47

Women and Pool

After listening to Julie's many questions and requests, Quip finally replied, "Of course we can do that, but I want to know WHY you want to do that. EZ keeps getting woken up out of a sound sleep repeatedly, launches some Yaqui Indian programs she got from Carlos, but then won't tell me anything. I want to know what's going on before I start chewing up processing resources on ICABOD."

Julie was contemplative for a moment. Before she could respond with her carefully chosen words, ICABOD offered, "Dr. Quip, I surmise that her project is on a need-to-know basis. It is not imperative that we know all the reasons why Miss Julie is asking for these routines to be run or put into place. I would submit that the routines can be quickly deployed to further her plan of attack and that we will be given more information in due course. In the grander scope of things, her requests are quite modest and will not impact my other duties. Her isolated computing space is sufficient to meet the requests."

Quip eyed Julie's face and ICABOD's current image on the video conference call suspiciously and then accused, "You know, you two haven't been quite the same since that last date night. ICABOD, you always seem to be on her side in these discussions, and, frankly, my quality time with you seems to be coming up short. I'm…I'm a little bit peeved at this situation, as the Brits would say."

Julie, struggled with her chuckling. "Oh, ICABOD, we've talked about this. We might as well put all the cards on the table. I simply cannot leave my husband and children to run away with you. You are so very sweet, but can't we just be friends like we were before?"

ICABOD quietly offered, "Miss Julie, I am unsure if I can continue processing without you. You see, only you have ever reseated my blade servers so…thoroughly…and with such tender determination. You use my fiber optic cable so lovingly. With the last expansion you helped support, you gently, but firmly, applied the supporting cable ties in such an aesthetic manner. No one could ever work in my data center hot aisle again without me thinking of your tender actions. But for the sake of the children and even your husband, whom I have the utmost respect for, let's soldier on as friends, per your request."

Quip, half-crazed with confusion and darting his gaze back and forth between Julie's stoic face and ICABOD's unchanging image, was not quite certain what to believe.

Julie relented and announced, "There, you see, Quip? Our fling is over, and, yes, I will fill in the details of my request as they evolve.

"Since we are in full disclosure mode now, you should know that we have those two data link end points, and EZ is trying to break the encryption. But honestly, we could use ICABOD's processing muscle to see what exactly is being exchanged down that tunnel in such a torrent of ones and zeros. We have traced some of the ransom monies in proximity of one of the end points, but not the other. I think that finding that other end point is key before we reengage with Wolfgang on the ownership of these targets."

Quip listened as Julie continued, "The other end of the encrypted tunnel seems to land in Russia, but there is no corresponding money trail there…yet. I need some disruptive routines for this questionable data tunnel to be able to play a man-in-the-middle intrusion routine. But, if we are successful in inserting ourselves into that data torrent, we will have to interpret what is being exchanged. That may be too easy to be observed in that activity though. What I want to do is capture some of the traffic and then exit the encrypted tunnel. Then we should be able to analyze what is being exchanged without too much suspicion. Comprende?"

Quip studied Julie's video image a few moments and then agreed, "That's actually a pretty good idea. We'll get to work on it right away. Oh, and one more thing, Jules. I don't want you leading ICABOD astray. He's a good lad, and I don't want him being seduced by a more experienced, older woman."

Trying to project a shamed attitude, Julie hung her head and offered, "Quip, you heard me break it off, didn't you? I promise he won't have to steal his daddy's cue and try to make a living out of hustling pool, like some young bucks are forced to do."

Quip looked rather sullen as he stated, "Okay, I'm going to end this video call now, Miss Julie May. Just remember your promise. And think about how you are going to admit it to your husband. He should be aware of your wandering ways."

Julie flashed smile. "He already knows it all and is working on helping me reform and learn to perform."

She laughed as she signed off the call.

CHAPTER 48

There's two of them?

Mohawk was adamant in his petition to McLaren. "Look, McLaren, she's my lady and all that, but she's one of the best long haul truck operators in the country. We're short on mates for this project, and she's available for hire. You hired your nephew, Hoyt, to drive one of the big rigs, and he doesn't have anywhere near the experience she does. Why won't you even interview her?"

McLaren, stalling for time by cutting his stare between the two of them, as well as determining how to make his case without hurting any feelings, stated, "Your orange mohawk took some time getting used to, but I don't think the team is going to be able to deal with her blue mohawk as well. No offense, but all the body piercings, uh, the ones we can see, would strain everyone's concentration for what is going to be a rough trip. Also, as the only female, I can assure you there won't be any segregated toilets, so feminine privacy will be non-existent until we return. Why don't you save us all a lot of headaches and withdraw your name from consideration, Tina?"

Tina was about the same size as Mohawk, only a little burlier. Her blue mohawk stood out in stark contrast with her amber, cat-like eyes and bold body piercing hardware that started with her face and then disappeared under her clothing. The story around the team was she was in a bomb disposal unit early on in life with the Australian military and got caught by a blast that embedded several metal shards into her upper body. After she got out of the hospital, she became fixated on body piercings, adding several done using the reclaimed metal from that blast. She considered them good luck pieces. It was never discussed among the team, even as locker room discussion, exactly where those good luck pieces were installed on her person.

Tina drew so close to McLaren that he could hear some of the metal piercings clank before she offered, "McLaren, you asked for skilled drivers, for top pay to do a job. I've been through combat, defused bombs for a living, driven long haul trucks across Australia, and I can assure you that I'm not a shy retiring violet who is worried if somebody will see her tinkling out on the desert! I can say tinkling, right? As far as my other body piercings that are under my clothes, if I show them to you, can I have the job then?"

Not many confrontational conversations ever brought McLaren up short, but Tina's challenge left him incapable of a reply. Before he could gather his wits about him and respond, Tina moved closer and offered seductively, yet loud enough for Mohawk to hear, "If I show you mine, I want to see yours."

McLaren was visibly distracted by the sultry voice, but Mohawk laughed uproariously and boldly stated, "That's my Tina. Always derailing a man's thoughts so she can get what she wants. Har! Har!

"McLaren, how about giving Tina that driving assignment we just discussed, so I can get the crane boom loaded and we can be on our way?"

Tina stepped back a few paces with a smirk on her face, knowing that she had won the job over McLaren's protest.

McLaren sulked somewhat but grumbled, "Alright, but no whining when you get all that I told you would happen."

Still smirking, Tina nodded her head.

Mohawk continued, "Come on, honey. Let's go get you suited up to drive that rig. Oh, don't forget to pack some traveling clothes and gear, but not too much as we must travel light. Just don't forget that real sheer black nightie that I like so well. Growl."

McLaren said under his breath as they hurried away, "I'm going to regret this. What a pair."

The caravan's journey was not a forced march, nor was it a leisurely pace. The crew groused as all crews do, but Mohawk and Tina were surprisingly quiet and certainly did their fair share. By the time they got to the Kookaburra mine, McLaren had forgotten his objection to having a woman on the team.

When they arrived at site, there was an eeriness to the huge open pit mine that made everyone feel uneasy. There was none of the usual sounds that one would hear if all the equipment were in full swing, and the quiet itself was somewhat unnerving. Even the old timers seemed a little reluctant to boldly drive into the operational area so close to dark.

McLaren sensed the crew's uneasiness but recognized they couldn't let that overcome their mission. He stated, "I want the crane and booms driven into the pit where we can begin assembly tomorrow. We'll need it operational so we can hoist the buried earth movers out and then place them where they can be worked on.

"Tina, you, and Hoyt check your loads before you head down that steep grade to the staging area. We have just enough daylight to get that far before we call it a day."

Tina and Hoyt scrambled to their rigs and dutifully checked to see that their loads were secure before setting off down the steep incline to the target area with Tina in the lead. Hoyt gave her enough room so that both flatbeds were not competing for space to maneuver once at the bottom. Tina's experience required she use the lowest gear as she cautiously drove down the steep incline. To the untrained eye, it seemed slower than necessary. Once she got to the bottom, she waved for Hoyt to follow.

By now the sun was dipping lower, and everyone wanted to get the other flatbed down there so they could clean up for supper and sleep. Hoyt was a little tired from the drive but was convinced that if she could do it, he could do it too. It was a poor judgement call.

The lower gear would have given him a slower descent, but he chose a higher gear which had him traveling too fast and picking up unnecessary speed. Once the rig was traveling too quickly, he naturally responded by braking. He then applied too much brake, which set the fastening ties used to hold the boom to the flatbed against the weighted inertia of the boom that only wanted to keep traveling forward. With the extra weight and unnatural strain, the ties gave way and the boom shot forward, crushing the cab and Hoyt in the blink of an eye. The rig stalled out with no driver at the controls and slowly ground to a halt in full view of everyone.

Tina leaped from her cab and ran to Hoyt's flatbed, only to see that she was too late. Realizing that he never knew what hit him, she sank down to her knees, crying for poor young lad. Everyone stared in disbelief at the surreal event, which even had McLaren in tears. Mohawk noted to himself that in all the years he and Tina had been together, he had never seen her cry.

After what seemed like an eternity, Mohawk, with tears running down his cheeks, turned to McLaren and softly offered, "I'm sorry, McLaren. I truly am."

The event was considered by all to be a bad omen, and McLaren knew that superstition could ruin any operation, if left unchecked. He resolved that this kind of fatality wouldn't happen again and that they would restore the site to operational status as soon as possible. He felt he owed it to Hoyt for his sacrifice.

McLaren finally steeled himself and faced George as he asked, "George, can you use our communications gear to get a chopper out here, please? We need to send someone home early."

George, also struck by the horrible scene, could only nod and quickly left to make the necessary call.

CHAPTER 49

Time - Out

Brayson was sullen and very introspective, but Mayor Perez was livid at the edict. While Perez was busy setting up a conference bridge, Brayson took out his cell phone and sent a text that read:

> Julie, Mayor Perez is being forced to go forward with the full ransom payment.

After the text was sent, Brayson quietly put his phone away to get ready for the conference call. Before she connected to the call, Brayson asked, "Do you want to alert your father not to put the art treasure diversion in play? It will save him and the museum a lot of trouble. They get the added benefit of being able to rest easier that it's not going into the hands of these extortionists."

Baby Perez paused the conference bridge setup tasks. After a long moment, she turned to Brayson. "I'm sorry you must watch my city council knuckle under to the ransom demands. I think you know that I'm not supporting this course of action, but time has run out and the vote is to pay the ransom. You and the IT team were unable to find or seal the breach in our security perimeter. The decision is out of my hands."

Brayson calmly offered, "Mayor Perez, I know you think that offering the painting was a useless exercise, but it did lead us to a massively encrypted data tunnel that we wouldn't have otherwise discovered. With your permission, I'd like to send a reply to the extortionists to see if we get any other clues from the backwash of our message. I won't pretend that it will give us enough to change the current strategy, but my team is working this problem and several others like it, so any additional information that we can provide will help."

Mayor Perez nodded, then with a slight smile said, "It pleases me to know that there is a team of people like you trying to fight the digital evils of this world. Yes send back a return message saying to stop the onslaught against my city, and we will complete the ransom transfer as demanded.

"You do realize once that transfer is completed your assignment here is over. I will see to it that you and your company are paid for your time here, but we are done with your services. I'll probably take some grief for paying your consulting fees because of the lost cause. However, we didn't take your advice, so I will simply point out that we contracted for technical consulting that we didn't choose to use. It's exactly like going to a doctor or lawyer but not taking their recommendation. The fees still stand, so I will have my way on this issue."

Brayson laughed softly. "It is exactly like what my former college coach used to say when we lost a game. He always got interviewed after a game. One important game that we lost, some journalist tried to pin him with a lousy question of, 'So your team lost this game and now you're out of the finals. How do you feel about that?' Always quite the gentleman, the coach replied, 'Sir, we did not lose the game. We only ran out of time.'

"Mayor Perez, we haven't lost completely, but for now we are out of time. I have some things to close out before departing. I need your permission to continue working them, off the clock of course."

Mayor Perez nodded and offered, "Don't stay too long. As they continue to see you, it will be a reminder of our failure to stop the extortionists. I don't want them taking out their hostility on you. That I cannot tolerate."

Brayson nodded. "I understand. Thank you, Baby, for everything. I wish I could have done more in the allotted time."

Mayor Perez face softened. "Me too." Then she gave him a quick hug and launched the conference call.

Julie asked, "Wolfgang, Quip, how soon can we have everything in place to trap the funds disbursement out of Spain? We received word the city buckled under the demands and are paying the ransom. While this is unfortunate, it does give us another chance to follow the money."

Quip responded, "ICABOD has Wolfgang's banking transaction tracking system already loaded. We weren't sure when the next opportunity might occur, so we left the program in idle mode. We can bring it up immediately. How much is this case's ransom?"

"It's for €50 million to be paid out of the city's operational checking account. Brayson gave me the bank routing code numbers, and they're in the chat window."

"Ah thanks, Jules. That's what we needed to launch the Watcher program. Wolfgang, are you ready?"

Wolfgang nodded.

ICABOD interrupted, "Gentlemen and Miss Julie, the funds are now in flight. I have initiated the Watcher program."

The video screen shifted to the visual tracking journey of the transfer. They saw the money as it traveled through the sanitizing metamorphoses designed to ultimately cloak the origin and destination bank accounts. ICABOD had added a 3-D graphic model perspective to Wolfgang's program so they could see how transactions moved or jumped from one system to the next. Each step added more destinations but sent ever smaller chunks of money down each route. They were all tense as the process took them through multiple layers of cascading accounts at different banks.

Finally, the trail led them to what Wolfgang had originally classified as an aggregating account. It was the one they had seen before. After a few minutes, Wolfgang announced, "Okay, we 'll leave it there for a while to see if all the €50 million ends up here. Julie, check back with us in twenty-four hours and we'll discuss what has accumulated."

Julie nodded her approval and agreed, "Let me know if anything unusual happens before then. I'll check back then. Thank you."

CHAPTER 50

Good game

The *Game Over* emblem was on the screen, which suggested the scenario had finished, but from the grins on their faces, it was difficult to determine who won and who lost. They both altered between grinning and chuckling.

Chairman Chang caught his breath and conveyed, "Dmitry, you old fool, you nearly had that last bag of euros. I can't believe you missed it, and I snagged it. Even though you amassed the most points, I think the intermediate profits I made were substantial."

Dmitry nodded and chuckled. "Chang, it was a well-played scenario with just enough changes from the last time we played to be fresh and exciting. The overall monies to be transferred are even more than I had planned. These incremental winnings are so much fun.

"This session was great. Did you like the female that looked as if she was going to be had by Groddo? The lifelike screams were, well, exhilarating to say the least. Though, if I want to take a woman, I prefer she beg for more. How about you, Chang, how do you like your women? Have you ever been so attracted to a woman that you were tempted to give her anything?"

Chairman Chang looked thoughtful and then faced Dmitry's image and answered, "All my women have begged. It's the way of them. I do like it when they ask for more and show off, really suggesting they like it all, not just as an obligation. Love, hmmm… no, I don't think I have ever really been in love, though I have desperately wanted one or two to the point of distraction. Why do you ask, old man, are you finding your way with a new woman?"

Dmitry grinned and replied, "Finding my way, what an interesting suggestion. I think that is a valid suggestion. Each woman is different and requires a different finesse, I think. But, no, this was just an idle question. I'll let you know when the funds are available for us to select the door. I get first choice. Tomorrow. I have a full day, so the day after at the earliest."

Chairman Chang replied, "That suits my schedule as well. Good modifications to the games, Dmitry. Pass along my congratulations to the team. We might want to consider a more commercial version of a few of these. I bet we could find a market for these games in Europe."

Dmitry agreed and disconnected after a modest salute.

Dmitry waited until things were shut down from the game perspective and moved toward his desk, looking as if he was going to do some work. The game had been good, but if he was honest, he was distracted. The staff had all left, and he decided to try and engage in conversation with Natasha, if she was in the chat room. He logged in and found that she was logged in as well. They acknowledged each other and moved to a private room.

Natasha chatted, "Mikael, I was hoping you might find some time to reach out. I hope all is well with you."

Dmitry replied, "I have been busy but have thought about you a great deal. How is your grandma?"

"We both get along as best we can. She needs some additional help getting around our apartment, so I was able to get her a walker, which helps when I am at work. And you, Mikael, how are you? Solving all the problems of the world?"

He replied, "Har, har, my dear Natasha, I don't really solve world problems, but I do get to influence many things. I like to think that I give people enough details to make an informed choice. Do you think that you make a difference in your place in the world?"

After a long pause she responded, "I think I make a difference for my family. I long to do more and be more, but I need to help my grandma."

He asked, "Is this something you wish to escape?"

Again, a long pause on her part before she typed, "These days, I escape into my books and online. That is enough for now. Perhaps in the future I can be free to go out and see more of the world, to laugh and perhaps hold hands with someone special."

Dmitry felt this was a critical response to capture her interest. He thought about the best way to respond and perhaps gain some of her trust. He decided on the direction of his next move and entered, "Natasha, it is so brave of you to tell me. Wouldn't it be a good end to a workday to sit in front of a fire and discuss a good book, or plan an escape of sorts to a park, with the colors of fall blazing like a raging fire of reds, oranges, deep purple and yellow? Or perhaps you'd prefer the ultimate pilgrimage for touring one of the world's most impressive collections of Impressionist art treasures housed at the Hermitage in St. Petersburg?"

Natasha quickly replied, "Oh, you taunt me with such lofty travel destinations, but yes, I'd love to be a part of that scene you create so well with your words. You seem to have a touch of poet. Hum, a sensitive man and one so powerful. I had no idea from your profile that you possessed this complexity. It's not found often in a man. It makes me wonder if your spoken conversation would be as delightful as your written words, my dear."

Dmitry grinned and asked, "Would you consider an escape with me for a few hours of walking through a park, and you could judge for yourself? I'd furnish a picnic if you like."

A long pause again for her response. He worried that perhaps he had pushed too much too fast. He looked at a few of the photos she had published that captured her womanly lines and wondered what it would feel like to touch her. Worried she might have left, he typed, "Are you still there, Natasha? I am sorry if I was too bold, but you seem to bring that quality out in me, like no other before."

She finally replied, "I'm here. I'm simply sad. You sound like someone I'd like to get to know, but I cannot afford to leave my grandma and spend hours with you. As much as I think I would like to get to know you, I simply cannot leave her for long periods of time, possibly repeatedly. I must consider the long-term results of my actions. I'm sorry, Mikael, so sorry."

Dmitry was back into the military mode of 'identify the target and go get it'. He responded, "I can help with that aspect, and it seems only fair, if I am taking you away, that I would help you find help to stay with your grandma so you can relax and enjoy yourself. You do leave her alone some now when you work, correct?"

"Mikael, I don't leave her alone ever. I have enough to pay someone I trust to stay and watch when I do work, but not when I am not working. That would be wasteful, and we have nothing to waste. No, I think it better we stop meeting in the chat room, and I go back to chatting with people of no consequence like your friend Andrei. He is just a flirt and has no plan of action. Silly, online, meaningless conversations. You, I fear, offer more than I can accept."

Dmitry was bordering on frantic. He wanted to continue this relationship. This beautiful lady was different from anything he had ever known. The barriers to attain her were nothing he had ever encountered. He finally replied, "I do not want to end our chats. I want to find a solution to this problem. Please don't let a small thing like a caretaker for your grandma stall our getting to know one another. I can help. I have funds. I can send you money, just tell me how much."

She quickly replied, "I cannot, would not do that. I do not do anything that I cannot earn. It is my responsibility. I need to go now. Goodbye, Mikael, I will think of you."

He quickly entered, "Not goodbye, Natasha. Think about our reading books, discussing art, and walking in the park. I will be online tomorrow around the same time. Please consider my offer to help. I can transfer funds to anywhere, and no one need ever know. Please reply that you will at least consider my offer."

"I will think about it, Mikael."

He was lost when the chat room signaled, he was the only one in it. Having no idea where she really was, he thought about asking Konstantin more details that he might have uncovered regarding Natasha. Tomorrow, he would figure out a way to get that information. It shouldn't be difficult. Konstantin was, after all, devoted to him.

CHAPTER 51

Once kind, now shy

Ernesto kept a leisurely pace as he took in the sights of Macau. He was doing the Western tourist thing of taking pictures with his cell phone and annotating each picture with a brief comment as to where and when the photo was taken. He stopped in what looked to be an Internet café and ordered a light snack to go with his coffee so he could use the free Wi-Fi access. Once he was linked up with the Wi-Fi, he launched an encrypted tunnel so he could exchange messages without the Chinese government knowing what was being said.

His first message began:

> Hi Julie. I'm in the destination city and will begin snooping as we discussed. I'm not far from the target

Julie responded:

> Good. Now, we are tracking you using our satellite geolocation program but that also means someone else can monitor you as well. Recommend you use boisterous, obnoxious Western tourist from one of the fly-over states in the U.S. routine number three

Ernesto typed back:

Julie I'm already there with my hair moussed and brushed straight up in front to really capture the goober look

Julie took a little longer to respond but sent:

Uh E don't try to hide with a spotlight and megaphone as your cloaking apparatuses, okay? We'll monitor your progress. If a problem occurs hit the panic button and we will access you from here. Use the key word Mother anywhere in your sentence and we are in rescue mode

Ernesto shot back:

Har! Har! I just love it when you worry about me! Yes, I know my exit strategy is Chen. Well wish me luck 'cause I'm on the prowl now

Ernesto fully embraced his role as the stereotypical, never-been-out-of-the-county tourist. Anyone nearby got asked to take a photo with him in the foreground of whatever artwork/decoration that he came across. He played the part of an excited Western tourist, in Midwestern plaids and jeans, with occasional bursts of country/western songs, so well that he was forced to do mostly selfies after performing for twenty minutes. The hostesses and greeters gave up on trying to steer him to more obscure areas where he wouldn't be such a spectacle, which left him to range freely throughout the casino. He toned down his antics for some more serious watching, but he occasionally flared up with a little song and dance just so the camera monitors had something to watch.

Ernesto surveyed the casino floor and the modest cafés in the adjoining areas. He was about to move on when he caught sight of a couple of very familiar faces. He moved over closer to their intended walking path and turned around to take a selfie just as they moved past him. He turned the video portion on to record everything. As if not content enough to get the selfie, he turned to the two powerfully built Asian men and stated, "Fellas, I'm from the U S of A, and I was hoping to soak up some of your local culture before heading home. Would y'all mind if I get a picture of you two boys and me for my mother's sister, Aunt Inez? She would be so tickled at seeing her nephew with some local boys. What do you say? I got a couple of shiny coins for each of you to make it worth your while."

As the two men studied the hick version of Ernesto, the third man offered, "I don't believe these two local boys are interested in having their picture taken with a Midwestern boy."

Ernesto, not willing to drop the request too easily, wandered a little closer to them. He was about to hand them each the promised shiny coin when he stopped short. Studying Won's facial scars, Ernesto blurted out. "Whoa! I bet that wound must have really hurt! Ouch! How about two coins for each of you, but I want a good side view of that bear scratch on your face. Say, buddy, do you mind taking a few snaps for me while I pose with these two fellers?"

Won was not amused and grabbed Ernesto but, as usual, said nothing.

Ton moved closer to Ernesto and quietly conveyed, "Mr. U S of A, you have worn out your welcome in our casino. Unless you want to have the same kind of wounds across your face, I suggest you apologize and leave quickly. He hasn't enjoyed his mid-morning tourist dismemberment yet, but you could be the lucky recipient."

Won was now tightening his grip on Ernesto's collar to the point that air seemed hard to get. Finally, after a few tense moments, Ernesto offered, "Geezus, fellers! You seem a might edgy. Okay, so you don't want your picture taken for my Aunt Inez, alright! No need to go off the deep end and act like a couple of junkyard dogs! I'll get someone else who's not quite so edgy. Forget I ever asked."

Won smiled his usual crooked smile just before he delivered a hard punch into Ernesto's stomach, causing him to double over. Ton quickly raised his arm and summoned one of the security guards over to where Ernesto was still gasping for air, and stated, "Security, this man has had too much to drink and has become belligerent to our staff and patrons. Please show him off the premises immediately."

Ernesto soon found himself outside the casino and harshly tossed to the cab area where he stumbled to the ground. Ernesto raised up off the pavement in time to see his escorts issuing instructions to the doorman not to let him back in. The cab operator quickly hustled Ernesto into his cab and sped away. Once out of the area, Ernesto said, "Thanks, Chen. I appreciate the quick response. You'd think those two would have been a little gentler with me after our earlier kindness."

Chen queried, "You know those two? I mean, everyone in this part of the world knows them, but I am surprised you knew them. How is it that they didn't acknowledge you?"

Ernesto smirked and replied, "Oh, you know how some people are. Once they get back on top, they don't acknowledge those kind folks that got them back home after they were so far down on their luck. Not to worry though. I got my pictures for my Aunt Inez. I'm sure these photos will be very interesting, once they get where they are going."

CHAPTER 52

It always matters

Summit concluded, "That's it, fellas. The CAs are installed on all the machinery here, and every piece of equipment must have the three-way handshake with the issuing CA to proceed with its next instruction. Massoud, if our theory's correct, nothing should try to operate out of sequence. And any bogus instruction sets from an untrusted source should simply be ignored."

Massoud, David, and Marco all nodded in unison.

Then Summit asked, "Are we ready to test our theory? And, more importantly, do we have our protocol analyzers in position to watch for malicious code or bogus instructions trying to enter the environment?"

David questioned, "What's our contingency if we do see malicious code enter the system, and equipment begins to malfunction again?"

Massoud, somewhat indignantly, stated, "That's not possible. The main reason these systems went berserk was because they were not configured correctly. We have corrected the installation oversight, and now machine-to-machine instructions will only be accepted if it comes with positive proof that it is a legitimate participant in our closed system. This center can operate as designed."

Marco politely offered, "Massoud, David is only thinking of our next steps in case there is a repeated failure. It's good to have plans of fallback positions in the unlikely event that the center goes sideways. Your theory is sound, and I agree that the machine-to-machine instructions should not deviate. But if they do, what is our response? I believe it's a fair question."

Summit quickly added, "It's a smart question, gentlemen. Marvin just got most of the center in shape to resume operations, and we are going to ask to reengage the same routines that threw everything into chaos and trashed the entire center. I really don't want to face Marvin and ask him to stand by while we turn every-thing back on without the contingency plans clearly outlined. If something goes wrong, and we're not prepared for that possibility, I'm sure that *we*, gentlemen, will be put into the next shipping containers to Honduras.

"Now let me ask, do we have a KILL program that we can launch at a moment's notice that will terminate all machine activity?"

David grinned and nodded. "Yes, we do. It's the electric power feed going into the building. We throw the power switch to off, and none of the distribution equipment can execute another instruction set whether it is good or bad."

Summit studied them a moment with his *Uh-huh* look before stating, "I had something with a little more finesse in mind, David. I was thinking of an overarching command to simply have everything freeze in mid-operations. Then we wouldn't have to work in the dark with flashlights in hand. This is relatively expensive equipment, and simply doing a power-off action might cause some major equipment damage."

Marco offered, "We could have Marvin's people standing by each machine and, on our signal, power cycle down each piece of equipment, which would leave the lights on for us to work through our next steps."

Massoud boldly stated, "I'm with you one thousand percent, gentlemen! But I'm confident your extra planning is not going to be needed."

They all grinned at Massoud.

Summit said, "Alright, let me bring Marvin into our discussion, so he is on board with the plan."

Massoud suggested, "Should we go with you in case we have to tie Marvin back into a chair for his own good?"

Summit chuckled at the image, though he was certain Marvin might not feel the same. "While I don't think that will be necessary, I think it would be good for all of you to hear the discussion. Let's go do it."

Marvin listened politely to the plan and responded, "Gentlemen, I have reservations about executing on this plan. We just got everything flowing again, even though the center still needs a lot of work. I'm sure you've got your agenda ordered to your liking, but frankly, it's not to mine. To be blunt, I really don't want the center to go back to the way that it was with all of us out of work.

"If you've fixed everything and it works as advertised, then all these people will only get a modest, one-time paycheck. If we say no, then at least we have jobs and a purpose. Tell me how we can see it from your point of view?"

Massoud, David, and Marco were all chastened by the honest statement looked at the floor.

Massoud offered, "You're right. If this all works as before, we three go back to being guards again. I'm not anxious to have that happen, but I want to know that I made a difference. I'd like the headlines to know that I helped restore the situation, as well as made it more secure. Don't you want to see if we can beat the problem?"

Summit intervened, "Gentlemen, we're near our 48-hour deadline to prove or disprove our cure to this problem. You should also know that the Constellation is being blackmailed to the tune of fifty million U.S. dollars. If they pay, then there certainly won't be any jobs left as overseers to the site operations. The company won't simply go back to the way it was doing business. But perhaps there's a labor compromise to be had, but only if we can stop the machine-to-machine poisoning from occurring ever again. We need to try this theory. Marvin, please let us try and help us."

Marvin sighed and looked beaten. "Yeah, I figured you'd have to play that card. Alright, let me get some people rounded up to watch the equipment and pull out the non-essentials. If the machinery goes sideways again, I don't want anyone unnecessarily hurt. Not on my watch."

Marvin began to put people in place at all the key areas to monitor and, if necessary, disconnect equipment should it go rogue again.

Summit turned to his three teammates and announced, "Gentlemen, we are a go. Massoud, let's throw the switch and give me the good news."

Massoud, David, and Marco scrambled to their machines, and Massoud hollered, "Okay, my one thousand percent confidence is in play, make my day."

The distribution floor shuddered as the electricity surged forward to supply the equipment with the power to perform the instructions in a carefully orchestrated manner. From their elevated command center, they could see the equipment behaving per the instructions. Materials were moving from station to station correctly again, and the distribution center returned to its original symphony of product distribution.

Then David bellowed, "I've got him! I've got him. The rogue code. I've got him coming in trying to access the equipment."

Marco yelled, "Me too. Whoa, what a flood. They're hitting everything at once."

Summit ran outside to the catwalk with his cell phone and started video recording all the equipment to see if their theory had worked. Summit's grin evolved into shouts of glee as he videoed the distribution floor. Not one piece of equipment deviated from its programming, and no disruption occurred. He waved to Marvin and gave the all-clear sign. The man that had rectified the order dutifully acknowledged.

Summit went back inside to the command center and reported, "Gentlemen, all's good on the distribution floor. I videoed the normal operations, and I'm now going to send it to the contracting officer with our success notes. Please keep tracking on the bogus code flooding into our systems and give me any information you can on the source."

Summit happily uploaded the video to his contracting officer and sent another text saying the systems were back online. Everyone in the command center was pumped and elated at the digital victory.

Momentarily, Summit's phone went off, and he promptly answered in his cheeriest of voices. "Good day, sir. I trust you found the text message and video proof to your liking?"

Summit was stunned to hear the caller say, "Summit, the good news comes a little too late to improve the situation. The ransom was disbursed. The 48-hour window expired thirty minutes ago, and when we didn't hear from you…well, you must understand our position.

"Thank you for trying, but the show is over. Your contract is now complete. We need to debrief here, so gather up your belongings and let's close this chapter out."

Summit slumped into the closest chair almost completely numb and unable to speak. Massoud came over gently and patted his shoulder as he quietly offered, "I suspected that, even with all our efforts, it wouldn't matter anyway. But, Summit, I want to thank you for letting us at least try because it mattered to us."

David and Marco both nodded with frowns.

CHAPTER 53

Are we there yet?

Juan launched the video conference bridge for the meeting, and the team promptly joined. Not everyone's bandwidth allowed more than the audio. Juan noticed those on video appeared tired and unsatisfied.

Julie and Juan felt alive and fresh for the call. Julie greeted the team with a bright smile and warm tone. "Hi, all! Good to see everyone. I know you aren't on the same time zones, so I want to express my thanks for the effort to join. We all have a lot of activities in motion. Some of this briefing is to relay what's happening in the background, as well as a quick update of current happenings. We need to know where you need extra help. I'll cover my piece last. Please, Tyler, you begin, and we'll go around the screen."

Tyler began. "The items fenced from the highly engineered robberies here in Pittsburgh have led us to an address in Amsterdam that routinely functions as a drop point for questionable goods and tainted services, or what I like to call QGATS. We got as far as that QGATS hub before our jurisdiction authority dried up. Then our questions received no response. We're fairly confident the package was forwarded on, even though the wire transfer got clipped a modest percentage for services rendered.

I suspect it had only the single additional hop to the last destination. We've poked around trying to find any other clues, but without help from Interpol we're stalled."

Julie inclined her head with a smile. "Good tracking, Tyler. The money trail you tracked to Amsterdam gave us a good clue for where to look. You should know we watched the funds transfer make it into Russia. They were careful to run their acquisitions through a third party, but the receivers were sloppy. Lazy mistakes are beginning to show. Who's next?"

Ernesto seized the opportunity to report next. "Julie, you saw the video of those gents at the casino I sent you. I thought you might have laughed at seeing the Asian twins again, only this time we didn't have to transport their drugged bodies out. Although it would have been better on my stomach if they had been. Good catch by you and Juan on the third person. His name is Jamie.

"I did some digging, and it appears he's got an IT job at the casino. What is odd about his relationship here is that he seemed like he was being escorted by Won and Ton, rather than functioning as a network computer technician. What I got from his teammates is that he is apparently on special assignment for the big cheese here at the casino. His team members complained about having to pick up his workload. I was also told about his girlfriend; however, I could get nothing useful out of her. Her name is Frieda, according to one of the team members. Frankly, she's too scared to say anything."

Juan mused out loud, "Most likely he was caught pilfering from the slots. We witnessed that activity while we were there. If he's any good to the casino boss, it may be that his special assignment is probably the price for them both to stay alive. Good sleuthing, Ernesto. See if you can get some additional information on his specific talents."

Brayson reluctantly took his turn. "I'm afraid that my news isn't good. The city council overruled the position Mayor Perez and I maintained against these bandits and paid the ransom. I've been instructed to disengage from this assignment and leave. I indicated that I had a few more things to do, but that won't last long.

"Basically, I'm hoping to catch a new attack in progress so we could stay engaged. But that may not happen. If you have any other suggestions, please let me know."

The team remained quiet. Julie commented, "Stick with it for the time being."

After a few moments of silence, George asked, "Alright if I take a turn? My news isn't much better. The Consortium paid their ransom, and I'm working for free here.

"I'm hoping to get into some of these equipment sensors and controllers and learn how they were commandeered to ruin everything and force the machines to fight.

"The on-site effort didn't start out well. We transported one of the equipment drivers after he was crushed. It was not a result of the vehicles being commandeered but more that he was simply driving too fast on the slippery sand. It put a real damper on the effort, so I would really like to stay engaged for the time being."

Everyone on the conference fell silent at George's report for a moment.

Julie offered, "Let me express our sorrow for the loss there, George. That was McLaren's nephew, right? I'll have flowers and a sympathy card sent on behalf of the team."

With a very glum face, Summit offered, "Julie, I'm sorry, but we weren't able to reprogram the equipment here at the Constellation distribution center and bring everything back online fast enough to meet the deadline. The ransom was paid thirty minutes ahead of us bringing everything back online. The solution to add in the certificates of authorities prevented any reinfection, though an attack started the moment that we put things back online. I feel like I let the locals down."

Juan interrupted and looked sternly into the video camera. "I'm sorry, I disagree. You commandeered on-site technical resources at a moment's notice, bargained for a time extension, and defeated the poisonous code that took a distribution center the size of Rhode Island offline. Keep failing like that, mister, and we'll all be working for you!"

The team laughed a bit, and the humor helped take some of the edge off everyone's nerves. Even Summit managed to smile.

Julie added, "Also, we have had our money tracking programs up and in watch mode just for this kind of contingency. Summit, we followed the ransom monies. We've confirmed that each one of you are working on extortion cases that use the same money anonymizing trail to move the ransom monies.

"Ernesto, you're local to one of the final destinations, with Juan and me working on the other. It is important that each of you continue to try and work your respective cases for the likely reoccurrence of another extortion round. At the very least, you can now help to stop or slow the attacks with the information we've collected. Review each other's reports so you can know what else to look for.

"Yes, I know several of you have been told to pack your bags but stay the course. Continue to hunt for more digital forensic evidence. Our customers may have paid the ransom, but they are not rid of these bandits."

Mercedes chimed in, "Julie, our airline was seriously considering paying their ransom as well. Then Jim put his foot down, with the authority of the FAA, saying no. The planes are still grounded, but no ransom monies are in flight. Of that, I'm certain."

EZ contributed, "I've been setting up satellite communication tunnels in some of the affected areas to keep team members talking. With Quip and his computer's help, we have been able to insert ourselves into the encrypted communication tunnel and have a better understanding of what is going on. Not enough to stop it yet, but I am working on it.

"Juan, George, and Tyler, the geolocational disruption that affected your areas is also a top priority of mine. I have a routine to at least allow for it, but I have yet to find the real start and stop routine. This has the potential of hurting thousands upon thousands, so it cannot be ignored. Once these bandits are caught, they will be prosecuted or worse, I promise."

George and Brayson both offered, "Thanks for your help, EZ."

"Yes, EZ, thanks for all the support you give us." Julie agreed, "We know more than when we started these cases. They're related. Even though the extortionists have their attack vector, we now have ours. Excellent work, team. Please stay the course and keep working your respective assignments. We are almost there."

Everyone nodded, and the video conference quickly disbanded.

Several hours later, Juan listened intently and asked, "Do you think that'll work? I mean, I like to gamble as much as the next guy, but this seems like a bit of a reach."

Julie frowned, then presented her thoughts. "We can't go file a complaint or go to court for a cease-and-desist order. Plus, there are the ill-gotten gains that, even if they wanted to surrender, their governments won't. No, this is the only way to put a stop to it. I think in this case, we are the only avenue for judge and jury.

Justice and fair play scripts were removed from their playbooks as soon as they decidedly affected the many individuals and organizations with such harmful intentions."

Juan solemnly nodded, knowing the difficultly of his wife's decision. "Point taken, sweetheart. Let's get started. We have lots of buttons to push in perfect sequence to gain the proper outcome."

Juan began the outline for the plans, and Julie added various details and steps, then moving details around. The plans took shape becoming like a movie in slow motion. Juan paused and smiled as he stated. "You know, darling, I must tell you the first time I met you, I had no idea of your many talents. I'd like to go on record and add," he wiggled his eyebrows, "I just love playing with our babies' mother."

Julie smiled and leaned over adding a generous kiss.

CHAPTER 54

Now, how that works...

Pittsburgh's Mayor Barker, practically shouted into the speaker attached to his phone set. "Are you out of your mind, Como?! You haven't figured out yet how these jerks got into and poisoned the ALI database for 911 calls and now you want two tickets to follow your lead to Amsterdam? Your badge barely gets you a cup of coffee here in Pittsburgh! How much weight do you think a U.S. city detective is going to pull in any European city?"

Tyler muted the phone, looked Como in the eye and quietly indicated, "I told you this was a poor idea. He won't be receptive to our recommendation without some proof points."

The mayor barked, "Tyler, I thought we had an understanding. I said you could work with Como on this case, but only if you kept his tedious, self-serving, boneheaded brain-freeze ideas formulating. Please tell me that you're not infected with his mental debris from the moronic halo spheres surrounding him?" He inhaled and growled "Or worse, received a near lethal dose of stupidity injections by working too closely."

Tyler unmuted the phone. "No, sir, I've not received any transfusions of nonstandard or undesirable mental coagulates. However, I would point out that Como's request is not a completely self-gratifying request to get the city to pay for our sleuthing efforts. We are confident that the source of the attacks originated in Europe, close to Russia. Tracking the funds back to the source, we can potentially intercept the assailant. This can lead us to how these criminals were able to poison the ALI database."

Mayor Barker considered Tyler's logic for a few moments. His steady voice mandated, "Look, no more cranial flatulency, gentlemen. I've got my hands full with political blowback at not having the perpetrators behind bars. Having to pay for you two to go to Amsterdam before all the analysis is finished is a non-starter. But, if you can find where the corruption occurred here in our emergency services and if those results point to Amsterdam, I'll authorize your captain to fund the travel. If you get that far, please make sure that Interpol is looped in before you board a plane. Do you understand, Como?"

Not wanting to debate this issue any longer with the mayor, Como grinned at Tyler and confidently replied. "Yes, Mayor Barker. We'll work the issue and get back to you." With that he disconnected the call.

Como looked at Tyler a moment, then wrinkled his nose and questioned, "Cranial flatulency?"

Tyler nodded. "Yeah, I thought that was a harsh comment too."

Tyler studied the screen and ignored Como's return to the conference room. Without glancing in Como's direction, Tyler said, "Thanks for getting us in to talk to PSAP to go over their records for the evening of the downtown heists. I also went back a ways to see if there were any other anomalies for 911 calls, and I found one not long before the big incident we're working on.

"In that case, the PSAP agent told the emergency caller that they should hang up and call for emergency service in their own country of Poland. It took a little convincing on the part of the caller to persuade the dispatcher that the location coordinates on her screen were hopelessly wrong. For that to be true, someone would be inside the wireless carrier's network. I'd bet this incident was a proof of concept and precursor to our event.

"What I find stunning is that the ALI database that everyone uses in their building of a local PSAP appears to be accurate, with no tampering. My original thinking was that the ALI database was tampered with and that was the source of the problem. However, all the information looks to be correct and there is no evidence of tampering with the database twice."

Como tilted his head appearing confused. "What do you mean, twice?"

Tyler turned toward Como using his hands for emphasis, clarified, "If they uploaded or tampered with the database, they'd have to do it twice. Once to modify it for their nefarious purposes and then a second time to restore it to make it appear untarnished. There's nothing but the standard routine uploads, all done according to procedure. This suggests that their attack entered and arrived from somewhere else."

Como frowned and squinted as he asked, "Okay, so where could this disinformation impact the dispatch process? The public carrier routes the call to the proper PSAP based on the ALI database, and the call lands in the emergency services center where they do a cross reference street locator look up. This process lasts a few seconds to promptly answer the caller and map to their location. Where would you put equipment to change that process, bright boy?"

Ignoring Como's taunt, Tyler's eyes returned to the screen and noticed something in the database which made him smile. He let go a soft whistle. "Well, I'll be. Como, look at this." He pointed at several items on the screen. "Apparently, all these downtown locations had their electronic alarm systems upgraded to run over shared media alongside their Internet data. They've all upgraded to run Voice over IP for their voice services. Their alarm systems are also using this upgraded technology."

Como began to fade from the technical explanation, which Tyler noted. When Como started to nod off, Tyler spoke up, with a slight smile on his face. "Detective, I sense this briefing is putting you to sleep. It would be embarrassing in this public setting to inadvertently have your clothes fall off again."

Como snapped to full alert. "I'm not drifting off. I was merely contemplating what you said with my eyes closed. Please continue."

Still smiling, Tyler continued, "These businesses all were using IP addresses that were supposed to be hard coded to each of these locations. Can we get the alarm company on the phone to see if their mapping of IP addresses was tampered with?"

Como with eyes wide, answered, "Yeah, but wouldn't that be as easily spotted as tampering with the ALI database? Like you suggested, it requires two changes which would be readily spotted."

Tyler nodded and concurred, "Correct. If they say no changes were done before or after our event, then one explanation remains. Someone or something issued machine-to-machine code instructions at the point of the signaling event and told the reporting alarm system to use a different IP address. The result of that would put the emergency vehicle en route to the wrong location."

Como struggled to grasp the explanation. Tyler sensed Como's technical expertise wasn't on par for this level of detail.

Tyler clarified, "At the point when one machine is handing off information to another, a vicious software program gave instructions to give incorrect information to the next piece of equipment. The new bogus instructions were preplanned and done in real time, resulting in record tampering in the admin logs.

"Think of it like this, if you're directing traffic at a busy intersection following a tried-and-true process things are golden. If your relief comes in to take over and routes traffic in a destructive manner while you are gone, there's no record just the traffic jam or wrecks."

Tyler saw the light bulb shimmer to a glow over Como's head, but in seconds it faded to dark. Como asked, "How could we prove that? Is there any place where we could catch those malicious instructions being given or what piece of equipment was issuing those wrong instructions?"

Tyler thought for a moment and said, "The information being sent from the location appears to be fine, and the PSAP lookup appears to be accurate. However, as it is not, the only place you could make the interception is inside the public carrier. Wouldn't it be nice if we could look at their records the day of the downtown event to see if their logs show any anomalies? Like maybe an unaccounted-for IP address in their system logs?"

Como smiled and offered, "You know, the last time I had to work with their technicians, they groused about having to keep those log files and calling records for so long in their systems. The reason they disliked it was because we kept coming in to access their records and finding important information in our investigations. Funny how that works."

Tyler smiled slightly and agreed, "Indeed."

CHAPTER 55

The games continue

Dmitry felt on top of the world. He skillfully extracted some critical data from Konstantin on the potential whereabouts of Natasha. The unsuspecting confidant provided the details, along with a whining session on her not taking their conversation to the next level. Dmitry hadn't the fortitude to relate the lost battle that Konstantin faced on that front. Dmitry felt that he had a real argument in his favor with Natasha's grandma's care that he was anxious to propose. She joined him in the chat room twice since he'd first offered the walk in the park, with a book discussion and simple picnic. No doubt she was interested. He needed to find a way, just like designing any other battle plan. First though, he wanted to select the correct door in the session with Chang and play a new game.

Dmitry launched the video conference call a bit early. Konstantin briefed him on some recent changes to the games and provided a total amount for the door selection. Dmitry's confidence soared as he smiled into the camera once he noticed Chairman Chang connecting. His opponent's face appeared with his normal inscrutable look, but with a distinctive tilt to his chin that reminded Dmitry of a cat that had swallowed the mouse. Dmitry discarded the thought.

"Good day, Chang. I'm pleased the timing worked for us. I wanted to alert you that the technical team added a few changes to the airfield scenario, along with some new challenges in the desert entanglements. I'm promised these both offer new exciting incremental rewards, if either of these are selected from the wheel of misfortune, which of course is your choice this round.

"Two million euros have not cleared, but the rest completed its travels and is ready behind one of the doors. Before I choose, I wanted to tell you how much I'm enjoying our game sessions. You've helped me hone my skills in this area and kept my interest as a viable competitor. Who would have ever thought that two gentlemen of power and distinction would become so instrumental in next-generation video gaming?

"Now, my friend and business partner, to your point during our last conversation, there is an upcoming video gaming festival in London that I think we ought to consider attending as expert players, but also to test the waters as gaming developers and publishers using our hands-on demonstration facilities. I wanted you to consider this as a possibility with each of us contributing, say, two percent of our winnings for some marketing material development and general use applications for our different gaming scenarios into a game set. The pull to this London venue has been outstanding for users, players, developers, and those curious sorts. We could select another location, but I recalled you spent some time during your formative educational years in England and might enjoy the visit overall."

Chairman Chang had leaned closer to the monitor during this portion of Dmitry's discussion and raised an eyebrow that accentuated his interest. He appeared deep in thought, as if considering the proposal. He lifted a hand slightly in view of the screen as if to make a point. A few moments later, he commented, "Dmitry, I think you've done valuable research. I'm pleased that you appreciated my idea of commercialization as a product for the public. The amount you suggest is high but not outrageous. I'd recommend that the oversight of the games and marketing angle would require staff from both our organizations. I'd like you to consider that during your planning. There's a young man from the UK that I'm considering adding to my permanent staff for technology support. I hear he comes with recommendations. Would you consider this as an additional expert?"

Dmitry grinned and nodded. "My old friend, I think we need to draw up some papers of incorporation for this project and set the plan in motion." He chuckled and added, "Right after I win the doors and we play the next match. I am hoping for you to choose one of the newly refined versions."

Dmitry pressed the doors icon, and the screen displayed the three doors toward payout. He carefully looked at each of them searching for the winning sensation. He frowned at the lack of insight in the selection and chose in the middle. Door two opened to reveal an empty space that then displayed an image for an empty pot of gold. His spirits were somewhat dampened as he stated, "Your turn, Chang."

Chairman Chang stared at each of the doors, with the appropriate amount of concern and apprehension. He finally looked with almost defeat into the camera and grumbled, "I guess I'll select door one."

The door dissolved and inside was the picture of piles upon piles of euros with images of fireworks and flashes of what might be paparazzi photographers. He basked in the moment of triumph and broadly smiled. "Dmitry, I must say I'm delighted. I was uncertain when I picked the door. Your turn will come around again, old friend. Plus, we now have the potential for ongoing residual income from all our gaming fun with the new business venture. Spin, select, and let's play."

Dmitry brightened noticeably and pressed the application for the game selection. It seemed to spin a bit longer than usual and ended up on one of the newly revised game scenarios. He grinned and said, "Ready your avatar and let's play. I have a new gaming controller that I have been waiting to test drive. Today is the day."

Chairman Chang looked at Won and Ton, with their game faces in place out of view of the video camera, then grinned as he readied his avatar. After the preliminary activities were completed, he stated, "You're right, old man, today is the day to win!"

Dmitry and Chairman Chang had completed their session after nearly twelve hours of battle. No big prize was won by either of them, but some incremental pots were accumulated by each. The score was a bit in Dmitry's favor, with the euros from the levels in the chairman's count. They agreed to continue the game and see if the rest would provide a richer outcome. Dmitry had rested after sending the technicians home, knowing that on this holiday day he wouldn't be disturbed.

Dmitry woke in the late afternoon and heated up a meal he'd found in the office breakroom. It was quite good, and he didn't mind fending for himself in this matter. One of the benefits of his role was that he ate heartily, and the kitchen was well stocked, Evgeniya made certain. The woman loved to cook almost as much as she loved to eat. He added a touch of vodka and settled into his desk with his plate of food to munch on. He got ready to go to the chat room and make his proposition to Natasha. He chuckled as he realized that while he'd rested the scenario played out in his mind, which allowed some additional caveats to be inserted into the grandiose plan.

Dmitry logged into the now familiar chat room. He noted the current room participants, grateful that Konstantin was not present, though he doubted Mikael would be noticed. After a bit of hunting, he was pleased to locate Natasha. He used their agreed signal, and they both retreated to the private chat room. He used the tools to scan her uploaded pictures and settled upon the newest one, which also happened to be his current favorite. It was the one he had seen during his most recent dream of the woman.

She entered the room and typed, "How nice to see you, Mikael. I hoped you'd be on a break from your vast responsibilities. We must have some sort of fated timing as I've only been here myself for a few moments."

Dmitry smiled and felt even more confident in his planned approach. "I too am glad you are here, Natasha. I'm looking at your latest picture with pure admiration in your beauty. How is your grandma today? Is she well enough to move about and eating well?" He then did something very uncharacteristic and flipped the view to the larger screen on the wall in his office. She looked even more beautiful as her smile filled the empty wall. He realized he was thoroughly smitten.

Without hesitating, she replied, "Today is a good day. I even told my grandma about you. She'd like me to just leave her to see you, but I told her I could not. I have asked for some extra classes with the chance to do some tutoring in a month or so, which would result in some additional income if I'm accepted. We might then arrange that walk you keep mentioning in a couple of months, if you are still interested."

Dmitry faltered at that timeline and took a breath before he entered, "My dear Natasha, I fear I simply cannot wait that long to see you, or my heart will break. We must meet sooner. Of course, if I offend you, you don't have to share in the picnic or the three new books I acquired for you. Three of the ones you mentioned I was able to secure first editions of, which I want you very much to have."

A long pause occurred before she replied, "Mikael, I think that is way too extravagant of you. I cannot, however, resist knowing which ones, please?"

He laughed at his success and then inputted, "That is to be a surprise. Now let me tell you what I have in mind…"

He explained his plans to woo her by providing enough funds for her to care for her grandma with no strings attached. He wanted to immediately transfer the funds to her account and would not be put off. Dmitry carefully described what he thought he knew about where she worked, and if she did not agree to this small consideration, he would come on bended knee and beg her for a walk in the park. The exchange continued for over an hour with her offering objections and his resolving them one after another. He felt he had worn her down to the point of agreement and waited for her response.

Natasha entered, "Alright, Mikael, the account number to wire to is as follows …"

"Thank you, my dear one. It shall be done immediately. Once that is completed, would you please get a phone so we might actually speak to one another? I long to hear your lyrical voice, and then we can make our plans. I cannot wait."

"I will do it, and thank you, Mikael. I look forward to our meeting and finding common ground. I am sorry, but I need to disconnect and take care of Grandma and then do what you asked."

Dmitry logged out of the site but continued to stare at her picture on his big screen, envisioning her in his life for a while and perhaps soon naked beneath him.

He turned at the sound of a ragged breath to see a look of dismay on the face of Konstantin in the doorway of his office.

CHAPTER 56

Truce or consequences

Mercedes and Chuck worked on isolating the viral code spotted during the data extraction from the automated onboard devices. Once isolated, they executed various command programs against the virus to determine the entire range of its behavior. The two worked methodically from the lowest to the highest level of commands. Several times at the lower levels, there had been a response, which, when isolated, seemed relatively innocuous. Their back-and-forth conversation focused on the process, with one testing and the other documenting until they grew bleary eyed and switched. It was a tedious effort at best.

Jim and Sean reviewed and categorized the other data sets that Mercedes previously extracted. Their line-by-line manual comparison between each type of devices, to the manufacturers recommended settings in the prescribed technical documentation. To avoid missing a key difference through the boring effort, Sean wrote two short programs to automate a part of the review efforts that also ensured nothing was missed. The eyes could play tricks after a while, looking at the tiny groupings of letters and numbers.

The conversation in both areas of activity was limited to completing the tasks. Consequently, the fighting between the two men had not resumed. It was clear that time was a factor that would benefit from them cooperating. Mercedes getting stiff from the lack of movement and hunched position, broke the rhythm of their calling sequences and suggested, "Chuck, would you mind if I grab Jim and we go get some food? I need a bit of a walk, and I know we're all hungry. The noise from my stomach is annoying to me and I fear you'll bust out laughing when it gets too loud."

"He might not," interrupted Jim, "but I sure as hell would. Come on, Mercy, I am starved too."

Mercedes grinned when Jim reached out with his hand to assist her to her feet. He had startled her when he spoke so close. She hadn't realized he moved. That signaled it was past time for a break. Jim glanced down at her notes and looked at the pattern she'd highlighted.

"Does that mean that we're close to finding the problem, the solution, or both?" asked Jim with a hint of hope in his voice.

Mercedes replied, "I think both. There are a few more tests to run, but it seems clear. I just don't want to short cut the review too short. Chuck agreed with that approach earlier."

Chuck added, "That's correct. I think it is very close but doing all of the tests ensures we won't be surprised.

"In answer to your question, I think I have about two hours to go, so go walk around and grab a bite to eat. You two have been at it for too many hours without eating."

Sean interjected, "Yeah, I am sorry about the food. Chuck, I should have found a better way of telling you, man, sorry. You two take a break, and we can wrap this up. Jim and I are close to wrapping up the stare and compare, but Chuck and I may team up." Sean held up his hand at the look of apprehension between Jim and Mercedes and reassured, "No more fighting. We both have the same enemy, and it is not one another. I was wrong, and that won't happen again."

Chuck grinned and said, "Take off, you guys, we got this."

Jim and Mercedes decided to go back to the hotel and order lunch delivered to their room. The timing turned out impeccable as the waiter arrived exactly when they reached their room.

After the cart was set up and the waiter left, with a generous tip in hand, Jim turned in time to see Mercy's sweet little bare bottom dash into the bathroom, and he heard the shower begin. Making certain the deadbolt was in place, Jim quickly followed suit. A shower seemed like the perfect way to unwind.

Later, they sat, sampled the food, and sipped on the tea. Jim thoroughly enjoyed watching her, looking all pretty, and relaxed with a glow to her cheeks. His face displayed his slow smile on his mouth as he asked, "Mercy, are you feeling better now?"

Her face bloomed with a fresh pulse of color as she coyly replied, "Is that a question or a statement? You already know that answer, honey. And, yep, I heard you beg for mercy at least twice in the shower even though my ears were thundering with my heart beating in overdrive."

He looked at a loss, so she let him off the hook as she added, "The shower was fantastic, the calisthenics you added were without equal, and the food was really needed. I think that we're better than ever.

"What I am dreading is going back to the staging area and separating the two babies exhibiting testosterone overload. Once they start working together, they're an effective team. I don't get it with you guys and the competitive *mine is bigger than yours* thing. I'm just glad that you aren't like that. You know you're great, and what others think or say doesn't matter."

Jim interjected, "Oh, honey, it always matters. It just takes years of practice to not let it get to you. You think I'm great. Very..."

Mercedes's cell phone let out a horrible scream like a guy being flayed. Jim asked, "What the hell, or who the hell, is that?"

Mercedes released the lock on the phone to stop the text alert in mid-second scream, then she laughed. "That's my new text tone for my buddy, Chuck. I changed it after their shouting match earlier. Wanted to be prepared for a quick response."

"You are somewhat strange, Mercy."

She barely heard him as she read the lengthy text and finally looked up. "Jim, come on, we need to get back. Apparently, they found the source of the viral code. Sean created a block he wants to show us. We need to see if it works so you can release the hold on the planes. They were able to successfully block all access to the control center PCs. No one wants to pay these bandits now. Come on!"

CHAPTER 57

How about it, Cowboy?

Jamie cautiously smiled at the unwanted greeting from Ernesto. The two men studied each other for a long moment, and Ernesto finally explained, "They are busy elsewhere, so we have time for some coffee. Your treat, of course, since you work here. Or, should I say, are a hostage here?"

Jamie's smile quickly turned into his game face, specifically designed to show no emotion. Jamie shifted to move around the man but was promptly stopped by Ernesto. He voiced, "It seems Jamie doesn't have a sense of humor anymore, Juan."

Jamie looked to the top pocket of Ernesto's shirt where the voice of a man originated/

Juan stated, "Ernesto, I'll authorize the coffee expense for our friend here. Jamie, why don't you join us for a coffee and some discussion on how to avoid having to take more sledgehammer hits from Won and Ton?"

Jamie uneasily studied the smiling Ernesto. Juan continued from the cell phone. "You know, for a man who's likely risked so much more, you don't seem willing to gamble on hearing a way out of this debtor's prison. Here you were, so clever at getting the both of you out of Africa, but you haven't moved a muscle to leave this isolated hellhole. That suggests, the odds of getting out alive are quite low, from your perspective.

"Let's go over those odds, shall we? If we wanted to force you to work for us, we'd grab Frieda to put the squeeze on you, like your current guards. If we wanted you whacked, we'd simply invoke the wrath of Won and Ton's boss, Chairman Chang, and poof, you'd be tiger food. Now how about we sit down to discuss what we've got in mind? If memory serves, I believe the café behind you has great coffee and not quite the number of cameras that the gambling floor does."

Jamie struggled to maintain his game-faced exterior, but the fear and anxiety that washed through him threatened to undo all his efforts. Finally, the desperation in him took over, and he moved towards a discreet table with Ernesto. Jamie motioned to the only waitress in the entire area. Their coffee order was taken, then promptly brought to the table.

Ernesto pulled the cell phone out of his pocket and placed it flat on the table. He indicated, "Jamie, allow me to introduce my esteemed colleague, Juan, who's on the other end of the phone. The signal on the phone is such that it is not heard by the many AI forms that are here to listen and then help the patrons. I can control the level of avoidance. My name is Ernesto, which you already know. We'd like to discuss your, oh, how does one say it, um…your current job description."

Juan quickly jumped in. "More importantly, we would like to know about your special assignment that has your casino IT irked because they're doing your work. Can you tell us, instead of just being a cowboy?"

Jamie studied the phone resting on the table as well as Ernesto's face and said, "What makes you think I'm a captive here? You know, the last time you were in here, Ernesto, the twins worked you over while I stood and watched. What if you've got it all wrong and my role here is one of significant importance? Heck, all I'd have to do is signal security that you're outta here.

They could alter several bone and muscle patterns in your physiology as they haul you out to immobilize you permanently. So, put something on the table besides coffee that might gain my attention."

Juan chuckled. "Quite the bluffer, aren't you, Jamie? And with quite a history, I might add. Those people in Africa are still looking for you. Oh, and those investors that lost everything they'd been persuaded to invest in that toilet paper manufacturer venture, are still annoyed. They might've been a little more understanding if you hadn't raided the remaining funds before vanishing. You know, it's bad form in most investing circles, but especially those quasi-legitimate investors. They haven't given up looking for you. Then there's…well, you see, we've done our homework on you. With a psychological profile such as yours, we're confident that you're in it up to your eyeballs in something you can't flee."

Jamie lowered his head and nodded slightly in silent agreement. Ernesto felt some sympathy for poor Jamie and his circumstances, but before he could offer words of encouragement, Juan argued, "Jamie, this hand is played out. You can't run, Frieda is your Achilles heel. Once your usefulness is consumed, you'll be eliminated. We know how the chairman works. If you believe there's a payday waiting for you with a happy-ever-after, think again!

"Now, we're willing to get you and Frieda out alive. You need to help us understand what we don't know, for us to break you out. That's the deal. There's no money promised, but we will drop you anywhere in the world with fresh identities, and you can start over. How you interpret starting over is entirely up to you."

Feeling annoyed with his situation and the underwhelming offer, Jamie sarcastically asked, "Oh, so you mean there's something you don't know about, as far as what is going on here? Oh, dear me! Here I thought you knew everything about the past, present, and the future. But then again, when you know everything about the past, present, and future, the situation gets tense."

Both Ernesto and Juan chuckled at the comment for a moment, and then Juan countered, "Kid, you play your hand well. I can see that you don't want to help us and that is probably because the stakes aren't enough. Well, okay then, let me add more to the pot. Frieda is now with child and nearly scared out of her wits. You need to get her out and home if she is to have a successful delivery. As in, the sooner the better. Does that improve your motivation to assist us?"

Jamie flinched noticeably, and for the first time in a long time, he felt hollowed out inside at the news. Trying desperately to reel in his emotions and get back to his gambler persona, he started, "Now, how am I supposed to believe …"

Ernesto interrupted, "You know, prenatal care here in Macau, in many ways a frontier country, is quite a bit different than what you get in a developed nation. They have a lot of the same technology, but somehow an expectant mother doesn't quite trust doctors in foreign surroundings. This is especially true, where societal views on children have traditionally had some gray areas. Mothers-to-be tend to have more anxiety and more problems than if they were at home with family. Jamie, you need to take her home, and we all know that you can't under these circumstances. Why won't you let us help you two? After all, she didn't ask for this lifestyle, but she followed you here anyway. Are you ever going to do what's right for Frieda?"

Jamie was now so choked up that he was on the verge of tears. Sensing the emotional tsunami crashing into Jamie, Juan quietly offered, "Jamie, we want to help you, but you must trust us. You help us so we can help you. How about it, cowboy?"

Frieda was sleeping peacefully as Jamie watched in the semi-darkness of the early morning. She finally blinked her eyes open and rotated her head around to see Jamie staring at her. After a few moments she asked, "What's wrong? I mean, besides everything. You never just watch me sleep. What's going on?"

Jamie quietly asked, "When were you going to tell me?"

Frieda, a little uncomfortable with this line of questioning, requested, "What do you mean?"

Jamie offered, "I found out about the OBGYN visits and made some inquiries. How far along are you, Frieda?"

Frieda, shocked at being discovered before she was ready to tell, evaded, "Oh, that's fine, coming from you! Mr. I'm Going to Get Us Out Jamie! Well, instead of us getting out, I'm now in deeper, dammit!"

Frieda's emotions went into overdrive, and she began crying. "Jamie, I want to go home. I'm trapped here, fours month pregnant. We don't have any support, and I'm just plain scared. Let's just run, the hell with the money. Use your accursed magic to get us home, please."

Jamie closed his eyes, gave a ragged sigh, and quietly said, "It's in play as we speak. I'll get us out, babe, trust me. But there won't be any diamonds as big as horse turds, like I wanted. But I'll get you home and your mom will help, I promise."

CHAPTER 58

Misunderstanding or lies

Chairman Chang arrived early and completed some work before the next challenge. He was delighted with the winnings that Jamie helped to secure for him. He considered letting the gambler off the hook with a bit of payout but decided for the time being to allow Jamie and Frieda a bit more freedom around the casino. Ton had reported that their work was being done, and Frieda was subdued.

Won and Ton entered along with Jamie and went to dress for the game, even while Jamie made subtle inroads with Nikkei. She seemed to enjoy Jamie's scratching on her head as her deep purring increased. It was interesting watching the Irishman get along with his prize.

Chairman Chang asked, "Do you like my Nikkei? She seems to enjoy your petting."

Jamie continued to focus his attention on the feline while he quietly responded, "Your tiger is a powerful animal, able to change attitude with little warning. I'm glad she's partially sedated, but I think she'd prefer her freedom. How long have you had her?"

Chairman Chang replied, "I've had her a few years now. She is a rare and special animal that I've grown very fond of in that time. She's a huge area to roam in for long periods and stretch her legs, but it's still an enclosure. I doubt she'd remain healthy back in the wild as she's been domesticated since she was a small kitten. The man that I acquired her from treated her like a spoiled house cat, which I've continued. She's got a large carnivorous appetite, so we make certain she's well fed.

"Today, I require you to do a bit of probing around in the programs. These are gaming applications, and I'm considering modeling a smaller commercial version of them, using static, pre-packaged avatars for the gamer to select from and making it purely a points game. Outside wagers could of course be enabled, but that is not my concern. The other thing is that the drawing for funds is rather small by comparison, so my opponent should win it. That strategy's been good and kept his suspicions down."

Jamie thought through the steps of the request as well as the other items he planned to accomplish today and decided they aligned. Jamie warned, "I can do as you ask, but the timing is such that I will need to be inside this room so I can pick when to do the probes you request. I suspect that your opponent has a technology staff monitoring the actions. I don't think either of us want them alerted. I suspect that would result in an immediate game shutdown."

"If that's the case, how do you propose to proceed without alerting the technicians?"

Jamie moved slowly away from the tiger to continue the conversation without upsetting the tiger with rapid movements. He needed his hands to make gestures as he explained. Before he began, he asked, "Might I ask for a bit of your drink of the gods before I explain? I'm a bit parched."

Chairman Chang nodded, and Jamie went and poured them each a small portion. He knew that the Chairman Chang was not a big drinker before a contest. Glass in hand, Jamie began to outline the details of his plan, including his adding code to the chairman's avatar to enable him to probe undetected. Jamie suspected the avatars were reasonably independent. That characterization provided cover for the request by the chairman and Jamie's strategy. Chairman Chang agreed after explaining several times that Jamie needed to remain out of sight, no matter what.

At the end of the discussion and close to the start of the game, Chairman Chang allowed, "If this succeeds in the way you have outlined, I'll add a small bonus to your nest egg."

During this same period, on the Russian front, Dmitry arrived early and spent several minutes trying to gain the attention of Konstantin. Konstantin's anger at the image of Natasha on the screen the previous evening when the man returned for his topcoat, was raw and explosive. Dmitry admitted he was infatuated with the woman and suggested they both compete for her hand. Konstantin discredited Dmitry and stated, there was no honor in Dmitry's behavior. Further he was profoundly disappointed their business relationship had inadvertently crossed the line to a farce of a friendship. Konstantin vowed, before he stomped back to his operations role, "I'll never make that mistake again." He turned at the doorway and added, "You are free to take any actions you see fit."

After that event, Dmitry was relieved to find Konstantin working when he arrived. He took solace in the thought that Konstantin was doing the job he was supposed to do and would earn his share of the profits. Evgeniya's behavior was unwaveringly the same, so Dmitry knew Konstantin hadn't complained to his secretary. Even with all of that, he'd slept well and dreamed of meeting Natasha. He'd sent the money to her account after Konstantin had left. He also requested an email confirmation upon receipt, which he received. With her email address committed to memory, he would work toward a more consistent communication outside of the chat room. He did want to reach out one more time in the chat room, after this contest, and clarify some items with her, as well as secure a phone number.

Dmitry launched the video conference right on time, and Chairman Chang joined.

Dmitry smiled. "Good day, Chang. The door selection first, as the remaining funds have arrived, and then we can play. Without further ado, let's begin."

Chairman Chang nodded agreement and play began. Chairman Chang lost the door, and he was correct in that it was a minor amount. He, however, was extremely successful at capturing several of the items in this sandbox game. They'd played this game a couple of times, and the sound effects were superb. The surround sound stereo was ideal and immersed Chang into the experience. Chairman Chang absentmindedly hoped that this was one of the games they would be able to use in the business venture for the common user consumption.

Both men playing rapidly and effectively through each level of the game. Chairman Chang won out at the end, and as the session turned off, he complimented, "Dmitry, old friend, that was well played by us both. I do think I won this round."

Dmitry allowed, "Yes, you played excellently. Why, even your Szechuan seemed to play a bit better this time around. Your familiarity with the game is showing, you rogue.

"Have you given more thought to a possible partnership on creating games? If this is something you'd like to pursue, I accept your suggestion of our technician pools getting combined to create the finished product. I've not yet spoken to my lead, Konstantin, but I'm certain he'll agree to your proposal."

Chairman Chang grinned at the text he received from Jamie. He looked at the video conference screen and replied, "I think that's a great idea, Dmitry. I'll get my suggested lead tech vetted and let you know."

Dmitry appeared pleased. "Good, let me know during our next session, day after tomorrow. London is a go too then, so I will reserve a couple of suites at a hotel in proximity to the venue."

"Sounds good."

Dmitry entered the chat room and immediately located Natasha. He typed, "Hello, Natasha. Did you begin completion of the steps we discussed?"

She entered, "I did, Mikael, and your generosity is without equal. I believe it's far too much for an unknown like myself. I was unable to secure the phone, but I was able to secure a companion for my grandma. The time was allocated for tomorrow. I got awarded some additional tutoring sessions which pay very nicely. I'll begin to start paying you back."

Dmitry was surprised at this action and typed, "No, my dear. I don't want you to pay me back. I want to take our walk in the park and get to know you better. I want you to learn about me."

"Oh dear," she entered, "I already promised that I'd do the tutoring sessions for the next three days. I cannot break my promise as it is my honor at stake. I'm so sorry. Now you're angry with me and won't want to see me on Saturday."

Dmitry backpedaled and entered, "No, I couldn't be angry with you. Saturday at the Muzeon Park of Arts is perfect. There's a quiet area where we can have a nice picnic if you are agreeable. Can we do that, my dear?"

A long pause occurred before she typed, "I'm so glad you are not angry. I think that will be lovely. I'll plan to arrive in midmorning. I'll pick up my own mobile phone before then and try to call. Can you provide me a number, please?"

Dmitry typed a number into the chat window and then alerted her that his friend Andrei was aware that they were doing side chats. He didn't want her to communicate with him but hesitated to add that caveat. She was a woman; it was her choice. They exchanged a few more comments, and he promised to bring an extra book to their meeting. They concluded the conversation, wishing each other well.

Dmitry was so engrossed in the conversation that he failed to notice Konstantin as he leaned against the doorway. Konstantin glowered at his boss in a manner that conveyed volumes of anger at the betrayal between two men who knew each other so well. Dmitry finished shutting down his machine and tidied up his desk while Konstantin watched. He'd reviewed everything he had entered on the screen. He decided it was done and not worth reviewing or defending. He said nothing and waited for Konstantin to yell, or shout, or confront in any manner. As he stacked up the rest of the correspondence and placed it into his completed tray for his secretary to retrieve. He glanced up at Konstantin's unwavering stare from his unmoved station. Angry discussion could be dealt with, but this was almost to the point of unnerving. Dmitry stood and faced Konstantin and finally asked, "Are you going to simply stand there like a jilted lover or make a statement?"

Konstantin looked like a man on the verge of losing control. He stood to his full height and set a steely, intimidating look on his face. Through clenched teeth, he stated, "You, sir, haven't a shred of honor."

Konstantin turned and exited as silently as he'd arrived.

In another place, Natasha had disconnected from the chat room and shut down her computer. She smiled at the recap of the chat conversation and looked up at her companion. Her companion smiled, then laughed and asked, "We kill moose?"

She replied, "We don't kill moose, we get moose and squirrel."

Port or Starboard?

After the tragedy of Hoyt's death, McLaren had somewhat withdrawn into himself. He hadn't slowed the project and had tried to be everywhere at once, barking orders. The dust and heat made the work more taxing to everyone, but the over-helping orders and reminders from McLaren made everyone edgy. The crew members gave McLaren some slack at first as they could all see that he was wounded by the death of his nephew. As the days wore on and the work pace never seemed to let up, McLaren's mothering of the crews increased to the point that it was understandable that something or someone would snap.

The team had assembled the crane under the constant direction of McLaren, and collectively they were able to pull out four giant dump trucks from the burial ground they had been pushed into. Mohawk, Tina, and George were ready to do a trial run with two of the giant units once the cleaning crews had removed all the sand and crushed rock from the engine compartments. McLaren chose the two obviously serviceable units and had the engine cleaning crews scramble to work them. McLaren was right to have the service crews bring batteries for the dump trucks since the two chosen units either had dead or leaking batteries after their near-death experience.

Once everything was checked out by the crews, McLaren loudly stated, "Lady and gentlemen, we are gathered here today to do a reverse burial of our dearly departed. Having them finally exhumed from their hot, baking graves, we are now ready to breathe life back into their system.! Mohawk and Tina will be our drivers. George will move between the units and work on the computer systems.

"We'll start in manual mode with Mohawk. Then I want George to fire up the onboard computer that runs the servo-mechanical equipment to see how it behaves. As soon as I give the signal and George launches the program, the dump truck is in auto-pilot mode and could go wonky again. George, I want you to be prepared to disengage the onboard computer system on my signal, which means that, Mohawk, you will be back to manual mode. Now, if…"

Mohawk, unable to contain his irritation at having all the obvious orders being issued like he was back in grade school, promptly raised his hand. Then he shouted, "Teacher, request permission to be excused to run to the toilet so I can throw up."

People within the immediate area and hearing distance were taken aback by the verbal volley by Mohawk. Tina sensed Mohawk was at his limit and gently tried to reel him in with a touch. He shrugged her hand off and continued, "McLaren, let me go ahead and just put the wallaby on the crew cab. I'm here to tell you, we're all sick and tired of this attitude you've developed. I'm sorry, as are we all, that Hoyt is gone, but for god's sake please stop taking it out on us with your overbearing instructions! We know what's needed, so stop digging your cleats into our backsides."

McLaren appeared speechless. His emotions raced rapidly between anger and remorse. If the hot desert wind hadn't been so oppressive, you could have heard a pin drop.

Finally, George broke the stalemate. "McLaren, we know you've suffered. We all sympathize with the loss. You've been driving yourself very hard. We can see your pain like a tattoo on your face but allow us to contribute to the efforts here as the professionals you hired."

McLaren took several ragged, deep breaths but said nothing. Finally, after visibly struggling to gain control of his emotions, he proclaimed, "I'm sorry that I've become a silly ass worrying about my chickens. I'm sorry that the loss of Hoyt made me too protective of this crew It was hard sending Hoyt's body back to his mother alone. We're stuck here, unable to attend a proper funeral for him. I want no more losses on this project, so, yes, I have over-helped in many instances. I refuse to lose ANYONE else on my watch. Please understand my perspective."

Mohawk clucked his tongue and sarcastically asked, "Is this where we all do a group hug and sing *Kumbaya?*"

Tina punched Mohawk in the back to get him to soften up just a little bit. Wincing from the pain of a modest kidney punch, Mohawk turned with some difficulty and asked, "Tina, does this mean you're ready for sex right now?" Managing a slight smile, he added, "You know I like it rough, sweetheart."

George rolled his eyes at their antics, then attempted to get everyone refocused as he asked, "McLaren, what about the replacement drone we need for our satellite uplink to actually control these units remotely?"

McLaren transformed back into character as he responded, "You're right, lad. Let me go get the drone…I mean, I need one of you lads to ready the drone for launch.

"George, can you use your communications uplink to alert the command center that we are ready for a trial? Also, how about that communications expert of yours, EZ. Is she going to be watching the data traffic to see if the digital pirates are still in our waters?"

George grinned widely and in a mock pirate's voice stated, "Arrr! We be talking pirates now. Aye, aye, Captain! I'll be alerting the EZ to be in the crow's nest looking for any pirates in our peaceful sandbox."

McLaren gave him his best look of disbelief over the tops of his glasses as he watched everyone scamper to execute their expected tasks. A slow smile came over his face as Mohawk gave him a knowing wink and nod before climbing up into the cab of the first dump truck to run through the preliminary checklist.

Shortly after the noon meal break, George hurried back to the dump truck staging area. McLaren dispatched the cleaning and moving crews to retrieve the rest of the equipment.

George reported, "McLaren, the command center was alerted of our test run and is ready to connect with the drone once it's airborne and stabilized. Additionally, I asked EZ to have a tunneled conference bridge open with the command center so they could communicate in real time while we bring everything back online. To conserve battery life on my satellite phone, I'll only join at the top of each hour unless the site goes sideways again. Argh! I need to apologize for waking EZ up again."

McLaren chuckled a little and commented, "It's a good thing when a lass doesn't grouse too much about being woken up in the middle of the night by a man to discuss tunneling. Alright, let's see if the drone is up and online, shall we?"

George brought the portable remote communications terminal up and began the connection process with the drone's video transmissions. When he had good visuals feeding to the portable terminal, he dialed into the conference bridge and said, "Hi, all. This is George at the Kookaburra site, checking in.

We've got the drone up and online. I'm checking to see if you are getting the same satellite feeds that I see here."

The operator at the command center and EZ both responded with a description of the transmission. Then the operator added, "Everything looks like we are used to seeing from the site. The drone's flying pattern is as expected, and it's transmitting video for the entire site. The drone's camera zoom is working nicely, but…uh, you might tell Mohawk to use a little more sunscreen on his noggin. It's getting sunburned, and his fly is down again."

McLaren did his *Why me?* look to the side while trying to get the bad taste out of his mouth at the operator's comment.

George chuckled a little and responded, "Roger that, command center. Good zoom video to give that much detail. I'll alert Mohawk that the cave is open, but that the beast is asleep."

George looked at McLaren and announced, "Alright, we are ready for the onboard computers to come up for their first trial in truck one. Mohawk and I will be in the cab to take it from manual to automated mode. Once it is up and running, operations, can you provide it some simple commands to exercise the program?

"After that is done to everyone's satisfaction, I'll need to get out of the cab and go over to Tina's machine and repeat the process. If that's successful, then, command center, can you stop the second unit so I can get out?

"Please understand, both Mohawk and Tina will remain in their cabs, observing the activity. If the equipment goes sideways again, they will turn off the computers and jump back into manual mode. Sounds simple, right? Any questions?"

McLaren studied George for a moment and offered, "You're doing fine, lad. Let's go do this."

George trotted to Mohawk's giant dump truck. Then Mohawk started the process as described. The machine shuddered to life as the massive diesel engine came up and began to respond to manual operations dispensed by Mohawk. Mohawk brought the massive truck to a stop and, turning to George, stated, "She's all yours. Launch the computer program, lad."

George brought up everything on the computer and launched the program from the command line. As the program came up to operational effectiveness, he confirmed, "I've been all over the external sensors, the internal servo-mechanical programmatic devices, and the only place the poisonous code could be running on is this onboard computer. I loaded up some newer anti-virus programs and turned logging on to capture anything that unexpectedly comes through. I even renamed the admin account and gave it an impossibly hard password-phrase. This should slow down even the most gifted hacker from taking over the system. The way these systems were setup, it looks like no one expected a hacker to get in and take over the program. Other-wise, they'd have used a separate account that only had enough privileges to run the program, not modify its functions."

Mohawk somewhat absentmindedly acknowledged, "I'm glad you know your trade, because I've no idea of what you're talking about. Besides, I'm still focused on that love punch from Tina, and I can't wait for more foreplay. You know she has this routine where she…"

George uneasily offered, "Let's just have you wait for Tina until later, okay? It's kind of close in this cab, and I don't think your amorous …, hey, we're up on the computer. Let me dial into the conference bridge to see how it appears to the command center."

George dialed into the bridge and said, "Hi, gang. The computer shows to be online, and Mohawk confirms that we've passed from manual mode into automated mode. If that's true, put us through some test scenarios."

The operator responded, "We're in verification mode now, folks. At this point, everything looks…"

EZ barged into the conversation. "Gentlemen, we have a BitTorrent surging through the satellite link, aimed at your destination. I recommend all precautions commence."

McLaren was listening in and asked, "George, what are your recommendations?"

George replied, "Honestly? I want to see if our re-deployment measures will stop the poisonous code so we can operate normally.

"EZ, can you work the BitTorrent backwards to see its origination point?"

EZ responded, "Hey, it may be too early here, but that doesn't mean I'm asleep at the wheel, bucko. I'm on it."

George sheepishly apologized, "EZ, I promise, from now on the only man that will ever get to wake you up early with crude jokes and unnecessary commentary will be your significant other."

EZ smirked and countered, "You just enjoy hearing me talk about going into my work area buck naked to work on a communications exercise. That's all you care about."

McLaren chuckled and confirmed, "Actually, I'd like to hear a little more myself."

EZ snickered and joked, "Ha! I bet you would.

"Alright, the BitTorrent is well cloaked. The signal for the attacking code is being uploaded from Costa Rica. Hmmm… looks like it is getting its stream from another satellite. Pretty good fellows, but I'm not buying it.

"So that was a nice hop, but I'm now back down from… yeah, just as I expected, a bank of anonymizing servers in…are you ready? May I have some dramatic announcement music, please? The signal is originating in Russia. Okay, folks, we have our general location but not an exact one."

George jumped in and exclaimed, "Great work, EZ.

"Let's watch to see how this bad boy behaves now that his administrative rights have been cranked down to the off position! While that is in play, EZ, is there any way for you to alert Julie to see if she can throw some more computer resources into the fray to find exactly where the originating signal is located?"

EZ shot back an agreeing comment. "Already in play, mister. Geezers, George, to hear you talk, you'd think this was my first time to rodeo. Now tell us about the systems there."

George refocused on his systems and, watching the ruggedized computer screen, stated, "Team, we are being pounded! EZ, you were right to call it a BitTorrent! I'm watching the logs fill faster than they can be emptied, and the entries are all the same! Request denied! Hah! As you young people would say, 'We be jammin', mon!'"

Mohawk was getting into the spirit of the win as he laughed and indicated, "Har! Har! They got their hands up me dress only to find I'm wearing a steel knickers-guard!"

McLaren, appalled at Mohawk's crass statement, closed his eyes and simply shook his head. Then, gathering his thoughts, McLaren asked, "So, George, does the system look like it'll hold? Right now it appears to be functioning normally, but that could change if they find a way in."

George watched the screens and logs a while longer before he responded, "That's true, but right now everything seems within our normal parameters. If the poisonous code can't get in to take over, it is simply a nuisance. I've set the log files to overwrite after one megabyte, and it is doing so every ten seconds. So far, we have the BitTorrent at bay. Do you want to bring another dump truck or ride this for a while?"

McLaren thought for a moment and decided, "Let's bring up the equipment as planned. As long as we have operators to watch the computers in the cabs, we are winning the battle, so the more the merrier."

George grinned and replied, "Arrr! Aye, aye, Captain. We've got those bloody pirates in our gunwale sights. Let's give it to them and board their scurvy decks."

McLaren wondered if his crew hadn't all gone mine-pit happy when he suggested, "Alright, team, let's try and stay focused."

The noise in the cab made it hard to hear, and Mohawk asked, "What did he tell us?"

George absentmindedly responded loud enough for Mohawk and the people on the conference bridge to hear him. "He wants us to focus."

Mohawk, wide-eyed and apprehensive, shouted, "Both of us?!?"

The command center operator laughed out loud, then voiced, "Okay, but I have dibs on Tina. Har! Har!"

Before McLaren could get past another *Why me?* moment, the operator hollered, "Hey, what's wrong with the drone? I've lost the video feeds."

McLaren quickly shot a glance to the portable terminal and responded, "I've lost video as well. Let me pick up the drone visually with my binoculars."

Sure enough, McLaren could see the drone buzzing over the mining area in a hopelessly erratic pattern. McLaren watched it for a moment and then asked on the bridge, "George, you did reprogram the drone before we sent it up, yes? Like you did for the trucks?"

George sighed and responded, "No, I didn't. I was only focused on the trucks' onboard computers because that was where all the heavy processing was being done. I didn't consider the drone."

McLaren clucked his tongue and agreed, "Yeah, I didn't think of that either. But the drone is the communications point for the whole site and all the equipment reporting back to the command center. My guess is, when the bandits discovered that they can't destroy the trucks or loaders, they vented their frustrations on our drone. It is the necessary upload communication point for the whole site. Any chance you guys can interrupt the BitTorrent that is about to wreck our drone and re-establish its authorized flight pattern?"

Before any more discussion could occur, the drone augured into the wall of the mining pit but caused no casualties. The whole crew saw it go into the wall and explode, but it was McLaren who uttered, "Oops. I wish we'd brought two drones. Operations, please let corporate know we need another drone dispatched as soon as possible."

CHAPTER 60

Cleansing Time

Julie cheerfully greeted, "Hi, Quip! I'm calling to see if I can get you and ICABOD engaged on a real time problem we are working on that has…."

A sullen Quip answered, "Yeah, I know about it already. EZ alerted me, so we high-tailed it to the data center."

Julie sensed some tension, so she asked, "What's up? You sound like something's wrong."

Quip accused, "I thought I was about to engage in that special couples' activity when EZ came boiling back to bed with nothing on, but instead, she rushed us to dress and get to the data center. That wouldn't have been bad except when we got there EZ spent so much time consoling ICABOD about his difficulties with two of his supercomputers buddies that she barely spoke to me. I feel like my lady is being finessed away from me."

Julie rolled her eyes but managed to empathically offer, "You poor thing. How awful for you to lose your wonderful, caring, beautiful lady to a room full of rack-mounted blade servers. Do you think that because ICABOD and I are no longer…well, that is to say…" Julie's pouted as though filled with remorse and moved her eyes to watch the ceiling. "When you told me to break it off with him…, maybe as a jilted lover reflex, perhaps he's now after EZ?"

Annoyed as well as sullen, Quip groused, "Oh, that's just fine, coming from you…"

EZ barged into the video conference call and barked, "Hey, knock it off, you two. I don't like being referred to in the third person when I'm in the room. We have a BitTorrent onslaught originating from an unidentified data source. I want to capture the source before we lose the signal, and you two are acting like brain-dead teenagers. Let's concentrate on our digital enemy."

Quip pouted and pointed toward Julie's image as he stated, "She started it!"

EZ glared at Quip. "And I'm ending it."

Quip quietly countered, "ICABOD, where are we with the BitTorrent traces that I asked you to work on before we got here?"

ICABOD politely offered, "Per the information feeds that EZ provided from her communications terminal, I was able to thread through the anonymizing servers and discover the source of the digital attack. I'm disappointed to report that the Russian supercomputer BORIS is the source of the BitTorrent. However, I also discovered that the Chinese supercomputer, LING-LI, was at the other end of an encrypted tunnel, working in concert with BORIS. As delicately as possible, I have queried them both on this activity, but both declined to provide an explanation. The only commentary offered was that the digital activity in question was designated as classified. As such, per prior agreements, it cannot be discussed with members of the Algonquin Round Table. I took their attitude as embarrassment at being used by their masters for childish game play."

Quip stated, "Do you want to guess who is behind this machine-to-machine communications disruption and blackmail scheme in Russia and China, Jules?"

"Juan and I believe we know the culprit in China. We need a bit more proof on the Russian connection. Good hard evidence will dictate our next steps."

Quip commented, "Jules, you said that the Chinese perpetrator is known. I imagine that problem is headed for prompt resolution. What about our Russian instigator, whom we now have dead to rights? Do you want me to launch our favorite cleansing routine, or do you want to handle it?"

Julie studied EZ and Quip on the video monitor with an emotionless expression. "We were certain of who it was, as well. I needed you, Quip and ICABOD, to confirm the MACDOR in this game. Quip, in case you were wondering, that would be the *Malicious Acting Characters Deserving Ostracism and Retribution.* Our cleansing routine is already in flight!"

Quip chuckled. "Good one! You're learning, little girl."

"Why don't you take EZ home now, and I'll get with Wolfgang for the final scene of our adventure of messing around in all the wrong places?"

Quip brightened up as he nodded. "That's a great idea, Julie! Come on, sweetheart, let's get you home and back into your jammies. Bye, Julie, must dash."

Just as Julie was disconnecting from the video call, she heard EZ.

"But, honey, you know I don't wear any jammies when sleeping." And then with a giggle, "Or, for anything else, for that matter."

Quip gave a grin and wink into the fading video image as the connection ended.

Wolfgang appeared chipper as the video camera displayed his face.

"Greetings, Wolfgang."

"Good morning, my dear. Do you have the additional proof you wished to verify? And, more importantly, were you able to gain the details on the accounts you wanted to access and reconcile?"

Julie gave him a thumbs up and said, "Indeed we do, Wolfgang. But permit me to be a little remorseful on the execution of our plan. There's something a little bit sad about destroying an adversary, regardless of how deserving.

"I am also not certain on what the right steps are with regards to their technology and how that should be neutralized. I'll need ICABOD to provide options at the next group meeting. That option process is outside of CATS charter, I think."

Wolfgang was taken aback by the statement and shook his head. "I might be tempted to agree with your first concern, if people hadn't had their lives upended or that young man been killed in Australia. Also, I noticed that you didn't say worthy adversary.

"When powerful men deliberately harm others without cause, they should be held accountable, regardless of their political position or wealth status. When the justice system cannot touch them, then it's time for people like us to swing into action. The world doesn't need men like them dishing out misery. I'm not even sure I would consent to pitying them either, based on what they've done."

Julie nodded. After a big sigh she concurred, "Point taken. Too bad that medical science hasn't progressed to the point where we could perform an ethics-conscience transplant to rescue some of these people, rather than destroying them."

Wolfgang grinned and lifted his eyebrows. "I could see you as a frequent donor in this area, my dear."

They both chuckled.

Wolfgang continued, "Let me get the access and validation for all the final proof points of your theory. I should have it within forty-eight hours. By then, hopefully you will have the remainder of the plans outlined and finalized for any necessary reviews."

CHAPTER 61

Spin it Again, Please

The plainclothes Chinese officer stood patiently at the casino slot machine. He casually but intently placed coins into the slot, not expecting any reward. Now and then his spin on the slot machine would yield a modest return, but always less than what he was feeding the machine. His activity was unobtrusive. He had said nothing to anyone, not even the hostesses who kept wandering by to see if they could engage with him.

Finally, after about forty minutes of casual slot play, Jamie nonchalantly strolled up. He stood by and watched the patron feeding in the coins, saying nothing. His cell phone chirped, and he discreetly looked at the text message before a slight smile came to his face. Putting the cell phone away, he said in a guarded tone to the patron, "Colonel Guano, I presume?"

Not moving his attention from the slot machine, the man responded, "That depends. Are you called Jamie?"

Somewhat annoyed, Jamie sarcastically replied, "Oh great! Here we are designated to meet each other, but neither one of us admitting who we are to one another. I can see THIS scene easily being an outtake from any spy movie.

"Yes, I'm Jamie. I'm here to meet Colonel Guano who's supposed to be playing this machine in nonmilitary attire so as not to attract attention. Yes or no, are you Guano?"

The slot player clucked his tongue in annoyance as well, then replied, "It was your organization that contacted me with these silly cloak and dagger routines. If you are irritated with the nonsense, then we have a quorum on this situation.

"Yes, I'm Colonel Guano. I need to understand what you're trying to sell. However, it's very well known in my organization that this establishment has no place for secret conversations. Thus, you are either a fool, or this is a very shabby attempt to trap me in a web of deceit."

Jamie studied the colonel for a moment and then, after a quick text, offered, "We're in a digitally isolated bubble. We're hidden from the internal surveillance cameras and voice microphones. I'll prove it to you by having you win the next five pulls on the slot machine to more than replenish your losses. We're meeting here so I can prove my claims with demonstrations of what I've engineered.

"More importantly, I'm on a strict leash, and any meetings between you and I off-premises would put us both at risk. Hope you brought a sturdy sack for what you are about to win."

True to Jamie's statement, the next five spins on the slot machine filled the tray to overflowing, but the colonel showed no emotion. Jamie grew uneasy at the dispassionate look the colonel gave him after the fifth winning spin. The two men studied each other for a moment.

Jamie said, "If you feel this meeting is a waste of your time, then simply take your winnings. You can leave to pursue what the money can buy. If you suspect I might have hard evidence of our claim, then slowly feed the slot. It's now programmed to take everything you put into it with no return."

The two stony-faced men again studied each other, before the colonel began methodically feeding coins back into the slot. The previous win had been noticed by one of the few hostesses on the floor, and she provided a congratulatory drink to both men.

Colonel Guano returned his attention to the slot machine as he sipped his victory drink, while maintaining his view of the slot output. He remarked, "The drinks are not watered down. I would have expected the house to have cut the drink with water to conserve their losses."

Jamie smiled. "No, we offer up good straight liquor to our winners. The alcohol has a tendency to embolden the player and keep them at the slots until we win back everything and more. Watered down drinks are ineffective. Plus, they tend to leave the machines too quickly to reach the head."

Still studying the slot output, the colonel commented, "You indicated you had evidence of a public official's misconduct. Yet here you are plying me with good quality alcohol and allowing me to win at a game of chance. Ordinarily, I'd have no chance at any of this occurring. Am I the rogue official you seek to destroy?"

Jamie remained stone-faced and explained, "My girlfriend and I came here to seek our fortune yet have found nothing but grief. I learned how to beat the house by deceiving the machine-to-machine communications. I got caught. I want to take my lady home. However, we are prisoners here in this casino. I want to trade our freedom for what we know about the silent partner of this casino who is a powerful Chinese official, Colonel Guano. We know that China is trying to crack down on corruption, and it occurs to me that a nice showy official might be just what you need. Someone who likely earned his enemies and too much wealth accumulated for his own personal account. With what I know and can provide you, I believe your government can realign the political power structure very nicely."

Guano, still sipping his drink, asked, "You're not asking for money then?"

Jamie nonchalantly shrugged his shoulders and offered, "I wouldn't turn any down if some were being offered. I must admit that a few shekels would allow us to fly home, rather than work on a freight cargo ship to get back. I know my girlfriend would appreciate a flight rather than hard work since she is now expecting.

"That, Colonel Guano, is my big motivator in all this. Probably hard for you to believe since that wasn't my motivation in coming here."

Colonel Guano peered at the man. "What a quaint story. And you were right. This slot is taking everything I feed it, so it appears I should quit while I am ahead. I guess there's the lesson for all of us, don't you think?"

Jamie swallowed hard but said nothing.

The colonel politely asked for a container for his winnings from a passing hostess. After she left, he stated, "You've made a compelling offer, but I must insist that you stay on here until all prosecution is complete. You see, we'll undoubtedly need your testimony for such an important case. I'll grant you the right to send your lady home, provided, of course, that everything falls into place as you suggest."

Jamie felt so alone and vulnerable with the implications of the offer. He felt afraid to have Frieda depart alone. Jamie sized up the situation and handed an envelope over, then stated, "She leaves immediately as my down payment. She must get to the States and her family without being dragged into this mess of my doing. Send her immediately or no deal."

Colonel Guano deftly pocketed the envelope, finished his drink, gathered up his winnings with a tiny smile, then quietly stated, "We'll be in touch, Jamie. Good day, for now."

CHAPTER 62

Retrospect

Julie smiled as she mentally reviewed the changes in the team's cases over the last few days. Each member made some real progress on not only the identity of the perpetrators for their specific cases but also on linking four of their contracted assignments. The team had performed flawlessly—nothing short of amazing.

After supper Juan suggested she go take a leisurely bath and relax. Julie thought he just wanted to spoil their children for a while, since he was more recovered. She imagined him playing their favorite game of *Don't Get Off the Couch*, which caused the children to squeal nearly nonstop. Maude would be close by in case the game got out of hand.

She'd finished her long, hot soak, and the bathroom smelled like lavender. She brushed her hair until her golden highlights sparkled as they caught the light. After she applied lotion to her skin, she moved into the bedroom and snuggled under the sheets to get warm. Closing her eyes, she promised herself just a few minutes, and then she would get up and check on Juan.

Julie's eyes flew open as she realized she'd not only been sleeping but that someone was touching her. The room was dark, and it took her a few seconds to return from the odd dream that had vanished as she had awoken. She settled as she realized the hands roving her naked body were familiar and desired.

Juan kissed her neck as his arms encircled her, pulling her tighter into his embrace. He murmured into her neck and ear, "How beautiful you are. I want you so much, Julie. I love having you this close. Your skin is like silk, and your scent is like a field of new flowers."

Julie responded with a passion that seemed endless. Her hands roved his skin, delighting in touching every available inch with no impediments. Vaguely, she realized she must have been deeply asleep as she kissed and licked his freshly showered skin.

For what seemed like hours, they touched and enjoyed one another, giving and receiving passion in turn. No hurry, and yet there was an underlying urgency that prevented each of them from feeling totally sated. First, she'd be on top, tasting every inch of Juan's skin, until he felt so close to release that he shifted and licked and touched her into several back-to-back pinnacles before he buried himself deep inside her. His insistent strokes and her grabbing him closer ultimately joined them in that place only they shared, floating together in total bliss. Sometime later they realigned, and Juan cradled Julie's head against his shoulder and chest.

"Hmm," she murmured with a sigh of satisfaction. "That was lovely, honey."

"Yes, you are," he lazily replied. "I'm not sorry I woke you. You looked so sweet, so kissable."

"What time is it? I planned to shut my eyes for a moment, but now I know it was longer."

"It was after ten before I came up to shower. And, before you shout at me, I didn't play with our children that long. Brayson called, and we talked about a few of the details he wanted to complete. He kicked a couple of good ideas around."

Julie chuckled, "You know, our team that we picked is amazing. We did a good job, honey."

Juan scooted into a sitting position and fixed the pillows against the headboard. Then he pulled her up beside him and carefully tucked the covers around her and fluffed the pillows. He reached over and grabbed a glass off his bedside table and offered it to her. She took it with a grin, and he poured a small glass of wine for her.

"Seems kind of late for wine, honey," she remarked.

"It's never too late to lounge in bed with my pretty wife and sip some wine. We haven't taken time to simply enjoy each other. Frankly, I like it. So there."

He raised his glass to hers and the soft chime was in perfect pitch.

"This morning you have a call with your family resources, right? I thought we might discuss the next steps to take so you get the right help to finish these cases."

Julie remarked, "Good idea. I'd like to make certain that we tie up all the loose ends and extract our team as quickly as possible. Ernesto is at the most risk at this point because of his location. Do you think we can trust Jamie? And what do we need to do for him?"

Juan stared across the room for a moment. "My darling, I think we can trust that Jamie will do what he says because it's the option that gives him a money stake and a viable escape route with the girl. Guys always want the money and the girl, right? It won't be too long before we find out if we made a good bet. Look at it this way, I've been gambling a lot longer than that kid, and I got the girl."

Julie laughed. "So true, honey. Good choice on your part, I might add.

"Tracing these incidents back to the source is delicate like tracing my mother's lace doilies. I'd never have thought we'd have gone to some of these extremes. I think they'll pay off. Unless you disagree, I'd like to recommend that, if our arrangements don't take them out indirectly, we marshal all the appropriate authorities to insure this can't happen again. I get so darn mad when I think about the arrogance of terrorists, thinking they're above the law. I want to do something about it."

Juan hugged her close to show his support. "I think our foundational plans will achieve those results. Agreed though – if not, there are extra steps we can take. You've been brilliant in leading the charge. I'm so proud of you."

"CATS is lucky to have you, sweetheart."

With that commentary, Juan took her glass and set it on the table then pulled her back into his arms and soundly kissed her. They scooted down into the covers, and before passion overtook her reason, she replied, "I am lucky to have you. You may not get hurt again, Juan. Stay with me."

Early the next morning Julie slid out of bed and looked lovingly at Juan while he slept. She donned her dressing gown and retreated to the study to join the conference call. Connecting quickly, she smiled and said, "Good morning, gentlemen. Anything new?"

Wolfgang replied, "Good morning, Jules, you look refreshed and lovely. I trust you rested well." He cleared his throat looking more serious. "I've tracked the recent transactions back to the account you suggested. I'm not certain how you identified it, and I'm not certain I care to know. I documented the information you requested and am sending that to our shared drop box. The sum of the transactions is certainly not everything that your team noted, but it's nonetheless a substantial amount. We've set up an alternate administrative access to this and the prior account we identified, which will allow you or me to redistribute the funds."

Julie outlined the next steps she and Juan had planned for CATS members to deliver. for their team. She summarized how each of her team hoped to conclude their assignments and ensure that the right safeguards and follow up reviews were contracted. She and Juan expected some business in the form of residual maintenance from each of these locations. Wolfgang and Quip asked for some clarification at various points in the conversation but overall agreed with her plan.

Quip interjected, "Jules, I remind you not to take too many risks. It's bad enough that Juan had his accident, but I don't want you lost or anyone on your team. Should I worry that the methods used to acquire that account information are not entirely based on a simple Internet search?"

Julie flashed a conspiratorial smile and laughed. "Quip, you worry too much. I've worked as an expert in the shadows for a long time. Besides, Juan wouldn't let me take any unnecessary risk. He's fully onboard with my activities. In fact, he's provided some outstanding pointers. At our next total team call, I'm requesting that Juan be allowed to listen and partake in our meetings moving forward. He's just as committed to this business me. He can speak for me anytime."

Quip raised an eyebrow and then looked very serious as he replied, "I don't know, Jules. That seems like too much of a risk to the rest of our business. For example, I wouldn't tell EZ some of the details about the family business, and she lives with me. For the business, I should have the details."

Julie's color brightened as the anger bloomed in her cheeks. Her eyes flashed like daggers as she barked, "You're not the boss. And as far as EZ goes, you're stretching the truth.

"I know exactly how much you tell her. She can be trusted. Just like my husband. Maybe if you married her, you could bring her closer into the fold. She even promised to stop having the affair with ICABOD, you idiot!"

ICABOD commented, "Miss Julie, you know that she was just teaching me how to tease, don't you?"

Julie felt ashamed. "I'm sorry, ICABOD, it's not you but Quip that tries to have his cake and eat it too. Juan doesn't know about you at all. Without you in all these cases, I'd be a mess and my team would have suffered."

Wolfgang cleared his throat and suggested, "Quip, you run your business here. Julie and Juan have made a successful business that we can be proud to be supporting. They, however, make the decisions on that business, and we'll support them as long as I'm here.

"Julie, you can bring it up at the next meeting, but I don't think you will receive any pushback. Let's go forward, shall we?"

Julie chuckled and smiled. "Wolfgang, you're always the one to maintain the peace. Quip, sorry I shouted."

Quip looked thoughtful before he replied, "Me too, Jules. She tells you all that, really?"

Julie flashed another great smile, nodded, and disconnected.

CHAPTER 63

Venture capitalists

Chairman Chang alerted Jamie that the winning door would be his during this morning's selection, and on the first pick. He was willing to give up the game selection to Dmitry, but the pot behind the doors this round was substantial, per the text he'd received earlier. He had also committed to Jamie a percentage of this door as an enticement to consider staying on to work on the next stage of business partnership with the Russian. Jamie was noncommittal with regards to taking the gaming to a higher level. However, both Won and Ton commented to their boss on Jamie's skills, especially in the Western marketplace. Chairman Chang would never trust the man, but he had proved useful and did as he promised.

Chairman Chang launched the sequence for the video conference with immediate success. Dmitry looked ready to play. Chairman Chang greeted, "Dmitry, you are looking fit today. Before we start door selection or a new game, I wanted to discuss the potential business partnership you have mentioned in the past."

Dmitry looked a bit surprised and wary as he replied, "I am always up for a good business discussion, Chang, so please go ahead."

"We discussed taking the games to a commercial level. I've decided to be in England as you had suggested. I've also done some research. It makes sense to get the perspective of the millennials. However, I think there's a real market for the older successful businessmen who are either retired or maybe just need break now and again, like us. I must admit that I've enjoyed the games and, of course, the winnings.

"As a public endeavor, the winnings might be an angle that they can sign up for, like a subscription or as a service. For obvious reasons, the power of the games would need to feel the same, but the ordinary person wouldn't have the same level of computing resources we've got. If we offer it as a service and in the Cloud, which is all the rage, then we could lease time on the supercomputers to the players and keep it isolated."

Dmitry looked thoughtful, then replied, "I think that your ideas have merit, especially renting some computer time and Cloud delivery. We would need to mimic what we have going on in the final games, or likely it would attract all the wrong attention. I think we could easily form a partnership and call it R and C or RC. I would consider a ninety/ten split with you for share time on your supercomputer, and investing, say, all your winnings in our competitions to date." Dmitry grinned into the video camera and nodded.

Chairman Chang shouted, "You've got to be kidding!" Then he composed himself and continued, "Dmitry, I don't mind you claiming first place on the partnership name. However, it'll need to be a fifty/fifty arrangement. I'm prepared to offer some computer time as a service. Additionally, I'm adding a chief marketing officer that I feel is both technical and of an age that target the correct consumer personas. I'll get the draft of the agreement over to you toward the end of the week."

Dmitry smiled a bit and said, "Fifty/fifty really doesn't seem reasonable as my team invested all the ideas and turned them into a digital reality. That investment cannot be ignored in our agreement. I am no fool, Chang."

"No, old friend, you are not a fool. However, the rework on the games to a consumer platform will require support, and I will lend some support to transition the games and invest half my winnings, as will you."

"Chang, you're a thief, I say. I'm not sure I can partner with a thief!"

Chairman Chang's face grew very dark and imposing on the screen as he glared at Dmitry. "Thief? You old snake! How dare you call me a thief! We've played this game with your rules, and quite honestly, the changes you order to be made to the games have put me at a disadvantage over and over. If I was not increasing my skill with every contest, I'd be out far more. We'll table this discussion for the long term and choose the doors now."

"Chang, that is no way to negotiate. If you want to win, you need to argue, use give and take. It is how the barter system was designed. We aren't even investing our own money, you fool."

Chairman Chang fumed and set his jaw firmly, then finally responded, "Alright, here's a negotiation for you. It's my turn to pick the door first, correct?"

"Yes."

"And you created these gates and tests to essentially play at the edge. Isn't that so?"

"Why, of course, that's a huge part of the fun, isn't it?"

"Agreed. However, my track record in selecting the correct door the first time is poor at best. Right?"

"Yes, you have, um…well…not done well on that front but far better on your second round. It is all luck, sir."

"Okay, then we will start this partnership on luck. Agreed?"

"Luck is good, but what am I agreeing to?"

Chairman Chang put on his inscrutable face and waited. Then he offered, "If I can pick the winning door the first time today, I'll give you the spin on the wheel of misfortune, and you'll agree to the contract terms I outlined. How do you feel about that, Mr. Russian Roulette?"

"Since you put it that way, you old goat, yes! Let's do it. Both of us will make money."

Dmitry had headed home after the long game with Chairman Chang. When he awoke in the morning, he lay in bed and stretched, then mentally reviewed the success from the day before. True, Chang collected at the door money, but Dmitry won the game. The payout would be considerable, even if it took additional games to convince the victims. Once the payout occurred, he had the advantage of selecting the door first. He also thought about the partnership. Upon review he felt it provided an avenue for security in his older years when he stepped down from his government role. The best part, though, was the personal side, he thought, as he stretched again. He had received a text from Natasha that she had her new phone but was teaching last night and this morning. She had, however, suggested they meet at the park at noon. He felt delighted him beyond belief. He reached over to the intercom and told his staff to prepare a picnic basket and ordered his valet to get his best jacket and slacks, a fresh white shirt, and boots ready. Then he proceeded to the bathroom for a shave and shower.

It was a grey, cold day, but his heart was warm. Dmitry wore his dark grey great coat and *ushanka* as he enthusiastically, almost jauntily, walked from his home to the driveway. The driver assisted Dmitry into the back of the limousine and promised the picnic basket with the fresh delicacies was packed in the front. The driver indicated he'd added a heater as the air was a bit colder than predicted earlier in the week. Dmitry reviewed the targeted conversation he planned with Natasha, even as he handled the presents in his pocket that he planned to present over lunch. He planned to escort her for a walk around the garden area even though most of the plants were hibernating.

They arrived and the driver opened the door. Before Dmitry could exit, the driver was pushed aside, and a man bent down and looked in the door. Dmitry was startled until he recognized the number two man to be the Prime Minster, Vladimir Kaskalfi.

Dmitry smiled and greeted, "Vladimir, what a surprise, sir. How are you? To what do I owe this honor?"

Vladimir's expression showed nothing as he replied, "We need to talk, Dmitry. Move over. It'll be more private in the car."

Dmitry slid over on the seat to allow Vladimir to enter. Vladimir held his hand up to the driver, then closed the door. He faced Dmitry and assessed him with a critical eye.

"Vladimir, what is it? How can I help you? Is something the matter?"

Vladimir shook his head slightly, then asked, "How could a man of your military background be such a fool?"

Dmitry was taken aback and scrunched up his features. "Sir, I am afraid I don't know what you mean." His stomach roiled at the thought of his meeting with Natasha being discovered. "I am here to take a little walk, clear my head, and have my midday meal. Granted, it is a bit cold, but that's not foolish for a Russian."

Vladimir glared at Dmitry and stated, "Shut up, old man. This is not the time for a walk and eating. This is a time for you to thank the powers that be that I don't shoot you where you sit.

"How could you be so stupid as to get caught doing what you have been doing for however long in an alliance with the Chinese? Then the money and using the state's resources for your own gain? You should be ashamed. I know I am."

Dmitry was shocked at the detail Vladimir conveyed. He knew without a doubt that he was lucky to be living. He hung his head and asked, "What's to become of me?"

"All of your property now belongs to the Federation. All your accounts are frozen. YOU will provide details of any accounts I don't yet know about."

"Yes, sir, I will do that. What of my faithful staff? Can they be spared if I tell you everything?"

"Your secretary is in interrogation right now. She's expected to turn state's witness against you. All your personal computers were seized early this morning. The data files are being reviewed for any traitorous communication exchanges you might have been involved in. You were a fool to use our resources, then get way too close to an international incident with all you've been involved with."

Dmitry's eyes filled slightly but refused to overflow. His world was dissolving, and he had come this close to meeting his destiny. With his fate sealed, the only thing that mattered was to try and catch a glimpse of Natasha in the park waiting for him. But Vladimir, in his highly agitated state, moved to block the window. It occurred to Dmitry that if Vladimir knew of her existence, she'd receive Russian justice as well. Rather than tip off Vladimir about Natasha, he swallowed hard and begged, "Konstantin, my second, please spare him. He like a son to me."

Vladimir laughed and then said, "Like a son? Well, your son turned you in with enough evidence that we might still shoot you. I want you to think about my next question. Do you want the formality of a public trial, or do you just want to move to the guilty verdict that most assuredly awaits you?"

Realizing his fate, Dmitry lightly chuckled with resignation and responded, "Ah yes, the Russian efficiency of an expedient trial. Funny how I used to believe that Russian justice was something that worked to my advantage. The perspective does change when you become the target."

CHAPTER 64

And then ...

Juan started the video conference early, to make certain the group saw him when they joined. Julie needed to take care of an activity with the twins but would join shortly after the start time. Juan felt it important that he focus on success after the recent weeks of work on these wild yet connected cases. He wanted to ensure each person completed the timely wrap-up details for their assignments. Two new work order requests had arrived shortly before lunch that Julie wanted to allow the team to bid on if they wished.

At first blush, each of the new assignments appeared to need two people. One request originated from the Caribbean, while the other was centered in England. After vetted the preliminary details, Julie deemed them unrelated.

The first indicated a protection type of assignment for the entire family of a high-powered official from the British Virgin Islands.

The second appeared to be more of a technology review and refresh for a powerful financial institution in England. That assignment required potential support from the family's R-Group staff. Julie would fill that role until the family agreed to her stance on Juan. Juan knew it was a topic of discussion in an upcoming meeting. Juan would be fine regardless of the outcome of the meeting with the family at dinner in Zürich the next day.

Mercedes joined first. Juan could tell by the smile on her face she'd tidied up with her assignment. Jim, the U.S. government's liaison was assigned due to the policies of the U.S. Homeland Security. Juan suspected Jim would be briefing his agencies during the same time as this call. Brayson sent a message earlier that he was almost finished but would miss the call. EZ quietly joined with a smile and quick hello from Zürich. Tyler and Ernesto both joined the call at the same time and started some lively banter. Summit was connected about the same time that Julie entered the video call and took the seat to Juan's right. Juan noticed that George joined, looking like he'd lost his best friend and totally exhausted.

Juan opened with a smile and an even tone. "Ladies and gentlemen, I want to thank you joining this meeting on time. I hope to stay inside the scheduled time, but if we finish early, we all get time back. You've each been working to finish up the work effort and write those pesky reports. Ahead of those reports, we'd appreciate a quick summary, especially if you need additional support. Then Julie will discuss a couple of new assignments. Let's get started."

Mercedes volunteered, "The problem at the airport was based on some vulnerabilities in the firewalls and procedural issues with maintenance. Overall, it really was one of those good news stories in that humans and machines need to share the workload with defined processes and ongoing reviews. With the help of the Homeland Security, we were able to force certain changes as well as help some capable individuals rejoin that airline.

"Julie, when you hired me, you said part of what you liked about the jobs you worked on was making people connections.

I'm happy to report that I am overnighting the final signed contract for three years of quarterly maintenance reviews as well as software update oversight with the targeted airline."

"Alright, Mercedes," several voices chimed in along with nods and electronic claps from everyone.

Mercedes smiled and continued, "It was a great ending to a stinky situation."

Groans were chorused from everyone, along with a laugh from Julie.

"I know it was a poor attempt at humor, but honestly, I learned everything I want to know about the sanitary facilities of an aircraft. Jim was a great help. I appreciate your letting me work with him."

Julie grinned and interjected, "As if any other choice would have been acceptable to you or your man. When are you guys headed home?"

Mercedes laughed and made a funny face and shrugged. "We have a flight out in a couple of hours and are returning to Zürich for the weekend. Then Jim goes back to work, at who knows where. You know, those three letter agencies of the U.S. simply don't share destinations. If you have any insight on the where, I'd love to hear it.

"Anyways, the best news is I heard my cat is fine but misses me." Mercedes laughed and added, "Just kidding, guys. The best news is that because of the close-knit community of airlines, we have requests for three additional contracts for similar services. I'll forward them now, Juan."

"Mercedes, that's great news," Juan stated. "If they are even close to the first one in annual revenue, we'll be in great shape. Perhaps even ready to begin adding some new talent. I received a note, which I tend to take with a grain of salt, from Jim that outlines in detail some of your accomplishments during the negotiations with the two opposing groups. Those are always tricky situations, so thumbs up, Mercedes."

Julie stated, "I second that, well done."

Ernesto interjected, "Good for you, Mercedes. I'd like to update next and then drop the call to finish up here."

"Of course, go ahead," stated Juan.

"The motion that was put in place with Juan's help appears to be moving in the right direction for stopping one point of origin. We drafted, Jamie, the person on the inside to gain some insights to the operations. His commitment is completed I plan to remove him and his girlfriend soon, regardless of the overall outcome. Have you verified that your father is good with sending them to the ranch in Georgia, EZ?"

EZ replied with a sweet smile and her vibrant, bouncing red hair catching the light on the high-definition screens. "It's all set. You merely need to send the flight arrival information as well as the photos of them. He'll pick them up. He's looking forward to a little company as the place is quiet these days. His girlfriend is also looking forward to it. They will help Jamie and his girlfriend get a fresh start."

"Thank you, EZ.

"Juan, I'll check back in when I am finished, in case you want me in a different destination from Luxembourg. I've not booked a flight yet, so I can be flexible.

"Sorry to miss the updates all, but I promise I will catch up and read all reports."

As Ernesto disconnected, EZ responded, "You're welcome.

"I think that I will just continue then with my updates, unless there are objections." EZ grinned and said, "I'll take the silence as a no. We were able to track the transmission origins for the bandits. Though we are still sorting through some of the captured routes for the electronic money laundering, we have not been successful at tracing all the funds. Based on the figures our customers shared, we feel confident we can recover roughly seventy percent of the funds paid out to meet the ransom demands. The time spent, manpower used, and mental anguish will not even come close to being recovered, ever.

"Julie and Juan, I, for one, find no satisfaction is just getting some ransom recovered and a few new customers from these cases. These bandits, or assholes, as my daddy would say, make me mad enough to spit. I want to find them and have them strung up for causing the undue pain and suffering. Sorry, but that is just how I feel. How can we hurt them back?" EZ looked so fierce and sincere on the screen that all hints of happiness were erased from her face.

Julie looked very stone-faced as she replied, "We do not take revenge ourselves, but we do facilitate justice in all the right places. We are well connected, EZ. These criminals won't get away with their crimes. Someday, when we are all together sipping a bit of celebration, we will regale you with a bit of the behind-the-scenes action that also occurred. Trust Juan and me to be right there with you, perhaps more so.

"Tyler, how about you next?"

"Thanks, Julie, sure. The geolocation problems that my case had, in addition to the ransom stuff, had a high risk for serious injury due to the inability for emergency services to respond efficiently in this region. A lot of businesses were affected when emergency services did not respond properly to their 911 calls.

"The good news from this case is also a small city contract. I also want to thank both Julie and Juan for agreeing to the start of a special outreach program for veterans. I've met twice now with a vet named Sarge, who I think we can jointly work with the local police to help him readjust to society. It is a totally different program defined in part by Detective Cormorant, known here as Como, to really get involvement, not just handouts. He has a passion for it. Thank you both for agreeing to help with the financing for this outreach program."

Juan replied, "Tyler, you found a good need and made the business case. I feel we can take it international, and so does Julie. A fantastic idea, to be sure. I've already signed up for some time in the program. Once you show the details to your co-workers, I suspect they'll volunteer time too. We have a lot of military background in our ranks. By the way, did the package make it back intact?"

Tyler studied the video feed a moment. "Yes, it did. I've given it to the mayor with the understanding that Detective Cormorant see that it's distributed equitably among the vandalized stores since all markings of ownership were removed. How did you manage to find these stolen goods and get them shipped back? I didn't see any customs stamps on the package, so I'm curious how it sailed through to me."

Juan grinned. "Oh that! It was easy! We just declared that it was a fruitcake that was being re-gifted!

"Summit, I think that leaves you."

Summit laughed. "Yes, sir, and I'll sign up for some time, Tyler. I scanned the report just before the meeting and am impressed with the openness of the ideas you've incorporated into the plan.

"My case was interesting and reminded me that we are in a team sport. I am happy to report, we've added a contract here with the new IT staff who are focused on this organization with a holistic view to processes and procedures. The idea of total automation is one folks keep toying with but it's not quite ready, yet. There's really nothing shining out in this case outside of folks reaching their potential. We'll maintain an ongoing consulting relationship by the project.

"Over to you, George."

George looked at the video camera, and the lines of his tired face showed. He looked so sad that Juan nearly interceded. George said, "This was a tough one for me, Juan. I thought it was bad enough when we nearly lost you in the once-in-a-century sandstorm. We had the geolocation issue, like Tyler, which thankfully EZ discovered early on how to work past. The struggle between a remote workforce and management was a contributor to the problems faced here. I wish I could've helped spare the life of that young man. My paperwork is all current. I fly back six hours from now.

"Julie, I think you are working on a contract with these folks. I want to just come home and rest for a couple of days, if you don't mind."

Julie and Juan both nodded. Julie said, "No problem, George. I will forever be in yours and EZ's debt for helping find Juan in time. Just so you know, bonuses for outstanding performance will be included in your next paycheck. I know word will spread, and we'll get new cases flowing." Julie went on to explain their new cases and the details for each of them. Very quickly Mercedes, Ernesto, Tyler, and Summit agreed to take them. There were discussions with regards to the fixes they had completed each done for their respective customers before the call ended.

Once the screen was blank, Juan pulled Julie into his arms and said, "I think that you did very well in your role, my Natasha. Your seduction skills are without equal, in-person or online."

Julie flashed her trademark smile and suggested, "I think the in-person is preferred. Let's go make love then get ready to meet with the family in Zürich. Our flight time is approaching far too fast for my liking."

"Yes, sweetheart." Juan swept her off her feet and into their bedroom and said with a mock Russian accent, "Darling, talk to me like you do in those chat rooms. You know how it drives me wild and makes me plead with you to get into my bank account!"

Julie giggled and said, "Yes, darling, it is how I leave all my men; emotionally and financially drained!"

Farewell and Adieu, Spanish Ladies...

Brayson was focused on the computer screen and failed to detect Mayor Perez move up and lean against the doorway behind him. She stood there for several minutes before she cleared her throat to gain his attention.

Gently snapped back to awareness of his surroundings, Brayson turned to face the mayor and offered, "Sorry, Mayor Perez, I didn't hear you. I know you said for me to disengage, but I wanted to follow through on my commitment. I'm almost finished here. Is there something else?"

Baby Perez studied Brayson a moment before she answered. "When were you going to tell me about it? You weren't going to leave and let me discover it on my own? It would have made me very sad to have found out about it after you had left. That would have been most unfair."

Brayson smiled. "I didn't think a big announcement would have done any good. I trust you to make the appropriate disclosure to the council for the maximum political traction. Our organization prefers the shadows and anonymity when going about our work. Being famous is not something we add to our resumes."

Mayor Perez smirked. "Exactly how am I supposed to tell the city council I got our ransom money back? I don't think they're going to accept a story that our €50 million check was marked *Insufficient Funds* and returned with a €20 charge for being overdrawn."

Brayson chuckled and agreed, "Let me know how that works out for you. I'm glad you're here so I can brief you on the other piece of business contracted by your city. We got a trace on the breach into your systems with the help of my offsite counterpart in concert with your IT group. The reviews showed that all the security protocols were in place, but the bandits entered through the internal certificate authority server and issued their own valid cert. This allowed them to issue destructive messages to all your internal servers and appliances throughout your connected smart city. We reviewed the security procedures that let the bandits in so that doorway is closed now and forever. We also ran and updated the proper security measures for your internal cert server.

"As a precaution, the cert server has a twin of itself on the network that's in read-only mode. That prevents it from being made to issue new certs. Yeah, your IT group will have to hand carry the certs generated from the primary to the twin server. However, it's a simple step that will prevent this from reoccurring.

"In addition to the ransom payment being returned, the other contract deliverable of securing your city's network is finished, Madam Mayor. You have a good IT group here. The bandits simply found a very obscure vulnerability to use. The risks are neutralized, per our contract."

Baby Perez grinned. "The city thanks you, Brayson, and your talented team. Please express our gratitude to your organization for a job well done. And now I sense you are in a hurry to leave for your home surroundings. May I assume that you have a significant other who tires of your absence? I might recommend you bring her here for some well-deserved rest and relaxation. Our cities in Spain are famous for our history, architectural achievements, and cosmopolitan night life. It is an easy city to help rekindle a stalled romance."

Brayson went cold and pale at Baby's recommendation. His smile faded, and he struggled to neutralize his dormant emotions for his lost love.

Baby realized the emotional trigger she had inadvertently pulled and hastily offered, "I'm sorry, Brayson, I didn't mean to derail our farewell discussion. I can see that I hit a raw nerve. I apologize. You don't make many friends in this line of work, and I just wanted to say…well, you are always welcome to return to our fair city as a tourist. I'll even be your tour guide." Then, with a wry grin, Baby added, "Of course, it can't be during my reelection campaign."

Brayson struggled to release the painful memories. After a few moments he commented, "Mayor Perez, I'd like to return to your city as a tourist at some point. I'll likely be alone when I do. I apologize for raising your concern. Thank you for all your hospitality. It's been much appreciated."

Brayson collected his things and rose to leave, but Baby intercepted him with a kind hug. Then looking into his eyes, she squeezed his hand goodbye. He gave a gentle but forced smile, then left without another word.

CHAPTER 66

Things to Come

Chairman Chang was already in an irritable mood and snapped at his administrative assistant. "I told you I wasn't to be disturbed! Whatever it is, Professor Lin will just have to wait with his request. Everything seems to have piled up at once, and he's not at the top of the list."

Professor Lin kept the cyber college running and maintained the supercomputer. Typically, Professor Lin requested additional funding for some special programs or software to forward the curriculum at the college. Chairman Chang simply wasn't interested in funding someone's pet project.

The assistant knew that tone of voice always meant not to try again, but she persisted, "Sir, he is not asking for anything. He only wants to give you something. He maintains that the requested conversation is important and, judging from his continual insistence, urgent. He won't leave a message, which must mean it is classified information for your consideration only. I recommend you take his call, sir."

Chairman Chang contemplated what the young assistant had petitioned him with and, with a resigned but irritated tone, relented, "Alright, send his call through, but if he has oversold his petition to you, count on late night work again."

The young assistant swallowed hard and hesitated briefly before sending the call through. Chairman Chang, in his cheeriest false speech, greeted, "Good day, Professor Lin. I trust your day is proceeding to your liking, sir. How may I be of assistance?

"My administrative assistant indicated that you were most insistent to be put through with all due haste. What can we talk about?"

Professor Lin had always been intimidated by having to deal with the powerful Chairman Chang. It took all his intestinal fortitude as he responded, "Sir, we just were visited by a representative of the Ministry of Internal Cyber Security, a Colonel Chew Guano. I won't trouble you with all the details, but the bottom line is that we failed our security audit on the supercomputer."

Chairman Chang's face gave way to a dismayed look, and he asked, "Okay. What does this have to do with me?"

The discomfort the professor experienced in advance of the conversation merely grew in proportion as he offered, "Sir, he knew to hunt for the secondary login files that were not scrubbed. I know we talked about covering your access trail, but he somehow already knew where to look."

Professor Lin drew a deep breath as he continued, "Basically, he pulled a report that shows your login ID into the system, and most importantly, the amount of supercomputer access time being used. The look on his face when he bypassed the scrubbed login files to see the unvarnished files left me feeling a little cold. He stared at me a moment, then printed off the report and left. I am almost certain he's en route with evidence in hand to discuss this with you."

Chairman Chang rolled his eyes and commented, "Now he has a list of times and dates that I logged into the system for my mathematical analysis. Is this what was so important that you had to interrupt my morning?"

Professor Lin struggled to maintain his professional demeanor, and he clarified, "I don't believe Guano will be convinced that you were compiling state sanctioned mathematical models after seeing the graphic rendering of your digital avatar. He also inspected your gaming executables while he looked around."

Chairman Chang, now indignant bordering on irritation, growled, "Alright, sometimes I run a personal gaming program to ease my tense state of mind. You can't run a state organization without some emotional release and mental recreation. What's the harm in that?"

Professor Lin practically choked but continued, "Sir, we failed the security audit, and your name is high on the list of excessive unexplained usage. They should have taken me in for questioning, but they didn't even give me so much as a warning. I feel certain that they are on their way to see you. I felt compelled to call and warn you. This new digital police force is very intimidating, sir. People are known to vanish when they fail a security audit. Your usage placed us at the top of the list for computer resources across the entire country."

Chairman Chang made a disinterested face before he announced, "Professor Lin, Guano has worked for my organization for some time now on a dotted line basis. I don't believe there's any real danger here."

Professor Lin, only able to manage to drive his voice barely above a whisper due to his anxiety, suggested, "Sir, perhaps you've forgotten that he worked in this facility under your orders and my direction when he was a major. He was recruited by the new Ministry of Internal Cyber Security.

"In the scant fifteen months since he did that, they have promoted him to colonel. This is the digital secret police, sir. By all accounts, they simply don't have a sense of humor when it comes to disobeying state security laws."

Chairman Chang, almost unable to hide his disgust with the implications of the conversation, stated, "Alright, fine. Guano is going to show up and complain about my department's excessive use of the supercomputer, with elevated access rights. I'll deal with it. Thanks for calling. Go back to your job now."

The chairman disconnected the call but sat, contemplating the warning. For some reason his normal political confidence was at odds with an unusual deep foreboding of things to come.

Chang's administrative assistant quickly escorted an expressionless Guano and his two officers into the chairman's meeting area of his offices. With as few words as possible, everyone declined refreshments, to which she uneasily nodded and then left.

After a long quiet pause while the men looked one another over, Chairman Chang finally stated, "I believe you had something to discuss, Guano."

Again, with no expression and with a longer than necessary pause, Guano finally asserted, "It is Colonel Guano, Chairman Chang. We are using formal titles since my team is here on state business."

Chairman Chang, a little annoyed at his former employee's attitude, offered, "Ah, yes, Colonel Guano. I see that they disregarded my advice and promoted you anyway. Be that as it may, what is the nature of this visit?"

Again, with no hint of emotion on his face, Guano flatly stated, "Chairman Chang, we are here to arrest you for crimes against the state. We'd like to have this event unfold with no undue dramatics and, of course, with your quiet cooperation."

Completely floored by this turn of events, Chairman Chang did a double take that threatened to have him fall out of his chair.

After a moment of supreme discipline, he was able to reel in his disoriented state and asked, "What did you say? Do you remember who I am, Major? I am Chairman Chang. I do not take lightly your disrespectful attempt to unsettle my authority in this country. If this is a joke, it's in extremely bad taste. If you are serious, then the next time we meet, you'll be begging for cigarette butts from fellow prisoners. I demand an explanation."

Guano almost smiled as he watched Chairman Chang squirm, but explained, "You've used the state-paid-for supercomputer to conduct an elaborate gaming exercise with an equally detestable partner in Russia. You're part of an extortion game of global businesses and municipalities. The results of said gaming exercise was not to enrich the state treasuries, but rather fill your own secret bank account. Or, at least, that was your original intention, except it's no longer a secret.

"As if that weren't hostile enough to your Chinese government, you have also funneled state funds into a gaming casino while trying to maintain yourself as a secret partner, not revealed. Following our investigations, I was instructed to collect you as quietly as possible for your trial."

Chairman Chang's mind was swirling with the accusations and any possible actions that might get him out of this. But before he could respond or challenge the statements, Guano stated, "As for Nikkei, your white tiger, she'll be remanded to the state zoo and given suitable quarters to the end of her days. She'll have better accommodations than where you're going. We both already know the outcome of your fair trial, but I felt it was the right thing to do for her. After all, a pet can't always choose their owners."

Chairman Chang, coming to grips with his destiny, solemnly asked, "And what of my two wards, Won and Ton? What is to be their fate considering my alleged misdeeds?"

Guano reflected thoughtfully and responded, "We've given it some thought, and we would like to have them continue to run the casino, but the proceeds would now be directed to the state treasuries. The third person in your casino enterprise and your supercomputer gaming competition seems quite well at home here, provided that enough leverage is applied to his partner. I believe it best for the time being to have them left to operate as before but to support a different master, provided of course that they don't ask any questions."

Chairman Chang, in a full-scale panic, retorted, "I have the funds to make amends for my alleged misdeeds. Let me make everything whole again. Tell me that there's another option."

Guano frowned and dispassionately offered, "Ah, the alleged misdirected funds in exchange for clemency. What a noble gesture, Chang, except there's nothing in your secret accounts. You should know that we weren't the first to find your account with the intention of seizing its contents. You have nothing to bargain with. It's now time to leave."

In his final plea, Chairman Chang offered, "I have five million euros in diamonds that I will put up for ransom. Surely that will hold some interest for the decision makers, and only I know where they are buried."

Guano again nearly smiled as he gently replied, "We removed Nikkei's collar when we transported her earlier. Not to worry, she'll get a nice collar in exchange. The new one doesn't have electrodes embedded in it to send her into a frenzy when you're mad at someone."

Chairman Chang sat numbed in his chair, hearing that his last hope fade to silence. He quietly asked, "May I then have the other way out, Colonel?"

Guano studied Chang for a few seconds, then unholstered his side arm, checked that one bullet was in the chamber, removed the clip, and sat the semi-automatic on the table. Then Guano and his two escorts moved outside into the reception area. As soon as they heard the shot, Guano dialed a number on his cell phone and said, "It's done."

CHAPTER 67

Is it my Turn Again?

Wolfgang and Otto wore grave faces as they faced each other in Otto's office in the Zürich operations center of the R-Group. Otto asked, "Where are we on it?"

Wolfgang replied without moving his eyes from the monitor. "Someone or something is driving commodity prices down to the breaking point. At this rate, world order will be irrevocably changed in six months."

Otto asked, "Do we know who yet?"

Wolfgang, with his eyes still focused on the monitor, replied, "We only know what's occurring, not who's driving it. What usually happens in a scenario like this is that prices are driven so low that the producers cannot sell enough to cover their costs and simply exit the business. Then someone with deeper pockets scoops up the failed businesses for pennies on the dollar. The problem here is that there are so many industries affected, and no one is buying the distressed property. It almost looks like an assassin's game."

Otto wrinkled his brow and questioned, "Which commodities are you referring to? You didn't specify."

Wolfgang took an exaggeratedly deep breath and responded, "All of the important ones. Oil, gas, copper, basically anything used in manufacturing. What's curious is that the precious metals like gold and silver aren't being driven down like the others."

Otto studied the screen output some more and then inquired, "Is this a cloaking effort? By that I mean, drop the price of, say, oil to the point that competing technologies like solar or electric battery can no longer compete, thus disrupting the disrupting technologies from growing. With oil at a very low price point, competing technologies cannot be price competitive. In that case, no investment monies find their way into the development cycle, which drops costs. But if you can buy your investments cheap enough, then you can compete and beat the low-price incumbent. We might even consider this a political play against raw material producing nations. In other words, which countries suffer from commodity pricing that is too low?"

Wolfgang considered the question and commented, "Good question. Even the most unlikely possibilities can sometimes just step on to the stage of life with no warning. Therefore, I'm not ignoring any option."

Otto frowned and stated, "This many commodities being controlled at the same time? That's simply impossible by a single individual. I'm not even sure that a highly disciplined evil organization could pull that off without making their presence known before now"

Wolfgang blinked several times and added, "Agreed. But I'm looking at abnormal market forces driving all of them down simultaneously. The one that caught my attention was the copper market. I've got ICABOD crosschecking the multiple events driving down commodity prices, but no single thread connecting them all has taken shape. As a great detective once said, 'When you eliminate all the improbable answers then the last one left must be the right answer, no matter how impossible.' I suspect that we are facing a highly disciplined group with an agenda we've yet to ascertain."

Otto offered, "To play effectively in the world of commodities trading, one must have excellent computer knowledge, formidable computer processing power, and deep pockets to cover the kinds of positions that would affect each market in this manner. I'd expect movement in these areas would be observed by our people sooner or later. Since we've spotted the anomaly, I'd expect us to find clues sooner."

Wolfgang nodded, with his demeanor becoming increasingly serious. "I concur. Our next full team meeting is tomorrow. I believe this is our lead topic of conversation."

Otto looked at the screen. "ICABOD, please continue your scanning efforts of the digital horizon for any other intersecting attack vectors. I've got a feeling there's more in store for this scenario."

ICABOD responded, "While there is currently no basis for your feelings, Otto, there has been ample evidence in the past of your premonitions to be accurate as to the suggested outcome. I will continue my surveillance, gentlemen."

CHAPTER 68

Dining challenges

Julie and Juan reached Zürich shortly after the noon hour. When they arrived at Wolfgang's spacious home with its lavish landscape, Bowen, Wolfgang's trusted butler, showed them to a private suite of elegant rooms decorated with European collectables from earlier decades. Each of the suites had a primary color theme, and this one was in a mix of burgundy and rose. Julie had played tour guide as she'd shown Juan some of the details of the home and the gardens. Juan had attended a family affair at the residence but had not seen any of the private rooms. He enjoyed the animated manner Julie exhibited and the tidbits of information she shared about her early years. Juan wanted their twins to see the magical gardens and planned to suggest that during the evening's conversation.

Julie insisted they change for dinner after a leisurely shared shower. She was ready to lead the discussion and make certain her husband was an equal in the eyes of the family in all ways, period. Bowen knocked on their door and alerted them that cocktails were being served in the library and informed them that dinner would be in three quarters of an hour.

Once downstairs, Julie flashed her smile when she saw Wolfgang and hugged him. Juan wasn't nervous, per se, but he knew this was important to Julie. He had met the entire family at his and Julie's wedding, but this was somehow different. There was no wedding distraction or well wishes, but rather a family getting together to assess him. Juan took quiet stock of the fact that he had already passed the personal evaluation as Julie's husband. The difference was that this was a business meeting.

He first shook Wolfgang's hand and asked for a glass of red wine. Julie chose a white. Otto and Haddy rose from a couch, welcoming him with hardy handshakes and hugs. Petra and Jacob, standing by the fire, approached and shared hugs, handshakes, and well wishes too. By previous agreement, Quip and EZ would be arriving for dessert so that Julie could speak her mind to gain consensus. EZ did not need to hear any part of the conversation. The conversation shifted from the decor to the children, to the trip in Macau, and then to how the new business was faring.

Julie decided to lay out her issue. "Wolfgang, it's so nice of you to host this gathering. Thank you for making us feel so welcome."

Wolfgang inclined his head and added, "You and your family are always welcome in my home, for short or long visits."

"Great," said Juan, "I really want the twins to see your lovely gardens and explore this big house the way Julie said she and Petra did when they visited as children."

"Of course, my boy, anytime."

Julie continued, "I'm glad everyone could make it. I've been thinking about the best way to approach this subject. I decided to just tell it straight out.

"Juan is my husband and the father of our children. We took vows to love one another, to honor and protect each other. We like to share our thoughts and ideas around the business we're building. There are too many times when I have had to bite my tongue to avoid revealing things to Juan, and I need it to stop today. He's either a total part of this family or I will need to avoid any further integration into the family business. I prefer we agree to remove the barriers so Juan can contribute."

Otto asked, "Julie, now that we know how you feel it becomes a discussion with Juan. Son, how much do you know, and how much do you want to know?"

Juan looked at each of the people in the room and replied, "Otto, to be honest, I don't know what I don't know. I do, however, want to make certain we continue to work together and avoid secrets. I don't want to mess in your affairs, nor have you mess into our business. I get the sense, from this latest round of cases we faced, that you have some resources that we might leverage. I suspect some of the work I did on contract via Julie was based on filling a gap your group may have had.

"We work in an arena that can be dangerous. Julie wants me to have the same access she has to those resources. Your resources could improve our successes."

Julie smiled at her husband. "Exactly, my darling.

"Dad, Wolfgang, Petra, and Jacob, I want our operations to be transparent for Juan because it makes us stronger and more flexible in our business model with the CATS team. To be fair and efficient, you should be able to contact either of us for assistance just as we would want in return. Every conversation shouldn't have to go through me for filtering.

"Mom, you know everything about the business, but you don't attend all the family meetings, and you don't have a vote, though your opinion might be requested. Heck, I don't have a vote either and honestly don't want one. I just want to talk to my husband and work through issues when they arise."

Haddy nodded and stated, "I do understand, Julie.

"Juan, in case you weren't aware, for years I have worked as Otto's executive secretary because I wanted us to be together and even travel after the girls were grown. The result was I have learned a great deal about the family business over the years. It puts me at a bit of a risk with those that we outsmart. The fear is that if they found out any members of the family and their relationships it might be used as a leverage point. This business was started during the turbulence of the Second World War. As such, trust doesn't come easy."

Juan listened intently to Haddy and finally realized that the issue was to protect everyone. "All, I understand not giving up information to those that don't have the privilege of the inner circle. I also can relate well to protecting one's family. That said, I still intend to be my wife's partner for life, and if she feels this is important then I am right beside her."

Julie beamed and added, "I certainly don't intend to give him all the details of activities over the decades since the war. We need to focus on our business, first. I will, however, from tonight forward discuss everything with him."

Wolfgang stated, "For the record, Quip is not keen on this, as we discussed it this morning. He did admit, however, that he was finding it a challenge even with EZ.

"Juan, you've earned the emotional trust Julie has for you and mine by proxy in her trust. I believe that based on that good first step I am prepared to take my trust to the business level so I, for one, am fine with it. My vote is yes! I don't believe for a second that you would hurt Julie or the twins. You have certainly proven yourself on one or two occasions, though you do keep getting in harm's way, my boy. My recommendation is that you might want to curtail those types of scenarios in the future."

Petra, Jacob, and Otto agreed and were quick to congratulate Juan.

Otto asked, "Can we eat now? I am starving. We'll fill in Quip during dessert if you don't mind."

Wolfgang agreed, "Yes, let's. I think we're a bit late. I hate to annoy Bowen. He's so punctual."

The dining room, adjacent to the library, was inviting. Aromas wafting in from the kitchen promised a delicious dinner, as always. Just as the second course was removed and the main course was being readied, Juan felt the vibration of the third call on his cell phone within fifteen minutes. He discreetly glanced at the caller ID and realized it was the third call from his brother, Carlos. After apologizing, he rose to call Carlos back in the hallway outside of the dining room.

"Hey bro, what's up? Sorry, but Julie and I are having dinner with her family in Zürich."

Carlos replied, "Tough duty, bro." His voice took on an ominous quality as he continued, "Sorry to interrupt you, but I wanted to let you know we have a bit of a problem."

Juan glanced around to make certain he was still alone. "How so, and what can I do to help?"

Carlos continued, "Our monthly stipend has hereby ended. JC, Robert, and company have all been arrested by the Mexican police, and the items in storage appear to be missing."

"How is that possible? That place is secluded, and the boys know better than to bring just anyone there."

"I don't know, nor do I have the details yet. I only know this much from the On-Brothers, who were supporting the operation. Don and Vaughn were picked up as well, but Ron was in town shopping for supplies when the hit came so he's currently in hiding. There's something else."

The tone of Carlos's voice hit a nerve with Juan. He asked, "What else, bro?"

"I am sorry to have to tell you, but our uncle, Jesus, is missing. I have exhausted all my avenues to get a hint of where he is, but there is nothing. He is simply gone."

Juan's mind went through all the implications as he suggested, "You think maybe he got picked up by the police first and that led to the whole drug operation being uncovered?"

Carlos responded, "Again, I have no good information to go on. I thought that maybe with your new sleuthing job you might do some poking around to see what happened."

Juan thought for a moment and then said, "I'll go to Mexico and start looking for Uncle Jesus and see what I can do to help JC, Robert, and the others..."

Juan turned to see Quip and EZ staring at him. Quip motioned EZ to join the dinner, and then he walked up to Juan.

"Heard they want you more aware of the family enterprises. Cool, man. I was looking forward to having you persuade me to bring you into our business circle. It's so hard to find good people to trust in our line of work that we are constantly looking for new candidates.

"How you will explain to Julie and the others that you have not dropped your prior identity, with its sordid lifestyle, as instructed? Doesn't bode well, man."

With that Quip lowered his head and, with a fatalistic sigh, turned and walked away.

Anguished at the thought of being caught, Juan closed his eyes while still holding the phone, unable to respond to Carlos.

Specialized Terms
and Informational References

http://en.wikipedia.org/wiki/Wikipedia

Wikipedia (<u>wɪki' pi: diə</u> / *WIK-i-PEE-dee-ə*) is a collaboratively edited, multilingual, free Internet encyclopedia supported by the non-profit Wikimedia Foundation. Wikipedia's 30 million articles in 287 languages, including over 4.3 million in the English Wikipedia, are written collaboratively by volunteers around the world. This is a great quick reference source to better understand terms.

Air-gapped Or **air wall** is a network security measure, also known as **air gapping**, employed on one or more computers to ensure that a secure computer network is physically isolated from unsecured networks, such as the public internet or an unsecured local area network.

Anonymize An anonymizer or an anonymous proxy is a tool that attempts to make activity on the Internet untraceable. It is a proxy server computer that acts as an intermediary and privacy shield between a client computer and the rest of the Internet. It accesses the Internet on the user's behalf, protecting personal information by hiding the client computer's identifying information.

Automatic Location Information (ALI) Modified in Wiki in September 2015 to Enhanced 9-1-1 services. **E911** is a system used in North America that links emergency callers with the appropriate public resources.

Avatar In computing, an **avatar** is the graphical representation of the user or the user's alter ego or character. It may take either a three-dimensional form, as in games or virtual worlds, or a two-dimensional form as an icon in Internet forums and other online communities.

BitTorrent is a communications protocol for the practice of peer-to-peer file sharing that is used to distribute large amounts of data over the internet. BitTorrent is one of the most common protocols for transferring large files, and peer-to-peer networks have been estimated to collectively account for approximately 43% to 70% of all internet traffic (depending on geographical location) as of February 2009

Blade server a stripped down server computer with a modular design optimized to minimize the use of physical space and energy. Whereas a standard rack-mount server can function with (at least) a power cord and network cable, blade servers have many components removed to save space, minimize power consumption and other considerations, while still having all the functional components to be considered a computer.

Certificate Authority (CA) is an entity that issues digital certificates. A digital certificate certifies the ownership of a public key by the named subject of the certificate. This allows others (relying parties) to rely upon signatures or on assertions made by the private key that corresponds to the certified public key.

Encryption In cryptography, encryption is the process of encoding messages (or information) in such a way that eavesdroppers or hackers cannot read it, but that authorized parties can. In an **encryption scheme**, the message or information (referred to as plaintext) is encrypted using an encryption algorithm, turning it into an unreadable cipher text (ibid.). This is usually done with the use of an encryption key, which specifies how the message is to be encoded. Any adversary that can see the cipher text should not be able to determine anything about the original message. An authorized party, however, is able to decode the cipher text using a **decryption** algorithm that usually requires a secret decryption key that adversaries do not have access to. For technical reasons, an encryption scheme usually needs a key-generation algorithm to randomly produce keys.

Enigma Machine An Enigma machine was any of a family of related electro-mechanical rotor cipher machines used in the twentieth century for enciphering and deciphering secret messages. Enigma was invented by the German engineer Arthur Scherbius at the end of World War I. Early models were used commercially from the early 1920s, and adopted by military and government services of several countries — most notably by Nazi Germany before and during World War II. Several different Enigma models were produced, but the German military models are the most commonly discussed.

German military texts enciphered on the Enigma machine were first broken by the Polish Cipher Bureau, beginning in December 1932. This success was a result of efforts by three Polish cryptologists, working for Polish military intelligence. Rejewski "reverse-engineered" the device, using theoretical mathematics and material supplied by French military intelligence. Subsequently the three mathematicians designed mechanical devices for breaking Enigma ciphers, including the cryptologic bomb. This work was an essential foundation to further work on decrypting ciphers from repeatedly modernized Enigma machines, first in Poland and after the outbreak of war in France and the UK.

Though Enigma had some cryptographic weaknesses, in practice it was German procedural flaws, operator mistakes, laziness, failure to systematically introduce changes in encipherment procedures, and Allied capture of key tables and hardware that, during the war, enabled Allied cryptologists to succeed.

Gamification is the application of game-design elements and game principles in non-game contexts Gamification commonly employs game design elements which are used in so called non-game contexts in attempts to improve user engagement organizational productivity, flow learning, employee recruitment and evaluation, ease of use and usefulness of systems, physical exercise, traffic violations, and voter apathy, among others. A review of research on gamification shows that a majority of studies on gamification find positive effects from gamification. However, individual and contextual differences exist.

Public Safety Answering Point (PSAP) sometimes called "public-safety access point", is a call center responsible for answering calls to an emergency telephone number for police, firefighting, and ambulance services. Trained telephone operators are also usually responsible for dispatching these emergency services.

Sirocco is a Mediterranean wind that comes from the Sahara and can reach hurricane speeds in North Africa and Southern Europe.

Supercomputer a computer with a high-level computational capacity. Performance of a supercomputer is measured in floating point operations per second (FLOPS). As of 2015, there are supercomputers which can perform up to quadrillions of FLOPS.

VoIP is a methodology and group of technologies for the delivery of voice communications and multimedia sessions over Internet Protocol (IP) networks, such as the Internet. Other terms commonly associated with VoIP are IP telephony, Internet telephony, broadband telephony, and broadband phone service.

Yaqui Indians Native Americans who inhabit the valley of the Rio Yaqui in the Mexican state of Sonora, Mexico and the Southwestern United States. The Pascua Yaqui Tribe is based in Tucson, Arizona.

Lost in the blink of an action

TEN YEARS EARLIER

Darkness encapsulated his dreary dorm room, like a cave with no entrance or exit. He hadn't bothered to eat after answering the university chancellor's endless questions. The fear of school expulsion gripped his innards like food poisoning. He realized illness such as that a better punishment than the humiliation to his family if his records carried the permanent exclusion from this college. The conversation ended without threat or decision but promised a disciplinary decision before Monday morning.

The consultations and joking that had led up to today played in his mind like a b-movie. The day's events begged to be changed and forgotten. Choices that seemed so innocent in theory had turned so horrible after the fact.

For three years, dedicated time to his studies in the highly acclaimed program and avoided a social life. Semester after semester his grades reflected his efforts. On the rare occasions that the instructor insisted on student workgroups, he found that he spearheaded the work to complete a given project. The focused work ethic he delivered proved worthwhile because the inadequate students and laggards were weeded out at the end of the prior year. The remaining Type A personality classmates joined his unyielding drive to succeed. Finally, he felt surrounded by men who possessed equivalent capabilities in logic, reasoning, and forward thinking, even from their different disciplines.

From the beginning, he had focused on database programming, using the logic and advanced views of the times to leapfrog the generally accepted thinking. The thought leadership that was coming out of the Ivy League schools or newly emerging technology businesses was dwarfed by visions he and the few classmates he considered near equals roughed out. His late-night studies and conversations with these men had allowed him to lower his guard, as he thought about being accepted as one of them. He had honestly believed that he could step out from his old, structured world and easily move into this new one. He was confident that this new world was filled with people who spoke and understood the possibilities of the digital realm.

Sadness with the weight of his choices caused him to shake his head in disbelief. How would he be able to honor his family name with this hanging over his head? Even though the others laughed it off and cried 'college prank', he would clearly not be able to make this excuse the focus of the upcoming discussion with his uncle. Guilt had slowed every thought, action, and response today.

He had not spoken to his co-conspirators at all since they had been taken away from the hospital, even though, as he passed, one of them grinned and quipped, "It will all work out. Keep a stiff upper lip, old chum, and your inscrutable face intact."

At that moment, regardless of the punishment meted out by the university, he knew he needed to plan how he would make amends. He practically choked every time he considered how he had come to the university robed in honor but had now replaced it with unendurable shame.

As the oldest son of the patriarch of a long line of an honor-bound tradition, he had no excuse for tainting the family name. True, he was thousands of miles from home in a culture that usually shrugged its shoulders at college indiscretions, but he knew distance was not a safety net as it might have been before telephones, fax machines, or even telegrams. He had been given the opportunity to gain advanced education at the European university. His uncle and other family members had sacrificed to meet the costs even though he had qualified for some scholarships. Those might even be at risk after this stunt.

If he were able to complete the program, he needed to increase his course load and finish faster to save the family any additional expenses. In the forthcoming discussion with his uncle, he planned to lay this out as one in a series of steps in his path to forgiveness. He also had been outlining for months a series of programs, a bit before their time, which could gather information in new ways and use his yet-to-be-completed programs to make deterministic decisions. He was destined to create technology for the future. He had the brains, the dreams, and the tenacity to use what technology was available, and imagination to stretch it to the limits and beyond. The cruel luck of this escapade sadly made the focus of his next avenues become clear.

Armed with the confidence of his plans and cash to pay for the privilege of using a semi-private telephone, he went to purchase his cellular phone. Until this time he had been confident enough to send long letters home at the end of each semester, along with his grades and class standing. Now a private conversation was needed, and to hear the voice of his uncle was critically important. Getting the device, some instructions, and a plan that afforded international calling with a controllable cost element, he placed the call to his uncle's offices, which were just beginning their day. When connected to the receptionist, he formally asked to be connected to his uncle.

His uncle answered quickly with concern in his voice. "My esteemed one, are you ill or in danger?"

"No, my uncle, but I am in trouble and need your forgiveness."

With all the concern removed from his tone, he sternly replied, "Why would my ward and the son of my deceased brother need forgiveness? What have you done?"

He could feel the stern iciness in his uncle's voice but was determined to petition for a second chance. As had been outlined in his head in his dorm room, he related his activities, point by point. There was no soft-pedaling on his culpability in the matter at hand as he related the activities to his uncle and sketched his go forward plans. After thirty minutes of one-way conversation, he went silent.

As the seconds stretched into minutes, concern heightened in the young man's chest, threatening to crush his heart and stop his breathing. He finally could take no more as he begged, "Uncle, can you not speak to forgive me?"

"Silence!" his uncle demanded. "You have disgraced your family and your ancestors. There is no amount of planning you could do to rectify the steps already taken by you. You will never call here again or show your face to your former family. You are dead and gone. The funds you have in your account as of now is all you will get from me, ever. You will never amount to anything good or pure again. Do not embarrass this family again by using our name from this day forward. You chose dishonor as a life's course, so make the transition complete and answer to another name. You are a ghost in shame and will be alone for eternity."

With that last remark, his former uncle disconnected the call, as well as cast him out alone into the world. Each of the statements made by his uncle replayed in his head, growing colder and harsher each time he rewound the conversation. He made his way slowly back to his dorm room and replayed all the events that had led to his demise. As he finished packing his bags, turned out the light, and shut the door, he completely accepted that his past was now gone.

Those simple activities, coupled with the realization that his past had been stripped from him, had helped him reach a decision. As he stared into the night's darkness, a new resolve grew within him. He announced loudly and with deep-seated conviction as he strode through the darkness toward the bus stop, "I will show you all! I have the patience to endure this obstacle, but I will win back my honor even if it is only for myself! A man without a past is free to reinvent himself into the image of his choosing! I will become the ghost, not mourn the loss, and I will win for my new family of me."

CHAPTER 1

Number Crunching Issues

PRESENT DAY

Mike Patrick was looking at the big wall screen in his opulent office overlooking the recently expanded Suez Canal as data streamed in. His tailored shirt strained at the buttons following his typical oversized lunch with his cronies. As the head of ePETRO, Inc., he felt he could eat daily at a five-star restaurant and never have to work out. He was too important to have anything look amiss, even though his valet was constantly letting out the seams of his tailored suits or simply buying larger sizes. An outsider might consider him powerful, rather than simply full of himself.

Mike behaved as if he was at the limits of his patience as he ran his hand through his salt-and-pepper hair and demanded, "How in the hell is that possible? We have agreements…uh, I mean understandings, in place that oil production quotas should not be overrun. Roslyn, are you telling me that world oil production is hovering well above its allowance? Who's violating their understood production limits?"

Roslyn had worked with Mike for several years as his number two. She kept extensive incriminating pictures and reports hidden, though he was aware of some. Roslyn was a large woman and slightly taller than Mike at 1.83 meters. Her red silk suit, though quite expensive, had been sat in for way too long and looked like no amount of pressing would remove the wrinkles. Her hair was well cut, but its color of old wheat was not attractive against her sallow skin.

Roslyn opened her eyes wide in obvious bewilderment and, through her generous lips painted red to match her suit, stated, "According to the report, no one, Mike. That's what doesn't make any sense. If this report's correct, then no oil producing country or corporation within our organization is violating their understood quotas."

Mike was grinding his teeth in anger as he complained, "At this price point we can't make back the cost to drill, let alone bring up, the damn stuff. And, Roslyn, if you try and tell me that stupid old joke about losing money on every barrel of oil but that we can make it up in volume, I will box your ears."

Before Roslyn could offer anything else, Mike practically hollered, "Get everyone on the phone. We are going to get to the bottom of this. I want to know who is violating our agreements and why."

Roslyn was hesitant and her eyes were awash in reluctance, but she finally managed to respond, as non-offensively as possible, "Uh, sir, I've been fielding calls from all of them already, asking us the same question. The last few phone calls were from people as agitated as you are, sir. I think we need to do a little more homework before we round everyone up on an encrypted video call."

Mike rolled his eyes as he asked, "So, what are you saying? You don't believe anyone is lying about boosting their numbers?"

Roslyn shifted uneasily as she sat in her chair. She blinked as she searched for the right word choice and offered, "Sir, I believe everyone is holding firm on their oil production numbers because our satellite surveillance cannot confirm the extra forty percent of oil from any of the known locations. That suggests that this increase in product came from somewhere else.

"Even if someone was sneaking out that much extra oil, my question is why and how would we not have known of additional production areas? If it is a new entrant to the market, they would be as hurt by selling prices that are lower than production prices, just as we are. Or, if someone is bringing up oil with newer, lower cost extraction technology, we would have already heard about it."

Mike, now calmed down to a just seething level, queried, "Okay, so let's just say, for argument's sake, no one is fudging on their quantities. The only other possibility is…"

Roslyn finished his sentence. "…the numbers have been tampered with."

Mike huffed and rolled his eyes at the remark. He was about to respond when his personal line rang. Not wanting to waste any effort, he answered it on speakerphone, and his administrative assistant quickly began, "I know you told me not to disturb you, but the chairman of the board is on the line with what is most probably the rest of the board as well. She was not taking no for an answer and did not provide her usual jovial greeting to me. When I complete the connection, I suspect you will be on with the entire board of directors, sir."

Mike didn't get a breath to respond before he was on live with the chairman. Using the speakerphone and trying to buy a little time to realign his thought process, in his cheeriest voice he offered, "Good day, Madam Chairman, and of course to all the other conference call attendees. I rarely get a social call from the board since I know you all to be quite busy.

"I am confident that I didn't miss a regularly scheduled meeting, so I am wondering…"

Marge, the chairman, promptly broke into the monolog. "Cut the crap, Mike! I called this emergency meeting with the the mealy mouth doubletalk you give to the reporters!"

Mike had to mute the phone again to bring his breathing back under control. He shot a stern look at Roslyn and pointedly asked, "Are you going to let her talk to me that way?"

Roslyn, completely on the spot and with a puzzled look, responded as naïvely and sincerely as possible, "Uh…what way, sir?"

Seething at the dressing down he was getting and more that was about to come, Mike unmuted the phone and evenly stated, "In looking at all our data, documentation, and numbers of all partners, rivals, and peers that produce oil, no one can be accused of overproduction. Our shipping to market, our insider information, and our satellite imagery all point to the same piece of information. No one is overproducing, Madam Chairman."

Marge sputtered for a second, then boomed, "What? Are you insane? At forty percent over-capacity production, prices on the commodity markets are dropping to fire-sale pricing, and you claim no one is flooding the supply chain?

"Mike, you aren't stupid enough to think I would believe the entire planet is lying about its production numbers just to make us look bad. Since you truly have nothing else better to do, why don't you find out who or what is playing this little joke on us, hmm?"

Mike could feel the ice from Marge coming through the phone with her last comment. Marge was a thoroughly unpleasant woman, but with her enormous bulk and intimidating manners she usually got her way. Her management style was a combination of coercion, threats, and psychological beatings until she got the answers she wanted. Marge the Barge was a formidable opponent in the business world, and it was better to stay clear of her. You couldn't really call her cruel because that would have meant that she enjoyed her brutal effect on others. She cared for nothing, not pets, not family, not her community, and probably not even her life. Her rise to the top had cost her all of her human emotions, save one. She had to win at all the global business games she wanted to play in. Nothing else mattered. And, like any psychological addiction, the momentary rush didn't last long enough before a new rush was required. She was a very sad excuse for a human being.

Mike, feeling calm again, realized that she would have her way. If it meant that he was out of the way, then so be it. He smiled at the corporate combat barrage that was being shoved at him, so he countered, "Madam Chairman, we are working this issue with all due haste. If that is an unsatisfactory answer to you and the board, I shall, of course, tender my resignation. Will that make the situation more palatable for the board?"

Without the benefit of a video to observe the impact of his statement, Mike was sure that all the board members were staring at Marge and waiting for her answer.

After a long pause, she finally conveyed, "You are one of the few people who can get me to reel in my temper when it gets a little out of line. I will not accept your resignation but will charge you to get to the bottom of this mess. I want order restored in the marketplace as rapidly as possible. To do that, I am prepared to offer additional resources to make sure you are successful. Do we understand one another, Mike?"

Mike muted the phone and retorted to Roslyn. "Oh good, we aren't going to reenact the Jonah and the Whale story." Roslyn smirked slightly.

Mike unmuted his phone and stated, "As usual, Madam Chairman, you have not understated your position. I understand completely. Allow me to disengage from this call so that I can return to my analysis. Good day."

After he disconnected from the call, Mike studied Roslyn for a moment, then questioned, "How is it that markets have different production figures than the producers of a raw material?"

Roslyn added, "We know all the players and we know within three to five percent how much they can pull from the ground. I'm working to discover how and who could be distorting those numbers."

Mike asked, "Why can't we just publish our numbers to the markets? That should be enough to make this go away and get oil back to where it should be priced."

Roslyn offered, "Our word against the commodity traders and brokers that make this economy go round and round? Their numbers are usually quite close to ours. At this point, our figures would mean a huge jump in oil futures and probably lots of angry people decrying the big bad oil producers of rigging the supply figures to raise the price. I'm sure we would be painted as self-serving opportunists trying to squeeze the average consumer. How big of a private army would we need to surround ourselves with to survive?"

Mike clucked his tongue and said, "Yeah, I can see that as a classic run-for-your-life moment. I don't think those are the kind of resources Marge the Barge was suggesting we call on.

"This is just great. We can't tell the world their numbers are wrong for fear of starting a firestorm, but if we don't we will be out of business selling our product for less than what it costs to bring it to market. Let's run the numbers one more time to see if we missed anything. If it comes up the same, then try to set up a full video conference with the others to discuss potential solutions."

Roslyn nodded her head and said, "Yes, sir."

CHAPTER 2

Board Games

The office was suitable to the man who had been ensconced in it for several years. Old European styling of the desk and chair was tastefully offset with a tile floor and an area rug that displayed woodland creatures and birds. A high-definition screen was mounted on the wall, and a simple keyboard was accessible on the desktop. Papers were neatly stacked with a clearly determined order of priority. A matching filing cabinet was modest in size due to most information being maintained digitally in the secure data center adjacent to this office. Quiet music was playing lightly in the background with infrequent interruption by the chimes of the antique wall clock.

Otto lifted his head from the documents he was reviewing and smiled broadly as he noted the incoming caller ID on his cell phone. He warmly greeted the caller, "Thiago, my good man. How nice to hear from you again. I know we haven't had a chance to chat, but I had noticed on my calendar that our semi-annual business call is coming up next month. I wouldn't want you to think that I am remiss in our discussions. I trust you are well, and that delightful daughter of yours, Lara, is prospering with her fashion endeavor.

"How can I be of assistance, kind sir?"

A sullen Thiago asked, "Otto, do you remember those 13th and 14th century maps of the world where Europe was thought to be the center of the universe? The fear of the times was if one sailed a ship too far in any one direction, one would fall off the world into the abyss."

Somewhat taken aback by the tone of Thiago and his odd introduction, Otto cautiously confirmed, "Yes, I recall pictures of those maps, as well as the associated fear of the times.

"Tell me, is there a subtle parallel to ancient but wrong impressions of the world and your present state of affairs?"

Thiago lamented, "It feels, Otto, like my business world is sailing off into the abyss. Do you have a few minutes to visit? I know I sort of sprang this call on you, but I feel I need to talk to someone if for no other reason than just to hear it stated out loud."

Otto responded, "My friend, I actually do have other activities scheduled, but if you hold for a moment, I can move a few things around so I can visit for a while." Otto put the phone down and quickly rescheduled a few things on his calendar and then stated, "Okay, now can you net this out for me, so we don't have to revisit the last six hundred years of history to get to your issues?"

Thiago chuckled slightly and allowed, "Point taken, Otto. How well you know me. Where to begin?

"For years, we, in Brazil, have tried to build a business portfolio that operated on the different cycles of commodities, up or down. Our energy holdings, mining operations, and, of course, shipping businesses have come close to being an ideal model until recently. We were about to sink several offshore oil wells here in Brazil when we watched the floor pricing buckle under the oil oversupply problem. We were also planning to sign a deal with the Chilean government to launch a new copper mine when that commodity's price began to flatline as well.

"With no demand for raw materials or oil to ship, I now have so much excess shipping capacity that I am going to have to do layoffs and idle my shipping fleet."

Otto listened sympathetically to Thiago and offered, "My friend, we both know that business cycles come and go. I'm sure you are not overstating your position, but in every business, there are ebbs and flows for products, whether finished or raw materials. I am confident that we can provide some useful guidance on how to weather this business storm, as well as be properly positioned during the next upturn."

Thiago countered, "Otto, I was fairly sure that this would be your position on the matter. Before calling, I and my staff played a little game of *Let's Pretend to be Otto* so we can see what our options are. Now, what we found as a result of that exercise is really what I'm calling about."

Otto, somewhat perplexed, responded, "Please, Thiago, go ahead. I'm decidedly interested in hearing how the Otto game went."

A slight grin blossomed, transforming Thiago's initial scowl. He explained, "We began digging into our numbers, trying to understand how we missed the oversupply issue of both oil and copper, when we discovered something, I can't explain.

"In each commodity area where we were planning to invest, we had diligently analyzed each of our competitive producers. We came up with a figure that simply doesn't match what's being stated on the world markets. We even discovered that production figures from my organization are being advertised as well, even though none of what is being attributed to us is, in fact, accurate."

Otto did a double take as he asked, "Thiago, how is that possible? You seem to be suggesting that your intended commodity production values are being input into the world commodity markets, but you did not physically have the materials up for sale.

"Hold on there! If your materials were being listed in the commodity markets and a sale was transacted, then it stands to reason that you had revenue coming in but no corresponding outflow of goods. Wouldn't that show up on your corporate books?"

Thiago grinned a little more and continued, "Ah, good, we are tracking to how the pretend Otto would think. We reasoned that as well, but, alas, no free money. I come to you with this issue to see if you can make any sense of it.

"I'm not out anything, except my future. I've plenty on my plate to worry about. I'm hoping you and your team can look at this anomaly to see what can be done about it. Because, right now, it appears from the outside looking in that we are selling commodities onto the world market, yet not recording the income. If the government saw this, they'd accuse us of income tax evasion and become most unpleasant. At least more than usual, anyway. If we found it, then someone else is bound to find it and start pointing fingers. I need your help sleuthing out an answer, my friend."

Otto thought for a moment and then queried, "Do you think we can turn your exercise into a board game? We could name it *Being Otto*. A board game of strategy that does combat against intrigue, with financial digital crime. I bet we can make an online subscription version as well.

"I know you thought of it, but since I'm Otto, I want a 70/30 split for the revenue. My favor, of course."

Thiago clucked his tongue and replied, "You're right, I shouldn't have teased you about being Otto. But the rest of the story is true. Can you and your team work this for me, please?"

Otto chuckled slightly and admitted, "Yes, of course, old friend. But, in the meantime I need you to design some swell board pieces for *Being Otto*. Don't tell Lara, though, as she'll want a share of the royalties. Maybe one of the pieces could be a commodity trader getting ready to jump out of the window. Or maybe one of your oil tankers loading up an order of tennis shoes. Oh, and hey, how about turning one of your offshore oil drilling platforms into a water park slide?"

Thiago chortled and stated, "Now I remember why we only visit twice a year and do lunch. Good day, Otto."

CHAPTER 3

May I have this dance?

The dark walls of the room were made more somber by the minimal amber lighting that circled the edge of the ceiling and the candlelit sconces at wide but equal distances along the walls. Floor and ceiling were covered in mahogany with darker stains pooled along the floor. No carpets muffled the sounds of the heavy chairs as they moved with the occupants sitting and shifting. Table lighting fanned out from the leader's position of power, minimizing the view of his features.

The meeting leader and organizer gave a slight smile as everyone took their respective seats and waited quietly for him to begin. No idle conversation or whispers came from the attendees. Before they were all seated, a large black female enforcer approached the leader and quietly whispered, "The room has been swept. No unauthorized electronics are present."

Then she took up her post behind the leader and stood at attention, aware of every movement made by everyone in the room. She looked quite menacing as she stood still as granite.

The leader seemed tall even while seated. His dark, straight, thick stock of hair was well groomed, if a little long. His eyes appeared black and dead in the muted light. His hands were sculpted, with long fingers. No jewelry adorned his hands or neck. His dark suit nearly blended with the color of the massive armed leather chair.

After a few moments, he finally offered, "I appreciate everyone breaking free from their daily routine to attend this meeting. I know you find travel to this monthly meeting tedious, but I do not trust the importance of our meeting content to encrypted voice/video tunneling controlled by the very people we seek to, uh…re-orient.

"I wanted to advise you that monies from our standard business practices are being funneled into our newest project. We need to have clear milestones at the computer-projected intersect points so that our goals can be achieved while we remain an anonymous entity. Let's go around the table, and give me short, crisp bullets of each of your assigned projects."

Before the third attendee could begin their report, the leader interrupted him, "Moncrieff, can you explain your failure to the group? Your actions in the copper commodity area were picked up by a most dangerous adversary who has been scanning for other examples, which could potentially expose our carefully orchestrated plan."

Moncrieff tried to swallow, but his dry mouth would not cooperate. After several deep breaths, he managed to regain control as he haltingly offered, "I, um…saw an opportunity, rather, that is, a trading anomaly which would let us, um… I accelerated our earnings with that trade. I thought that…"

The leader raised his hand to gain the silence he wanted. Moncrieff struggled to keep his terror under control as the leader stated, "We have very simple rules in this organization. That way, when someone doesn't comply with them, we have very simple solutions."

The leader cut his eyes over to his other enforcer who, in an instant, was behind Moncrieff. The enforcer's bulk had pinned

Moncrieff between his chair and the massive mahogany table. His large, powerful arms quickly wrapped themselves around Moncrieff's head and abruptly twisted it 180 degrees, producing a sickening crack loud enough for all to hear. The large black man then dispassionately stepped back to let Moncrieff's body slump to the floor.

The leader, moderately pleased with the demonstration, stated, "For the group's consideration, I need someone in this role who can be trusted to follow instructions succinctly. As you all are aware, we want to discourage independent thinking that deviates from our plan or risks our detection. If there are no objections, I would like to appoint LJ to immediately step into the role and responsibilities so recently vacated."

No one dared to do anything except nod their heads in agreement. LJ, the enforcer, smiled broadly, revealing several gold-encrusted teeth, and then promptly took the seat at the table which Moncrieff had occupied. LJ's head to shoulders had no clear neck delineation. He too wore no jewelry, and his black leather slacks and black satin long-sleeved shirt completed the look of the enforcer turned player. The other enforcer kept her smile in check, even as she gave a barely perceptible congratulatory nod to her associate.

The leader added, "LJ, you have a week to determine the extent of the possible breach into identifying our team. All available resources transfer immediately to you, including housing and vehicle arrangements."

LJ nodded agreement. He recognized time was of the essence in his complying with his new task. He would use all his own computer resources to make certain the breach was obliterated. He thought back to those he had worked with as he considered the best way to make the data shifts remain untraceable. All his work had been to achieve this point of power, and one misstep would end more than just his career. If his faith had ever been real, he might have prayed. But prayers would not keep him alive or on top with this crowd.

Breakfield – Works for a high-tech manufacturer as a solution architect, functioning in hybrid data/telecom environments. He considers himself a long-time technology geek, who also enjoys writing, studying World War II history, travel, and cultural exchanges. Charles' love of wine tastings, cooking, and Harley riding has found ways into the stories. As a child, he moved often because of his father's military career, which even helps him with the various character perspectives he helps bring to life in the series. He continues to try to teach Burkey humor.

Burkey – Works as a business architect who builds solutions for customers on a good technology foundation. She has written many technology papers, white papers, but finds the freedom of writing fiction a lot more fun. As a child, she helped to lead the kids with exciting new adventures built on make believe characters, was a Girl Scout until high school, and contributed to the community as a young member of a Head Start program. Rox enjoys family, learning, listening to people, travel, outdoor activities, sewing, cooking, and thinking about how to diversify the series.

Breakfield and Burkey – started writing non-fictional papers and books, but it wasn't nearly as fun as writing fictional stories. They found it interesting to use the aspects of technology that people are incorporating into their daily lives more and more as a perfect way to create a good guy/bad guy story with elements of travel to the various places they have visited either professionally and personally, humor, romance, intrigue, suspense, and a spirited way to remember people who have crossed paths with them. They love to talk about their stories with private and public book readings. Burkey also conducts regular interviews for Texas authors, which she finds very interesting. Her first interview was, wait for it, Breakfield. You can often find them at local book fairs or other family-oriented events.

The primary series is based on a family organization called R-Group. Recently they have spawned a subgroup that contains some of the original characters as the Cyber Assassins Technology Services (CATS) team. The authors have ideas for continuing the series in both of these tracks. They track the more than 150 characters on a spreadsheet, with a hidden avenue for the future coined The Enigma Chronicles tagged in some portions of the stories. Fan reviews seem to frequently suggest that these would make good television or movie stories, so the possibilities appear endless, just like their ideas for new stories.

They have book video trailers for each of the stories, which can be viewed on YouTube, Amazon's Authors page, or on their website, *www.EnigmaBookSeries.com*. Their website is routinely updated with new interviews, answers to readers' questions, book trailers, and contests. You may also find it fascinating to check out the fun acronyms they create for the stories summarized on their website. Reach out to them at *Authors@EnigmaSeries.com, Twitter@EnigmaSeries,* or *Facebook@TheEnigmaSeries.*

Please provide a fair and honest review on amazon and any other places you post reviews. We appreciate the feedback.

the Enigma Rising
Breakfield and Burkey
the Enigma Ignite
Breakfield and Burkey
the Enigma Factor
Breakfield and Burkey
the Enigma Wraith
Breakfield and Burkey
the Enigma Always
Breakfield and Burkey
the Enigma Stolen
and Burkey
the Enigma Gamers
Breakfield and Burkey
the Enigma Broker
Breakfield and B
the Enigma Source
Breakfield a
The Enigma Dragon
A CATS Tale
the Enigma Beyond
Who Won the AI Wars
Breakfield and Burkey
the Enigma Threat
Breakfield and Burkey

We would greatly appreciate
if you would take a few minutes
and provide a review of this work
on Amazon, Goodreads
and any of your other favorite places.